The Parihaka Woman

Witi Ihimaera

16

EasyRead Large

Copyright Page from the Original Book

ReadHowYouWant partners with publishers to provide books for ALL Kinds of Readers. For more information about Becoming A **RHYW** Registered Reader and to find more titles in your preferred format, visit:
<u>www.readhowyouwant.com</u>

The Parihaka Woman is the twelfth novel to be published by Witi Ihimaera (Te Whanau-a-Kai), who began his writing career with the short-story collection *Pounamu, Pounamu* in 1972 and became the first published Maori novelist with *Tangi* in 1973. His best-known novel is *The Whale Rider,* which was made into a hugely successful film in 2002. He has published six short-story collections, written for stage and screen, and edited books on New Zealand arts and culture. His recent awards include the inaugural Star of Oceania Award, University of Hawaii 2009, a laureate award from the New Zealand Arts Foundation, 2009, the Toi Maori Maui Tiketike Award, 2010, and the Premio Ostana International Award, presented to him in Italy, 2010. He was co-producer of the documentary, *What Really Happened At Waitangi,* screened in 2011, and his work was set to music by well-known contemporary musicians in *Ihimaera,* commissioned for Auckland Festival, March 2011. The television film of his novel *Nights In The Gardens of Spain* screened at the Hawaii Film Festival in 2010 and premiered on New Zealand television in 2011.

ii

*Ko tenei 'e ma'i aro'a,
ei w'akamana i nga poropiti
i a Tohu Kaakahi raua ko
Te Whiti o Rongomai,
'ei tautoko 'oki i nga kuia,
i nga tau'eke, me nga tangata
katoa o Parihaka*

The Parihaka Woman is dedicated to Ray Richards, my literary agent, mentor and dear friend. Ray flew Corsair ground attack fighter aircraft from Fleet Air Arm aircraft carriers in World War II and was awarded a Distinguished Service Cross. Later, for services to book publishing, he became an Officer of the New Zealand Order of Merit.

Always ahead, guiding me on the wing.

A Note on Taranaki Dialect

In deference to Taranaki iwi, the magnificent Taranaki dialect is used throughout the novel. Some spellings and word usage will therefore strike some readers as unusual, for example, 'mounga' rather than the standard 'maunga', and 'tauheke' for old men rather than the standard 'koroua'. As well, because Taranaki Maori do not sound the 'h', this usage has been marked with a single apostrophe, e.g. ''aere' instead of 'haere', 'mi'i' instead of 'mihi' and 'tau'eke' instead of 'tauheke'.

Taranaki Maori pronounce the 'wh' as in 'whare' not as an 'f ' sound but rather as a soft 'wh' as in the English word 'whine'. This usage is also marked with a single apostrophe, e.g. 'w'are'.

The exception to the above is that names, such as Te Whiti o Rongomai, Tohu Kaakahi, Parihaka, Horitana and so on, are not marked in this manner. Please note that these names would be pronounced as Te W'iti o Rongomai, To'u Kaaka'i, Pari'aka and 'oritana. In fact in some nineteenth-century manuscripts Te Whiti and Parihaka are rendered as 'Te Witi' and 'Pariaka'.

A further exception is that where quotes have been taken from other sources and commentaries, the quotes are as rendered by the original authors.

PROLOGUE

Taranaki

CHAPTER ONE

Always the Mountain

1

I'm a retired high school teacher who once taught history, and I'm not important.

I was born in the Taranaki and so was my wife, Josie, whom I met in the 1960s. In those days, if you were a young bloke like me, you got drunk after playing rugby with your mates and hoped you'd meet some nice girl at the pub. That's where Josie caught my eye. She was out painting the town red with some of her girlfriends, though she likes to change that story now and tells people we met at the local Sunday school picnic. Yeah, right.

Josie and I got married and, a few years later, bought our three-bedroom bungalow here in New Plymouth. We honeymooned in Australia and, since then, we've had a trip to London and another one to Hong Kong to see New Zealand play at the Rugby Sevens. We've lived in New Plymouth all our lives, and have three children and seven mokopuna. Josie's saving up to take them to Disneyland.

As for the bungalow, well, we bought it for the view of Taranaki Mountain. New Plymouth at that time was a small town with oil rigs off the coast. Look at it now: prosperous port, tourism, an art gallery, even a mall. A lot of the original outlook has gone as other houses have mushroomed around us but we still have a great view from the sitting room, and the bathroom too, if you open the window when you're sitting on the lav. Doesn't the mountain look majestic today? When Captain Cook saw it in January 1770 he thought he had naming rights and called it Mount Egmont; apparently there was an Earl of Egmont and, for all I know, Cook might have known him.

To Maori, of course, the mounga has always been Taranaki. Geologically speaking, it's a volcano, dormant right now, and it is very sacred to us. People have taken to calling it 'The Shining Mountain', which is how it looks in winter when it is snow-capped, but also in summer the peak sometimes glistens. Forgive me if I boast, but can you see how perfectly shaped it is? Its symmetry is similar to that of Mount Fujiyama in Japan, and I guess that's why Tom Cruise made his movie, *The Last Samurai,* here in the Taranaki. Josie got a part as an extra, but I was offended that somebody would borrow our mountain and pretend it was someone else's.

The mounga has always been ours.

Of course Taranaki is more than a mountain. It is a tipuna, an ancestor. Born in a mythical past when mounga were able to move, Taranaki had an unhappy love affair with another volcano, Pihanga, and shifted west to get over it; the Whanganui River now pours along the deep channel scored in the earth by Taranaki's passing.

Taranaki lived through amazing historical times. How did the mountain feel, I wonder, when, some seventy years after Captain Cook, it saw European ships bearing settlers from across the sea? I'm talking about the early 1840s, when English migrants from Great Britain bought inland bush country from Taranaki and Ngati Awa tribes, and six ships of the Plymouth Company arrived to settle it. Between 1841 and 1843 around 1,000 settlers raised *New* Plymouth.

By 1859, however, the migrants wanted more land. They cast their eyes to the north-west: if they purchased land there, they could have a harbour.

That's when the troubles with the Maori, here in the Taranaki, started.

From the very beginning, the purchase of what became known as the 600-acre Waitara Block was disputed, and Wiremu Kingi Te Rangitake refused to let government surveyors onto it. 'I have no desire for evil,' he protested, 'but, on the contrary, have great love for the Europeans and Maoris.' Although there were such verbal objections from Maori, no violence was offered. One contemporary newspaper account relates, instead, that the surveyors were ignominiously overcome by one aged kuia who embraced a member of their party, and another woman who removed a protective chain.

This provocation was apparently enough, however, for the government troops to fire on Te Rangitake's pa at Te Kohia, on 17 March 1860. The defenders withdrew, but soon retaliated with warrior reinforcements from as far south as Waitotara. Although the Crown had the greater firepower, and the battle had a disastrous impact in terms of the number of chiefs who were killed, Te Rangitake rallied and was victorious at the battle of Waireka thirteen days later. The great chief Wiremu Kingi Moki Te Matakatea, already renowned for years of fighting, sided with him. His name, which meant 'The Clear-Eyed One', referred to his lethal marksmanship.

Humiliation is a good word, I think, to describe how the government troops must have felt, but the Pakeha exacted their revenge the next day. They had a warship, the *Niger,* off the coast of Taranaki, and the captain was ordered to punish the Maori victors. Not by direct bombardment of the rebel force, though; no, by targeting the Maori settlement at Warea in the kind of lateral and *in* direct retaliation on civilians for which they were to become famous.

Warea was a small, tranquil village led by Paora Kukutai and Aperahama Te Reke. It had also become the home of two remarkable young chiefs, Te Whiti o Rongomai and his uncle, Tohu Kaakahi, and their band of followers. Some twenty years earlier they had returned to the region from Waikanae, further south. Te Whiti was baptised by Minarapa Te Rangihatuake—a Maori missionary who had migrated with them—and from the beginning Te Whiti was marked for leadership.

Minarapa set about raising a Wesleyan church and pa at Rahotu. In addition, by agreement of Te Whiti and Tohu, a mission station was established at Warea by the Reformed German Lutheran missionary, Johann Friedrich Riemenschneider, otherwise known as Rimene. It was there that Erenora, the Parihaka woman, was born. At the time of the bombing, she was four years old.

When she was an old woman in her eighties, Erenora told of the terror of the occasion in an unpublished manuscript that's lodged in Anglican Church archives at St John's Theological College in Auckland. As it was written in Maori, it has been overlooked and forgotten, but it is from this document that we, her descendants, have been able to access the information that is contained in this narrative.

2.

'As well as the mission station,' Erenora wrote, 'Warea comprised a small group of houses with a flour mill, livestock and crop plantations; there was good trading with New Plymouth.

'We knew, of course, that the Pakeha war with us had started. By prior arrangement, a young girl lit a huge fire at Waitara to alert all the tribes it had begun. But we had not expected Warea to be a target, so we had been carrying on our lives as normal. The deadly bombardment continued for two days, most of the shells falling short, the deafening explosions sounding all around. The *Niger's* guns finally calibrated the range and pinpointed the village and, very soon, the missiles were falling on the flour mill. I was sheltering with my teachers and other children in the nearby schoolroom, aware that our situation was becoming dangerous.

'Then the shells began to fall closer to us. I saw Te Whiti come running to the rescue. My parents, Enoka and Miriam, who had just returned from working on a nearby settler's farm, were with him.'

Te Whiti took quick command.

'Take the children to the pa,' he yelled to the teachers.

Enoka told Miriam to take Erenora's hand, and together they followed the others from the schoolroom. They were halfway across the square in front of it when, suddenly, the earth exploded beneath their feet. One minute Erenora's parents were there, the next minute they were gone. But their bodies shielded Erenora from the blast.

Of that horrific event, Erenora had only flashes of memory: maybe she tripped, or perhaps that was when the shell which killed her parents blew her off her feet. Suddenly her mother's hand was no longer pulling her across the compound. A voice in Erenora's own head called, 'Mama? Kei w'ea koe? Where are you?'

She stood up and saw two bodies on the ground; one of them was her mother's. She ran to Miriam, shaking her, telling her to wake up. Her mother's eyes were closed and blood was issuing from her lips and nostrils. Then Te Whiti lifted her away. He was saying something to Erenora like, 'Your mother is dead.' Her ears were ringing from the blast as he took her to the pa.

Erenora was frightened, in shock; she didn't know what was happening. Nor could she understand why her parents were no longer there. Around her, in the underground chambers of the fortifications, people were praying. She couldn't hear the words of the karakia; all she saw were the lips moving. 'Oh God of Israel,' the villagers prayed, 'hear our karakia and take pity on your people in their misery. You, God of deliverance, rescue us as you did the Israelites out of Egypt.'

The *Niger's* bombardment was just the beginning of the assault on Warea. Soldiers, seamen, marines, artillerymen and others followed in an overland attack; they numbered 750 or so. Some reports say that the actual target of the shelling was the pa rather than the settlement and mission station; if so, it is puzzling that the invading force avoided the pa altogether and, although they spared the church, ransacked the rest of Warea and then retreated.

In the darkness of the pa Erenora met a young boy, about five years older, who held her tightly in his arms as the redcoat soldiers went about their business. He must have heard her whimpering at the sounds of the pillaging: rifle shots, and whooping and hollering as the village was razed.

Was it true about her mother? And father? What did being dead mean?

The young boy had tender, shining eyes and his voice was strong and comforting. 'Don't worry,' he told her. 'I'm an orphan too. Cast away your fears and don't be sad. I will look after you.'

ACT ONE

Daughter of Parihaka

CHAPTER TWO

Flux of War

1.

This is not a history of the Taranaki Wars. After all, I'm only a retired teacher who obtained my qualifications from Ardmore Teachers' Training College, Auckland, in the 1960s. I will therefore leave it to you to read the accounts of university-trained historians on the subject.

When I was younger, my elders would often talk on the marae about what happened to Maori way back then, but I really wasn't interested. I had a well-paid job, Pakeha friends—and a Pakeha girlfriend that Josie doesn't know about. Although I copped the occasional Maori slur or racist remark—'Hori' or 'Blacky', you know the sort of thing—I generally laughed it off. If it got a bit too out of hand, as in, 'Hey, you black bastard, can't you find a girlfriend among your own kind?' I was handy with my fists. On the whole, however, Pakeha and Maori got along pretty well really.

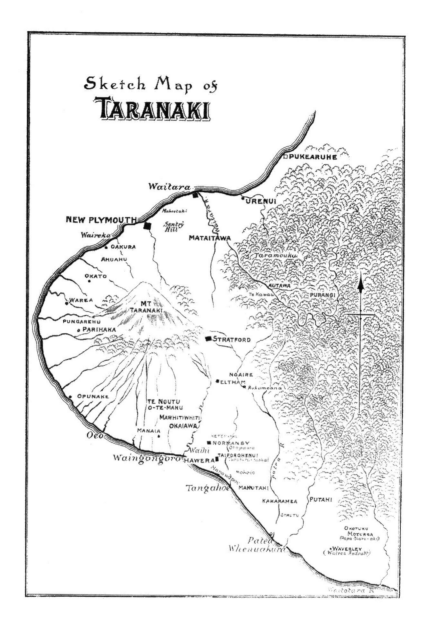

I think my tau'eke and kuia were affronted that I was teaching our kids about the kings and queens of England when there was all our own Maori history around us. In my own defence, I guess it was easier for me to look somewhere else, where history belonged to the victor and happened to other people, rather than locally, where we were the vanquished and it was a bloody mess. 'Why bring up all that old stuff?' I'd say to my elders. 'We're all one people now.'

It took the 1970s, when Whina Cooper led the land march from Te Hapua at the top of the North Island all the way down the spine to Parliament in Wellington, for me to confront the fact of 'that old stuff ' and that, actually, we weren't one people at all: history's fatal impact had also happened here, in my own land.

I joined the march because my Auntie Rose came around to pick me up, no buts or maybes. She said to Josie, 'I'm borrowing my nephew for a while.'

Josie answered, 'Good, don't return him if you don't want to.'

The protesters carried banners proclaiming *Honour the Treaty* and *Not One More Acre of Maori Land;* while some of the stuff they spouted was pretty offensive, there I was, right in the middle of it all, and it started to rub off on me. It wasn't long before I looked around and realised: Hey, where was *our* land, here in the Taranaki? What had happened to *us?* My eyes were opened.

They stayed opened.

But this isn't my story; it is Erenora's.

I've done my best in telling it because, of course, Erenora wrote it originally in Maori. When the family gave me the task of translating the manuscript into English, I must say I found it daunting. A lot of her handwriting had faded, making it difficult to read. And some of her phrasing—well, I've had to explain it a bit for the modern reader. But I've tried to ensure at all times that it's my ancestor's voice, not mine, in the translation.

Better a family member to do the job than a stranger, eh?

2.

'Mine were not the only parents who were killed by the *Niger's* shells. All of us who were orphans were taken in by other families at Warea. In my case a couple by the name of Huhana and Wiremu took a shine to me. Even so, I felt I owed it to Enoka and Miriam to remember them as long as I could. As old as I am now, I have never forgotten their a'ua, their appearance. I know they loved me.

'Following the attack, I returned to the mission's classroom, my Bible and my books. After all, I was a little Christian girl, somewhat serious, and although I was puzzled that my parents were dead, I knew they would be together in heaven. But I did begin to wonder why, when the Pakeha professed Christian love, they would fight on Sundays, destroy the very churches we worshipped in and burn our prayer books. And why did they want to take land they did not own?

'There was also the matter of Rimene. He had left Warea before the *Niger'* s shelling, and some people even said that he had probably given the Crown details that enabled them to target the community. Although, under Te Whiti and Tohu's guidance, we rebuilt Warea, especially the mill, the people were suspicious of him. Whose side was he really on? He made several attempts to convince us that he loved us but, clearly, the assault on Taranaki placed all missionaries in a difficult position: they were shepherds with Maori flocks, but their masters were Pakeha. This was why, I think, many Taranaki tribes turned against the missionaries and also rejected the baptismal English names that had been given them.

'Notwithstanding the suspicions about what Rimene did, or might have done, I will always remember him for a particular kindness. He must have had a soft spot for me. On the last occasion I saw him, he gave me a gift, a book of German phrases, and he stroked my chin. "Leb wohl, mein Herz," he said. "Go well, sweetheart."

'I never forgot the words or him. But when Rimene abandoned us, we had already learnt to fend for ourselves.'

3.

The situation between Maori and Pakeha escalated to full-scale war, and the Pakeha soon discovered that the love of Taranaki iwi for the land was greater than their own desire to steal it.

In 1860 Maori fought battles at Puketakauere and Omukukaitari and faced bombardment at Orongomai-hangi. In 1861 they faced off troops under Major-General Thomas Simson Pratt for almost three months as he advanced by a series of trenches and redoubts.

Facing strong Maori resistance, however, and the huge costs of maintaining his troops, in May 1863, Governor George Grey declared the abandonment of the Waitara purchase and renounced all claims to it. At the time, Grey was in control of all military operations in New Zealand; he was in his second term as governor.

The troops may have retreated from the Waitara but they appeared within weeks to occupy the Tataraimaka Block and were closing in on Warea again.

Erenora was seven years old by then, and Te Whiti and Tohu had stepped into the gap left by Rimene's desertion and become the people's leaders.

4.

'We had already faced bombardment three years earlier by the *Niger.* This time, under supporting naval fire from the *Eclipse,* forty of our warriors died at the outer trenches of our pa. They had been protecting the rest of us; as was our practice we were sheltering within.

'Te Whiti and Tohu kept us at prayer in the darkness but I saw Huhana stealthily leave our huddled congregation. "Where are you going?" I asked her. She replied, weeping, "You stay here, Erenora. I have to see what has happened to my husband. If Wiremu is dead, I must find out what the soldiers have done with his body or where they have taken him." Even though Huhana told me to remain, I followed her.

When she saw me dogging her footsteps she said, "'aere atu, go back, you'll only get in the way." But I wouldn't listen to her.

'The bodies had been laid out in a long row in front of the trenches and rifle positions where they had fought. Two important-looking men came to inspect them. I didn't know it at the time but I later found out that one of them was Governor Grey. He seemed like a king on his white horse; it was such a pretty horse, stepping lightly along the trenches as, from his saddle, Grey inspected the dead warriors. Then he nodded to the soldiers and left.

'Poor Huhana was distraught when she saw Wiremu's body being dumped into a pit with all the others; some of the warriors were still alive, and one arm appeared to reach up before the dirt covered it. Our hearts were thudding as we waited for the soldiers to leave. Some of the bluecoat sailors stayed to have a smoke; how I wished they would just go. But once they had departed, Huhana called to me, "Kia tere, Erenora, quickly!" We ran to the pit to dig the men up. From all around, other villagers, having ceased their praying, were also running to dig, dig and dig with their hands. Huhana began to wail loudly when she found Wiremu; she hugged him close to her chest.

'Among those who were kua mate, gone, I saw a twelve-year-old boy; his was not the only young body among the warriors. I recognised him as the same one who, three years earlier, had soothed my fears. I had come to know him as Horitana and had grown accustomed to seeing him from the schoolroom window, sometimes waving to me as he worked in the potato plantations.'

Erenora cleared the earth from Horitana's face. He was still and wan with the waxen pallor of death.

'When we first met,' she said to him, 'my heart opened to your aro'a, your love, but now you are dead. And every now and then I have seen you watching me in Warea to see if I am all right. How will I live without you?' She lowered her face to his and wept and wept.

All of a sudden, Horitana coughed dirt from his mouth ... then more dirt. He was alive! He began to take deep breaths and, once he had recovered, looked into her eyes and smiled weakly. 'God has saved me for some purpose,' he said. 'He took me down into death so that I would get the taste of the land in my mouth and, behold, I am resurrected. Now that I have savoured our sweet earth, I will always serve it.'

Erenora cried out to Huhana, 'Kui! Help me!'

Other women hurried to her side. They lifted Horitana from the earth. 'We must keep digging out our other men, Erenora,' Huhana said. 'You take Horitana to the stream and wash the dirt from him.'

Erenora led him away but, when they reached the waterway, Horitana was embarrassed. 'No, I can wash myself,' he said.

Afterwards, when he was huddled in blankets, Erenora sat with him as he ate bread and drank some water.

5.

The following days were a blur of men digging graves for those who had died and women wailing at tangi'anga, the burial rites. In the aftermath, Horitana stayed with Huhana and Erenora, chopping wood, gathering potatoes and catching fish for the cooking fires of other villagers. Huhana may have hoped that, now that she was a widow, Horitana would stay and become as a son to her. Every now and then, however, she saw him looking at the faraway hills; she knew he was restless.

A few days later, Erenora saw Horitana talking to Huhana. Then he knelt before the old woman. 'What's going on?' Erenora asked.

'Horitana has asked my blessing,' Huhana answered. 'Maori chiefs are fighting to the south, and he wishes to join them.'

'What about us?' Erenora was panicking.

'Erenora!' Huhana reprimanded her. 'We can look after ourselves.' Ignoring the young girl, she began a prayer for Horitana's safety.

At the end of the karakia, Horitana saw that Erenora was still disconsolate. 'Don't worry, I'll be back,' he assured her.

That evening, he said his goodbyes to Te Whiti, Tohu and the villagers. He asked Erenora to walk

18

with him to the perimeter of Warea. Although he was tall, he was still a boy and not yet a man.

They stood watching the moon, and then Horitana turned to Erenora with his shining eyes. 'Will you wait for me?' he asked.

Erenora was much too young even to know what he was talking about. She knew, however, that she couldn't say no.

'If you want me to,' she answered.

She watched with sadness as he melted into the bush and headed north.

Not long after that, Te Whiti and Tohu decided to take leave of Warea. They called upon those who had always followed them, and any others who wished to join them, to trust in another journey.

'When I brought you here from Waikanae,' Te Whiti said, 'I thought we would be safe. But we have already been attacked twice. What happens if the soldiers come again? We have lost enough of our people. It is time to leave.'

At his words, the followers began to weep. Abandon the village they loved? But Te Whiti was adamant. He had already begun to fashion a remarkable new fellowship in God, a Maori brotherhood of man. After all, while the beliefs taught him by Minarapa at Waikanae and Riemenschneider at Warea had been based on Christian brotherhood, the offer of true fellowship to Maori was often lacking. But did not Christ also love the Maori? If He did, better to interpret the Bible and its many promises to the

Chosen People from a Maori, not Pakeha, point of view. Better to act for *themselves.*

'We are the more'u,' Te Whiti continued, 'the survivors, and God will succour us as we continue our travels. Although we may die many times, we will rise again in the face of adversity. Let us leave Warea for another sanctuary, another haven, our own Canaan land. Therefore gather our belongings, our children and our livestock, all that we can carry.'

He led the people swiftly away, and their pilgrimage in the wilderness began.

'Me 'aere tatou,' he said. 'Let us go.'

CHAPTER THREE

Te Matauranga a te Pakeha

1.

As for Horitana, he was soon in the midst of the fighting.

Like many young boys of the time, he was simply a foot soldier. His young mind scarcely comprehended the traumatic machinations of the Pakeha as they established their settler society in Aotearoa. All he knew was that, although he was only thirteen, he was needed in the fight against them.

Alas, the Maori throughout Aotearoa found themselves facing increasing odds: government forces, local militia and, propelling it all, more and more Pakeha wishing to settle in New Zealand. They also faced an arch manipulator in Governor Grey, who, with one piece of legislation, achieved two goals: punishing Maori for fighting against Pakeha; and obtaining more land for Pakeha settlement. Thus his New Zealand Settlements Act enabled him to confiscate land from Maori because they had rebelled against what he considered to be his legitimate government.

Here's how historian Dick Scott describes what took place: *In 1863 all of Taranaki except the uninhabited hinterland was proclaimed a confiscation area. From Wanganui to the White Cliffs this involved a million acres and with that bonanza, fortune hunters, younger sons without prospects and Old World failures of all kinds need moulder no longer in the colonial dustbin to which they had been relegated.*[1]

What else could Maori do except continue to defend the land?

We know from eyewitness accounts that Horitana fought with such defenders, led by Te Ua Haumene, the founder of the Pai Marire religion, at the battle of Kaitake Pa in 1864. Te Whiti and Tohu acknowledged Te Ua who, two years earlier, had been visited by the Angel Gabriel, bringing a message from God. The angel, whose Maori name was Tamarura, told Te Ua to battle the Pakeha and cast their yoke from the Maori people. Some say that Te Whiti and Tohu inherited the mantle of Te Ua as a cloak, which combined with theirs in creating Parihaka.

Let's imagine Horitana running, with other boys—bearers—along the trenches: older warriors are firing at the government troops and calling urgently for more ammunition. The battle is not going well for the Pai Marire; the ground shakes with the sounds of exploding shells and gunfire.

Horitana is passing one warrior to supply another with bullets when the man slumps down, a bullet through his head. Horitana picks up the dead man's

---

[1] Dick Scott, Ask That Mountain: The Story of Parihaka, Heinemann/Southern Cross, 1975, p.19.

tupara—his double-barrelled shotgun—loads and, sighting above the trench, fires. What are his thoughts as he watches a fresh-faced young soldier fall, his chest blossoming red?

The record shows that 420 redcoats and eighty military settlers, together with supporting bombardments and devastating artillery fire, finally triumphed over the Maori defenders. 'Come, boy, time to go,' one of the warriors tells Horitana. 'You've earned the shotgun, bring it with you. Live to fight another day.'

Blooded in the battle, Horitana flees. On the way he stumbles over a dead warrior with a tattoo on his buttocks—a spiral rapa motif. Later it would catch the eye of one of the redcoats; sliced from the body it was made into a tobacco pouch.

Once, Horitana had been a boy. Now, before his time, he is a man. Fighting a desperate rearguard action through the enemy lines, he goes on to further guerrilla action against the Pakeha soldiers at Te Morere, Nukumaru and Kakaramea.

2.

You know, a lot of people are unaware that at one time there were more British troops in New Zealand than in any other country in the world; that's how great the odds were against Maori.

Michael King offers some details:

In 1863 Grey used the opportunity provided by the second outbreak of fighting in Taranaki to prise further troops from the British Government.

By early 1864 he had as many as 20,000 men at his disposal—imperial troops, sailors, marines, two units of regular colonial troops (the Colonial Defence Force and the Forest Rangers), Auckland and Waikato militia (the latter to be rewarded with confiscated land after the fighting), some Waikato hapu loyal to the Crown and a larger number of Maori from Te Arawa.[2]

The Taranaki Military Settlers were also formed, in 1865. Many were recruited from Australia, attracted by the prospect that they would be settled on the land, once they had gained it.

Under the command of Lieutenant-General Duncan Cameron, an imperial field force of some 3,700 men descended in what we Maori call the murderous Te Karopotinga o Taranaki, the slaughtering of the people and the encirclement of Taranaki. Yes, 3,700.

Imagine Horitana again, now a fully fledged warrior. War had made a hardened killer of him. Whenever he pressed the trigger of the tupara, he no longer wondered about the soldier or settler caught in his sights.

As for the people of Warea, they were on the run, trusting completely in their two prophet leaders.

---

2 Michael King, The Penguin History of New Zealand, Penguin, 2003, p.213. The figure of 3,700 field forces in Te Karopotinga o Taranaki also comes from King, p.216.

3.

'You want a description of Te Whiti?

'Aue! Well, he was the son of Honi Kaakahi, a chief of Te Ati Awa. His mother, Rangikawa, also came from a rangatira line and was the daughter of a Taranaki chief. His height was similar to Horitana's as an adult, so that must mean he was around 5' 10''. His forehead was narrow and his face was marked by piercing eyes. He had a strong build and his movements were always dynamic, agile and spirited. I can remember that one of his fingers was missing; I think he had an accident at the mill at Warea. In all his life he was humble and gentle and, you know, he lived as part of the people and not apart from them. His wife was Hikurangi, a lovely woman. Actually, it was her sister, Wairangi, who was the wife of Tohu Kaakahi. Although he was Te Whiti's uncle, Tohu was only three years older than him.

'Our patriarchs likened our situation to that of the descendants of Joseph, the same Hohepa of the Old Testament who was sold into Egypt by his brethren. In some respects Te Whiti and Tohu saw in Joseph's story a parallel with what the Treaty of Waitangi had done: some "brothers" signed it and others, like Taranaki, did not. They were thus enslaved by Pharaoh without their consent but, just as Hohepa and his descendants had done, the two prophets and their followers kept strongly to the belief that, one day, would come their deliverance from the Pakeha.'

Te Whiti and Tohu took the more'u along the coast.

There were around 200 of them, a rag-tag bunch of pilgrims: old men—the young having gone to fight—women and children. Te Whiti and Tohu and some of the men scouted ahead, carrying the very few arms they possessed. The main party was in the middle, the old women on horses, but the others on foot pushing handcarts or shepherding a few milking cows, bullocks, horses, pigs and hens before them. The rest of the men brought up the rear.

They were spied by a gunship at sea, probably the *Eclipse,* which was still in the vicinity. Next moment there was a small puff of smoke from the ship and its first shell exploded close to them.

'We are too exposed,' Te Whiti yelled. 'Quickly, strike inland.' The sound of cavalry pursuit followed them as, crying with alarm, they ran into the bush and climbed to higher ground where the cavalry's horses couldn't go and where they wouldn't be easy targets for rifle fire.

They were all exhausted by the time they came to Nga Kumikumi, where Te Whiti thought they would be safe from the dogs of war. There they raised a kainga. Well, it was more like a camp really, with the scouts patrolling the perimeter, ready to tell the people to go to ground whenever soldiers were nearby.

The more'u didn't stay there very long. A small band of other Maori trying to flee a pincer movement of the field forces came across their camp, and it was clear to Te Whiti that the soldiers would not be far behind. 'Time for us to move again,' he said.

Huhana woke Erenora. 'Quickly, rouse the tataraki'i.' Women were helping the men on sentry duty, and Huhana had a rifle in her hands. 'We must leave before dawn.' Her eyes were full of fear.

The word tataraki'i referred to the many orphan children in their ranks. It was the word for the cicada, which rubbed its legs together and made a chirruping noise. The great chief Wiremu Kingi Te Matakatea was credited with the symbolism surrounding the tataraki'i. 'Watch the cicada,' he said, 'which disappears into its hiding places during winter but reappears in the summer.'

The children were the embodiment of Matakatea's concept, always reminding the people to look beyond their current troubles to when the sun comes out. There must have been about seventy tataraki'i in the pilgrim band.

As the more'u departed Nga Kumikumi, Erenora was given a special job: Huhana told her to take charge of the young ones. 'If we are attacked,' Huhana said, 'take them into the bush, and don't come out with them until everything is clear.'

Erenora nodded, and crept around the tataraki'i, waking them and warning them. 'Not a sound, all right?' She even cocked her head at the dogs. 'That goes for you too! No barking from any of you either, you hear me?'

Those dogs were good; they obeyed her.

With smoke rising behind them as the cavalry torched the camp, the survivors embarked again on their pilgrimage. This time their convoy included horse-drawn wagons as well as bullock sleds. They set down their belongings at Waikoukou, where they made another kainga, another makeshift camp; this was in 1866. However, their cooking fires gave their position away and when they were attacked there—Major-General Trevor Chute had taken over from Lieutenant-General Cameron in this, the last campaign of the Imperial forces in New Zealand—the running battle through the bush forced them to leave the protective embrace of Mount Taranaki and move to the foothills beside the Waitotoroa Stream.

'I have a half-brother, Taikomako, living on a block of land there,' Te Whiti said. 'He will take us in.'

Erenora never knew how they managed to get away. All she recalled was the pell-mell flight, the sound of rifle fire, and her shame about one incident: she was with other children, herding the bullocks, when two beasts took flight and there was no time to go back for them. The villagers had to keep on going because if they were caught, what would Major-General Chute do to them? Finally evading the troops, they burst out of the bush. Lungs burning, they flung themselves down to rest in an area sheltered by small hillocks. It was there that Te Whiti and Tohu walked among the people. They could see how tired and distressed everyone was.

Huhana asked them, 'Will there ever be an end to our running?'

Te Whiti hesitated ... and then he looked up at Mount Taranaki, arrowing into the sky, and posed the question to the mountain. The mounga began to *shine,* and it answered him.

The prophet raised his hand for the attention of the people. 'Put down your weapons,' he began. 'From this time forward, we live without them.'

There was a murmur of anxiety, but the mountain nodded and blessed his words.

'Enough is enough,' Te Whiti continued. 'We will run no longer.' He bent down and took some earth in his hands. 'In peace shall we settle here, for good and forever, and we will call our new kainga Parihaka.'

CHAPTER FOUR

Oh, Clouds Unfold

1.

By musket, sword and cannon, Major-General Chute cut a murderous swathe from Whanganui to the Taranaki Bight.

Just in case he missed Maori standing in his path—whether or not they were warriors or civilians didn't matter—he smote them down when he turned back to Whanganui. He destroyed seven pa and twenty-one kainga. He also burned crops and slaughtered livestock; if he couldn't kill Maori, he would starve them to death. 'There were no prisoners made in these late engagements,' the *Nelson Examiner* reported, somewhat chillingly, 'as General Chute ... does not care to encumber himself with such costly luxuries.'

Astonishingly, although the Angel of Death flew over Taranaki, Parihaka escaped in what some people called the Passover. Instead, as the trumpets and bugles of war faded, a sanctuary was born beneath unfolding clouds and, with the mountain looking on, the pilgrims built a citadel.

2.

'It was winter and bitterly cold, the wind coming off the flanks of Taranaki, when our prophets put an end to our pilgrimage. The peak was wearing a coronet of snow and the landscape all around was fringed with ice and snow drifts.

'In the beginning, the only cover to be had from the driving rain was provided by the bullocks. The old people herded them to form a circle and then commanded them to lie down. Then they said to us, "Tataraki'i, huddle close to our beloved companions." Oh, I will never forget the heat coming from those noble animals as they pillowed our heads and blew their steaming warmth over us.

'When the weather was really stormy, the adults had to provide extra shelter by standing and becoming the roofs above us; they were like sentinels, and they sang to each other to keep themselves awake until the storm passed. Why did they do that? Well, as Huhana told me one morning, "Our children are our future. Without you, why keep going?"

'Eventually we erected makeshift tents like the camp we had at Nga Kumikumi, but we couldn't start raising our kainga quite yet, oh no. From my recollection it was 1867 and the spring tides, nga tai o Makiri, were especially high and strong. At those times when the moon switched from full to new, our people gathered kai moana, our staple diet. You can't tell the spring tides, "Wait, we're not ready!" or the fish to stop rising at the most propitious time of all for fishing! We were soon busy harvesting both shellfish and sea fish, like shark, and also trapping eels when they swirled upwards to suck at the surface of the water.

'At the same time as this was happening, Te Whiti and Tohu were also concerned to get some seeds into the ground. If we missed the planting time, there would be no food in the coming year. Not until we had some cultivations under way were the two prophets satisfied. "Now we raise Parihaka," Te Whiti said. And so we began the work of clearing the site. We were so happy to start building the kainga. Even the tataraki'i, how they chirruped!

'Meanwhile, Huhana had fully taken me to her breast as my mother. She also took in two other orphans, Ripeka and Meri, as w'angai or adopted daughters. She said to Te Whiti, "If I have to take in one it might as well be three", which was her way of saying that she had an embrace that could accommodate us all.

'I can remember only hard-working but happy times through that warming weather. Ripeka and Meri and I helped the adults smooth down the earth and take the stones away so that the houses could be built. Ripeka was the pretty one, with her lovely face and shapely limbs. As for Meri, she always tried to please, and that endeared her to everyone.

'Both my sisters were older than me but somehow they were followers rather than leaders. For instance, we had a small sled on which Ripeka and Meri would pile the stones, but I was the one who pulled the sled from the construction sites. Even in those days, although I was always slim, I was strong. Ripeka would follow my instructions but Meri was often disobedient. One time she thought she would give me a rest and pull the sled while I wasn't looking, but she took it to the wrong place and unloaded it there. "I was only trying to help," she said to me plaintively as I reloaded the sled. "Please, Meri, don't *try*," I answered.

'It took us the best part of the season and then the summer to raise Parihaka. I think one of the reasons why it happened so quickly was that Te Whiti discouraged the carving of meeting houses or any such adornment on other w'are. He was more con-cerned with us concentrating on food-gathering and sustaining ourselves. He also wanted to discourage any competition between the various tribal peoples who came to live with us.

'The days turned hot, and we sweated under the burning sun. Te Whiti ordered the men to build the houses in rows and very close together. Those men were out day and night selecting good trees to cut down for all the w'are. They sawed the trunks into slabs of wood, two-handed saws they used in those days, one man at each end. When a w'are's roof was raised, we would cheer, sing and dance in celebration!

'My sisters and I graduated to helping the women thatch the roofs with raupo, which the men brought from the bush. Huhana was always yelling to me, "Erenora, hop onto the roof." Men mostly did the thatching but, sometimes, they were busy on other heavier work—and Huhana knew I had good balance and was not afraid of heights. The women threw the thatch up to me and I laid it in place. After that, my sisters and I helped the women as they made the tukutuku panels for the walls of the houses: I sat on one side pushing the reeds through the panels to my sisters on the other side; they would push the reeds back and, of course, Meri's reed kept coming through at the wrong place. Why was she so hopeless?

'Everybody was vigorous with the work. Later, my sisters helped to make blankets, pillows and clothing, but I had no patience with such feminine tasks and preferred to work outside with the men. Te Whiti and Tohu had marked out the surrounding country for cultivations and there were a lot of fences to construct, and small roadways and pathways between them. As we worked, we sang to each other and praised God for bringing us here. There could have been no better place really. The Waitotoroa Stream was ideal as a water supply, and it would have been almost impossible to sustain ourselves without it.'

'It must have been around this time, as autumn descended and the leaves began to fall, that Te Whiti had word from the South Island that the Reverend Johann Riemenschneider had died. Apparently, after he and his wife had left Warea in 1860, Rimene had spent two years in Nelson. Then he accepted an invitation from a society in Dunedin to do mission work among the Maori people in the city. He lived four years there, and his body was committed to the earth in Port Chalmers.

'Te Whiti mourned the German missionary, telling us, "Rimene did not achieve great victories but he sowed the seed of God so that the harvest was sure. What more can you ask from a servant of Christ?"

'We all said a prayer for him. Now he was forever with the Lord. And I found my own karakia for him from the German phrasebook:

'"Selig sind die Toten. Blessed are the dead."'

3.

The next few years flew by. Sometimes when Erenora looked back on them, it was as if the raising of Parihaka, so that it would stand triumphant in the sun, had taken place on one long day. Of course it hadn't, but certainly Parihaka grew as Maori fled from the British soldiers in Taranaki.

'From 200 people we increased to 500. Word got around, you see, that Te Whiti and Tohu were building a city, a kainga like the Biblical city of Jerusalem. We therefore mushroomed to over 1,000 as refugees poured in, driven by the encirclement of Taranaki. They were all hungry and thirsty, and some were grievously wounded. Once they had been fed and recovered, however, they had to pitch in straight away—no mucking around and having a rest! The consequence was that we were building all the time, and Parihaka was quickly forced to become a large kainga.

'Still the refugees sought us out. Sometimes we would see a cloud of dust and know they were painfully making their way to salvation. Or the rain would part like a curtain and there they were, ghost-thin, crying out to us from the space between. At night, we lit a bonfire so that the flames would show those who were searching for us. During the day, a pillar of smoke, like the sword of an angel, revealed the gateway to Eden:

'"Here be Parihaka."

'And when the pilgrims arrived, nobody was turned away.'

'Depending on our skills, Te Whiti organised the iwi into working groups to ensure a continuous food supply. Farmers tilled the cultivations mainly of potato, pumpkin, maize and taro to the north and between us and the sea. The sea, of course, remained the source of our primary sustenance; whenever nga tai o Makiri came, down we would go to harvest the kai moana as it rose to the surface of the sea. Some men even ventured in waka out to the deep water to fish, but usually we kept close to shore. You could drown so easily in those dangerous seas; the weather could change even as you were watching it.

'At the beginning Te Whiti didn't like us to eat meat but, rather, to use our oxen and cattle as our beasts of burden. He wanted us to be self-sufficient but later we began to run sheep, pigs and poultry.'

'One day the villagers were all busy storing kumara and kamokamo carefully away for the winter. Huhana happened to notice that some tataraki'i, bored with helping us, were baiting each other. She gave me a shrewd look and said, "Erenora, the children have stopped chirruping and are pulling each other's wings off. Go and teach them something."

'I was astonished! After all, I must have been only eleven. Te Whiti was passing by and he said, "Yes, you go, Erenora. Plenty of others can store food but not many have your brains." My sisters were affronted by Huhana's remark that I was "too clever" and even more by Te Whiti's acknowledgement of it. They were practising a poi dance, their poi going tap tap tap, tap tap tap. Ripeka sniffed and said, "You may have the brains but we have the beauty." And Meri said, "I can do anything that Erenora can do," which was true, but she always did it wrong.

'Now, about Te Whiti, don't forget that he himself was not without Pakeha education and knew the value of such learning. He was a scholar, had been a church acolyte at Waikanae and Warea; later he became a teacher, and he even managed the flour mill. Both he and Tohu were good organisers too. As Parihaka grew even larger, they were the ones who promulgated the regulations every person had to comply with; we all knew our civic duties. As well, they organised the daily and weekly timetables by which we conducted our work.'

'Parihaka continued to grow and I grew up with it, leaving childhood behind. Apart from farm, forest and fishing teams we also had village officials, kitchen workers and maintenance staff. Teams regularly swept the pathways, collected the rubbish every day, kept the drains clear and cleaned the latrines. We still had scouts patrolling our perimeters but, now, we also had our own police! They were on duty day and night ensuring law and order. You don't think that Parihaka became a great citadel by accident, do you?

'I was so proud of Huhana. She was appointed the kai karanga, the strong-voiced woman, who would call us all awake before first light. She would call again at the end of the day to finish our labours.

'Meanwhile, the refugees always brought news of what was happening in the rest of Taranaki. One of them sought me out.

'"Are you Erenora? I have a message for you from Horitana."

'My heart skipped a beat. "How is he?"

'"He is alive and still fighting," was the answer.

'"Where is he?" I asked.

'"He is now defending the land with Titokowaru's guerrilla army."'

4.

Ah, Titokowaru.

All you have to do is mention the name and Maori throughout Aotearoa will recognise it as belonging to one of the greatest warrior prophets our world has ever known. He was perhaps seven or eight years older than Te Whiti and, like him, as a young man had become a Christian of the Methodist persuasion. The four prophets—Te Whiti, Tohu, Titokowaru and Te Ua Haumene—created an astounding Old Testament framework for Maori in Taranaki.

Titokowaru's warrior ways began when, along with everyone else, he took up the fight against the Pakeha's continuing predations upon our land. Under military provocation, he led a raiding party near New Plymouth in protest. From that time onward, he became a dreaded presence, waging an increasing number of attacks against the Pakeha in the lands south-west of Parihaka.

You can't pinpoint Titokowaru. He was both civilised and savage, peacemaker and rebel. He bestrode both the spiritual and temporal worlds. He was a man about whom Maori wove legends, but he was not invincible. At his army's assault on Sentry Hill in April 1864, a Pakeha bullet took the sight from the old leader's right eye. It was Horitana who, along with Titokowaru's lieutenants, treated the wound. From that moment, the young man became like a favoured son to the great chief.

While Te Whiti was raising Parihaka, Titokowaru was rebuilding Te Ngutu-o-te-manu, just north of the Waingongoro River. Sixty houses were centred on an imposing marae in front of the awe-inspiring meeting house called Wharekura. Like Te Whiti, Titokowaru wanted to live in peace. The trouble was that his lands, too, continued to be encroached upon by Pakeha and, in 1868, his defining moment arrived.

And all his previous military actions paled against what was to come: the campaign known in history as Titokowaru's War.

For two years, Pakeha New Zealand *trembled* before Titokowaru's military genius and brilliance. The narrative of his army's astonishing field tactics, fought with a blend of intelligence and savagery, makes the hair stand on end; and Horitana fought with him in five do-or-die campaigns.

Historian James Belich describes the encounters in this way:

At the outset, the odds against Titokowaru were immense, twelve to one in fighting men, and the chances of victory minuscule. Yet Titokowaru and his people destroyed one colonist army (at Te Ngutu-o-te-manu on 7 September 1868); comprehensively defeated another (at Moturoa on 7 November 1868); and scored several lesser victories (including Turuturumokai on 12 June 1868, and Te Karaka and Otautu on 3 February and 13 March 1869). Their least successful tactical performance was a drawn out battle at Te Ngutu-ote-manu on 21 August 1868, and it could be argued that even this was a strategic success.[3]

Belich goes on to point out that at Turuturumokai, on 7 September 1868, Titokowaru deployed his fearless lieutenants against the best that the Pakeha military could offer; it was at this same battle that the great Prussian general, Gustavus von Tempsky, fell.

What a life von Tempsky had lived. Adventurer, artist and news paper correspondent, he had fought twice in Central America, mined gold in California and Australia and, in New Zealand, his name was attached to the Forest Rangers. So great was his mana that when he was killed both Pakeha and Maori honoured him.

Titokowaru's victories 'brought the colony to its knees', Belich says. However, inexplicably, the tide turned against the warrior prophet. At Tauranga-ika he built a fortress—but his own army abandoned it before any attack by colonial troops. Some people say that he fell out of favour with whatever gods supported him; as easily offended as any of the Greek deities of Olympus, they lightly tapped his knees and his stride began to falter. What was the reason? Nobody knows. But soon, with £1,000 on his head, Titokowaru was on the run. His followers melted away from him and by the time he returned to his homelands in 1871,

---

[3] James Belich, 'Titokowaru, Riwha—Biography', from the Dictionary of New Zealand Biography. Te Ara—the Encyclopedia of New Zealand, updated 18 April 2010.

he was a different man. He was older and less turbulent in his ways. With his own dream fading, he established a close liaison with Te Whiti and Tohu and *their* dreams at Parihaka.

Meantime, Parihaka had, indeed, become a sanctuary. And Erenora was a young woman now, certainly no longer a girl.

5.

'As young as I was, I had become a good teacher. I loved the children and enjoyed teaching them the English language, knowing it would enable them to converse with Pakeha and understand European ways.

'My greatest thrill, however, was taking time off from my teaching duties to help the men break in the bullocks so that they would accept the yoke of the plough and pull the scythe cleanly through the dirt. With so much acreage to plough, the village needed good teams of strong, obedient beasts and, for some reason, I was able to calm their fears. I would stroke them, saying, "Thank you for being our beloved companions on our journey through the vale of the world. Will you not continue to be partners with us as we go further together?" Then I would introduce them to the yoke and command them, "Pull now."

'Huhana wasn't too sure how to take my masculine habits. "Oh, Erenora!" she would sigh, "I don't know what to make of you! And if I feel this way, you must be a puzzle to the young men too!" I think that was why she began to get a bit more persistent in pushing me, and, to a lesser extent, Ripeka and Meri, towards attachments with suitable male candidates. "We need men in our family," she would chastise me, "and babies for the future."

'My sisters were not backward in taking up our mother's prodding, especially Ripeka, who loved flirting. I might not have been as pretty as them but I wasn't without suitors. None of the boys, however, like one called Te Whao, were at all desirable to me—and some of them couldn't even plough a straight line.'

Then, in the summer of 1873, when Erenora was seventeen, while she and her sisters were carrying calabashes of water from the stream they heard someone coming towards them. As the stranger drew nearer, they saw that it was a young man. Around him a few excited tataraki'i were buzzing.

He happened upon Ripeka first, no doubt because she had seen him approaching and wanted to flirt accidentally on purpose. But she wasn't fast enough in pretending to slip and fall at his feet because Erenora felt his shadow cutting the sunlight across her path. One moment the sun had been hot and spinning, the next, Erenora was shivering, not because of the sudden eclipse of the light but because she knew her destiny had arrived.

'May I have some of the cool, sweet water that you carry from the stream?' the young man asked.

Erenora could not look up at first; she knew immediately that the stranger was Horitana, and her heart leapt because he was still alive and had finally returned home. Thank goodness, as he had a price on his head for fighting with Titokowaru. However, when she appraised Horitana her heart sank. Although there was some sadness about him, he still had his shining eyes and he was so handsome now, and, well, her sisters had always been the attractive ones—surely he'd be more interested in them. His hair was thick, long and matted, and he looked as if he'd been walking for years. Across his back was a haversack and slung in a pouch across his chest was an Enfield rifle; it was a sharpshooter's weapon, now his favoured gun, which he had looted from a dead British soldier.

Heartsick, she nodded. 'Yes, you may have some water.' She didn't even bother to try to push her hair back or wipe the sweat from her brow. What would be the use? She gave him the dried pumpkin shell.

The tataraki'i pressed closer, wanting to look at Horitana's rifle. ''aere atu,' Erenora said to them. She began to motion them away and would have followed except that Horitana reached out a hand and stopped her.

'No, don't go,' he said. Despite his war-weary appearance, he was attentive and polite. 'It would be even nicer if your lovely hands would tip the calabash so that the sweet water can pour between my waiting and eager lips.' His voice was low, thrilling and slightly teasing.

Erenora had never liked being addressed in such a familiar manner, so she said petulantly, 'I do no man's bidding! Tip the shell yourself or ask one of the other women to do it for you!' Ripeka would have loved to do *that*.

Horitana didn't take offence. Instead he laughed, 'Don't be angry with me.' In a softer tone he said, 'I haven't had the opportunity in my life to know what is appropriate to say to women, and what is not.'

Erenora gave him a look of acceptance. She watched as he lifted his face, opened his mouth and held the calabash above it. Some of the water splashed down his neck. If he only knew how she wanted to lick the water. And the masculine smell of him: it was like the musk of the bullocks.

For a while, there was silence. Then Horitana coughed. 'You waited for me?'

'For someone who has a reward posted for him?' Erenora retorted, her usual sense of independence returning. 'Maybe I have, maybe I haven't. And you should know better than to bring a rifle into Parihaka.'

His eyes clouded, as if the memories of the wars were painful to him. Then he looked her up and down. 'You've grown as tall as me,' he said, as if that were a problem, 'and you sound very proud. Perhaps I should reconsider the plans that have always been in my heart to make you mine.'

He had the gall to wink at Ripeka in Erenora's presence. Ripeka was lapping it up.

'Alas,' he sighed, 'I am a man of honour...'

'You had better be!' Erenora said. Was he deaf? Could he not hear the loud beating of her heart: ka patupatu tana manawa? 'As for my height,' she continued, 'the problem is easily solved ... you must get used to it.'

Of course Ripeka was jealous but, really, she was never in the running.

Erenora was finally reunited with the orphan boy she had always loved, but she wasn't an apple that fell too readily off a tree. Yes, she *was* proud and she knew her own worth. Horitana would have to do much more than simply profess his love to win her.

After a suitable time of wooing, throughout which Huhana was a vigilant duenna, Erenora and Horitana finally tied the knot. Although it was difficult to retain her virgin status in the face of Horitana's persistent ardour, she *was* a virgin when she married him; he was twenty-two.

Te Whiti himself presided over their wedding and led them to their marriage bed.

'My love for you is like a cloak of many feathers,' Erenora said to Horitana. 'Let me throw it around your shoulders.'

His voice was full of gratitude. 'Erenora...'

'And now, let me plait and weave the flax of our desire into each other's heart and tighten the tukutuku so that it will never break apart.'

This time, Horitana's voice flooded with urgency. *'Erenora.'*

CHAPTER FIVE

Parihaka

1.

PARIHAKA.

> *Taranaki Prov. Locality in Egmont County. Farming. Twenty-six miles south-westward by road from New Plymouth. Access by side road from a turn-off three-quarters of a mile below Pungarehu. About two miles eastward from the main highway between Pungarehu and Rahotu. This village, now a curious mixture of the ancient and modern, was once a celebrated Maori centre, but is chiefly remembered as being the headquarters of Te Whiti and Tohu, who taught the doctrine that the Maoris were Israel and that the British were Pharaoh and the Egyptians who enslaved Israel ... Name means, perhaps, 'Dancing on the cliff '.*

I quote from *The New Zealand Guide,* published by H. Wise, noting the date: 1962. Up to the mid-1960s, when I was studying at training college, there was very little mention of Parihaka at all: G.W. Rusden's *History of New Zealand* (1883), James Cowan's *The New Zealand Wars* (1923) and then thirty years of virtual silence until Dick Scott's booklet, *The Pari-*

haka Story (1954), and Bernard Gadd's 1966 article on Te Whiti in the *Journal of the Polynesian Society.*

Erasure from the official histories and memories seems to have been the order of the day. With some disgust I record that the first edition of the New Zealand government's *Descriptive Atlas of New Zealand,* published in 1959, went as far as to expunge Parihaka entirely and overprint it with a Pakeha name.

2.

I wouldn't be surprised, therefore, if you haven't heard of Parihaka or its remarkable history. From the very beginning, Te Whiti and Tohu practised conciliation, and in Parihaka they set up a kainga on land which they truly believed the government had acknowledged as theirs. They also went one step further and set themselves up as negotiators for the return of other lands in Taranaki that had been confiscated without proper legal basis.

This is my interpretation, of course, and the situation on the ground is murky only because the Pakeha made it so. For instance, despite the New Zealand Settlements Act, the Crown didn't exercise ownership over the great tract of land that amounted to almost half of the Taranaki Bight.

Let's look at a map of the time as that might show more easily what Pakeha occupied as Te Karopotinga o Taranaki continued, and what, for want of a better description, was still Maori territory. This is the Taranaki Bight, ne? Josie will dislike my comparison with a woman's breast but think of the top side of the right breast at the armpit as the location for the Stoney River. Now draw a line across the breast, across the top part of the nipple, Mount Taranaki, like so, and continue it down to the centre of the chest to this place, the Waingongoro River: all the land to the north-east of the line was in the process of being taken by the Pakeha. But all the w'enua, the land to the south-west, was still ours! Indeed, ex-*rebels* had been allowed to return to it, and an area of 70,000 acres given back. Surely this was a sign that the government was honouring the prior ownership of this territory by Maori?

And here, immediately west of the mounga, was Parihaka and the land that became known as the Parihaka Block. Within, as it were, a demilitarised Maori zone. Indeed, some people say that Te Whiti actually told Robert Reid Parris, the government's land purchasing agent, in words that brooked no argument, 'You stay behind.'

Do you get the picture now?

Thus, with the Pakeha wars—at least the effective fighting—to all intents and purposes over in the Taranaki, Te Whiti and Tohu moved swiftly. They formally established themselves as the owners of 'Maori territory' and facilitators for the return of disputed Maori land.

Why did they take up this leadership role?

The answer was that the wars in the Taranaki had taken a huge toll on Maori tribal leadership. This may sound cynical, but there was a reason why European generals sat on their white horses and sent younger soldiers onto the battlefield: if they became cannon fodder or fell to withering enemy fire, the generals could carry on, no matter how bad they were as leaders. Not so Maori chiefs.

Thirty Maori leaders were killed in one battle alone, at Waireka in 1860, and Te Karopotinga o Taranaki harvested many others. But Te Whiti and Tohu's strategy was not to continue leading by the sword. In 1869, therefore, they summoned all Taranaki tribes to meet at Parihaka and, there, they unfolded a new plan.

The proposition was unveiled on the day that we call 'the first Ra'. It was the day of prophecy, the Takahanga, marking the occasion when the two prophets stepped up to the plate and took upon themselves the roles as leaders of our eventual resurrection as tangata w'enua, the original people of the land. On that day the world held its breath as the prophet Te Whiti proclaimed Maori freedom from Pakeha authority.

'This land is ours,' he said.

Clouds had gathered above Taranaki and from the guts of the earth came a sudden quake—a quivering of anticipation. Birds arrowed sharply through the air and the bullocks were bellowing.

Then Te Whiti made an astounding proclamation. Certainly there would continue to be struggles with the Pakeha, but Maori would participate *unarmed.*

'We will hold the land by passive resistance,' he said.

Te Whiti and Tohu's positions may have been firm, but the government had given itself wriggle room.

Hazel Riseborough cleverly puts it this way:

The Government had confiscated the land on paper, but it did not have the means to enforce confiscation on the ground, and for the time being the people at Parihaka were left in peace to cultivate their land.[4]

I don't like the sound of that 'for the time being', do you?

3.

Yes, *for the time being.*

During that peaceful interval, Erenora and Horitana settled into married life. He was astounded at the growth of Parihaka and the great leadership skills of Te Whiti and Tohu.

'When I left you,' he said to Erenora, 'I was just a young boy and you were still at Warea.' He was sitting with her, watching the tataraki'i as they sent kites dancing into the air. 'And now, from out of the

---

4   Hazel Riseborough, 'A New Kind of Resistance' in Kelvin Day (ed.), Contested Ground: Te Whenua i Tohea—The Taranaki Wars 1860–1881, Huia, 2010, p.233.

ground where once there was nothing, has arisen Parihaka.'

Horitana was welcomed into the village with open arms. From the very moment he returned, Te Whiti sought him out too, even though the prophet was, initially, cautious. 'You have been fighting so long with Titokowaru,' he began. 'Parihaka might not be for you.'

'Rangatira,' Horitana answered, his eyes haunted, 'I have witnessed many dreadful things and I myself have killed men in the name of war, I acknowledge that. I have shot them and seen them fall in the battlefield without knowing who they were. And yes, I admit that the bloodlust has come upon me when I have witnessed terrible acts of butchery: soldiers taking heads from our warriors because of the beauty of their moko. That has only made me rage all the more, and to fight at close quarters with them, kano'i ki te kano'i, face to face.

'But always, when I have slid my bayonet into their hearts and their blue eyes have gone white, I have realised just what it means to take the life of another. How I have clasped them to my breast and grieved for them.'

'Are you therefore able to put that life behind you and ascend the whirlwind path of Enoch?' Te Whiti asked.

Horitana swayed, cried out in great pain and nodded. 'I am still a young man. If God will forgive me, I will work for Him.' He kissed Te Whiti's hands.

'Let me serve Him here in Parihaka and ensure that the kainga truly becomes the citadel where peace can reign.'

So it was that, one bright morning, Te Whiti took Horitana to the stream. Erenora, Huhana and other villagers stood on the banks to watch the baptism.

'Look!' Huhana gasped pointing. Eels were swirling around the two men.

Dressed in white, Te Whiti baptised Horitana, submerging him in the water. 'In the name of the Father, the Son and the Holy Ghost,' he intoned, 'arise from the water washed of your sins.'

When Horitana came out of the stream he sat on the bank, weeping. Then, crying out with passion, he walked swiftly to his and Erenora's house, where the Enfield rifle was hanging in its pouch. He took it out into the front yard and swung it by the barrel against a fencepost, slamming it until the stock splintered and broke.

'Husband, calm yourself,' Erenora said to him as he stood, panting.

'How was I to know, Erenora?' he asked, grief-stricken. 'Nobody as young as I was should ever go to war.'

She cradled him in her arms, soothing him.

Let me show you a photograph of Erenora and Horitana.

I'm not sure what year it was taken—it must have been after their marriage—and it gives a good indication of what they looked like when they were young.

The photographer is anonymous, but he could have been one of the Burton brothers, though if that were the case, why is the photograph not listed in their collection at Te Papa Tongarewa? That question aside, the photographer was like many others of his profession, compelled to capture pictures of the bold villagers who would eventually stand against the might of the Pakeha world.

The subject of the photograph is actually Parihaka itself, but the photographer has managed to inveigle a large group of villagers to pose for him just outside the settlement. It looks like he has found a rise outside the village—or he's taken the photograph while standing on a tall ladder—on the outer side of the road leading to Parihaka. From this vantage point, the photograph shows the fence perimeter of the village, broken by a large gap that was one of the entrances to Parihaka. It's not a gateway—there's no gate—but I'll call it a gateway anyhow, and the villagers are standing in front of it: eighteen of them in the foreground, six men and twelve women, three holding babies in their arms. There are eight more villagers in the middle distance, standing in a thoroughfare that runs between thatched houses, and way at the back are two men.

Most of the subjects in the photograph are women. The two in the front are Erenora's sisters, Ripeka and Meri. You can tell, by her overflowing beauty, that the one on the left is Ripeka; on the right, looking at her sister for reassurance, is Meri, always a little uncertain of herself, holding poi in her hands, tap tap tap, tap tap tap.

All the villagers, with the exception of Meri, are looking into the camera. They appear to be saying, 'Tenei matou, this is us.' They aren't taciturn and they don't look belligerent. Most of the men are wearing light-coloured trousers and shirts or jerkins, dark jackets, and all have hats. The women wear blouses and long, full skirts to their ankles. It must be cold as a few have wrapped blankets around their shoulders—and the babies have shawls to protect them from the wind. Like the men, some of the women wear hats too.

Of course the photograph doesn't show the entire village, only nine good-sized sleeping w'are. It presents a very tidy appearance indeed. Look: down one of the thoroughfares is a streetlamp. Beyond, there's scrub and a few tall trees. The rest is sky, so the photographer must be looking westward to the sea. Note the village is unfortified.

Now look at the two men at the very back of the photograph. They too stare boldly at the camera, but one stands on the balls of his feet, ready to defend. Horitana, you think?

No, it's Erenora.

'I remember the day the photographer took that picture. It was the beginning of winter and on the air was the acrid smell of many cooking fires; the smoke wreathed the sky.

'I was not surprised at what I looked like in the photograph. It only confirmed what I always saw in the mirror. All my life I was built like a man: tall, wide-shouldered, narrow-hipped and strong-legged. Not for me the ample breasts and thighs and other telltale signs of womanhood.

'In the photograph I'm wearing a plaid shirt and trousers—yes, trousers—cinched at the waist with a wide belt. I wasn't above scandalising other villagers, especially my mother Huhana—or even my husband, who sometimes was grumpy that I dressed like a boy. And the illusion that I am a man comes from the fact that my hair is pinned up, whereas Horitana—who also had long hair but wore it, as all the men did, in a topknot—has his long hair down! When that photograph was taken, however, I could sit on my hair.

'You see, Horitana had got over his shyness of that day when, as a child, I had rescued him from death and tried to wash off his dirt in the stream. Now he enjoyed my bathing him in an old tin tub, and sometimes I would get one ready for him on his return from whatever work Te Whiti had assigned him to do. It might be riding with a squad around the perimeter of Parihaka to en-sure that our borders were safe and protected. At other times it might be to keep guard on the fishermen as they went to the sea.

'I would hurry to get the bath ready, taking my bucket to the well and, one bucketload after the other, fill the copper. Ripeka and Meri sometimes liked to watch me and say to themselves, "Huh! She can't fool us! Pretending that she wants to wash Horitana's dust off or get the warmth back into him after a cold day, when we know that what she really desires is to admire his handsome and naked body!"

'My sisters were still unmarried, though on Ripeka's part it was not for want of trying, and they were still living with Huhana, whereas Horitana and I had the w'are next door. Ripeka was always the cheeky one, saying to our mother, "Can we go somewhere else to sleep tonight? All the noise as Erenora bathes Horitana, the splashing and the sighing. What can they be doing?" Ripeka's thoughts were so salacious.

'Once I filled the copper I lit the fire beneath it and heated the water. Then, bucket by bucket, I filled the bath ... and waited ... and when Horitana arrived home, I would put a candle on the rim of the tub and invite him to clean himself. "Oh, wife," he would shiver in anticipation. The tub wasn't very big, but I loved bending his limbs so that he could fit into it. He was tall and lean-muscled and, yes, I will admit that I got much pleasure in looking upon him.

'"Is the water hot enough?" I would ask. I washed and soaped him and asked him to let down his hair so I could wash that too. Sometimes I sang to him, to tell him why I loved him: "Softly, you awoke my heart, you put your arms around me and sheltered me from sorrows deep and asked the mountain me to keep! Since that day I have loved you so, wherever you go I go too!"

'I will admit that often I wished the tub was big enough for both of us.

'And sometimes Horitana would responded to my song with his own: "From the moment I first saw you, dearest wife, I carried your face in my heart! The thought of you sustained me even though we were far apart! Respond to me, my Erenora, respond again, Erenora..."

'We loved those times together, Horitana and I, except that finally that impudent sister of mine, Ripeka, would shout from next door, "Oh, hurry up you two and get *on* with it!"'

Look at the photograph again. In my opinion, Horitana has indeed just come from a bath, so the photograph must have been taken in the late afternoon; the photographer would have been anxious to capture the image while he still had enough light.

Horitana may even have come from lovemaking. His skin *glows,* don't you think? Everything about him glows, his eyes, his hair, even his chest, over which he has hastily thrown a blanket.

And Erenora definitely looks like someone to be reckoned with, eh? Even though it's only a photograph that's being taken, she has flung her arms around Horitana's shoulders as if he is imperilled in some way.

CHAPTER SIX

A Prophet's Teachings

1.

On what principles did Te Whiti base his creed?

Bernard Gadd has written about this in his article which covers the teachings of Te Whiti better than I ever could. He says that 'Te Whiti did not carefully systematize his theology, but the principal strands in his thinking stand out clearly.'

> *His fundamental conviction was that God was sovereign in His universe and that nothing existed or occurred but by His will. Te Whiti said in October, 1880 that all things were ordained at the beginning of the world ... namely wars and dissensions ... We could not have altered anything hoewever we might strive.*[5]

In Gadd's words, 'the heart of Te Whiti's creed and that which drew people to him was his confident reaffirmation that the Maori "had not been lost sight

---

[5] Bernard Gadd, 'The Teachings of Te Whiti O Rongomai, 1831–1907', Journal of the Polynesian Society, 1966, Vol.75, No.4, p.448. Te Whiti's quotation is cited from G.W. Rusden, A History of New Zealand, 3 vols, Chapman & Hall, 1883, Vol.3, p.259.

of by the Great Ruler, who kept all things in good order"':

> *'God has protected us and will protect the land and the people ... You are a chosen people and none shall harm you.* [6]

Aren't Te Whiti's utterances inspiring? I particularly like this one: 'The ark by which we are to be saved today is stout-heartedness, and flight is death.' No wonder Parihaka became a symbol of hope and an emblem of Maori sovereignty, not only to Taranaki tribes but also other iwi in Aotearoa. You have to shake your head, though, and wonder why did the prophet choose such open ground to build Parihaka on, and with no defensive walls and ramparts? What was Te Whiti *thinking?*

Well, first he was proclaiming pride in ownership. Perhaps he was also sending a message to Pakeha that he was not afraid of them.

He was certainly sending a message to Maori that he and the people of Parihaka were not in hiding. When you think of it, his full name, meaning 'The shining path of the comet', couldn't be more apt. It shouldn't be surprising that Maori were drawn to that flightpath, to follow in its glowing wake to Parihaka, as the three wise men did to Bethlehem.

---

6 Gadd, 'Teachings', p.449. Quotations are cited, in order, from New Zealand Herald, 18 October 1881; Rusden, History, Vol.3, p.291.

Maybe Te Whiti was also sending a message to God:

'Just in case you can't find us, here we are.'

2.

'The main tribal meetings,' Erenora wrote, 'took place on the 18th of each month, Te Whiti's special Sabbath—actually the 17th by calendar date, because Te Whiti argued that Pakeha had left out the day the "Sun stood still".

'Visitors arrived from all over Aotearoa to pray and to korero.

They came from the Waikato, Wairarapa and the King Country and as far away as Otago and the Chatham Islands. Scouts watched from the hilltops for them and came running to tell us so that we would be waiting with our welcoming party. I could never detain the tataraki'i in the classroom on those days. I had still kept up learning German from my phrase-book—I don't know why, perhaps it was a sentimental link to the missionaries at my place of birth, Warea—and I liked to farewell the first girl or boy out the door with the same German phrase that Rimene had addressed to me when I was a little girl. "Leb wohl, mein Herz," I would say to the child, "Go well, sweetheart."

'The children liked to dress up for the visitors. They wore ceremonial shoulder cloaks and feathers, and would welcome the arrivals with song and skipping ropes. Sometimes, the boys whipped their tops among the manu'iri and ran after them. At other times, up would go their kites to dance and soar in the capricious wind. We always said that if the children liked you and made a noise, they were happy. But if they sensed anything about you that was menacing, and they started to buzz or go silent, watch *out.'*

'In those days, the visitors were always greeted on Toroanui, Tohu Kaakahi's marae. It was the men who were prominent, welcoming the manu'iri with Tohu Kaakahi's foot-pounding, breast-slapping and vigorous 'aka:

'"E pari koe te tai, w'akaki ana mai nga ngutuawa o Waitotoroa kei Toroanui, i aa 'a 'a! 'aere ake aku waka e rua, 'ei! Ko te w'iu poi, ko te ringaringa w'iua! Taia!"

'Titokowaru was a frequent visitor, leaning on his sacred staff Te Porohanga. Whenever Horitana saw him, he leapt to the front of the men and urged them to greater ferocity. "Ringa pakia!' he would lead them. 'Flow in the tide, filling the mouth of the river up the Waitotoroa to Toroanui. Behold the prophet's two canoes to launch his message! The twirling poi! The action of the 'aka! Taia! Aue!"

'Horitana never ceased to acknowledge his great friendship with the old fighting chief. "This is the man who could stop bullets," he would tell me. "Even the winds of Heaven were his." How thrilling it was to see the way my husband's muscles bulged as he per-formed the 'aka.

'Other dances and songs of welcome greeted the many manu'iri who visited us. I was not very good at poi dancing, so I left that to my sisters and the other women. I envied Ripeka and Meri their dexterity and the ways in which they could make their poi whirr, whirr, whirr in the sparkling sunlight. My sisters were so pretty, especially Ripeka, who would shove herself to the front, twirling her poi for all they were worth. Meri liked composing her own poi songs:

'"Titiro taku poi! Rere atu, rere mai, taku poi! Look at my poi! It goes up it goes down, it flies around our sacred mountain Taranaki, which is the centre of our lives!"

'Sometimes, however, she would try too hard in the dance and lose one of her poi. Off it would go, flying like a bird into the crowd.'

'Such great rangatira came to Parihaka. Surely their coming only confirmed the growing greatness of our citadel. Among the chiefs were Wiremu Parata, Winiata Naera, Whakawhiria and, as always, the great Wiremu Kingi Te Matakatea. Despite a promise by George Grey, Matakatea's land had been confiscated and he smouldered, still awaiting its restitution. Te Kooti Arikirangi came from Poverty Bay and Raniera Erihana was a regular visitor from the South Island.

'Europeans were also welcomed, even government officials, like Robert Reid Parris and James Mackay, land purchase agents, who came to spy on us. They tried to bribe Te Whiti and Tohu or even speak against them on our own marae! We were scornful of their attempts to spread dissent among us and cast doubt on our leaders. They were like the money-lenders in the temple, moving among the people, asking, "Have you got land to sell?"

'There were also journalists and always the handful of curious sightseers. I liked to engage them in conversation about the world outside Parihaka. I think a few were surprised that I could read and write. I wasn't offended by their presumption that Maori were ignorant and uncivilised; it wasn't their fault that their newspapers portrayed us in this way. A few generously left me books to read, one of which was a tattered but soon revered copy of Shakespeare's plays.

'By that time, Te Whiti was around fifty and Tohu just a few years older. Although Tohu had the seniority, Te Whiti was the statesman, the one who always spoke first. He had his grey beard by then and his eyes were always alert. He was reserved and dignified and some Pakeha, forgetting about his education, were disappointed that, well, he was an equal to *them.* The mi'i over, Te Whiti would open his arms in greeting:

'"The twelve tribes of Israel are amongst you. Great are you amongst people! You are as a heavy stone not to be moved."'

3.

Of course, the many visitors to the tribal meetings had to be fed and housed. Although some brought supplies with them, the village men were kept busy cooking the kai: Parihaka now boasted a large granary and associated bakery, and the land and sea were bountiful with fish, beef, poultry, vegetables and other foods. The only drink served was water; Te Whiti frowned on the wai pirau, the Pakeha alcohol.

The visitors loved to wander down Parihaka's thoroughfares and, sometimes, indulge in inter-tribal games and competitions. They particularly enjoyed the sport of pitting the strength of one bullock team against another. By that time Parihaka had over 100 bullocks in the kainga's bellowing herd; you could tell by their vanity that even the beloved companions themselves enjoyed showing off their muscles, bellowing and straining to pull the rival teams across a line marked in the earth.

Ripeka and Meri graduated to being handmaidens, helping to serve the kai to the visitors.

'Anei!' the young men yelled as they moved among them, 'Nga putiputi!'

Erenora's sisters loved the many 'ui because they were able to meet eligible men; they were irritated that she had married before them.

It was at one such gathering that Ripeka met her husband Paora. Really, once she had him in her sights, he didn't stand a chance because wherever he looked she was standing there, giving him the eye. Paora was a fine young man from Whanganui, but when his companions left—hello, he did not return with them. 'I told Paora I didn't want to leave my sisters,' Ripeka sobbed happily to Erenora.

Not long afterwards, Meri met Riki from the Waikato during a friendly game of cricket. Well, what really happened was that Riki invited Meri to go for a walk in the dark and, as she was trying so hard to please him, she let him go all the way. The consequence was that she became pregnant.

Huhana wasn't having that. She bailed up Riki's elders and harangued them. 'This isn't just any girl he's had his way with! This is my Meri.'

Poor Riki found himself being told by his chiefs to do the right thing. The good part was that he truly did adore Meri and, as a token of his love, he gave her a beautiful greenstone 'eitiki, neck pendant. 'I will wear it always,' she said to him. But did she go back to the Waikato with him? No. She couldn't bear to be separated from Erenora and Ripeka either. Riki had to make a choice and, like Paora, he stayed in Parihaka too.

Horitana shook his head and mused to Erenora, 'Sometimes I suspect you sisters love each other more than you do your husbands.'

Erenora tried not to be envious of Meri's beautiful rounded pregnant body. No matter the strength of Horitana's and her lovemaking, sadly, she could not come to child with him.

One day she even heard other women of the village gossiping about her. 'Why is she still barren when to even look at her husband would make any woman pregnant? Her mission education has diluted her ability to have children.' It was spiteful talk and not to be taken seriously, but Erenora pondered her barrenness for weeks. Then she made up her mind. She prepared a good dinner for Horitana and, after that, sat him down for a talk. 'I want you to divorce me, husband, and take another wife.'

He looked at her, puzzled. 'What has brought this on?'

'I have not been able to bear you a son,' she answered.

He scratched his head, smiling. 'It might be my problem, not yours,' he began, 'and anyway I love you. No other woman comes close to you. Apart from which, I would miss the clever, beautiful and sometimes puzzling things you say—and I like all our trying!'

Most of all, Horitana admired Erenora's intelligent and questing spirit. Sometimes he would watch her on the marae without her knowing. He would see her eyes catch fire as the speakers rose, one by one, to talk about the future of Parihaka, of all Maoridom and Aotearoa. The cut and thrust of debate showed that the brightest minds were present at the many tribal meetings.

'What is our kaupapa?' they would ask. 'What is our purpose? It is to protect the land and the people and maintain our way of life for future generations.'

At one such gathering, Erenora caught Horitana's glance. She edged her way to his side and smiled at him. 'You don't mind my masculine interest, do you?' she asked.

'No,' Horitana answered, 'I'm proud of your enquiring mind, Erenora.'

Together they watched Te Whiti take command. The prophet never moved much, and his voice was so resonant and powerful that no matter how many people were there, it was as if he were speaking to each person alone. Well versed in kawa and korero, he was able to use a simple w'akatauaki, proverb or passage from the Book of Books, and it was enough to have people laughing or weeping or nodding in agreement. Assuredly he showed his rangatiratanga when he said:

'I do not care for the parliament that meets in Wellington, my Parliament is at Parihaka.'

Oh, the thunderous ovation that greeted his remark.

One image of Erenora on the marae imprinted itself indelibly on Horitana's memory. The day was waning, the debates between the chiefs reaching a climax. The night was pouring into the sky but there, silhouetted against twilight's striated pinks and reds, was Erenora. Even as the darkness deepened into purple, and other women slipped away to prepare dinner, she still stood there, listening.

This was his wife. She was holding up the sky. She turned to him and smiled and the first evening star came out.

4.

Aue, always hanging over Parihaka and Taranaki was that business about the confiscations which existed *on paper.*

The time came when the government *did* have the means to enforce confiscation on the ground. After all, there were already British and colonial positions along the coast from past campaigns; if you like, around the side of the breast—excuse me, Josie—from the armpit to the middle of the chest.

I'm talking about the era which began when Henry Albert Atkinson, known as Harry Atkinson, came to power as tenth Premier of New Zealand, albeit initially for only one year, from 1876 to 1877. In my opinion he was the worst of the land-grabbing leaders of our country. His curriculum vitae contained, for instance, a stint as one of the two captains of the Taranaki Rifle Volunteers formed from the settlers to defend New Plymouth when it was surrounded by Maori in the first round of the Taranaki fighting. He made no secret of the fact that he thought we were 'savages'.

Then the period's hostility to Taranaki Maori escalated when Sir George Grey, who had left New Zealand to serve as Governor of Cape Colony, returned and reinvented himself in New Zealand politics. He ousted Atkinson and took over as the eleventh premier, from 1877 to 1879. Under Grey, the government disclosed its hand: it rolled out its plans for the complete takeover of Taranaki, looking *inward* from the coast to that territory which Maori had claimed as theirs.

The moment had come for surgical removal.

You know, I think both sides were lucky that the resolution of land matters had moved from active military conflict between us. Otherwise, more blood would have been shed. One wonders why the government did not continue the conflagration?

I've heard that it simply couldn't afford the cost of maintaining the British Army—the koti w'ero, redcoats, and the koti puru, bluecoats—in Aotearoa. And it has to be said that men of conscience, speaking within Parliament and without, put the brakes on any further fighting: were Maori not members of the brotherhood of man?

That, however, may have slowed Premier Grey down, but it did not stop him entirely. After all, he had the economic woes of the country to think about: 1877 was a year of depression in New Zealand, and what better way of solving some of the financial problems than by going after land that wasn't yet in the Pakeha pocket? Like that interesting Maori territory in Taranaki. It could be worth up to half a million sterling.

And, by that time, the government had begun to institute a

different kind of 'army': a heavily armed police force known as the Armed Constabulary, supported by settler volunteers.

The Grey Cabinet moved quickly to advocate the survey and sale of the land by force.

In July 1878 the surveyors, that perennial metaphor for provocation, were ordered in. What had once been a demilitarised zone now became *active,* and although the land's ownership was still disputed, the Pakeha acted as if he owned it. Te Whiti and Tohu immediately protested, but the Crown went ahead with the surveying and then advertised 16,000 acres for sale.

Te Whiti took immediate action. After all, the ark was being assaulted.

centre of a new Maori republic. It had already become the largest and most prosperous kainga in the land and its many tribal meetings were forever increasing in size, sometimes past the usual 3,000 to, at times, 5,000.

The figures won't mean much unless I give you a couple of reference points from the 1881 census, even though it was still three years away. For instance, the census listed the total number of Pakeha in New Zealand at 489,702 and the total number of Maori at 44,099. That meant that up to 9 per cent of Maori in the country were meeting at Parihaka whenever there were significant 'ui. And if we look at the population of Taranaki, which was 14,852, any comparison with the figures of Maori living at the citadel must have made for alarming reading. After all, the population of New Plymouth itself was only 3,326.

The large gatherings could mean only one thing: Parihaka was also becoming a Maori 'parliament' and—the news just kept getting worse—a diplomatic precinct for Maoridom. A comparison with the Holy See of Rome wouldn't be inappropriate. Waikato sent twelve apostles to live at the kainga. Other tribes stationed emissaries to function as ambassadors at the court of Parihaka; there were at least nine such diplomatic missions, with their own meeting houses and dwellings.

I'll make no bones about it: merely mentioning the citadel was enough to sound loud alarm bells among the Pakeha populace. Thus Parihaka began to be demonised as the greatest threat to Pakeha progress in Aotearoa, *ever.* Why, it even had its own bank because, remarkably, Te Whiti had turned the citadel from a self-sustaining economy into an income-generating kainga.

The main item of trade was flax, the swamps were full of it, and gangs went daily to harvest and sell it to flax mills—in the 1870s there were over 160 mills nationwide and most in nearby Manawatu. The mills made the flax into rope and other fibre products for export to the UK and Australia; there was also huge demand from Maori tribes, who bought the flax for clothing and other domestic purposes.

Te Whiti and Tohu also built on the model of Warea by reestablishing trade in agricultural produce to both Maori and Pakeha. After all, they now had a vigorous horticultural industry centred on their plantations. Not all Pakeha were against them and, if they were, they turned a blind eye because the prices were competitive. The quality of the kainga's agricultural produce was often better than that of other suppliers.

Further money for Parihaka's coffers came from villagers' contributions by way of regular tithe. March, for instance, was a month when they would work on farms outside Parihaka, and all the wages they earned were given to support the citadel.

And of course ko'a—voluntary monetary funds—from the many Maori visitors added to Pariha-ka's wealth. Outside tribes like Whanganui Muaupoko

3.

'I remember the evening', Erenora wrote, 'when Te Whiti came to our w'are to talk with Horitana about the invasion of the Pakeha surveyors.

'It was raining softly and I was making the evening meal when he arrived. It was always an honour to have the prophet in our house. I took his coat and hat and motioned him into the warmth. "Won't you stay and have dinner with us?" I asked him. He looked in the pot, sniffed the stew and said yes.'

Erenora ladled out the stew. Te Whiti said grace and then began to eat.

'The Pakeha are cutting their lines in the ground,' he said after a while, looking squarely into Horitana's eyes. 'If that is a challenge, I shall accept it. I want you to take a squad and stop them. Only men of mana are to go with you.'

Since his baptism, Te Whiti had elevated Horitana to a position as a protector of Parihaka. All the men in the village had rejoiced in the decision because not only could Horitana look after himself; he would look after *them.* And he had experience in handling dangerous situations.

'The land is mine and I do not admit the Pakeha's right to survey it,' Te Whiti continued. 'My blanket is mine! Think you it would be right for them to try to drag it from my body and clothe themselves with it?'

Listening in, Erenora could only agree with the prophet. 'The Pakeha doesn't care that the Maori moko has been tattooed here long before they came,' she began, laying her spoon down. 'We can't let them continue to engrave their own moko over ours.'

Te Whiti was accustomed to Erenora saying her piece. He winked at Horitana, who kicked his wife under the table, but she would not heed him.

'And it is not only the w'enua—cultivations, burial grounds, villages or grass seed crops—that's at risk,' she continued. 'There's also the danger to our w'akapapa, for it is the umbilical cord between the past and the present which is being shredded by the surveyors' lines. If Pakeha continue to do that, the enriching blood of the pito, the afterbirth, will drain away and what therefore will give life to the generations yet to come?'

The prophet smiled at her as he finished his stew. 'Maybe you should be the one to go out and stop the surveyors?'

Erenora coloured, a little embarrassed, but Te Whiti patted her hand. 'Kei te pai, Erenora, your words are food for thought.' He pondered them, and then turned to Horitana again. 'I do not want you to take weapons with you. You are not to use arms against the surveyors.'

'How will I be able to get them to stop?' Horitana asked. 'What if they fire on us?'

'Let them do what they do,' Te Whiti answered. 'I am telling you what *we* do. The land is ours and I do not admit their right to survey it. You will find a way.'

The next morning, Horitana selected his squad. The rain had stopped but the clouds were hanging heavy in the sky. The group of men was large, perhaps seventy, including Paora and Riki and others like Te Whao, Ruakere, Rangiora and Whata.

Meri was unhappy that Horitana had chosen Riki. Swollen with child, she needed him. As the men rode out, she shouted after him, 'Don't do anything foolish.'

Ripeka elbowed her impishly. 'You should talk,' she said.

Meri was still upset. 'Horitana should never have picked Riki,' she said to Erenora. 'If anything happens to him, it will be your husband's fault.'

But, as it happened, when the squad had their first encounter with the surveyors, Horitana won the day because of the intimidating number of men with him. He had also decided, in talking to the surveyors, to try not to provoke, but to use reason and be firm.

The squad rode up to one of the surveyor camps, and Horitana called for the chief surveyor, a Mr Charles Finnerty. 'Friend,' he said, 'you and your men are trespassing. We have therefore come to pull up your survey pegs, take down your theodolites and...' with a twinkle in his eye '... if you would be so good as to dismantle your tents, we shall escort you safely back to *your* land.'

The surveyors may have objected but they were also obedient. It was all very reasonable and done without incident.

Came the dusk, however, and Erenora was in such a nervous state, worrying about the men. She ran with Ripeka and Meri to the road to watch for their return. A phrase in German came to her lips.

'Ich hab auf Gott und Recht vertrauen,' she whispered to herself. 'I trust in God and Right.'

The tataraki'i waited with the women, silent, but when the men appeared, oh, their commotion was deafening. Meri was so melodramatic, running towards Riki and wailing as if he had been away for years. All the women were making a fuss of their men, even Ripeka of her Paora, but Erenora held back. Even though Horitana had brought her a gift of some surveyors' pegs she said, 'Husband, you were only doing your job.'

As soon as she said the words, Erenora realised she should have been more forthcoming with her praise. Sometimes, however, her love for Horitana was so huge that rather than show it she limited its expression, especially in public. And Te Whiti was correct that she should have been the one to go out and lead the men: she was as good as any of them.

Later that evening, she saw that Horitana was still hurt by her slight. He excused himself after dinner, went outside with his axe and began chopping the surveyors' pegs into kindling. Erenora followed and stood watching him. The night sky was immense and full of wheeling constellations. All there was to disturb the silence was the sound of Horitana at work, cutting through the night. After a while he looked at Erenora and smiled shyly. 'The pegs will make a good fire,' he said.

'I'm so glad,' she answered, 'that you did your job well, husband, and that you've come back to me.'

'I will always come back to you, Erenora, always,' he said. 'Who else do we have in our lives except each other?' Then followed a long period when, every morning, Erenora and her sisters would farewell their men: ''aere ra ki runga o te kaka'u aro'a o te Atua. Go under the cloak of God's love.'

Erenora had spoken to Horitana about Riki, and, initially, he had commanded him, 'No, not you, e 'oa.' But would Riki stay behind? No. 'Men will always do what they wish,' Erenora sighed, threading an arm through Meri's. The women watched the men riding away through the reddening dawn.

During the day Horitana's squad removed more parties of surveyors. Sometimes they used packhorses and drays so as to quickly and efficiently escort them out of their lands. By nightfall the womenfolk would be waiting eagerly for the men's return. Nor was Meri's continuing nervousness any help: 'Maybe something has happened to them.' But Erenora would finally see Horitana leading the party back through the twilight and, as always, she continued to try to hide her overwhelming feelings.

Nevertheless, one evening, she asked him, 'Have you done your job today, husband?'

'As well as I think my wife would have wanted me to,' he said with a grin.

Although she wouldn't admit it, Horitana was the lord of Erenora's life. She pushed him reprovingly for teasing her, but her heart betrayed her. It thundered with love for him, ka patupatu tana manawa.

How come he could never hear it?

4.

'Parihaka's resistance by peaceful means truly began,' Erenora wrote.

'During this period, however, the kainga became sanctuary to a man named Wiremu Hiroki who had killed one of the surveyors, a European named McLean.

'The story is mangled and confused with conflicting accounts of which side was to blame. The dispute began over the killing of pigs owned by Wiremu and escalated into unreason. I will be honest: neither side was faultless. The killing, however, added to settler fears that our peaceful removal of the surveyors was only a prelude to a violent uprising. Wiremu was pursued by a number of different posses, one of them led by his own chief, to take him back to face Pakeha justice. But Te Whiti intervened and offered Wiremu haven. In doing so, however, the prophet appeared to affirm Parihaka as the centre where criminals were gathering to create a growing rebel stronghold.

'Te Whiti instructed me and Horitana to take Wiremu into our house and, of course, as a Christian I offered him sanctuary. This, even though he was not a person I was inclined to like—but he had been pursued, shot at, and was wounded. What shocked me, however, was that soon after Wiremu's chief departed, another posse pursuing Wiremu stormed into Parihaka. When I saw them coming I shouted to Meri, "Get into the house." As usual she disobeyed me and barely managed to move out of the way.'

The posse was led by a fair-haired gentleman, a settler who was a cut above the others. He wore a red riding jacket and black hat and jodhpurs and looked as if he was on a fox hunt; there was a whip on his saddle.

Erenora stepped in front of the horses. 'Stop,' she cried. The horses wheeled and bucked, dust swirling from their hooves. The men riding them cursed her, but she stood her ground until Meri was safely to one side.

'So this is what a Maori kainga looks like,' the fair-haired gentleman said. 'It is more modern than I had expected.' He looked somewhat bored. The hunt for Hiroki had developed around him and he had agreed to lead the posse only because it would provide a diversion in his day.

Angrily, Erenora stepped up to him. 'Where is your search warrant?' she asked. She looked for Horitana to support her but could not see him.

The gentleman looked at Erenora, bemused. 'This is a pleasant surprise,' he smiled. 'What does a Maori wahine like you know about such things?' The lilt of his accent was playful and slightly aspirated but, beneath, his intonation was inflected with all the assumptions of his class—*May-or-ree wah-hee-nee.* 'Is this where the fox has gone to ground?' He dismounted and pushed Erenora out of the way.

Her anger mounted as he went from one w'are to the next, walking in as if he owned them, as if he had some divine right. When he tried to enter her own house, however, she stepped into his path and barred his way. 'This is my w'are. Keep out.'

'You are annoying me,' he said. This time, he was not smiling.

'I will not stand aside and let you invade it without a legal document.'

Erenora's mission-educated accent gave him pause again, but not for long. His eyes widened at her impertinence and he tried to push past her.

Meri, trying as usual to be helpful, came to her aid. 'No, Meri,' Erenora cried, concerned that the settler might hit her. The tataraki'i, seeing Erenora struggling with him, tried to get in between, to protect her. At that moment Horitana spurred his horse along the thoroughfare, leapt from the saddle and joined the tussle. 'What's going on here?' he asked.

But the settler would not back away from the doorway and, with a laugh, Horitana slapped him.

The fair-haired gentleman fell backwards to the ground. When he rose, dusting himself off and rubbing his face, he had become a different person.

'How *dare* you put your *filthy* Maori hands on *me*,' he whispered, his words carefully enunciated. His growing hysteria was all the more frightening for being so contained. And then he caught a glimpse of Wiremu inside Erenora and Horitana's house and made an assumption that was clearly motivated by the merest visible connection. 'You were with Hiroki at the time of the murder,' he accused Horitana.

One of the men in his posse called, 'They both have a price on their heads for helping Titokowaru.'

The settler strode back to his horse. Erenora thought with relief, *He is leaving us.* But when he turned to face Erenora and Horitana, he had the whip in his hand.

'You should never have touched me,' he said.

The first lash of the whip was aimed at Horitana. It caught him around the legs and he cried out, 'Aue!' and fell to the ground. The second lash had an altogether different target, snaking towards Erenora. Had she known, she would have put up her hands to protect herself. And even when she saw the lash approaching she thought, *Surely a gentleman would not do that to a woman, even if she were a Maori.* But then the whip wrapped itself around her neck and tightened, taking the breath from her. Eyes wide with fear, she backed away but that only made the situation worse, and she was coughing and choking.

She saw Horitana picking himself up and though close to blacking out, retained enough presence of mind to wind herself even tighter into the whip so that the fair-haired gentleman could not use it again. A tug of war began that was somewhat comedic. The settler began to snarl, alarmed that Erenora appeared to possess the greater strength. 'Let it go, damn you, let it go.'

Horitana realised what Erenora was doing, and he sprang at the Pakeha. 'You, a man, would whip a woman?' His neck tendons were popping as he tackled the Pakeha to the dust—and the whip lost its master.

That's when Erenora unloosed herself from it. Her throat felt on fire as she stumbled away, gasping for air.

Horitana, seeing the settler trying to stand, picked the whip up and used it against its owner. 'As you do to my wife, I do unto you,' he cried. No, he had not yet been able to ascend the whirlwind path of Enoch.

One of the lashes caught the settler across the eyes and he called to his men, 'For God's sake, help me!' before falling again to the ground. Another stroke whipped across the planes of his face, the blood beading the skin like moko. But the men were cowards, standing off as Horitana continued to flay their leader, shredding his red riding jacket to the skin beneath. Even when the man attempted to writhe away, Horitana followed, lashing him again and again.

Erenora tried to stop him. She thought, with fear, *So this is what it is like when the blood-lust comes upon you.* She rushed up to him, grabbing at the whip, her voice hoarse and rasping, 'Horitana! No...'

Then another voice commanded loudly, 'Kati. Enough.'

It was Te Whiti. He wrested the whip from Horitana and stopped the song of the lash. For a moment there was silence, except for the groaning of the fair-haired gentleman.

Horitana reached for Erenora, then collapsed at Te Whiti's feet. 'Aue, te mamae,' he sobbed. 'I am so sorry, rangatira.'

That day marked all three men:

Wiremu would never escape implacable and vengeful justice.

Te Whiti was also marked, for in harbouring Wiremu he gave John Bryce justification for closing Parihaka down.

And Horitana had just made an enemy.

As Erenora watched the fair-haired Pakeha being helped away by his men, she began to feel very afraid. Such men did not like to be humiliated in front of their fellows, least of all by a native.

At some point she knew Horitana would be made to pay.

ACT TWO

Village of God

CHAPTER EIGHT

Do You Ken, John Bryce?

1.

Before I go any further I need to bring on stage a man whom I have already mentioned in this narrative:

John Bryce, enter, sir, and take your bow.

Born in Glasgow, Scotland, in 1833, Bryce arrived with his family in New Zealand in 1840, the same year the Treaty of Waitangi was signed between Maori and Pakeha. As a young man in the 1850s, he bought a farm near Whanganui and also went into local and then national politics until ill health put a temporary stop to his career.

But Bryce was a man on a mission: sort out the Maori and get on with the business of settling Pakeha in New Zealand. During Titokowaru's War he was a lieutenant in the Kai-Iwi Yeomanry Cavalry Volunteers and, in 1868, his detachment was reported as having successfully attacked Hauhau warriors, killing two and wounding others; some reports actually suggest the 'warriors' were unarmed ten-to twelve-year-old boys. He re-entered politics and rose quickly to prominence, mainly because his actions were so swift and effective against Maori opposed to the alienation of their land. Called Honest John by his supporters and, mockingly, King Bryce by his detractors, Bryce became Minister for Native Affairs in 1879, the politician with the highest power over Maori—and he did not hesitate to use it. His face became one of the most recognisable in New Zealand: already large, it was made bigger because of his receding hairline, and the small alert eyes could not hide behind whiskers and beard.

G.W. Rusden found him contemptible. Referring to his earlier life as a dairy farmer he wrote:

> The occupation of a cow-herd gives scope for the humane and for the brutal. If the lad be kindly he will reclaim an erring cow in a kindly manner. If he be inhuman he will inflict as much torture as he can by hurling stones at the eyes of the patient beast which unwittingly offends him. His admirers have not cared to record much of Mr. Bryce's boyish days, but his conduct as Native Minister justifies the inference that he was of the inferior order of cow-boy.[9]

What did Maori call him? We named him 'Bryce ko'uru': Bryce the murderer. How could we expect to obtain justice from a man who called Parihaka 'that headquarters of fanaticism and disaffection'?

---

9 Rusden, History, Vol.3, p.286.

Bryce served under four premiers: Atkinson, Grey, John Hall and Frederick Whitaker. Whether they liked him or not doesn't matter, and although John Hall privately criticised him, there was implicit condoning of his work.

He was their *familiar.*

2.

While I'm at it, let me get something else off my chest.

As I mentioned earlier, it wasn't until the Maori Land March of the 1970s that I woke up to my own history. Josie sometimes liked to say that even though I was a history teacher I had a thick head or, rather, a slow one. You had to go, 'Knock, knock, is anybody at home?' a few times before you got an answer.

After I returned from the march I said to myself, 'Right, I'll give it a go.' I decided to present the class with a lesson on the Maori Wars, except that from the very beginning it became problematic. That title, for instance—or 'Land Wars'—was a Pakeha definition. What did we call them? The *Pakeha* Wars!

Can you see my problem?

Now don't forget this was some forty years ago, and the Maori protest movement was only beginning: clashes with police at Waitangi, Raglan and Bastion Point and the pitching of tents in the grounds of Parliament itself. I should have expected that after the lesson there would be complaints and that I would be called in by the headmaster.

'Are you going radical on me?' he asked. 'What do you think you're doing! The Land Wars aren't in the curriculum and, even if they were, it wouldn't be your version. Go back to teaching British history so that the students can get University Entrance.'

Well, that really got my goat, and I couldn't have been the only Maori who was pissed off about that other 'version' where they won, we lost, end of story. Fortunately, as the decade progressed, other Maori—and Pakeha teachers too—began to make a fuss about the teaching of New Zealand history, including Maori history. Today, thank goodness, it's now an examination subject. That hasn't stopped me, however, from spending the rest of my life working out how to rebalance telling the history from a Maori point of view.

Is it difficult? Is it *what!* Even in this account of Parihaka and my kuia Erenora's life most of the details that I'm deploying about Parihaka in the narrative are taken from accounts by Pakeha historians. Why? Well, Pakeha wrote things down; Maori didn't.

Then the problem is exacerbated because of the inadmissibility of oral evidence as historical fact, although that's changing a bit now. And as far as Erenora's account goes, some Pakeha historians would question its validity because, although it was written down, there are more *reliable* sources—apart from which her account is judged subjective, at the very least.

Why should an oral account be suspect? Maori have had hundreds of years to hone the memory. Yes, it's oral: tough. Get over it. Perhaps the tribes need to resuscitate the old Maori schools of learning with their disciplines of memorisation. Let Maori write the history that we want to, from our own sources and our own perspective, that's all I'm saying.

3.

Let me now add a few words about the fair-haired gentleman.

Had he not ridden into Parihaka that day he, Horitana and Erenora might not have met as foes—and things might have developed differently between them.

This settler was building a large two-storeyed country house from which he planned to rule his estate. The fact that it was grander than most other houses did not bother him; he could afford it. The architecture was typically colonial, square and white with verandahs top and bottom, standing in the middle of a flat expanse that he was planting with English trees and a garden. A drive of loose pebbles led to a turning circle in front, where a flight of steps rose to double doors. Above the doors was emblazoned the motto, 'Fais ce que tu voudrais, Do what thou wilt.'

Of course I know who he was: Pakeha of the times tell us that he was a man of wit, charm and sophistication. He was single, and it was hoped, among the matrons of Taranaki, that he might marry one of their daughters. As to his personal history, he was the second son of an English lord whose estate had gone to his elder brother, and he had emigrated to Taranaki in the 1860s to the promise of land, riches and prosperity. His desire was to establish his own colonial demesne and breed horses.

Among the settler's hobbies were two that were highly desirable for a Victorian gentleman to pursue: science and collecting. In New Zealand he had begun to put both to use in the study of the Maori as an anthropological subject and in the collection of our tribal artefacts. Already he had submitted papers to learned British journals on the Taranaki Maori, believing that, in the light of their forthcoming extinction, it was more appropriate to write about them while they were alive and not when they were dead.

I hope you'll forgive my not giving you his English name; my research on him is unfinished, and I don't want to unmask him until I've completed it.

Erenora, however, had a name for him. In the encounter in Parihaka she had glimpsed the man beneath, the real person glossed over in reliable sources. She called him Piharo, from the Maori word pi'arongo, a very hard black stone, because what she had seen of his i'i, his life force, had been so dark and sinister.

Because she called him that, I shall call him that also.

Let me interpolate a scene from my own imagination as Piharo returns to his estate.

Thunder is booming overhead and lightning cracks the sky apart as he arrives at his house to await the arrival of a doctor who will stitch the places where the lash cut deep.

He still cannot believe the marks on his face are from his *own* whip. How could this have happened? Not three men but four have been marked on the day that the fugitive Hiroki was pursued into Parihaka.

The fourth is Piharo himself.

While the doctor's needle criss-crosses the cuts in his face, Piharo's rage mounts. He groans with pain as the doctor sews together the torn flaps of his left eyelid. When the work is finished, he looks in the mirror at the cicatrice of stitches and waves away the doctor's apologetic gestures.

'No,' Piharo says gallantly, 'it will be all right.'

All right? Nothing will ever be *all right.* From this day, for every day henceforth, people will look at his face and know that something happened to him, someone had got the better of him.

Piharo's obsession grows. The wounds to his face will eventually heal but not the black place the lash has uncovered where unforgiveness dwells. He will make the Maori named Horitana pay—have his pound of flesh—even if he has to wait years to exact it.

CHAPTER NINE

The Year of the Plough

1.

The fugitive Wiremu Hiroki remained in Parihaka under Te Whiti's protection. Meanwhile, the predations of the Pakeha surveyors continued, and Te Whiti decided that he had to step up the defensive measures against the Pakeha incursions.

Of these deliberate provocations, G.W. Rusden had this to say:

> *Confident that the Maoris could easily be crushed by the available forces, the despisers of Maori rights were not displeased at the prospect of collision which might at last sweep away the hated guarantees of the Waitangi treaty.*[10]

2.

'Despite our attempts to dissuade them,' Erenora wrote, 'the surveyors still kept unlawfully crossing the river into Maori territory, there being no evidence of its legal government purchase. Indeed, when James Mackay asked Te Whiti to cease preventing the surveyors from doing their work, the prophet answered,

---

10   Rusden, *History*, Vol.3, p.257.

"You had better go to the government and fix their side first. They are the active parties in the matter, not me. I am living quietly on my land."

'Te Whiti came to see Horitana again and his eyes were steely. "If the Pakeha thinks he can still come onto our land as if he owns it, we will go onto his as if we own it. I want you to gather the men and go out, this time with ploughs. I want to plough the belly of the government, and see how they like it."'

And so the Year of the Plough began, one morning when the wind was coming off Taranaki Mountain.

Erenora watched as Horitana inspected teams of ploughmen, fifty in all, waiting with their bullock teams for the order to move out of Parihaka; after all, Te Whiti had asked for a display that showed he meant business. Indeed, so eager had been the men they had begun assembling before dawn, talking amiably to one another. Some were watching the sacred mountain: it always inspired and guided them. Others, like Ruakere, Rangiora and Whata, were farewelling their families before they left for the sacred work.

Ripeka shivered and said to Paora, 'You will be careful, won't you?' And Meri, close to her delivery, told Riki, 'Don't forget that you're going to be a father.'

Erenora kissed Horitana on the cheek. 'Are you sure I can't come with you?' she asked. How she wished she could be one of the ploughmen. 'If I put my long hair up into a topknot, nobody would know.'

Laughing, he chided her, 'But *I* would know.' He put his hands on the back of her neck and pulled her into an embrace—and she winced. Where Piharo had used his whip on her the skin had broken. Now healing but still hurting, the weals were like a crusted necklace.

Erenora hid her pain. 'Do your job, husband,' she said, 'and bring your brothers-in-law back to my sisters.' She farewelled the bullocks too, calling, 'And you, beloved companions, no shirking!'

The bullocks stamped and bellowed, wanting to get on with it. Breath jetted from their nostrils. What noble, strong beasts they were, etched against the sky as it faded, lightened and became streaked with red. And then, lo and behold, ka ao, ka ao, ka awatea, the dawn came over the horizon.

Horitana looked to Taranaki; it *shone* with morning light. 'The mounga is watching,' he said. 'Let's go.'

As the teams left Parihaka one of the ploughmen, Tonga Awhikau, began to sing a passionate waiata:

'I te raa o mae'e ka iri kei te torona, ka mau taku ringa ki te parau e 'au nei te w'enua. Ka toro taku ringa ki te atua e tuu nei ko w'akatohe; ka puta te 'ae a te kaawana e tango nei w'enua e kore au e taaea, 'e uri noo Hoohepa, noo ngaa tuupuna. On a day in May I was suspended from the throne of God, my hand to the plough as it swept across the land. My hand, also extended to God, is resolute. The ill-feeling of the government emerges in the taking

98

away of the land. It will not deter me, a descendant of Joseph by way of my ancestors!'

The men whistled and stamped, urging the bullocks forward, 'Timata! 'aere tatou!' Dogs were barking as, slowly but surely, the bullocks dragged the gleaming ploughshares across the river and into Pakeha land.

3.

Te Whiti and Tohu's ploughing campaign began. Dick Scott describes the reaction to that first plough-ing, done at Oakura, in this way:

> *The settler could not believe his eyes. Long furrows broke his grassland and a team of silent ploughmen was steadily extending the area of upturned soil. This was land only seven miles from New Plymouth, it had been in undisturbed Euro-pean possession since the wars, the original owners, long ago killed or hunted off, had been forgotten. Courtney, the outraged farmer, rushed to stop them. But the Maori ploughmen who started work before sunrise at Oakura on the morning of 26 May 1879, serenely continued till dusk. And the next day was the same, and the next, until twenty acres were turned under.*[11]

In all of this we have to try to look into the prophet Te Whiti's mind. Why provoke Premier Grey and Mr Bryce?

---

[11] Scott, Ask That Mountain, p.55.

The prophet's answer was, 'You want to come onto our land? See how you like it when we come onto yours!'

Did the government have the right?

In Te Whiti's eyes, no, it did not, and he wanted to test that right.

But was the prophet aware of the risk?

I like to think so. His biblical vision saw the future of Parihaka in the long term. For instance, back in 1869, when he proclaimed the Takahanga, Maori freedom from Pakeha authority, he also prophesied two crises that Parihaka would have to suffer before the final phase of the kainga's resurrection and harvest.

The first of these was Akarama, otherwise known as the Aceldama, the transaction of Judas Iscariot, when Parihaka would be betrayed.

Was Premier Grey—or was Bryce—Judas Iscariot?

'Every day,' Erenora wrote, 'our plough teams went out in the bright mornings and returned safe through the twilight. I could always tell, even before seeing the teams, that Horitana and our men were on their way home. How? Our beloved companions, eager to get back to the kainga, would set up a bellowing and trumpeting loud enough to deafen the world. And there would be our men, trying to keep them under control, laughing as the bullocks pulled them over hill and down dale.

'As soon as they arrived, I would say to the tataraki'i, "Quickly, unyoke the bullocks from their traces and take them to the stream." You had to be fast because those noble animals wanted to be fed and watered and never liked to wait. While the tataraki'i washed and scrubbed them, I moved among their number patting them and inspecting their hooves but also upbraiding them. "You are all becoming like my husband," I growled at them, "accustomed to the pleasures of a bath after a hard day's work." Oh, how they loved being washed and brushed down and, just like Horitana, they shivered with sensuous delight. And they knew I didn't mean my grumpy words. After all, did I not also whisper my thanks to them, reaffirm the w'akapapa between us and the times of travail when they sheltered the more'u while we were building Parihaka?

'A week later, however, I saw that Horitana was becoming worried for the safety of the ploughmen. He came down to the stream one afternoon to stand beside me and wash the bullocks. The tataraki'i were clambering among the noble beasts, climbing onto their backs and diving into the stream. "We continue to take the Pakeha by surprise," Horitana said, "but, now, they are beginning to arrive where we are ploughing to stop us."

'I pressed his hand. "They must have scouts watching the kainga," I answered. "It won't be long before..." I began to tremble. I did not want to think about the possibility of the Akarama or to show Horitana how afraid I was. Suddenly, I was sprayed with water as one of the children jumped close to me, and that saved me from showing my concern. "You meant that!" I laughed. But I couldn't help fearing the coming of any conflict as Horitana and the teams expanded their ploughing.

'They went onto settler-occupied land along the coast between Pukearuhe and Hawera. At Manaia the great chief Wiremu Kingi Te Matakatea and his Ngati Haumiti followers joined them. Now approaching his eighties, "The Clear-Eyed One" was sick of waiting for the government to give him back his land.'

The conflict mounted as Pakeha settlers demanded immediate action. They held boisterous meetings and organised vigilante groups, and Pakeha tempers soared sharply to war-mongering fever pitch.

One newspaper of the time wrote:

> Perhaps, all things considered, the present difficulty will be one of the greatest blessings New Zealand ever experienced, for without doubt it will be a war of extermination ... The time has come, in our minds, when New Zealand must strike for freedom, and this means the death-blow to the Maori race![12]

And do you remember Harry Atkinson, ex-premier and now in opposition? At a public meeting on 7 June, he was reported in the *Taranaki Herald* as taking up the same theme, clearly keeping his enmity against Maori alive. 'He hoped,' the newspaper told its read-

---

[12] 'The Historian's View', Taranaki Herald, 27 January 1903, cited in Rusden, History, vol.3, p229.

ers, 'if war did come, the natives would be exterminated.'

Undeterred, Horitana followed Te Whiti's command to stay on the job. He and the ploughmen well knew the risk that they might be subject to lynch mobs. If some were shot, Tohu counselled them: 'Gather up the earth on which the blood has spilt, and bring it to Parihaka.'

It almost came to that. 'Someone could have been killed today,' Horitana told Erenora one night, his face creased and drawn. 'Why does the government remain silent? Surely it is time for them to negotiate with us over the land. Instead they allow the settlers to organise themselves and outnumber us. And today, for the first time, they arrived bearing arms. They had a flag and, when they came upon us, they took up a skirmishing line with loaded rifles at the ready. I saw murder in their eyes but as they advanced I shouted to the boys, "Keep going. Ignore them." Their line came right up to our furrows and, when they reached where we were ploughing, the settlers stood and raised their rifles. The others behind them knelt for the reload.

'I went over to their boss and said, as calmly as I could, "We will finish our job at five o'clock." I could tell that he was on the knife edge. I added quietly, "We're unarmed and you wouldn't want to kill unarmed men, would you?" Although his men called out to him with scorn, "Don't listen to the black bugger," he nodded—he didn't want blood on his hands. So we continued under their watchful and angry gaze for an hour. Then we packed up and left, but I don't know how long before the settlers lose their heads.'

Erenora kissed him. 'Everything will be all right,' she said. She tried to be brave but she trembled for him.

Not long after that, Horitana went out again with the ploughmen. He was not to know that the land he had chosen to work that day belonged to Piharo. This time, the ploughing was opposed with great belligerence and stopped. All the ploughmen were beaten and tied up.

'Well, well, well,' Piharo smiled when his farm manager brought Horitana under guard before him, 'how kind of you to pay me a visit.'

He ordered Horitana and the other ploughmen to be detained, pending arrest. The constabulary arrived to charge them.

'This time the law is, indeed, on my side,' Piharo said.

And the Akarama began.

4.

On that evening, Erenora was at Meri's house.

Meri's baby had arrived. When he slithered into the arms of the midwife, who was Huhana, she cried out, 'A son for the tribe!' Tenderly, she blessed the babe and placed him in Meri's arms. He wailed lustily, waving his fists in the air.

'We will name him Kawa,' Meri said.

Suddenly the women heard shouting outside. 'Something's happened,' Erenora said. She ran to the doorway and saw other wives and girlfriends gathering to look down the road where Te Whao, one of the ploughmen, was running towards them. When he saw Erenora he yelled, 'Horitana and the others have been arrested.' All these nights Erenora had known that this could happen. Now, the realisation that Horitana wasn't coming home tonight—and might not come home tomorrow night or the night after—made her double up with physical loss.

'Look after Meri,' she said to Huhana and Ripeka. 'I'm going into New Plymouth to find out what is happening.' She saddled one of the village's fastest horses and was soon on her way.

As she approached the outskirts of the town some Pakeha, who had been celebrating the arrests, halted her. 'Here's one that we didn't serve with a warrant, lads!' one of the men laughed. He tried to grab the reins. 'Take your hands off my stallion,' Erenora warned him. When he didn't obey, she commanded the horse, 'Kei runga!' It reared, its hooves flashing, and he and his friends scattered.

Sweating from the wild ride, she arrived at the gaol. As she forced her way through the crowd she saw that Te Whiti and a few other elders had arrived before her to remonstrate on behalf of the ploughmen. 'Aue, Erenora,' the prophet greeted her. 'It is the Akarama after all. So be it.' The hostility was palpable as she walked into the building with him. 'What is the charge? ' Te Whiti asked.

'Malicious injury, forcible entry and riot,' was the answer.

'Can we see our men?'

Erenora's heart was thundering as she followed Te Whiti and the elders to the compound where the prisoners were held; among them was Horitana. 'What have they done to you?' she moaned. His face was bruised and blackened.

Although Horitana saw her alarm, he tried to smile. 'I was only doing my job,' he teased. He traced the red marks on her neck, now fully healed; how he had wept when applying kawakawa oil to soothe Erenora's pain. 'Don't be afraid,' he continued, 'for I have been cast into the pit before and do not fear the darkness.'

But Erenora had good reason to be concerned. As well as the charge for the ploughing, the old matter of the bounty on Horitana's head might be raised.

If it was, what would happen to him?

Erenora went to the New Plymouth Resident Magistrate's Court a second time when the forty ploughmen were charged for malicious injury to property.

I beg your pardon? Surely it was the surveyors who should be put on trial for maliciously injuring the land itself.

Meri had insisted on being in the courtroom. When Riki was charged, he gave her a wan smile. She held up Kawa so that Riki could see him. 'Yes ... our son,' she called to him. Riki's face shone with pride. How he wanted to hold the babe.

The charges were read out. Horitana responded with a fierce declaration. 'My weapons were ploughshares,' he said, 'but yours were firearms.'

The ploughmen were returned to their cells to await sentencing.

In the interim, settlers showed their satisfaction that justice was being served. Listen to the editor of the *Taranaki Herald:*

> *If it should come to fighting then we have very little hesitation in saying the struggle will be a short one, and afterwards this district will never more receive a check to its progress from the same cause.*[13]

5.

You'd have thought that such a remark was a signal that any further Maori ploughing would end in certain death. But Te Whiti and Tohu had nerves of steel; the Akarama might be at hand but, until the government itself gave a response about the legality of the ploughing, the protest would carry on.

---

[13] Cited in Rusden, ibid, p.271.

'Although your brothers are in gaol,' Te Whiti said to the men of Parihaka, 'take the bullock teams out. Do as your brothers have done.'

No matter that every new team was arrested, another team took their place. By 5 July ninety men were in custody—this time Te Whao was among them—and the next day 105. Within three months, 200 men had been arrested.

On one matter, how the settlers must have fumed.

Why didn't the Maori take up arms? If they did, then there would be just cause to raise their rifles and fire on them all. Instead, all Te Whiti and Tohu's followers did was offer themselves up for arrest! And Te Whiti, too, kept out of reach.

'If any man molests me,' he said, 'I will talk with my weapon—the tongue. I will not resist the soldiers if they come, I would gladly let them crucify me.'

But the Pakeha had their day in court on 26 July with the sentencing of the first forty imprisoned ploughmen.

For the third time, Erenora attended the courthouse with Te Whiti and other elders. 'I want you to accompany me,' he told her; how proud she was of his regard for her. She shielded the prophet as they entered the courtroom and abuse was hurled at him. 'It should be you on trial, *Tay Witty,*' a settler called, 'but we'll get you.'

The party passed through the crowd to the public gallery where Erenora took a seat. Across the courtroom she caught sight of Piharo, the fair-haired gentleman settler. In a mocking manner he took off his hat and bowed his head to her. It was the first time she had seen him since the whipping and she was not prepared for ... his *face.* Now it was marked by a series of parallel scars across his eyes and nose. And despite the skill of the surgeon who had attended him, nothing would ever repair the loose flap that now functioned as his left eyelid.

Quickly Erenora turned away and tried to keep calm as the first batch of twenty-five prisoners was brought into the courtroom; Horitana, Riki and Paora were not among them.

Settlers in the courtroom began baying for blood. 'Give them the noose!' they cried.

The presiding magistrate found the twenty-five ploughmen to have caused damage estimated at 5 shillings. Was that all? Then surely they would only have to pay the fine to be let go. Instead, 'You are sentenced to two months' hard labour in Dunedin Gaol,' the magistrate said. 'You are also required to pay £200 bail to ensure that on your return to Parihaka you maintain good behaviour for a period of no less than ten months.'

Who had £200? 'Nobody?' the magistrate asked. 'In that case, you are all sentenced to hard labour for a year.' A loud wailing arose among the Maori women in the courtroom; this was tantamount to a sentence of death.

'Hip, hip, hoo-*raah!*' the locals roared. It might not be the noose but it was good enough.

The remaining prisoners were brought to the dock. Erenora saw Horitana, Riki and Paora among their number. When she gained Horitana's attention he smiled at her. *Cast aside your fears, Erenora, and don't be sad. I will always look after you.*

And then came the sentencing. 'You will all be taken to Wellington and there you will be held without trial,' the magistrate said.

The words flowed over Erenora. She swayed with puzzlement and her head started buzzing. 'That can't be right,' she said to Te Whiti. 'Held without trial?'

The magistrate went on to explain that, to accommodate the prisoners, the military barracks at Mount Cook, a rise on the outskirts of the city, would be removed and the site prepared for a gaol. 'Hip, hip, hoo-*raah!*' the settlers cried.

The magistrate waited for order to restore itself. 'Would the prisoner known as Horitana step forward?'

Erenora began to panic. She saw the magistrate exchange a glance with Piharo. 'Because of your previous involvement in the Taranaki Wars fighting with Titokowaru,' the magistrate said, 'you have had your sentence reserved pending receipt of all the facts pertaining to your actions against the state.'

Someone shouted, 'The Maori has a price on his head, Your Honour!'

The magistrate nodded. 'Until all charges are brought before this court and a separate trial can be organised, you will join the others imprisoned at Mount Cook.'

Erenora looked again in Piharo's direction; he was smiling in triumph. The smile chilled Erenora's heart. She rose from her seat and cried out to Horitana:

'Taku tane! Horitana! Kia tupato te 'e o te tangata nei! Husband! Horitana! Beware the evil of Piharo!'

6.

Ah, *Piharo.*

Erenora was right to be concerned. Piharo had been able to subvert the course of justice and, by brilliance and bribery, had taken his revenge against Horitana.

Let me therefore interpolate another scene as Piharo returns from the trial to his estate. At first he is elated by his triumph, consuming with great gusto the evening meal prepared by his housekeeper. But as the night deepens, so does his excitement diminish.

Think of him now, brooding through the evening and staring into the fire that has been lit for him in his library. He has a goblet of red wine in his hand and he holds it up to the fire's light, twirling it by the stem. Then, in a sudden movement, he stands and flings the glass into the flames.

'I thought, Maori warrior,' he rages, 'that putting you in prison would give me satisfaction ... but it is not enough. It is not ... sufficient...'

Piharo paces back and forth and his shadow is like the dark stone that Erenora glimpsed within him, a crookbacked *thing* pacing with him.

He looks around the room for support. Above the fireplace is the family coat of arms. Along one entire wall are Pakeha classics: Machiavelli, de Sade and popular novels by Poe, Dumas *père* and Hugo. Lining another wall are items in his developing Maori collection: carvings, weapons of war, greenstone mere and 'eitiki—and three tattooed mummified Maori heads of which Piharo is particularly proud. Trafficking in the heads is so brisk that warriors fallen in the most recent Taranaki battles against the Pakeha have been harvested for purchasers with sufficient money to acquire them; Piharo is such a buyer.

Frustrated, Piharo goes up the stairs to his bedroom. 'What can I do to punish you, Horitana?' he asks himself. 'What will be ... what is the Maori word for it ... fitting *ootoo?*'

Throughout the night, he moans, tosses and turns; he cannot let go of the question. Then, around dawn, he takes up a hand mirror and looks at the scars on his face. And though the doctor says his appearance will improve, actually, the scarring looks rather beautiful ... like the Maori facial tattoo.

He begins to laugh and laugh. That's *it!*

Piharo rings for his foreman. 'I require a silversmith,' he says. 'I wish to give him a particularly intricate and exquisite task. Bring him tomorrow.'

7.

Not long afterward, Erenora was able to have a few moments with Horitana before he and the other prisoners were taken away. Among them was Wiremu Kingi Te Matakatea. Too late the government realised the injustice of sentencing 'The Clear-Eyed One' and offered him his release; Matakea would accept it only if his men were freed also, a request the government would not entertain.

'Will I ever see you again?' Erenora asked Horitana.

'I will write from Wellington,' he answered. 'Once I know when my court case will be held, I will tell you. Have faith, forget your fears and look to the day when we are reunited.'

Erenora tried to smile at his gentle comforting, but tears began to stream down her face. 'I'm sorry, husband, I'm so afraid.' She didn't care that Riki and Hori and other prisoners—Te Whao, Ruakere, Rangiora and Whata—were looking on.

'Don't fear,' Horitana answered. 'Our imprisonment isn't a sentence of death. There is always the promise of release and of resurrection. Tell the other wives that, won't you? We're all orphans in a storm, but, like all things, even storms do pass.'

The day was darkly lowering when, shackled to each other, Horitana, Paora, Riki and the other men were marched on board the prison transport. Distraught, the three sisters watched as the ship set sail and turned southward. Just as it disappeared into the stomach of the night, strange lights began to illuminate the sky, and seagulls circled and clawed away as if trying to escape. Bitter rain came rushing landward.

'It's all Horitana's fault,' Meri screamed. 'If he had commanded Riki to stay home, my husband would never have been arrested.'

Erenora embraced her sister. 'Our husbands are brothers-in-law and loyal and loving friends,' she answered. 'They will protect each other.'

'And who will protect *us?*' Ripeka asked. Like Meri, she was looking for someone to blame for Paora's imprisonment.

'We will protect each other,' Erenora replied.

And still Te Whiti would not bow down.

The next morning at Parihaka he said to the ploughmen, 'Go, put your hands to the plough, look not back. If any come with guns and swords, be not afraid. If they smite you, smite not in return. If they rend you, be not discouraged—another will take up the good work.'

It was from that moment that the wearing of three white feathers in the hair was widely adopted as a symbol of honour and remembrance for the men sent to prison. When some Pakeha saw the feathers, they were reminded of the three plumes of Bohemia and thought that they may have referred to the days when Riemenschneider was at Warea.

No, the feathers had biblical and Maori inspiration: Glory to God, peace on earth and goodwill to all men. Thus, with God at their shoulders and peace and goodwill within them, the ploughmen, straight away, went back on the job.

And from that time can be dated this fact: all men who were subsequently arrested were gaoled without trial.

CHAPTER TEN

Te Paremata o te Pakeha

1.

Aue, I now have to go behind the scenes of Erenora's story for a little bit.

This is the problem with history. You think it's one narrative but most often it's three or four or more, all like a twisted rope, tangled and knotted. But Maori have always known this about history anyway. Look at the way we korero in the meeting house. The talk goes all over the place—backwards, forwards, sideways and circling on itself.

In particular, I have to take you away from Taranaki to Wellington and to the New Zealand Parliament, Pharaoh's Te Paremata o te Pakeha.

Why? From the time the Pakeha gained the upper hand in Aotearoa, the fate of all Maori throughout history has been decided there in that Valley of the Kings, presided over by Pharaoh's palace, temples, library, stelae and other memorials and, crouching nearby, his judicial sphinx: the High Court. It was therefore at Te Paremata o te Pakeha, in 1880, that the fate of the Parihaka ploughmen was also decided.

Now, what's interesting is that Parliament had actually tried to create a voice for Maori by establishing four Maori seats in 1867, albeit, initially, as an experiment for one term only. The seats were the government's way of fulfilling the third clause of the Treaty of Waitangi—that is, giving Maori the rights of British subjects. During the 1870s and 1880s the Maori parliamentarians included Wiremu Parata, Ihaia Tainui, Hori Kerei Taiaroa, Henare Tomoana, Hone Mohi Tawhai and Wiremu Maipapa Te Wheoro, the Member for Western Maori. Laudable as that was, how much real power did the Maori parliamentarians have? Well, Parliament comprised 88 seats. It refused to give Maori a just proportion of seats based on the value of their communal property rights because then Maori would have dominated.

No wonder Parliament was able to push through legislation about Maori virtually unopposed.

There were three main legal positions Parliament had to address about Parihaka.

First, what was the status of Taranaki land: who owned what and where it was confiscated, what had been the instruments enforcing the confiscations? Second, given these questions, was the government legally entitled to send in surveyors? Third, if it wasn't, shouldn't the ploughmen sent to prison be released?

Rest assured there's ample evidence that the Maori members of Parliament actively tried to resolve the Parihaka problem. They are often maligned today as Uncle Toms or as ineffective but, supported by Maori chiefs throughout Aotearoa, they continued to call for the surveys to be halted. And of course they were not lacking some support from their parliamentary colleagues: some members, acting on their con-sciences, also protested the process by which the ploughmen had been sentenced.

Then the Maori members and chiefs threatened to test the government's right to confiscate by taking it to Pharaoh's own Supreme Court and, if necessary, all the way to Queen Victoria in London.

Parliament quickly moved to stop that kind of legal action. Sir John Hall had taken over from Sir George Grey as eleventh premier of New Zealand on 8 October 1879. He had in his Cabinet Harry Atkinson, as an all-powerful Minister of Finance, and John Bryce—two men who, as has already been demonstrated, lost no sleep over Maori. It was Bryce who now, as Minister of Native Affairs, resolved the third big legal position by introducing the infamous Maori Prisoners' Trial Act. Not only could prisoners be sent to prison without trial, they could have their trials postponed *indefinitely.*

Although objections increased in Parliament about denial of justice, conflict with the principles of Magna Carta and suspension of habeas corpus, nothing could overturn the government's view that such a bill was required to deal with the threat of Te Whiti and Tohu. And after all, were Maori really British subjects?

Then, to deal with the first question, Bryce also introduced the Confiscated Lands Inquiry, which would investigate Maori grievances over confiscated Taranaki land. There was an added sting, however—to keep the Maori prisoners under lock and key, the Act declared that it was 'indispensable for the peace and safety of the colony that the ordinary course of law should be suspended, and [the trials] should take place under special legislation'.

Pharaoh was harsh, keeping the Children of Israel enslaved unto him forever.

2.

Even so, Horitana, when he heard the news in his Wellington prison cell, was able to send a message to Erenora.

'My darling,' he wrote, 'although the prisoners' chances of any early justice are bad, the overriding news about the Confiscated Lands Inquiry is good. I urge you to attend the first meeting of the commissioners in Hawera on 11 February. Let me know the outcome of their findings. The fate of the land is more important than my own. I am in God's hands.'

Horitana mistakenly assumed that the inquiry would happen quickly. He also expected it to be fair—but let's face it, how could Maori obtain such a hearing? Wouldn't you expect the commission, for instance, to go to Parihaka to talk to Te Whiti and Tohu? They were invited to do so but did they take up the offer? No.

I like the way Rachel Buchanan describes the nature of the hearings:

> *The commission was working in one kind of reality, Parihaka in another. In one of its three*

reports, the commission said: 'As on the Plains, even more so certainly at the doors of Parihaka, the establishment of English homesteads and the fencing and cultivation of the land, will be a guarantee of peace.' [14]

Dream *on*, commissioners!

As Horitana had requested, Erenora attended the first hearing. She realised with dismay that the sun would rise and set many times before any outcome would be known.

Even worse, Bryce was apparently not planning to wait for the commission to complete its hearings. Confident of sanction, the Armed Constabulary began crossing the Waingongoro River to ensure that the surveying and the associated business of roadmaking would proceed. More ominously, the constabulary were actively rebuilding the old beach road, digging trenches and adding blockhouses and a watchtower. By April 1880, as Buchanan describes it, 600 armed police and labourers were on the job. They had a camp and stockade south of the village and another to the north. The intention, so Bryce said, was to link Hawera to New Plymouth, but why then the fortifications?

Parihaka was in its path.

---

14 Buchanan, Parihaka Album, p.44. The quotation cites an opinion in the third and fi nal report of the commission, 4 August 1880.

3.

It was during this same time, while incarcerated at Mount Cook, that Horitana was woken in the middle of the night by sounds of consternation and alarm.

'What is happening?' he shouted.

He saw guards turning up the gaslights and, carrying lanterns, moving swiftly from cell to cell, rousing the prisoners and shackling them together. 'We're to be shipped to the South Island,' Paora cried to him, 'either to Hokitika, Dunedin or Christchurch.'

Suddenly, Horitana's own cell door was opened and a visitor was admitted, a distinguished fair-haired gentleman. Horitana leapt at Piharo but his chains held him back. 'You have finally come to kill me?' he asked.

'Oh no,' Piharo said, 'that would be altogether too easy a punishment. Here,' he continued, 'I have brought you a gift.'

In his hands he held an object that Horitana at first could not recognise: it possessed a terrible beauty. Then he realised that it was a mokomokai, a tattooed head, plated with silver. It flashed in the light and Horitana put his hands to his eyes to prevent being blinded.

The silversmith who had fashioned the mokomokai must have been a craftsman of the highest order. He had duplicated the mummified face beneath, finely layering it and etching it with the filigree of the original moko. There were no eye apertures and only an open gash for the mouth.

There was a sinister refinement. The skull of the mokomokai had been entirely hollowed and scraped out. It had been hinged so that it could be worn. Once the wearer's face was enclosed, it would be padlocked tight.

'You cannot do this inhuman thing,' Horitana said.

Piharo's revenge had twisted into something beyond human pity. He called five guards into the cell to restrain Horitana.

'No. *No,*' Horitana cried as the guards pinned him down.

And Piharo wrapped his whip around Horitana's neck and forced him so close they could have kissed. 'I vowed you would pay for what you did to me,' he said. 'You not only *touched* me, you marked me forever.' His words hissed out. 'You inflicted me against my will with your moko. Now, against yours, wear mine.'

The mokomokai was surprisingly heavy. The silversmith had been required to reinforce the skull with an iron plate. As it was fitted onto his face Horitana groaned at the weight; the bottom edge of the mokomokai cut into his shoulders so that they bled.

And when it was padlocked into place, immediately the temperature inside the mokomokai increased so that Horitana's face streamed with sweat. *How will I be able to live in this eternal darkness?* As fear overtook him, his heart accelerated, racing out of control. He began to gasp for air, pressing his lips against the mouth aperture.

Lesser men would have died from terror within an hour or two. Somehow, Horitana managed to calm himself. 'Oh, valiant heart,' he cried, 'practise the art of forbearance.'

'Still alive, are we?' Piharo was disappointed at first, hoping for a quick harvest. Then he smiled with joy. 'All right, live as long as you wish. I will have you imprisoned until you die and then you will be mine. You will never see your wife again.'

From that moment, Horitana disappeared off the face of the earth.

And now the question:

Why, in all the prison records of the time, was there no mention of the mokomokai? You'd think, if it were true, that we would all have heard of a dead man's face being used to cover that of a living man? Perhaps Piharo's silver didn't just cover the mokomokai but also the palms of a few warders to ensure their tongues remained silent.

Another question:

Where did the inspiration come from? Well, I have earlier mentioned some of the authors in Piharo's library. One of those was Alexandre Dumas *père,* and it is most likely from *L'Homme au Masque de Fer* (begun in 1847), the final part of his Three Musketeers trilogy, that Piharo got the idea—or stole it. Other *romans* of the time relating to torture and cruel imprisonment include Edgar Allan Poe's *The Premature*

Burial and Dumas *père'sLe Comte de Monte-Cristo* (both published in 1844) and Victor Hugo's *Les Misérables* (1862).

Whatever the influence, the rumour grew among Maori prisoners of the man who lived within the face of another, dead warrior. Just to look upon that face, which sometimes flashed blindingly in the light, was to bring you to your knees in awe at the abhorrent nature of the punishment—and at the prisoner's great agony.

They called him the man with the face of silver.

Te tangata mokomokai.

CHAPTER ELEVEN

Saga of the Fences

1.

Meanwhile, at Parihaka, the extraordinary saga of the fences began.

Picture this: the year is 1880 and villagers are working in the gardens of their expansive plantations north-west of the kainga. There is no school today and, early in the morning, Erenora has gone to the complex of barns and high-timbered paddocks where the bullock herds are kept. As soon as they see her, they crowd around her. 'No, no!' she laughs as they press in and nuzzle her. 'I only need two of you!'

She yokes the lucky bullocks to a sled and is soon off to the stream to fill barrels of water for the cultivations. As she passes through the village, some of the tataraki'i jump impulsively onto the sled. 'Can we come with you?' they ask. When Erenora reaches the stream the children happily help her fill the barrels; sometimes they playfully splash each other.

Further upstream, a group of kuia is harvesting watercress. They stand in the stream, their dresses stained dark with the water, gossiping as they pluck the cress from the banks.

June is an important month in the Maori calendar. The heliacal rising of the Pleiades star cluster ushers in Puanga, the Maori New Year. Falling at the end of the harvest, it is the time to prepare the land and plant the new crops.

The cultivations are all neatly divided by sod walls and manuka picket fences. They stretch from the citadel to the outer perimeter near the sea; there are also small shelters and huts between. The walls and fences are there not only to protect the crops from the village's bullocks, horses and pigs but also to contain and define the plantings: mclon, potato, pumpkin, maize and other vegetables, oats for horse feed and, also, tobacco. The gardens are tilled on a rotational basis, so every now and then there is an empty plantation, fallow the current year but to be planted next year. Pigs are fenced in. Domestic fowls roam wherever they wish. Small lanes allow the workers to move between the gardens.

An idyllic scene, you think? Not so. Bryce's roadbuilders are making relentless progress towards the plantations.

'I was driving my bullock team, taking the water to the gardens, when all of a sudden the children, who had been skipping beside the sled, pointed ahead, "Titiro! Look!"

'The road Mr Bryce's labourers were building had reached the outer perimeter of the gardens. How could you not notice it! The roadbuilders were loud and boisterous, and so was the Armed Constabulary protecting them.

'I saw an altercation taking place between the trespassers and some of our villagers. "Get out of the way," two of the constables were demanding. The labourers had broken two of our picket fences around fields where we were storing crops and preparing the land for the coming year. The invaders pushed one of the villagers and, with a cry, she fell to the ground. Then the labourers and constabulary pushed right through the fence onto our side. Quickly, I lashed at the bullock team, "'aere! W'ano!"

'The tataraki'i leapt aside as my beloved companions trumpeted and put their heads down. Oh, they were so inspiring as they approached the invaders; the barrels of water were falling left, right and centre, and the constabulary scattered. "The road is yours," I said, as I pulled on the reins of the team before they trampled the men, "but the fences are ours." I think the labourers and constabulary were more frightened of my pawing beasts than they were of me, but they wisely retreated.

'That evening, Te Whiti came to see me at my house. I expected him to chastise me for my intemperate action. Instead he said, "You are as bad as your husband."

'He told me he had called all the villagers to meet on the marae.'

2.

The space in front of the meeting house was ringed with blazing firelight. The sun had disappeared, and the temperature had plummeted. The villagers huddled in blankets, trying to keep warm.

Huhana smiled at Erenora. 'We were lucky to get our seeds planted before winter really arrives.'

Te Whiti and Tohu appeared. 'What are all you people doing sitting out here in the cold?' Te Whiti joked, stamping his feet and hugging himself. 'Waiting for me? Then I had better get on with it. It is makariri, freezing.'

The gathering laughed as the prophet got straight down to business. 'The government has still not proven its right to come onto our land,' he began. 'Why have they not stopped their surveying and roadbuilding until the commission reports on its findings? Although it appears that the inquiry is hostile to us we shall, as we always have done, trust to God's will.'

The people murmured, 'Ae. Yes.'

'Thus I say that until God shows us what that will is, we carry on as usual. Tomorrow, let us return to our gardens and put the fences up again where they belong. Kua pai?'

From the people came a strong, deep chorus. 'Yes, we are agreed.'

James Cowan describes this extraordinary reaction:

The dispute now assumed a new aspect. A party of forty to fifty men, styled the morehu, or 'survivors', marched out from Parihaka almost daily, each man carrying a tree-branch, and on arriving at the road where it entered the cultiva-

128

tion on the south side continued to march along the line, reciting an incantation, until within a short distance of the north boundary of the field, close to the Constabulary camp, and back again to the south boundary, where they planted the branches across the road.[15]

Every morning, the roadbuilders tore the fences down again and pushed on with their road. Came the evenings, however, and while the roadbuilders were asleep, the villagers rebuilt *all* the fences they had broken. What happened the next day? The constabulary tore those down. So what did the villagers do? Rebuild them again and again.

That's when Bryce ordered this, on 19 July: 'Any Maori who puts up a fence that has been taken down by the government will be arrested.' *Why?* Surely it was the government that should be arrested for removing the fence in the first place.

3.

'By now,' Erenora wrote, 'the winter had burst upon us, with squally rain sweeping across Parihaka from the sea. No matter the weather, Mr Bryce's challenge was too much for our men not to accept. They clamoured to work at the fences! Te Whiti and

---

[15] James Cowan, The New Zealand Wars: A History of the Maori Campaigns and the Pioneering Period, 2 Vols Government Printer, 1922–23, Vol.2, p.469.

Tohu chose who was to go and many men were disappointed when the prophets didn't pick them.

'Just as had happened with the ploughmen, the arrests of the fencers began, but to our amusement, the constabulary could only handle on average four arrests a day. Who were they going to choose from the large groups of fencers sent out by Te Whiti? Our men were calling, "Pick us! Arrest us!" When their colleagues were carted away to New Plymouth by the Armed Constabulary, those who remained turned unimpeded to repair the fences and fill the breach.

'Mr Bryce had no option but to post more constabulary to the area. The number of arrests increased. The men held vigorously to the pickets and wouldn't let go. Prised away, they would run back and hold tight to them again. It ceased to be a game for the constabulary. Bad weather made for short-fused tempers. After all, what constable would not want to be drinking beer in the mess with his mates instead of dealing in the cold and wet with Maoris? The invaders began to use batons to smash the men's fingers: the crunch of wood on delicate bone was terrible to hear. In pain, the men were wrested from the fences, handcuffed in pairs and taken to New Plymouth.

'Still, they refused to give in. One day, 300 men went out. This time, they resowed with wheat the very road the roadbuilders were constructing.

'In all this time, Te Whiti and Tohu stayed inside at Parihaka. They knew that Mr Bryce was awaiting any opportunity to arrest them. Cleverly they continued to keep out of his reach.'

It was a deadly war of attrition.

The male population of Parihaka was being depleted. Seeing this, Titokowaru sent warriors to reinforce the numbers of men at the village, but Te Whiti and Tohu would not let them go out to the plantations. 'This is our fight, not yours,' the prophets said.

The weather turned nastier. Taranaki was snow-covered. From July to the middle of August—an extraordinary space of six or more weeks—most of Parihaka's able-bodied men were arrested. One man, almost blind, was released. The prisoners were not deterred by the initial sentence of two years' hard labour and the threat of continuation.

By the beginning of September, the courts had sentenced 150 to be sent to the South Island. On 4 September, the last fifty-nine able-bodied men and thirty-two boys marched through snow drifts to the fences. The men were arrested.

'Who was left? Our prophets, yes, and aged tau'eke, old men, women and the tataraki'i. All the rest had been taken away to gaol.

'It would have been so easy to give up. Everywhere, women were weeping. "What shall we do now?" Ripeka asked me. I thought of Horitana and I looked at her. "We must do our job," I answered. "Rouse the rest of the wives, but not Meri—she will only get in the way. Tell them it's our turn now."

'The snow still lay on the ground. The women wrapped themselves up against the chill. Te Whiti didn't try to stop us. Instead he came to watch as I marched with the other wives out to the fences. "Good, Erenora, so the women now act as the men," he said. "Be resolute, be strong."

'The constabulary and the roadbuilders were shocked when we arrived. "What do we do now?" Ripeka asked.

'"Pick up the broken pickets," I replied. "Weave them together with flax and build the fences again."

'Piharo was among the invaders. "Stop those *wah-hee-nee,*" he ordered. He rode towards me, bent down and with his whip nudged my chin up so that he could look at the weals around my neck. Then he tapped his own scars and, smiling gently, said, "We have such pretty decorations, you and I."

'It began to hail, the ice stinging our faces. The constabulary cursed as they moved among us. Their body odour was rancid and bitter. Some of the invaders were lascivious, handling our breasts in an obscene manner. "Ignore them," I ordered. "Keep making a fence." One man tried to put his hand into Ripeka's groin. She spat in his face.

'And then Meri came running to help, almost slipping on the icy ground; Kawa was strapped to her back. "You left me behind," she rebuked me. "I know you think I'm hopeless, but I'm not entirely useless."

'"It's too dangerous for you," I answered.

'But the arrival of a woman with a baby made the constabulary nervous. I took the advantage and said to Meri, "Sister, sing us a poi song."

'"Titiro taku poi!" she began. "'Uri atu, 'uri mai! Watch my poi as it weaves the broken rakau! It goes up, it goes down, it binds the wood together, 'ei 'a 'ei, 'e 'a!"

'There was such defiance in the song. The constabulary threw up their hands in desperation. Arrest women?

'"Let them go about their useless work," Piharo said. "When they leave, as eventually they will, we'll carry on." He sidled up to me and asked, "By the way, have you heard from your husband lately?" He laughed and laughed.'

A few days later, Erenora was woken by singing.

She thought she had overslept and that the women were going to the fences without her. When she looked out of her w'are she saw the tataraki'i were walking into the bright morning, over a hundred of them. She ran after them, calling, 'Children, no!'

They took no notice. They were like little soldiers tramping through the melt-water and splashing through the mud. When they reached the fences, they didn't even care about the constabulary. Instead they looked around for every branch or twig they could find and laid them across the road.

It didn't matter that what they erected wasn't really a fence. What mattered was that they were trying their best. Their chirruping was loud and deafening and the steam from their lips created a large, hovering cloud.

Erenora had never heard them so *angry*.

4.

'A reprieve came, of sorts,' Erenora wrote. 'The government was forced to return some of the men who had been sent to the South Island.

'The weather was fitful now, sometimes very cold but most times struggling towards spring. In October I went to the port with Ripeka, Meri and other women to welcome the first of the prisoners home from Dunedin Gaol on the SS *Hinemoa.* Imagine our shock and consternation when, as they came to land, we saw that their time in prison had gravely altered their appearance?

'And then Huhana noticed a small group of a dozen men who were in worse condition; they looked like koiwi, skeletons. At first they stood stock still, almost disbelieving that they were back in the Taranaki. Then a loud sigh came from them like the moaning of a lost wind. Puzzled, Huhana approached them to give them comfort. Suddenly she gave a sharp exclamation and beckoned to me and my sisters, "Bring water and food. Quickly!"

'When we joined our mother she had tears in her eyes.'

'"Who are these men?" I asked her because none were recognisable to me.

'She answered, "They are warriors who fought in Titokowaru's war. Many were captured back in 1868 and shipped off to the South Island. These men must have been boys at the time and among the first to travel 'The Trail of Tears' to Te Wai Pounamu."

'We moved among the men offering them bread, fruit and water.

'"Weren't those men released in 1872?" I asked, referring to the warriors from Pakakohe, Ngati Ruanui iwi, sent to Dunedin in 1869.

'Huhana nodded, "Yes, and those who didn't return we presumed were dead. Let us rejoice that at least some are among us again."

'I saw Ripeka and Meri offering smiles and aro'a to the men. I knew their hearts were breaking that their own husbands were not among the returnees. I was so proud that even so they could turn to welcome others who had been released.

'"Perhaps next time," I said to them.

5.

The following year, 1881, all the cultivations ringing Parihaka were broken through by Bryce's men and the road finally reached the citadel itself.

Then Bryce's illegal process was *checked.* Questions had mounted in Te Paremata o te Pakeha about the welter of despotic acts afflicting both Parihaka and the exiles in prison. The consequences of such mass imprisonments were now being commented on both overseas and nationally. At this rate, it was said,

New Zealand could become a vast prison-house with every gaol a Bastille.

In an effort to ameliorate the bad publicity, the government released four further groups of prisoners from South Island gaols, among them Wiremu Kingi Te Matakatea. Although this appeared to be a magnanimous gesture, many of the men had in fact already served their sentences.

The returnees were landed by ship either at Opunake or New Plymouth. They came mainly by the SS *Hinemoa* from Dunedin and Lyttelton gaols in January and May, from Lyttelton only in June, and the fifth and last group arrived from Hokitika on the SS *Stella* in the same month. When they gathered to attend the monthly 'ui at Parihaka on 18 June, they were a moving sight. Some were so broken were they in health and spirit. Others, having been sentenced to solitary confinement for up to seven weeks, were seriously ill and still recuperating from the harshness of their prison conditions. They had not been properly fed. A number had been beaten for not working hard enough; some were whipped for minor or trivial infractions.

Te Whiti praised them for their travails. He reminded them that they had not suffered in vain. 'My heart is glad to welcome you,' he said. 'Though you be halt or blind you have conquered. You were not imprisoned for heinous crime, or theft, but for upholding the words of Te Whiti. In such a case prison-houses lose their disgrace and become houses of joy. You were imprisoned for the land, for the chieftainship, and for godliness. A sea of fish lying dead on the strand taint the atmosphere for miles around but the fact of your unjust imprisonment is now known far and near throughout the world.'

On their return, what did most of the men do? Why they joined the women and children repairing the fences and planting the road. They arrived home only to be arrested and sent back to the South Island again.

'Of course,' Erenora wrote, 'it was not easy for my sisters and I to have our hopes dashed again and again when our husbands were not among those who had been returned. Meri, in particular, took it very badly, mocking me unfairly with my own words, "Perhaps next time, Erenora?" However, we had good news from Whata, one of the men. "The last time I saw Horitana, Paora and Riki," he said, "they were still alive. That was, of course, almost a year ago, though," he cautioned, "at Mount Cook before we were shipped to Dunedin."

'Although our hopes rose, the rest of Whata's information was alarming. "Horitana was in solitary confinement. This was because the prison warden regarded him as a ringleader among us and, also, he had fought with Titokowaru. He made matters worse for himself by refusing to wear the prison clothing with its broad arrow insignia, and was thrown into the cell clad only in his loincloth. He must have suffered dreadfully from the bone-chilling cold, but he never thought of himself. He would call out to the other prisoners, 'Kia ka'a, kia manawanui. Have strength, and be of good heart.' One night, in an act of rebellion he turned up his gaslight when the order came for lights out. In solidarity with him, some of the other prisoners turned their lights up too. Guards warned him, 'You're only making things worse for yourself.' He was given a lashing for starting a mutiny. Two others, Tamata Kuku and Te Iki, were put in solitary confinement with him and fifteen more men—including Paora and Riki—were on bread and water for two days."

'"Do you know if our husbands are still in Mount Cook Prison?" I asked Whata.

'"No," Whata answered. "You should ask one of the other men."'

It was Rangiora who provided further news.

'I was in a later group of prisoners sent to the South Island,' he began. 'What I can tell you is that because Horitana, Paora and Riki were deemed to be resistance leaders, they were split up. Paora was sent with a batch of prisoners to Hokitika...'

'But all those men are back,' Ripeka cried. 'Where *is* he?'

'Perhaps he was transferred from Hokitika to another prison,' Rangiora answered.

'Do you have news about Riki?' Meri asked, her lips trembling.

'He is either still in Christchurch or Dunedin.'

'What about Horitana?' Erenora asked. 'Tell me the worst.'

'I will not lie to you, Erenora,' Rangiora answered. 'One early morning, a Pakeha was seen entering his cell. He had with him some of the gaolers. Horitana was heard screaming, "Kaore au ki roto i te Po, please, not eternal darkness." That is the last anybody saw of him. He could still be in Mount Cook. He could be in the South Island. He could be anywhere.'

Something in the back of Erenora's mind brought back Piharo's words, *Heard from your husband lately?* 'Taku tane kua ngaro ki te Po!' she cried out in agony, 'Horitana has been swallowed up into the Great Night.'

She fell to her knees in karakia. 'Oh Lord, protect him,' she prayed.

6.

Parihaka was between the pit below and, above, the pendulum.

And all around the build-up of constabulary and settler forces was escalating. Bryce, confident that the inquiry would find for the government, was preparing to move the recalcitrant villagers *out.*

Did that bother Te Whiti and Tohu? No, their nerves held. In defiance, they encouraged the people of Parihaka to rally. They embarked on a new construction programme.

To fly in the face of the odds ... what a gesture. New houses were built, in the European style, including the imposing two-gabled w'arenui, Miti Mai Te

Arero. Its name, 'To Defiantly Protrude the Tongue', defined its political role. By the time the new buildings were raised, Parihaka had become a settlement of 350 houses. And despite the deportations to the South Island, new supporters boosted the population to around 2,000.

Te Whiti and Tohu would not submit to the might of the Pakeha.

Nationally, however, matters outside the prophets' control were spiralling Parihaka into Te Po. The war-mongering talk among Pakeha reached the pitch of hysteria, as did the scare tactics that advised an up-rising was likely. The consensus was that the time had come to extinguish the Maori citadel.

And closer at hand, mustering at nearby Rahotu, was what the people began to call 'Mr Bryce's Army'. It came by ship, along the coast and by road from the north to surround the kainga.

This is how James Cowan described the scene:

> By this time [October, 1881] Taranaki was a great armed camp. Redoubts with tall watchtowers studded the face of the land; loop-holed blockhouses stood on commanding hills; Armed Constabulary tents whitened the plains.[16]

Then the Confiscated Lands Inquiry was completed and the 'betrayal' was confirmed when the commissioners, instead of affirming Te Whiti and Tohu's

---

16 Ibid., p.471.

ownership of the land, decided the government owned it.

But don't worry. Reserves would be set aside for the iwi where they would be resettled to live the rest of their days in happiness.

The inquiry congratulated itself on being able 'to do justice to the natives' and continue 'English settlement of the country'. Legislation was passed to bring the findings of the inquiry into law. To make sure that the law was obeyed, anyone who did not subject themselves to the findings, or who obstructed the continuation of further settlement in non-reserve lands, could be accused of sedition, arrested without warrant and imprisoned for up to two years with or without hard labour.

Regarding Bryce's roadbuilding, well, the inquiry realised that might have been premature, but their findings validated his action, didn't they?

Te Whiti and Tohu were ordered to submit to the authority of the Queen and prepare their people to move from Parihaka. Maintaining his position of passive resistance, Te Whiti responded with a message from within the kainga. This was man's will, not God's:

'Though the lions rage,' he said, 'still I am for peace.'

His was an act of brinkmanship.

Bryce disregarded it and decided to go *in.*

CHAPTER TWELVE

5 November 1881, Te Ra o te Pahua

1.

'We all knew that Mr Bryce and his army of constabulary and volunteer settlers were coming,' Erenora wrote, 'when, on 2 November, some of our villagers, going to a wedding, were turned back on the coast road to Patea. I rode out to the checkpoint to see for myself. A squad of constabulary was manning it. Nobody could get out. Nobody could get in.

'As soon as the news spread that we were imprisoned, we knew we had to expect the worst. "The man that is come to kill is standing in front of us," Te Whiti told us. "Behind is the dark."

'The next morning, 3 November, Huhana woke us as usual with her karanga. When she finished she said to me, "All these years I have always had a competition with the birds to see whose karanga is the most beautiful and loudest. I won today. There was no birdsong." Nature itself was showing its disquiet.

'The day was hot and the sky clear. Despite our anxieties, we all went about our daily duties. The men were still putting the finishing touches to some of the new houses they had added to the kainga. Heedless of Mr Bryce's army, the women went to tend the gardens. I took the tataraki'i for their school work but, in the afternoon, Te Whiti sent a message that the bullocks were playing up. They were lowing and shifting dangerously in their pens. Would I go to their enclosure and calm the beloved companions? Some of the tataraki'i came with me. We were halfway to the barns when, suddenly, I heard bugles and rifle shots.

'"What's going on over there?" one of the boys asked. I shaded my eyes and saw a rifle unit practising mock attacks, bayonets at the ready, raising clouds of dust which drifted over Parihaka.'

'On 4 November, Te Whiti and Tohu called us all together. There was still no birdsong. How could they sing when their homes as well as ours were being invaded?

'"Mr Bryce plans to surprise us," Te Whiti said, "but we know he comes to Parihaka tomorrow." When he said these words there was a moan of fear. Te Whiti called for us to remain calm. He told us that the best way to defend ourselves was not to take up arms. "If any man thinks of his gun or his horse, and goes to fetch it," he began, "he will die by it ... place your trust in forbearance and peace ... let the booted feet come when they like, the land shall remain firm for ever."

'Instead, he instructed us to offer peace, and said that the women should bake loaves of bread to offer

Mr Bryce's men. I asked, "Why should we bake bread for them?" He knew I was in a wilful mood and could not be pacified. He turned to Huhana and some of the other women and said, "Gather the tataraki'i together and teach them a song to sing to the troops as they enter our holy citadel, eh? And—" he turned to the assembly "—those of you who are concerned for your safety should leave while you can." He was referring to secret tracks out of the kainga.

'I couldn't help but hear Meri weeping quietly as she held Kawa close to her breast. She had always had a nervous temperament. "You should go, sister," I said to her. When she nodded, I was relieved; at least I wouldn't have to worry about her. That evening, Ripeka and I accompanied her and Kawa to the beginning of the track along the Waitotoroa Stream and said goodbye.

'Just as she disappeared, we saw some strange men and women sneaking towards us. "E a'a to ma'i?" I asked them. "What are you doing here?" The bush telegraph had been busy and supporters from far and wide were slipping through the army's cordon. "We've come to sit with your people," they said, "and to wait with you."'

'That evening, the sky was dark. There was no moon or wind. At 2 a.m., under the cloak of darkness, we had breakfast and karakia.

'"It is time," Te Whiti said, "to get dressed in our best clothing and to wait for Mr Bryce and his army. Let him see that his surprise is not a surprise and

144

that we are prepared to greet him in mana and with dignity."

'We reassembled on the marae, maybe from 3 a.m. onward. As the dawn rose, changing from deep red to blazing light upon our sacred mountain, Huhana gave her usual karanga, "O'o ake nga iwi ki o tatou ma'i o te ra!" I had never heard her voice so strong and so beautiful. "Rise up, people, and begin the work of the day!" But when she had finished she began to weep. "Will the birds ever return again to join me in welcoming the sun?"

'Ripeka and I were sitting together, and I pressed her hands. All around, everyone was greeting the person next to them, "Kia ora. Hello. It is so good to be together and to draw courage from each other." Te Whiti and Tohu were smiling at us. I saw that grand warrior Titokowaru and rushed to embrace him. "Aue, Erenora," he said, "I weep for you, I weep for all of us today and I weep for Horitana, who I have always thought of as a son." Nearby was Wiremu Hiroki, the man who had killed one of the surveyors when they had come onto our land. His face was sombre. He knew that once Mr Bryce came into Parihaka, Te Whiti's cloak of protection would no longer hold.

'But was that Meri, holding Kawa and stepping through the crowd towards me and Ripeka? Why hadn't she been obedient?

'"Don't be angry with me," she began. "I had to come back. Even though the soldiers surround us, I'm happier with my sisters." When she said that, Ripeka started to cry. My sisters both embraced me, knowing I was irritated. I resigned myself; there was a great love between us.

'And then Mr Bryce and his army came in.'

2.

It was 7 a.m., Guy Fawkes Day.

War fever was in the air as Bryce's army of 644 Armed Constabulary and 945 volunteers prepared for the action ahead.

The Armed Constabulary headquarters was at Pungarehu. Two companies had come from the Rahotu camp, along with the Nelson artillery and volunteers. To give you a better idea of their makeup, here are the units of Timaru Camp, just outside Parihaka: the Wellington Engineers, the Wellington City Rifles, the Wellington Guards, the Masterton Rifles, the Makara Rifles, the Greytown Rifles, the Marlborough Contingent and the Canterbury Contingent under the command of Captain Alfred St George Hammersley of the Timaru Artillery. Also on duty were support units, including a medical corps. A 6-pounder Armstrong gun was positioned overlooking the village on a nearby hill that the constabulary called Mount Rolleston.

The perimeter of the kainga *bristled* with men. The army's orders were to provide cover for Bryce as he rode in to arrest Te Whiti and Tohu for non-compliance with the order to submit and move with their people to reserve land.

Throughout the preparations, the army had been hyped up to expect the worst. 'We are expecting treachery from *Tay Witty* and *Tay Tow-hoo,* lads. Be on your guard, as his bloodthirsty warriors have been ordered to retaliate with arms from their cache of secret weapons. Don't forget, Titokowaru's with them! He has a squad of 500 warriors in hiding, ready to overcome us.'

Oh yes? The overwhelming army response was, 'Let the Maoris try! If even *one* black bugger fires off a shot, we'll rake the lot of them with covering fire and rip them all to shreds. And if we're wounded, well, they'll be honourable wounds. Our medical corps will patch us up good as new, eh lads, and we'll live to tell our children and grandchildren that we were there the day Parihaka was brought down.'

Around 9 a.m., was that John Bryce preparing to go through the gateway?

'Look at him, spick and span in his uniform, on his prancing white charger. Raise a cheer, lads, for our leader and the brave men with him as they advance fearlessly into the fanatics' den. Doesn't he look like the grand old Duke of York, boys! But what's this? Are little children guarding the way? Bloody savages! Mr Bryce, they may have weapons concealed on them. Don't trust the buggers, sir! Mow them down, go straight at them! Who'll be the first to kill a Maori, lads?'

3.

'I put my hands over my eyes to shade them and, from out of the sun, Mr Bryce was riding.

'Our tataraki'i awaited him. There were around 200 of the little cicadas. They were arranged in their usual lines of welcome, singing, chanting, skipping and playing with their tops. As usual they had dressed ceremonially in shoulder cloaks and some had feathers in their hair. The boys were in the front and, behind them, around sixty young girls. Among them Huhana and an old tau'eke led them in their song. If you come in peace and greet the tataraki'i with smiles, they spin their songs with brightness and beauty; if you come in anger, their song *changes.*

'My heart was in my mouth as Mr Bryce ordered his men to charge straight at the children and the old man. "Be careful, tataraki'i!" I called. I heard the drumming hooves, saw the horses' flowing manes and I thought the children would be cut down.

'They didn't care! They kept to their ranks and the soldiers had to wheel away at the last moment.

'The cicadas became loud and furious as Mr Bryce ordered another charge. Piharo was among the horsemen. I cried out to him, "They're only children." The sun flashed on him and I knew he would give no quarter. After all, was his soul not made of hard black stone, dark and sinister?

'But the tataraki'i were ready. Again they held their ground. At the last moment they clapped their hands loudly, took off their capes and waved them at the horses. The sharp sound of their hands split the air and the capes created unsettling whirlwinds. Take that, Mr Bryce! The horses reared, whinnying wildly and plunging away, unseating a few of their riders. Furious, Mr Bryce could only call a squad of his constabulary to come forward and bundle the children away. As the men did so, the children began to buzz loudly. Their song was one of prophecy:

'"Hear the sound of the cicada! Do not assume you have power over us. We filled the skies above Egypt in our millions and brought down the plague upon Pharaoh."'

Erenora and the women were watching and waiting.

'Not a good start to Mr Bryce's invasion, eh?' Erenora laughed, and the women laughed with her. 'Now, wa'ine ma, it's time for us to do our part.'

She put on a brave face for Te Whiti; she was doing this only because he wished it. As Bryce, Piharo and their accompanying contingent proceeded toward the marae, she led the women, carrying 500 loaves of warm bread, gifts for the visitors. The women had smiles on their lips as they held up the food, but Erenora was not smiling. She had no gladness in her heart. It took all her willpower to stop the derisive patere that threatened to rise unbidden to her lips.

Bryce, his horsemen and accompanying constabulary passed by, rejecting the women's offerings. Bryce's horse was prancing, its stirrups jingling, such a pretty horse, and Erenora gave a sudden moan. Her memory flashed back to the time when she had been a young girl, watching Governor Grey inspecting the bodies of the dead warriors at Warea. She could not restrain herself. 'Titiro!' she called. 'Bryce ko'uru kua tae mai i roto i a tatou! This is Bryce the Treacherous who comes among us! Beware of him!'

Breaking away from the women's ranks, she ran after the invading contingent. She wanted to leap up, drag Bryce off his horse and stop him from advancing any further. But she saw Te Whiti on the marae and, all of a sudden, she heard his voice in her mind saying, *No, Erenora, what must be will be.*

She faced him, defiant. 'No, rangatira, no.'

4.

The grand old Duke of York! He had ten thousand men! He marched them up to the top of the hill...

The sun was spinning, spinning, spinning in the sky. Ahead, Tohu Kaakahi's marae was shimmering with heat. Fronting it was the meeting house known as Toroanui.

Bryce's face registered surprise at the large number of Maori gathered with Te Whiti. Two thousand five hundred, maybe more, all most excellently dressed. A good-natured voice from the crowd called to him, 'Friend, you're a bit late. We've been waiting for you since one o'clock this morning.'

Bryce heard the laughter rippling around him. His throat was parched. He had to sit upright to calm himself. How had the Maoris known he was coming?

Piharo reined up beside him. 'The fanatics' den,' he muttered to his leader.

'We have lost the element of surprise,' Bryce said. Suddenly, light blasted from the meeting house, Toroanui, dazzling his eyes. He jerked the reins of his white charger. When the bit pulled at its mouth the horse pawed and stamped the ground.

Since first coming to New Zealand Bryce's greatest fear was of what he called the 'sacred medicine-houses' of the Maoris: the hideous carvings, the three-fingered monsters with their protruding tongues and serpent tails, and the other forms of beings half-human, half-inhuman. The house before him did not have such embellishments but, even so, it was still to be feared. His heartbeat rose as from out of the shimmering heatwaves came three voices, so loud that he put his hands to his ears.

Bring your treachery no further.

Bryce shook his head quickly to clear his hearing. Before him were Te Whiti, with Tohu, Titokowaru and other Maori elders. Wary, he turned to Piharo. 'This', he said, 'is as far as we shall go.'

Taking advantage of the moment, village women, in traditional dress and wearing the raukura in their hair, came singing onto the marae. Right in the front were Ripeka and Meri, with poi in their hands.

'Titiro nga putiputi!' the crowd roared as they began to dance: 'Takiri te raukura,' the women sang, ''aere koe i runga, 'uri 'aere ra i te motu e! Takiri te raukura, 'aere koe i runga, waiho te ture kia rere i raro e! Let the raukura dance, go forth the raukura, fluttering above and arise upwards! Throughout the land let the raukura dance, fluttering above while the laws are fluttering down below!'

Erenora slipped between the many men and women in the crowd. 'Let me through, let me through.' Her heart was pounding when she finally joined the ranks of the elders standing with Te Whiti. 'Must we allow Mr Bryce to come riding into our kainga?' she asked.

The prophet smiled quizzically at her. 'I have always relied on you, Erenora, to ask the difficult questions but ... tell me ... do you know the will of God?'

Chastened by the remark, Erenora bowed her head. Te Whiti kissed her on the cheek, 'Kei te pai, Erenora.' He turned to watch as the men took the places of the women to perform an 'aka. Raised to the dazzling sun, their faces were full of pride:

'Ko te tongi a Noa 'e aka te oranga!' they sang. 'Ko te tongi a Te Whiti 'e raukura e! The symbol of Noah is the ark! Likewise the symbol of Te Whiti is the white feather e!'

Te Whiti and Tohu were wearing fine cloaks. Te Whiti's eyes again alighted on Erenora. Without wanting to, she began to weep with frustration. He shook his head, 'No, Erenora, don't cry.' She heard his voice again, whispering to her like a warm wind through the din around them. 'Rather, gather your strength for the journey you are soon to undertake to te Pito o te Ao, the end of the world.'

Then the 'aka was over.

'We expected Mr Bryce to dismount,' Erenora wrote, 'so that Te Whiti and Tohu could begin the speechmaking. But what did Mr Bryce do? He remained on his horse. And Piharo and the accompanying constabulary, they also would not dismount.'

Nevertheless, Te Whiti and Tohu stood and welcomed Bryce ko'uru.

They waited for him to reply to their mi'i. But he remained seated on his horse, silent, his eyes looking straight ahead. What was he waiting for?

For almost an hour there was no reciprocal exchange of greetings.

'Then, at 10 o'clock, Mr Bryce finally made his move. He nodded his head and a Pakeha officer of insufficient mana abused the hospitality of the two prophets by speaking to them with unseemly directness. "What is your answer, Te Whiti, to the proclamation of 19 October?" he asked.

'When Te Whiti did not reply, Mr Bryce bid his underling to read out the Riot Act: "You are unlawfully, riotously and tumultuously assembled. You must disperse, otherwise you will be arrested. You have one hour to leave Parihaka."

'Nobody stirred. The silence remained. The allotted hour passed.

'And then Mr Bryce took upon himself the conqueror's right to read out the warrants of arrest for Te Whiti and Tohu. A warrant was also read out for Wiremu Hiroki, who stepped forward when his name was called.

'A bugle began to play, *Tatara-raa! Tatara-raa!* And the forest suddenly quaked as Mr Bryce's army emerged from it and burst into the kainga to execute the arrests. As they rushed in, the birds appeared. Disturbed by the army they shrilled in untimely song, flocking above Parihaka before seeking the safety of the sky.'

5.

O God of Israel, I ask of you, why didn't you come down from your glorious throne and smite the Pakeha?

You gave your divine assistance to Joshua when he blew his trumpet and brought down the walls of Jericho. You saved Lot and destroyed the twin cities of evil, Sodom and Gomorrah. You gave Samson back his strength so that he could demolish the Temple of Dagon. And you chose Moses, closing the Red Sea over the pursuing Pharaoh and his cohorts of the Egyptians.

O God of Ages, why did you not do the same for your prophets Te Whiti and Tohu and your beloved Maori people?

154

'After that,' Erenora wrote, 'everything happened quickly. Two Pakeha officers moved up with an arresting party armed with revolvers and handcuffs. The arresting officer was Captain Stuart Newall.

'Te Whiti said to us, "Be of good heart and patient. This day's work is not my doing. It comes from the heart of the Pakeha. On my fall the Pakeha builds his work: but be you steadfast in all that is peaceful."

'And as Tohu was handcuffed, he turned and said, "Be not sad. Turn away the sorrowful heart from you ... Be not dismayed. Have no fear but be steadfast."

'The arrests were too terrible to behold. There arose a sound of such grief, such a deep moaning, that you could not stop your own sadness spilling out. A surge like a deep sea swell compelled the people forward to try to stop the arrests. But I remembered that other prophets of the Holy Bible had suffered in the hands of despots, and I saw that as Te Whiti and Tohu were led away, they were not bowed down. I turned to the villagers. "Why are you grieved?" I asked them. "Look, they are smiling as they walk away with the Pakeha."

'The two prophets were taken by trap to Pungarehu. As soon as they left Parihaka, the rain came squalling down.'

Let me put it to you.

It didn't matter that the people of Parihaka were unarmed. All it would have taken was one shot. One rifle raised, one Maori sighted, one trigger pressed and...

Think about it.

And do you remember that Te Whiti had proclaimed four phases in the history of Parihaka? Some people say that the invasion of the citadel was the third one, Tupapaku.

It was the day that Parihaka died.

CHAPTER THIRTEEN

The Sacking of Parihaka

1.

'To the victor the spoils,' Erenora wrote, 'is a story older than the fall of Troy.

'For two days, however, the rain kept Mr Bryce's army at bay. It wasn't until 8 November that the weather cleared. Only then did the army enter Parihaka again, and the wolf came down on the fold.

'The pretext was that they were searching for so-called hidden caches of gunpowder, firearms and weapons. All the search parties found were fowling pieces, tomahawks and axes but in the process they stole many pounamu and other taonga, banknotes and savings.

'Piharo made a special visit to my house. "Aren't you going to ask me for my warrant?" he laughed.'

'Mr Bryce appeared on his white charger. "The time has come", he said, "for all tribes, who came to support the Parihaka people to pack up and leave."

'He posted a proclamation to all Waikato, Whanganui, Ngati Awa and other tribes on the west coast to get out. He called them "strangers" and gave them an hour to comply. If they did not, the Armstrong cannon would be fired on Parihaka. They refused to leave and, instead, sat with us on the marae, disregarding the order.

'Mr Bryce's threat was an empty one. The cannon remained silent.

'But then Mr Bryce began the forcible and savage removal of the "strangers" and the destruction of domestic village w'are—whether they belonged to our visitors or not. He had always considered Parihaka as a sanctuary for criminals and now he took the opportunity to rid himself of it: Maori supporters from Whanganui were targeted first, arrested and moved out. Next were those from the Waikato. Once they were "identified", rightly or wrongly, they were marched out of Parihaka and, just in case they thought of returning, their houses were destroyed.

'I was sick at heart as I watched men, women and children lined up and, at the word of a Maori informer, identified as one of us or not. More than 400 from North Taranaki were marched away, some in handcuffs, to New Plymouth; 200 from South Taranaki were escorted to Opunake.

'Mr Bryce ordered the destruction of the plantations. If any remaining "strangers" wouldn't leave, he would starve them out.'

2.

By 18 November, just over 1,000 people were left in Parihaka.

They were mostly women and children now, and the tataraki'i had assumed the front line defence on the marae, making loud sounds of anger whenever the constabulary appeared.

Over 400 more people were identified as not belonging to Parihaka and forced to leave. By 20 November, 1,443 people had been thrown out.

Mr Bryce then turned to destroying the wairua of Parihaka. He ordered the pulling down of the 'sacred medicine-house'.

By 22 November, 2,200 people had been evicted at gunpoint. The remaining villagers were given passes, not only to identify those belonging to Parihaka but also to prevent those who had been forced out from returning and resuming life in the village. 'Parihaka continued to be looted,' Erenora wrote. 'Houses were torched, crops destroyed and livestock—hundreds of pigs, cattle and horses—driven away.

'Among the livestock were the village's 100 bullocks. Some refused to be herded from the kainga and, escaping the constabulary, returned again and again to Parihaka. In the end, the decision was made to slaughter them in their enclosures. A small shooting detail was given the task but at the first gunshots the bullocks created havoc, bellowing loudly and crashing against the high wooden fences where the shooters were standing.

'I ran, crying, to the paddocks. I wrenched a rifle from one of the constabulary. Their shooting was so indiscriminate. They were too far away to give the fatal shot and some of the wounded bullocks were still writhing with terror.

'"I will do it," I screamed at the shooters. My will was so ferocious that the men stepped aside for me. They thought I was crazy to go into the paddock but, as soon as the bullocks saw me and heard my comforting voice, they stopped stampeding. And so I was able to move among them, scolding, "Why didn't you go with your new masters?" I knew, of course, why they hadn't but, oh, how I wished they had not turned back to the kainga.

'I gathered my strength and commanded them all to lie down. "Thank you for your companionship," I told them. "Look into my eyes now," I said to each one and, while they were looking at me, I put the rifle to their foreheads and pressed the trigger.

'Oh, what beloved companions they had been.'

'Within three weeks we were down to 400 villagers, mostly women and the tataraki'i, and we were starving. Ripeka and I would go out at night to pick over the razed crops and bring back kai for Meri's boy, Kawa, and other children.

'When the house of my dear adoptive mother, Huhana, was burnt down she decided she had suffered enough. "I'm going back to Warea," she told us. "Why don't you girls come with me? We can wait out the troubles there." My sisters and I said, "No."

'By the time Huhana was ready to leave, others had decided to go with her. We wept as they departed: such a small band of men and women. But Huhana called to us, "Don't cry. This has happened before and, no doubt, it will happen again. We have always been more'u, pilgrims."

'The kainga was at the mercy of kites and crows. We were unprotected and exposed to marauders. Not long after Huhana left, some men, their faces hidden, came with a more sinister intent. They stole into some of the houses, muffled the sounds of sleeping women, bound them and put them into carts. But I was roused by nearby screams. I went to Meri's house and told her, "Protect your son." Where was Ripeka? I took up a butcher's knife and went to find our sister.

'Three men had decided there was time enough to have their way with her. They were raping her, two of them holding her down and the third on top of her, grunting like a pig. Rage possessed me and I screamed at them. I lashed at the man who was taking my darling sister against her will and, howling, he fell away from her. Of course, Meri was never obedient and she showed up with the only weapon she could find—a broom—but her appearance was enough to make the other two marauders take fright. They ran away into the night.

'Meri comforted Ripeka. Our sister was moaning and swaying from side to side with grief. Then she began to scream, over and over again, "I should have fought harder." It took us a long time to calm her down. When she had done so, she became still and silent. With perspiration beading her brow, she hissed at us with great fierceness, "This is our secret, you hear, sisters? Ours. Paora must never know. Never."

'She became distraught again, so, to calm her down, Meri began to tap her poi and made up a song to go with it:

'"Titiro taku poi! Tapiri atu tapiri mai, taku poi, tapiri atu! Look at my poi, sister, as it dances up and down. It invites you to sing and dance with it! Come, sister, smile!"

'I don't know what happened to the women who were carted away from Parihaka. I hear that some were forced to become wives of settlers. Others were given as sexual fodder to constabulary in other parts of New Zealand. But I now knew how Horitana felt whenever the blood-lust came upon him. I wanted to follow the rapists to the end of the earth and geld them.'

'On 12 November Te Whiti, Tohu and Hiroki were transferred from Pungarehu to New Plymouth Gaol. They were remanded in custody, to await trial on 1 May 1882. Before that could happen, however, Mr Bryce passed a bill that rendered their trial unnecessary: they were lawfully imprisoned without appearing in court.

'To make sure that the presence of the prophets in Taranaki would not prove an inspiration to the people, they were taken by ship from New Plymouth to Wellington.'

3.

With the crops razed, Erenora took to slipping at night through the constabulary's cordon to the sea. There, she would throw her net for fish.

One morning, just as she had managed to get back into Parihaka, she saw a man on a horse riding towards her. It was Piharo. Her first impulse was to run. Instead she threw her catch into flax, moved quickly away from it and stood her ground, her fists bunched.

Piharo reined up beside her and leant down from his saddle. 'Your scarring has gone,' he observed. 'As for mine, never.' When Erenora tried to move past him he drove his horse into her, knocking her to the ground. 'Did I ever tell you that I have democratic tastes?' he asked. 'I'll let you starve just a little bit longer. Perhaps that might bring down a pride like yours sufficient for you to make the walk to my gateway, as many have already.'

'Never,' Erenora said to him as she stood up. *'Never.'*

Bryce tried to enforce a media blackout. He said he would arrest any newspapermen at Parihaka. His threat didn't work: two correspondents sneaked in and were hidden by Maori on the marae. Not only that, but photographers were able to take pictures of Bryce's army as it awaited orders to move against Parihaka. One, from the W.A. Price Collection in Wellington's Alexander Turnbull Library, shows serried ranks of men, arms at the shoulder, like toy soldiers. In the background among the trees you can see their tented camp. Another photograph shows the villagers of Parihaka in defiant waiata. Yes, the three women in front are Erenora, Ripeka and Meri.

Their mouths are opened as if they have swallowed the sun. 'Ka manawanui au i 'ei 'a!' they are crying defiantly. 'We are indeed of stout heart au i 'ei 'a!'

CHAPTER FOURTEEN

A Wife's Decision

1.

Flow on, bitter tears, flow on. Weep for the soul of the Maori people, weep. Shadows hide the light, dark as darkest night. Weep, o women, for the more'u, lost to the world.

'In the aftermath of Parihaka's fall,' Erenora wrote, 'Ripeka, Meri and I thought constantly of our husbands. By now, *two* years had passed since they had been taken away from New Plymouth. Since then, other men had also been submitted to imprisonment without trial. And when our two rangatira, Te Whiti and Tohu, were taken away from us, well, that was a black day.

'Piharo was still harassing me, wishing to enslave me. Even though his property was now unimpeded of Maori title, he liked to ride to Parihaka for the express purpose of mocking me with his success. He would follow me as I scrabbled for food, asking, "Are you not hungry yet? I have a place already set for you at my table. Will you not join me one evening?"

'Bedevilled by him, I sought escape by going down to the sea, and it was there that I had a matakite, a vision, about Horitana. At least I thought

it was Horitana, except that all I could see was ...
a mokomokai, but it was shining like silver. As I was
looking at it, the face began to sing, but the voice
was Horitana's. His song was full of pain and agony:

'"Aue, e Atua!' he cried. 'O God! Kua ngaro a'au
i te Po! How dark it is in this mokomokai! Aue 'oki
te pouri o tenei Ao! How terrible this silence!"

'I did not understand the vision and, although
my soul was filled with foreboding, I voiced the
thought that came to me: "Horitana is still alive! If
he had been dead his spirit would have visited me
to tell me he was waiting for me in Te Reinga."

'But why was he in so much pain? His agony was
so intense that I put my hands to my head, moaning.
Even when the vision ended, I could not rid my
memory of that tragic voice coming from the
mokomokai and the agony that inflected it. What
had happened to him?

'Yes, that was the moment of my decision. I
would go and look for him. What else could I do?
Ka patupatu taku manawa.'

With beating heart, Erenora began her quest to
find Horitana. But how would she, a Maori woman,
be able to travel through a hostile Pakeha land?

One evening her glance happened to light upon
the book of Shakespeare's plays given to her by a
kind visitor to Parihaka. In *Twelfth Night,* she recalled, the heroine, Viola, is wrecked on the coast
of Illyria and must masquerade as a man to survive
in a hostile land.

That made Erenora remember something she had heard from the traditions of another tribe on the other side of Aotearoa—the east coast. Their waka had just landed after having journeyed from Hawaiki and, while the men went to investigate the strange new country, the women waited in the waka. However, the tide came up and the canoe started to drift towards rocks. By tradition, women were forbidden to be paddlers but this was an emergency. Thus, a woman by the name of Wairaka shouted to the gods, 'Kia whakatane au i ahau. Let me make myself into a man.' With that, she grabbed the oars and rowed the waka to safety.

'I shall do the same,' Erenora said to herself. 'And I shall call myself Eruera.'

ACT THREE

Three Sisters

CHAPTER FIFTEEN

The Muru of Parihaka

1.

The graphic muru of most of Taranaki and the raupatu without ending describe the holocaust of Taranaki history and the denigration of the founding peoples in a continuum from 1840 to the present.[17]

These words come from the conclusion of the 1996 Waitangi Tribunal report on the invasion of Parihaka and the taking of Taranaki land.

I have the same opinion, although others might think the word 'holocaust' to be rhetorically deployed and overstating the case. I do not consider that any comparison was intended with the mass murder of six million Jews less than 100 years later. Rather, the word describes what the survivors of any great injus-

---

17 Waitangi Tribunal, Taranaki Report, 1996, p.312, cited in Buchanan, Parihaka Album, p.176.

tice and plundering of land, treasures, bodies and souls have had to endure. More important, the crimes in Taranaki were justified for very similar reasons—the superiority of one race over another.

My ancestors had to live through some relentless attempts at their extinction. The fact that I'm here, however, is evidence that the government didn't succeed in wiping us out. Administrations began to be dominated by peace lobbies attempting to demilitarise the situation between Maori and Pakeha. Frankly, though, it is my opinion that Pakeha escaped a return to war with Maori only by the skin of their teeth.

Why didn't Te Whiti change his tactics and fight Bryce? All I can do is point to the prophet's own sense of Parihaka's future. After all, the people of the kainga had experienced only Takahanga and Akarama, and were now undergoing Tupapaku.

There was still to come, Aranga, the day of resurrection.

Did not Joseph predict seven years of plenty followed by seven years of famine before the good years of the harvest?

2.

Ah well, timata ano. Let's start again.

By gender switching, Erenora was only affirming what Te Whiti himself had authorised when he said, 'Ko tama wa'ine, a woman is a man.' Indeed, it was this dual strength that he had always admired in her.

Women fought beside their men during the long war. Sometimes irritated at the long discussions of men when debating the welfare of the tribe, women would often step in to provide the solution. Most times, in good humour, the men would acknowledge their caustic and peremptory tone. Hence the saying, 'A man unties a knot, but a woman cuts it.'

I tell you, my darling Josie often acts in this way. You want to hear her when the local school committee has a meeting! Last time she looked at her watch, stood up and said, 'Enough talk. Time to vote now.'

'I woke early,' Erenora wrote, 'wanting to get away from the village before dawn. I lit a candle and dressed quickly in vest and trousers. When I looked at myself in the mirror I was heartened by my appearance; it helped that I had always looked somewhat boyish, with my broad shoulders and narrow hips. I saw, looking back at me, a young man in his mid-twenties.

'However, there was one problem: my hair. Certainly I could roll it up and pin it tightly under a farmer's hat, but what happened if someone knocked the hat off? I would be exposed. I realised I would have to sacrifice it before I could truly assume my new guise. Although many men had long hair, woman definitely didn't have short hair, so to avoid any questions as to my gender, it had to go. And I would make that offer because, oh, how I loved Horitana and...

'"Wie bitter sind der Trennung Leiden," I muttered from memory, words from the German phrasebook. "How bitter are the sorrows of separation."

'I made a quick decision. "Forgive me, husband," I said. I picked up a knife and with savage movements cut my hair off as close as I could to the scalp. Oh, and I felt a huge regret, remembering how Horitana loved to braid and wrap it, twining it with his as we made love.

'The huge hanks fell to the floor. When I looked again at my reflection, I hid myself from my eyes. I'd never been beautiful but now...

'Keeping my emotions in check, I finished the job with a razor. When I looked again, I saw Eruera, with unkempt hair, standing before me.

'No time to waste on self-pity. It was time to go.'

Erenora pulled on some boots and put on her hat. She put the large knife in her belt. Then she grabbed a shoulder sack, filled it with some food and went to blow out the candle. Before she could do that, Meri and Ripeka came in. 'Where do you think you're going?' Ripeka asked.

'I told you Erenora was up to something,' Meri said.

The two sisters had been watching Erenora like hawks. They pushed her back and glared at her. 'You think we don't know what you're planning to do?' Ripeka continued. 'Well, you're not doing it without us! Trying to sneak away, no wonder Meri got suspicious. We've got husbands too, and neither of us can cope any longer with having our hopes raised whenever prisoners are returned only to have them dashed when Paora and Riki are not among them. We're coming with you.'

Erenora was extremely sympathetic, but more to the point she was irritated that they had found her out. Not only that, however, they were all ready to go: coats on, scarves around their necks, knapsacks slung over their shoulders, and Meri had brought some poi with her. Did she think Erenora was going somewhere you could sing and dance?

'What are we waiting for?' they asked.

Erenora folded her arms. 'You two will only hold me up,' she answered, 'and it could be dangerous.'

'Not with a young *man* to look after us,' Ripeka sniggered, 'and don't think I didn't consider cutting my hair off too.'

'That would have been a sacrifice for nothing,' Erenora answered sarcastically, referring to Ripeka's overflowing beauty. 'Get out of my way, both of you.'

She was shocked when Ripeka and Meri pushed her back ... again. 'Either we go with you,' Ripeka began, 'or we'll raise the alarm and you won't have only us in tow. There are lots of other wives who would want to come with us.'

'Are you trying to blackmail me?'

'You're not the only one with brains, sister.'

Erenora glared at Meri, hoping to intimidate her. 'You, Meri ... you should know better than to abandon Kawa.'

'He's already gone to our mother,' Meri answered smugly.

What could Erenora do? 'It won't be easy or straightforward,' she argued. 'I was planning to go to Wellington first to follow Horitana's trail to wherever it might lead...'

'Well, you'll just have to include us, and our search for Paora and Riki, in your plans,' Ripeka interrupted her.

Oh, this was infuriating! Erenora realised that if she kept arguing, other women would indeed be attracted by the raised voices and decide to tag along. She gave up. 'If you lag behind, either of you, don't expect me to wait for you.'

They stepped outside the house. The darkness was shapeshifting with swirling light.

'Let me button your coat for you,' Meri said. 'It's cold.' When she had done the task, she touched Erenora's hair gingerly. 'You always did look like a boy,' she continued, 'but your voice should be lower.'

'Like this?' Erenora asked, demonstrating.

Meri grinned. 'That's a bit better.'

At the last moment, Erenora remembered she had left the candle still glowing. She returned quickly, cupped the flame and blew it out.

Dawn rose over the horizon.

CHAPTER SIXTEEN

The Quest Begins

1.

Let's look at a map of colonial New Zealand.

We know that Erenora, Ripeka and Meri left Parihaka on or around 15 November 1881. They stole past the sentries and the cordon of constabulary and soon made their way to the coast. They were all carrying food supplies, and Meri was in charge of their money.

The morning wind was blowing into their faces as they turned southward. 'The sea,' Erenora sighed when they reached it, 'so far so good, sisters.' But when they were passing Piharo's palatial homestead, his foreman saw them and woke his master.

Piharo called for his telescope. 'They are trying to escape,' he shouted.

The sisters made good time to Opunake.

Erenora was hoping to pass by the redoubt and other fortified positions undetected. Aue, the morning was very bright and they had no choice but to go to ground for the day or to chance it. 'The sooner we clear the district the better,' Erenora decided. She waited until the changing of the guard was under way and, while the constabulary were occupied in their drills, she ordered her sisters, 'Run for it!'

174

Just in time. Safe and laughing, the three women continued along the beach.

'That's when I heard the sound of pursuit. I thought it must be the constabulary but, no, it was Piharo's foreman and three Maori farm workers coming after us on horseback. They were brutish men and, when they caught up with us, they belaboured us with sticks.

'But my sisters and I had learnt a trick from the tataraki'i. We flapped our scarves at the horses and added shrill karanga, "'aere atu!" The horses reared, unseating the men. Cursing, our assailants took after us on foot. They had not reckoned, however, on my strength or that of my sisters. Although we were soon battling for our lives, we managed to fend off their attack. When they saw the flash of my butcher's knife, they kept their distance.'

'Ripeka,' Erenora screamed to her sister, 'get Meri away *now.*' She lashed out at the men and, as soon as she reckoned her sisters had cleared the beach, made her own escape.

The ruffians were closing in again and, in desperation, Meri threw half of the money she was carrying at them. 'Take it!' she yelled. The ploy worked; the men began to fight among themselves for the coins and, by the time they had lifted their heads, the women had disappeared. 'Let the bitches go,' they laughed.

Safe, the women dropped to the ground. 'I'm sorry, sisters,' Meri said. 'Throwing the money away like that was the only thing I could think of.' Really, Meri was so childlike you could forgive her.

'Don't weep, Meri,' Erenora consoled her. 'Money is only money. At least we have escaped with our lives.'

'Those men could have made vicious sport with us, Erenora.' Meri was shivering.

'Yes,' Erenora nodded. 'It's going to be dangerous all the way to Wellington. Are you sure you both want to come with me?'

Ripeka and Meri saw right through her. 'You can't get rid of us that easily,' Ripeka said, 'and we'll be safer with you.'

'All right,' Erenora answered. 'However, Meri,' she added grumpily, '*I* will take charge of the money.' It wasn't a reprimand, but the incident taught the three sisters a lesson—to avoid the Pakeha as much as they could—and if anything happened to their money again, Erenora wanted to be the one at fault.

Meanwhile, the foreman and his three Maori labourers returned to Piharo empty-handed. They may have gained some coins but Piharo saw through their fabrications and lies.

'I had plans for the *wah-hee-nee* Erenora,' he said regretfully. 'Never mind, one of these days she'll return.'

2.

The three sisters had never been out of Taranaki. Can you credit the courage it must have taken for them to make that terrifying journey on foot?

'Originally I had planned to make my way to Patea where I hoped to take passage on a ship to Wellington. With my two sisters in tow, and half our money gone, that idea was no longer possible. "We'll have to walk," I told Ripeka and Meri.

'"Not all the way?" Meri asked.

'I ignored her dismay. "We'll keep to the coast," I continued. "We'd better stay off the roads." Ripeka agreed, "Me 'aere tatou," she said, "let's go."

'I walked ahead, setting the pace. I was surprised at how strong and fit my sisters were. "We've been in training," Ripeka said in a droll manner.

'We soon arrived at Ohawe. Near this kainga, steeped in history, moa hunters had once pursued the fabled bird. We took shelter at the pa and then moved on to Patea. That kainga was one of greater importance to us, marking the place where our ancestral waka, *Aotea,* had landed in Aotearoa, bringing our forebears. The people there were kin and we rested among them for a couple of days. Like many other villagers in Taranaki, they were now living by leave of the Pakeha. Their eyes grew as wide as saucers when we told them where we were heading. "You're going *where?* Who will look after you when you leave your homeland?" We may as well have been heading to the edge of the world and over.

'From Patea we began the long walk to Putiki, on the Whanganui River. We made good progress along the beach, but I noticed that Ripeka and Meri were always looking back at our beautiful tipuna mountain, Taranaki. "Don't do that," I snapped at them one day, because their sentimentality was getting under my skin. "If you're already homesick, turn back now."

'That was when Meri cried out, "Wait." Tears were spilling from her eyes, oh, how they were falling. And *I* looked back. The mounga had diminished to a triangle between earth and sky. Any further, and we would no longer see it.

'And Meri called a farewell to the mountain. "E tu mai ra, te mounga tapu, e tu mai ra. Farewell, sacred ancestor, farewell." Taranaki began to *shine* as Meri turned to me and asked, "Will we ever see our mountain again, Erenora? Our people? And will I ever see my sweet son, Kawa?"

'We had reached the point of no return. "How should I know?" I answered, cross.

'Ripeka reproved me. "You should have a care for our sister," she said. She took some albatross feathers from her knapsack and threaded three into Meri's hair. Then she placed three in her own. "From this point onward," she told Meri, "people will know that we are women of Parihaka and come from Taranaki. And you *will* see Kawa again."'

3.

Ae, Erenora was correct: the point of no return. What lay ahead?

This should give you some indication: it's the 1881 census from which I quoted earlier. Look at the statistics: total population of New Zealand, 533,801 and, of this number, 44,099 Maori. Our population was declining so rapidly that by the turn of the century many commentators considered we were doomed.

Now think of the impact of the Pakeha population on the landscape. Everywhere saw tumultuous change to Aotearoa. The juggernaut of European settlement had rolled over the country Maori had once possessed and Pakeha were triumphant. Wherever Erenora and her sisters looked, had been farms built on the land, and towns had sprung up like taniw'a's teeth.

Fortunately it was now summer, with long days and warm nights. The women could sleep comfortably and supplement their provisions by foraging for shellfish or for edible roots in the bush. Sometimes Erenora was able to catch fish.

'The moko of the Pakeha was everywhere. We crossed his many roads, hurrying over them before we could be seen. However, we were often confronted with signs on fences which proclaimed "Private Property" or "Keep Out" or "Trespassers Will Be Prosecuted". When we came to such warnings we waited until dark before climbing through. Some of the fences were made of barbed wire, with clusters of metal thorns. One night Ripeka became badly entangled and, in freeing her, I tore some skin off my left hand. "It's all right, sister," I told her, but all she could say was, "Oh, look at my dress!" Meri and I rolled our eyes at our sister's vanity.

'As we approached Whanganui, we skirted loggers chopping down the huge stands of coastal forests. The ground quaked as the trees fell. It seemed that even Tane, God of Trees, was powerless against the might of the Pakeha. So too was Tangaroa, God of the Sea ... My sisters and I were having lunch on the beach when Meri said to me in awe, "Look at all the ships, Erenora!" They were like white-winged moths fluttering at the horizon or smudging it with their smoke.

'Suddenly there was gunfire. Crack! Crack! *Crack!* A Pakeha settler had decided to use us for target practice.

'"We must move on," I said.'

The three sisters arrived at the mouth of the Whanganui River and walked along the bank. Ahead they saw the powerful settler town of Wanganui, one of the first to be founded in Aotearoa. Already, with its busy harbour, town buildings, church spires and fine suburban houses, it dwarfed Putiki, the Maori kainga on the other side of the river.

A friendly Maori in a canoe took them across to the village, where Erenora sought out the chief Te Rangi Paetahi Mete Kingi. He had been the first

member of Parliament for Western Maori, a man
of pro-government leanings and a frequent visitor
to Parihaka.

Mete Kingi did not recognise Erenora at first
but, when she told him who she was, he greeted
her warmly. 'Why have you dressed like that? And
why have you cut your hair?' Then he added, 'I
still have much love for Taranaki and your iwi.'
They were generous words, considering how he
had been humiliated at Parihaka. When Bryce's
army arrived, he tried to persuade his people to
leave the settlement before it was sacked; they
rebuffed him by choosing to stay.

Erenora hoped that Mete Kingi might have a
tribal party travelling to Wellington. When he said,
'No,' she was disconsolate, unsure what to do.

'We can't go on without protection,' she told
her sisters. 'It's too dangerous.'

A week later, however, Erenora heard chanting
voices, 'Toia mai! Te waka! Ki te urunga! Te waka!' She looked upstream and saw a large sea-
going waka from Patiarero coming in to dock at
the kainga's landing.

The captain of the waka was named Aperahama. With him was a group of about forty men,
women and children—and some empty seats. He
was a cheeky one, looking Erenora up and down.
'Are you a boy or a girl?' he asked.

'Does that matter when I have money?'
Erenora answered gruffly. 'If you're travelling to

Wellington I will pay for passage for me and my two sisters.'

'Our destination is Paekakariki,' Aperahama answered. 'From there, my people and I will trek inland to kin at Heretaunga.'

At least that will get us halfway there, Erenora thought. 'Will you take us?' she asked.

'Of course,' Aperahama answered. 'We could do with another paddler, eh boys!' Obviously, he had decided Erenora was male—or had he?

The following morning, despite gusty winds, the waka cleared the busy rivermouth. Oaths and curses were exchanged as the canoe jostled with Pakeha vessels also wishing to go out on the turning tide.

'Get out of the way, you heathen bastards!' a sailor yelled.

'You don't own the river yet!' Aperahama answered. Quickly, because the currents were clashing at the rivermouth, he shouted instructions, 'Nekeneke! Nekeneke!'

Erenora paddled for all she was worth. Her arms were aching when the waka finally reached the open sea where Aperahama cried, 'Hoist the sail!' He winked at Erenora. 'Do you want to change into a girl now?'

The canoe was soon skimming before the wind along the curve of coast from Putiki to Paekakariki. Out to sea, Erenora glimpsed the South Island—the inland Kaikoura. 'So,' Aperahama asked her, 'who are you? And why are you going to Wellington?'

She told him about Horitana. When she had finished he looked at her with admiration. 'Your husband is a fortunate man. May you find him.'

Onward the waka sailed, reaching the Manawatu coast. Aperahama pointed out to Erenora the huge fires that ringed the coast with rising columns of smoke. Where the coast was not on fire, it was charred, smoking earth. 'The Pakeha burns the bush to make way for more settlement,' Aperahama said.

The wind changed direction. It began to blow from the land and soon the people in the waka were overwhelmed with the swirling wreaths of smoke, ashes and hot embers. Out of the dark clouds, bearing down on them, was a sailing ship making for the rivermouth at Foxton Beach. 'Kia tupato!' Aperahama cried. It was too late. The sailing ship scraped past but its powerful wake capsized the canoe. Clinging to it, the occupants struggled through the breakers to the beach.

Aperahama was seething but, as in all transactions with the Pakeha, he was powerless. Erenora stood with him, watching as the sailing ship unloaded its precious cargo: sheep. 'There are almost 500,000 between Whanganui and Foxton now,' Aperahama told her. 'When the Pakeha takes over the land, that's only the beginning. The towns and roads come next and then the pastures where his sheep may safely graze.' Then he looked at her and chastised himself for falling in love with women so easily. 'No need to pay me, Erenora. After all, I didn't get you to your destination. You and your sisters can travel overland with us as far as Otaki, if you wish.'

Offshore lay Kapiti Island, brooding in a sea of stars. Once, the great Ngati Toa warrior chieftain Te Rauparaha had controlled the region; no longer. And everywhere, other Maori were moving back and forth along the coast, landless, finding their livelihood only on the tidal fringes between land and sea.

'We go our separate ways now,' Aperahama said to Erenora when they arrived at Otaki's large Anglican settlement. It was difficult for him to leave her. He started to lead his people away, then he stopped and called, 'Erenora! When you get to Wellington, seek shelter at Kaiwharawhara. Tell Auntie Rupi that Aperahama sent you. That will make her laugh!'

4.

'From Otaki we negotiated the thin coastal plain with its sand dunes and river fans to Waikanae and Paekakariki. Wherever we went among Maori folk we were immediately recognised, not only by the white feathers Ripeka and Meri wore in their hair but also because of our Taranaki dialect. The news had also spread about Mr Bryce's attack, and the fall of our kainga, and we were shown great hospitality and sympathy. And, of course, our Ngati Mutunga and Taranaki connections secured us shelter among Raukawa and Ngati Toa, the iwi of the region.

'And then our odyssey took us completely into the throat of the Pakeha. Everywhere were Pakeha settlements, houses, roads and, also, railway tracks, as if a taniw'a had slithered across the land.

'We arrived at the mouth of the double-armed Porirua Harbour and found shelter at the Ngati Toa marae known as Takapuwahia. It was there that my sister, Meri, made a bad decision.'

Poor Meri! Ever since she had thrown half the sisters' money at Piharo's henchmen, she'd been upset. She decided to make good the loss by selling the beautiful pounamu 'eitiki Riki had given her. It was a huge sacrifice; from the time Riki had pledged his troth to her, she had never taken it from her neck. She sneaked off after breakfast while Erenora and Ripeka weren't looking and went to the local trading post to sell it.

It wasn't until half an hour later that Erenora discovered she was missing. She was thanking Hariata, one of their hosts at Takapuwahia, for her hospitality, and then she turned to Ripeka and said, 'Time to go. Where's Meri?'

'She left a message that we should meet up with her at the trading post,' Ripeka answered.

When Hariata heard where Meri had gone, she became very agitated. 'Arapeta's place has a bad reputation,' she said. 'Nobody from here ever goes there, not since the last time.'

'The last time *what?*' Erenora screamed.

'I'd better get some of the boys to go with you,' Hariata answered.

The tone in her voice made Erenora so alarmed that she said to Ripeka, 'We can't wait. We'd better go on ahead.'

Erenora ran from Takapuwahia.

'Wait for me!' Ripeka cried.

Erenora kept on running. Her heart was pounding when she saw the trading post with its hitching rail outside. A few Maori youngsters were sitting on the verandah passing a whisky bottle between them. 'Hey, what's the hurry,' one of them greeted her. 'Wanna swig?'

She went up the steps two at a time and entered the store. To one side was a counter with a display of sweets for little children. To the other was a big room filled with saddles, farm equipment and sacks of grain and sugar. A doorway led to a smaller room in which there were cheap cotton dresses hanging on racks, hats and shoes. There was no one in the store. Where was Meri?

The owner came out of a back room. 'What can I do for you, matey?' he asked. He was large, swarthy and smiling. 'You here to buy or do you want a woman?'

Erenora stepped up to him. 'Are you Arapeta?' she asked. In her fear for Meri she took up an attacking position; nobody would have thought she was anything but a young boy. 'I'm looking for my sister. She was supposed to meet us here.' She kept her voice low and level, pronouncing the words in an emphatic way.

Arapeta held her gaze, unblinking, still smiling. 'I'm sorry, matey, but I've not had a woman in here all morning.'

At that moment, Ripeka burst into the trading post. 'Have you found Meri?' she asked, distraught. The expression on Arapeta's face changed. He reached under the counter for a gun and levelled it at the two sisters. 'Get out of here, both of you.'

Then Ripeka saw Meri's 'eitiki around his neck. 'What have you done with her?' she screamed.

What was that sound...?

Erenora heard thumping from the back room. 'Get out of my way,' she said as she shoved past Arapeta.

'Stop or I'll shoot,' he roared.

She saw him raise his rifle and sight on her. He would be well within his rights: an unknown boy, wishing to rob him...

Before Arapeta could go further, however, Hariata arrived with two Ngati Toa men, one of whom wrested the rifle from him. 'Up to your old tricks, eh, Arapeta?'

Meri was cruelly lashed to a bed with ropes. She had a piece of wood in her mouth, tied tightly by a gag to prevent her from crying out. Her eyes were wide with fear, and even while Erenora was cutting through the ropes Meri could not stop trembling. When she was released it was to Ripeka she turned for comfort.

'Oh, sister,' she sobbed, 'I thought if I sold the 'eitiki we would have enough money to pay for our passage from Wellington across Raukawa. But when I got to the trading post the owner...'

Erenora grabbed her by the shoulders and shook her hard. 'Meri, be obedient to me. Don't *think*. It only gets you into trouble.'

They helped Meri out of the back room. Hariata and her men had surrounded Arapeta. 'A man's got to live,' he said, trying to talk his way out of the situation. 'And the bitch was struggling, see, so I had to tie her up. You understand...' He began to offer them goods from the store in exchange for letting him go.

Hariata turned to Erenora. 'Arapeta preys on young women,' she said. 'If he discovers they're travelling alone, he captures them, plies them with grog to keep them insensible and then sells them into prostitution.' Erenora walked up to him and wrenched Meri's pendant from his neck. 'Call yourself a Maori,' she hissed. She was so enraged—she could have lost Meri to him—that she slashed his face with her knife.

Arapeta yelled with shock and put his hand to the wound. When he saw the blood on his hands, his eyes widened with fear.

'Somebody should put you out of business,' Erenora said.

He staggered away, out of the store, crying for help.

'There's nothing we can do,' Hariata answered, 'except keep a watch on his activities. We've put the police on to him but he always gets off with a warning. And after all, Arapeta's one of us, he's getting along well ... and we need the trading post. You understand?'

Oh, Erenora understood all right. It was all so futile, really.

'You'd better go quickly now,' Hariata said. 'Arapeta will be sure to report you for what you've done to him.'

Meri was still weeping as, on Hariata's advice, the sisters set out on the old Ngati Toa track that would take them to Wellington by way of Tawa and the Ngaio Gorge. All the way up the track, Erenora refused to give her sister comfort.

Finally, Ripeka stopped Erenora. 'Our sister was only trying to help,' she said.

Relenting, Erenora cuddled Meri. 'Why don't you sing us a little poi song?' She smiled, unloosed the poi from Meri's belt and put them in her hands.

Meri looked at the poi. She was wan and reluctant but then her spirits lifted at having been forgiven and she began to sing a song, tap tap tap, tap tap tap:

'Titiro taku poi! Rere atu rere mai! Look at my poi! It swings up and it swings down! Aren't you lucky, Meri, to have sisters to rescue you?'

The sisters crested the Ngaio Gorge. From the top they beheld the harbour below and, encircling it, the city.

CHAPTER SEVENTEEN

Empire City

1.

What were Erenora's thoughts on seeing Wellington, Whanganuia-Tara?

In her manuscript she wrote, 'Such a large kainga! On first glimpsing the city I truly realised the great and overpowering might of the Pakeha. So confident were the citizens of its mana that they had built it without walls or other fortifications to protect it.'

Erenora's recollection invokes another thought:

Remember the Gustav Doré engraving, *The New Zealander* from *London,* 1873? For English men and women, New Zealand was no longer regarded as an outpost of England at the very edge of the British Empire. Could the New Zealander in Doré's engraving, come to look at a decaying London, have been a Wellingtonian? Was a 'new' London being built in the southern land among green and pleasant hills?

No wonder that, from the comfort of their armchairs, the English upper and middle classes could look with pride to Wellington, where British civilisation had begun anew.

They called it Empire City.

The three sisters arrived at Kaiwharawhara just as night was falling. The marae was crowded, and a camp of tents and makeshift huts spilt onto the beach where groups of Maori huddled around campfires.

Erenora immediately sought out Rupi, whom she found in the community kitchen. 'My name is Eruera,' she said.

Rupi didn't bat an eyelid. 'Kia ora, boy,' she answered. 'So that good for nothing nephew of mine, Aperahama, told you to come here, eh? It's usually his runaway girlfriends he sends for me to take care of! Ah well, we may be full up but room can always be found for three travellers from Parihaka. Eat with us and, later, you and your sisters can sleep with me and my w'anau.'

The sisters sat down to a meal of home-baked flour bread and broth. Some people, recognising the feathers in Ripeka and Meri's hair, came to greet them. 'Aue, we are all refugees,' they said. 'Even here in Wellington, ever since the Pakeha came in 1840 with his deed of purchase, we have been gradually forced out. His is the great white tribe who owns Whanganui-a-Tara now.'

Afterwards, Rupi took the sisters to her family tent on the beach. 'Put your blankets next to ours,' she said to them. She introduced them to others sitting at one of the nearby fires. 'You', she said to Ripeka, 'can have a place near the fire.' She muttered angrily at some who had already taken the privileged position.

Embers from the beach fire burnt tiny holes in the dark. The evening was cold but there was no wind.

The moon, shining full in the sky, was reflected in the water. Looking at the sea Erenora wondered, *How will my sisters and I get across Cook Strait to Te Wai Pounamu?* She began to get a headache, thinking about it. Sometimes a problem, like a knot, took a long time to untie and solve. Meanwhile there was a more pressing difficulty: seeking information at Mount Cook Prison about Horitana, Paora and Riki. The question soon attracted voluble opinions from the refugees at Rupi's campfire.

'Political prisoners aren't allowed visitors,' said one.

'No matter how long you wait at the gates, you'll never be allowed in,' said another.

'And if you get inside the prison,' said a third, 'how do you know the guards will let you out?'

The overall view was that the venture was hopeless. 'Don't listen to them,' Rupi scoffed. 'You should place yourself upon the mercy of one of the Maori members of Parliament.'

'Te Wheoro?' Erenora asked, her interest stirring.

'He's the member for Western Maori, isn't he?' Rupi answered grumpily, as if Erenora should know. 'Go and see him tomorrow morning.'

A vigorous debate began about how difficult it was for Te Wheoro and the other Maori parliamentarians to represent Maori interests in Te Paremata o te Pakeha. Was it their own fault if, in advocating for Maori, some members believed that survival lay in Maori turning to Pakeha ways? After all, if Maori efforts to maintain tino rangatiratanga had so far failed, what other option was there?

'Aue,' Rupi said eventually, breaking up the korero, 'the night is growing late. So you'll go to see Te Wheoro?'

'Yes,' Erenora answered. 'Thank you for suggesting him.'

Rupi looked around smugly. 'Everybody around here knows that if you have a problem, Rupi will fix it! Why do you think Aperahama sent you to me?' She roared with laughter, pleased with herself. 'But you,' she added, looking at Ripeka, 'you should stay behind tomorrow.'

Ripeka coloured. 'No. Where one goes, we all go.'

Rupi's remark puzzled Erenora. 'Why is the kuia so concerned for you?' she asked Ripeka.

'I don't know,' she shrugged.

The next day, Erenora had forgotten the matter. She and her sisters set off for Te Paremata o te Pakeha.

2.

'My sisters were dazed at the marvellous sights and, although I was in a hurry to get to Parliament, Ripeka pestered me, "Please, Erenora, can we look at the shops?"

'Of course Ripeka's reason was so that she could look at the fashions in the windows. However, I did not think that a small detour along Lambton Quay would be amiss. "Very well," I said.

'Well! I had completely forgotten that Christmas was coming. The street was crowded with citizens pointing at the Christmastide displays: holly and ivy, sparkling decorations, scenes of families skating on ice or riding sleds through the snow. It was like another world, so entrancing. I thought to myself, *Never will New Zealand be a place where, during our hot summers, snow will fall!* Then I noticed that our presence among the festive crowd, all dressed in gay apparel, was being remarked upon. "Don't linger," I said to Ripeka and Meri, as they tarried too long before a department store display. Ripeka had stars in her eyes, daydreaming about a particularly lovely gown of purple silk into which she could never have fitted.

'It wasn't long, however, before some of the revellers took exception to our passage through their fair city. You might have thought that good will to all men would prevail but some ignorant individuals, clearly affronted by our presence, wrinkled their noses and challenged us, "What are you doing here?" And when, at the corner of Willis Street, a dowager shook her umbrella at us and said, "Be off with you!" that was the last straw.

'I have always had a facility with the English language and, noticing that she wore a crucifix on a chain around her neck, responded to her with sharp words of my own. "Madam," I answered, in my deep *male* voice, "you would do well to say three Hail Marys when you next see your priest for your uncharitable and unchristian behaviour, particularly during the holy Advent." It was worth it to see her grow scarlet—she was in polite company—and step back to make way for us.

'It was satisfying, too, to note that the pavement suddenly opened to us as if God had parted the Red Sea. "Let us go back now and seek the Valley of the Kings," I said to my sisters.

'Aue, Te Wheoro was not at Parliament. "Come back in two days' time," his secretary, Anaru, said. "The House will be in session and Wiremu will return to Wellington for it. When he arrives, I will let him know you seek his help to visit your men in Mount Cook Prison."

'Two days ... and then what?

'I made a decision. Whether Te Wheoro could help us or not, my sisters and I would still carry on to the South Island.'

3.

The following morning the three sisters again ventured into Wellington but this time they headed to the port to book passage on a vessel across Raukawa.

'Be careful down at the docks,' Rupi warned them. 'They're all robbers and cut-throats there. Watch out that you're not overcharged for your billets of passage either. If anybody tries it on, just tell them Rupi will come and cut their balls off.'

During the night, Erenora had discovered why the old kuia had so much influence, and how she seemed to know, well, everybody. In the changing world of the Maori she was a new breed; a black marketer, her network extended not only among Maori like her nephew Aperahama—she had a lot of 'nephews'—and, possibly, Te Wheoro, but also among Pakeha down at the capital's port.

'And you, boy,' she said to Erenora, 'you should have known better than to encourage your sister to come with you.' The way Rupi said 'boy' made Erenora wonder if the old kuia had twigged to her disguise. But after all, people escaping from the law or with secrets to hide often said they were one thing when they were really another.

The women made their way to the port through the tangles of warehouses and commercial buildings, public houses and other drinking places. Meri clung to Ripeka as drunkards called out to them, 'You got time for a poke, girlies?' At the dockside, it was bedlam. Cargo was being loaded or unloaded from an array of coastal ships: 'Watch out below!' The quays milled with shouting sailors and workers, 'Clear the way!' Darting among them, gentlemen shepherded their ladies, 'Come, Millicent,' before they were soiled by the salty language and terrible odour of sweat and labour.

Erenora found a number of offices selling billets of passage. 'Do you have passage available to Hokitika?' she asked.

Rupi had been correct: sharks were indeed masquerading as agents. They named exorbitant rates and then leant back, folding their arms. Even though Erenora tried to bargain, the lowest offer for deck space was still more than she and her sisters could afford unless ... Well, Erenora ignored all the lewd suggestions made to Ripeka and Meri about alternative ways of paying to cross the strait. 'All your girlies would need to do', one scrawny ship's agent sniggered, 'would be to make the trip on their backs.'

Despondent, the sisters returned to Kaiwharawhara where Erenora mulled over the problem.

'The art of forbearance, Erenora,' Ripeka reminded her.

'I should have come by myself,' Erenora muttered. 'If no solution offers itself, I'll go on alone and send you and Meri back to Parihaka. It's the only way.'

Ripeka showed some spirit. 'You reckon?' she flared. 'Not without us you don't.'

When the time came to set off again for Parliament, however, Erenora saw a small schooner moored at a makeshift jetty off Kaiwharawhara.

'Quick, boy,' said Rupi, 'some pounamu hunters have just arrived from Auckland where they've been trading. They're on their way back home to the South Island for Christmas. So I've spoken to Whai, their chief, and he says you and your sisters could cross over Raukawa with them.'

Oh, that was such lucky news! The sisters immediately went down to the schooner, the *Arikinui,* and presented themselves to Whai. He had strong links with Taranaki. 'The old blackmailer tells me you need a passage across the strait. Well, if I don't take you, she'll spill the beans on me! As long as you're ready to leave tonight I'll take you as far as Arahura.'

Tonight? 'Let's hope Te Wheoro can help us by then,' Erenora said to her sisters as, without hesitation, she leapt at the offer. 'We'll be ready,' she answered. Arahura was just a few miles short of Hokitika.

'Okay then,' Whai continued. 'After all, if I don't help you the gods could get angry. Wasn't it a woman from the North Island whom my ancestor Poutini abducted and turned into pounamu? If that hadn't happened I might not have a livelihood today, eh?'

The sisters hastened to Parliament where they were welcomed again by Te Wheoro's secretary, who ushered them through the corridors to the public gallery.

'Right now, the House is debating the findings of the Confiscated Lands Inquiry,' Anaru explained. 'Te Wheoro and other Maori members have taken the floor to ask why Te Whiti, Tohu and their men are still being held without trial. Wiremu will see you once the debate is over.'

Anaru opened the door to the gallery and immediately the sound spilled over them. It was the sound of rage, the sound of hostility, the sound of people baying for blood. The object of their ire was a short, heavy-set man, who had taken the floor. Wiremu

Maipapa Te Wheoro was speaking in Maori, and the other members of the House were roaring their displeasure at his translated words.

'Behold, Daniel in the lion's den,' Anaru said to Erenora.

The roaring of the lions was so great that the walls shook from it. Te Wheoro happened to look at the public gallery and, seeing three figures, two of whom wore white feathers in their hair, inclined his head to them. *Yes, pilgrims of Parihaka, witness my humiliation that day after day I must come here with my fellow Maori members to be eaten alive.*

Despite the hostile debate, Te Wheoro was in a buoyant mood when the session ended.

'The lions were hungry today,' Anaru said to him as he made the introductions.

Te Wheoro laughed. 'Perhaps they'll eat me tomorrow,' he jested. He turned to Erenora. 'Are you the boy and his sisters who want to go to Mount Cook Prison?'

'Yes,' Erenora answered. 'If there's any way you can help us...'

Te Wheoro's eyes twinkled. 'Although, in the Parliament, I haven't yet been successful in overturning the laws inflicted on your two prophets, some compensation can be taken from smaller victories. Come! A carriage is waiting to take us to the prison where my good and faithful servant Anaru has made arrangements with the superintendent to admit us.'

'You will do that for us?' Ripeka asked, shedding tears of gratitude. 'And you are coming too?' Meri added, kissing his hands.

'One lion's den is like another,' Te Wheoro answered in good humour, 'and the lions of Mount Cook perhaps do not roar as loudly as the ones here in Te Paremata o te Pakeha.'

4.

'It was three days before Christmas, 1881. The weather had turned cloudy and cold. The Wellington streets were packed with horse-drawn vehicles of all kinds; men on horseback squeezed through the gaps. Te Wheoro's driver, oblivious of the shouted oaths, navigated expertly through the traffic, sometimes with only inches to spare between his vehicle and the next.

'"Bob's showing off for the country constituents," Anaru whispered to Te Wheoro.

'As the carriage turned up Taranaki Street, Te Wheoro pointed out a rise ahead. "Ah, we are approaching Pukeahu," he said. Mount Cook Prison crouched on the top of the small mounga. I caught glimpses of an encircling palisade topped with viewing platforms and sentry boxes. Guards holding rifles patrolled the walls.

'My sisters became nervous. In an attempt to calm them, Anaru engaged them in conversation. "Did you know," he began, "that the palisade was built by the very first contingent of prisoners from Parihaka? When they arrived they were put to work converting the original military barracks into the prison. They repaired and altered the buildings, put in the gas and water fittings, gravelled the yard and built the prisoners' wing—and then they moved into it."

'The carriage clattered up to the main gateway, interrupting him.

'"Ah, here we are," Te Wheoro said. He showed our credentials to the guard, and we were admitted. As Bob drove through, we saw that another guard was waiting at the steps to the administration block. He gave a snappy salute as we stopped. "Rank has its privileges," Te Wheoro continued.

'My sisters clung to me as we were led to the office of the prison superintendent. On the walls of the corridor were sketches of similar prisons in Tasmania and Norfolk Island. One showed a prison at night, its outer walls lit up and guards on constant patrol.

'"Let me speak for you," Te Wheoro said. It was fortunate that he did so because the prison superintendent was not helpful. No sooner had Te Wheoro introduced himself than that officious man responded by saying, "While I am forced to entertain your presence, I am not required to assist your enquiries."

'Te Wheoro almost lost his temper, but he maintained admirable self-control. "Sir, I quite understand your position. I am here on behalf of three of my constituents. Won't you help them? All they request is that you consult the manifest for the month of August 1879..."

'"That information is classified."

'"... and advise them if the names of three particular prisoners appear on it. The men were transported here with the original 170 sent from Parihaka. They were not, however, among those who returned and my constituents understand they may have been transferred instead to prisons in the South Island. Once they know that destination they will thank you and be on their way."

'"I repeat," the superintendent began again, "that that information is..."

'At his words, Meri gave a sob and, well, my sister had her uses: she could melt a heart of stone, even if it did belong to a prison superintendent. After a while, he coughed. "I will make an exception to the rules in this case," he said, and reluctantly called one of his men to bring him the relevant records.

'"The names of the fanatics?" he asked us. *Fanatics?* We gave him Horitana's, Riki's and Paora's names. He thumbed through the manifest. "Yes, we have their names entered in the register among the misguided men who were sent here."

'I could have hit him for his abusive words. "This prison follows the Pentonville model," he continued, "and therefore, for infractions, felons are subjected to the normal punishments. From the very beginning the fanatics you refer to were sullen, morose, refused to work and were disobedient. The ones named Riki and Paora were punished for insubordinate behaviour and the third, Horitana, was placed for seven days in isolation and solitary confinement."

202

'My heart lurched with fear. "The first two men were detained from transportation with their fellow fanatics to the South Island because they were undergoing punishment. The same applies for their misguided leader, Horitana. Upon completion of their sentences, however, the fanatic named Paora was conveyed to Hokitika..."

'"Those prisoners have already returned to Parihaka," Ripeka interrupted.

'The superintendent ignored her. "... and the fanatic named Riki was sent to Christchurch."

'"What was the date of their release?" Te Wheoro asked.

'"On 14 August, at 6.15 a.m., the fanatics were presented for transfer while the streets were still empty, so as not to disturb the harmony enjoyed by the citizens of our peaceful city."

'"What of the prisoner Horitana?" I asked.

'The superintendent thumbed through the register. An expression of puzzlement appeared briefly on his face. "His name appears to have been erased. There's no indication of his movements. Certainly, he's no longer imprisoned at Mount Cook."

'Te Wheoro asked the question I dared not ask. "Is it possible that the prisoner Horitana died in solitary confinement?"

'My heart skipped a beat as the superintendent turned the pages. Finally, he shook his head, "No, I have no record of his death. I do have the name of Tami Raiha, however. He was so ill he could not be sent with the others."'

5.

Te Wheoro turned to Erenora. While the prison superintendent looked on, he whispered to her, 'Young man, I think we have the information you and your sisters seek, yes?'

Erenora nodded. She felt drained and numb. *Oh husband, where are you?*

'So we are finished here?' Te Wheoro asked again.

'Yes,' she answered. She could not help the bitterness that flooded into her words. 'Let's get out of here and away from this disgusting man.'

Te Wheoro was more polite. 'I thank you, sir,' he said to the prison superintendent, 'for your assistance.'

They were just about to leave—Te Wheoro, Anaru, Erenora and her sisters—when the superintendent coughed for attention. 'We don't have many members of Parliament visiting us,' he began. 'Perhaps you might like to make an inspection of the fanatics so as to reassure your colleagues that they are well cared for by Her Majesty's prison officials?'

Te Wheoro looked at Erenora: this was manna from Heaven. 'Of course,' he answered.

The superintendent led them all toward the prisoners' wing. 'The fanatics are all at work,' he began, 'in our brickyard. Thus they serve a useful purpose during their confinement by making bricks to erect the proud edifices of our country's government. The current batch is destined for the Wellington courthouse.'

Even before they reached them, Erenora could hear the men singing:

'Fly, our thoughts, on golden wings! Alight upon the slopes of Taranaki Mountain, the slopes and hills where the soft and sweet breezes blow warmly over Parihaka! Oh, our beloved people! Our beloved country!'

Suddenly, there they were, toiling in the yard. Erenora's heart went out to them. Fanatics they were not, but fine and good men. Some were filling the moulds with clay. Others stooped at the kilns, stoking the fires. Even more were stacking bricks onto sledges.

All the prisoners were sweating. They wore the familiar prison garments with their broad arrows. Most looked in good health but a few were coughing and clearly ill from their incarceration. Ripeka and Meri recognised some of them and, before they could be stopped, called out to them, 'E nga 'oa, tena koutou! Titiro ki nga roimata o o koutou tua'ine o Parihaka!'

'No,' the prison superintendent cried, alarmed, 'don't do that.'

It was too late. 'Women of Parihaka, here?' the prisoners cried. Flinging down their tools, leaving the kilns, they rushed to the bars behind which Ripeka and Meri were standing and pushed their hands through the gaps to touch them. Tears flowed down their gaunt faces.

'How are our wives? Our children? Tell them that we think of them and yearn to be with them.'

Whistles were sounding. Prison guards rushed toward the men. 'Back! Back, fanatics! Get back!'

One of the men Erenora knew well. It was Ruakere and, despite her disguise, he recognised her. 'Erenora! Wait!' His eyes were wide with shock and desperation.

Te Wheoro and Anaru looked at Erenora, puzzled. 'You are a woman?' Te Wheoro asked.

She nodded, then turned her attention back to Ruakere. She saw him reach into his shirt pocket and try to thrust something through the bars to her. Too late—he was brutally herded away with the others. 'No! Please, I...'

All too soon the brief encounter was over.

6.

The three sisters returned with Te Wheoro to Parliament.

'What will you do now?' he asked Erenora. He and Anaru had accepted with equanimity her confession that she was not a boy.

'My sisters and I will go on to Te Wai Pounamu,' she answered. 'We came to find our husbands and we will not rest until we do.' She thanked him for his assistance. 'Keep fighting the lions,' she said.

She turned to Anaru. 'I will never forget your kindness.'

They hastened back to Kaiwharawhara. Had Whai and the greenstone hunters left without them? With relief Erenora saw that the *Arikinui* was at the jetty.

'You're just in time,' Whai called.

There was hardly a moment to say goodbye to Rupi and others gathered on the beach. Rupi patted Ripeka's stomach, gave her a kiss and Erenora and Meri a stern look. 'Look after your sister,' she said.

The schooner was casting off when Erenora heard a shout. Who was that? It was Te Wheoro's carriage, and Bob the coachman was still showing off his skills. He drove straight through the crowd and right up to the jetty. Rupi had to leap to one side and into the water. When she got up, she gave Bob an earful, 'A new dress is going to cost you a pretty penny.'

Anaru jumped out of the carriage and ran along the jetty. 'Erenora! Wait!' He was just fast enough to thrust something into her hands; any later and it would have fallen into the sea. 'A letter, Erenora,' Anaru panted, 'under the parliamentary crest, to whomever it may concern. Who knows, it might come in handy.'

The wind belled the sails and the *Arikinui* surged away.

'And I have a message.' Anaru was panicking. 'From Ruakere, who recognised you in Mount Cook Prison. It's about your husband.'

Seagulls were clattering in the air. 'Tell me!' Erenora shouted.

Anaru cupped his hands and his voice came across the water, pursuing the schooner, dipping on white wings, quickly, quickly, and then soaring above her head, dropping its message. 'Piharo came in pursuit of your husband,' he yelled. 'It was on Piharo's order that Horitana was put in leg irons and chains and placed in solitary confinement.'

He threw a second object across the waves. It came tumbling through the sky and clattered on the deck. Erenora ran to pick it up. It was a small figurine, about 8 inches long, of a Maori warrior; Ruakere must have whittled it in his cell. But around the warrior's head Ruakere had wrapped a shard of tin. As Erenora took a closer look, the tin silvered in the sun.

At the base of the carving, Ruakere had carved Horitana's name, followed by a phrase that Erenora had never seen before:

Te tangata mokomokai.

CHAPTER EIGHTEEN

Ever, Ever Southward

1.

From the calm of Wellington Harbour, the *Arikinui* approached the gap between the heads. Beyond, the southerly was whipping the water and white-tipping the waves. The swell deepened and, with Whai at the tiller judging the contrary currents, the schooner sailed out into the open sea. The *Arikinui* hesitated, then her canvas *cracked* and she leapt into Cook Strait.

'She's keen to get home,' Whai called to Erenora. 'We've been away a long time.'

Erenora nodded and smiled at him. The wind was in her face. Ahead were the cloud-encircled mountains of Te Wai Pounamu, the South Island. She was thrilled, not a little afraid, and said a quiet prayer of safekeeping. How undreamed of—to leave one island of Aotearoa for the other. It defied all her expectations to have made it this far.

In her left hand Erenora still clutched the wooden figurine thrown to her by Anaru. For a moment, she grew afraid of it: the carved indentations, the rough whittled surface and, especially, the suffocating tin enclosing the head. And the name Ruakere had given it, te tangata mokomokai, what did it mean...?

She nicked her finger on the tin and blood welled from it. Suddenly she felt nauseous, as if the figurine was a devil-doll. Something horrifying had happened to Horitana. If she cast the effigy into the sea, perhaps whatever malevolent spell or incantation that had been cast over him would be undone.

'Erenora?' Meri's voice interrupted her.

'I'm so afraid, Meri. Oh, I'm so frightened.'

The sky was turning crimson, and night began to fall fast.

A few moments later, Ripeka joined Erenora and Meri. 'There's something I have to tell you both,' she began. She was shivering with cold.

Meri grabbed her in her arms and held her tight. 'No, Ripeka, don't say it...'

'If you haven't already guessed,' she began, 'I am with child.'

Oh, and the glowing sun was falling quickly to the west, setting fire to the horizon.

'We thought as much,' Erenora said after a while. 'You've kept your morning sickness well hidden but Rupi's eyes unmasked you.'

'Of course the child isn't Paora's,' Ripeka continued. 'When I was raped at Parihaka, one of those bastards planted his seed in me. Ever since, I have felt it growing like an unbidden vine in my womb. How I have wished I could rip the plant out and watch it shrivel and die.' She burst into sobs. 'What am I going to say to Paora?'

'He'll forgive you,' Meri said, willing the words to be true. 'He'll know it wasn't your fault.'

Erenora remained silent but, in her head, a selfish thought took root. *If I am barren, perhaps I can ask Ripeka to give the child to me and Horitana to bring up.* Wouldn't that make it easier for Ripeka and Paora? They wouldn't want the child as a constant reminder of what had happened to Ripeka, would they? Almost immediately she had the thought, however, Erenora felt ashamed.

'Being with child is supposed to be a woman's crowning joy,' Ripeka continued, 'but there is no joy in my heart. I will place myself on Paora's mercy.'

'You'll have us with you when you tell him,' Erenora said, kissing Ripeka on her cold cheek.

It was the morning of Christmas Eve when the schooner reached Arahura.

As they were disembarking, Meri asked Erenora, 'Would you really have sent me and Ripeka back to Parihaka?'

'Yes,' Erenora answered. 'I would have purchased a single ticket for myself on a vessel sailing across Raukawa.' She sighed melodramatically. 'Oh, why did Whai and his schooner have to show up?'

Meri gave a wide grin. 'See?' she said to Ripeka. 'Our sister is all blow and no go.' They began to wrap themselves up against the cold, hoisted their shoulder sacks and prepared for the walk to Hokitika.

Whai was reluctant to let them leave. 'Are you sure you won't come with us to our kainga for Kiri-himete?' Already his men were waiting for him to join them on the last few miles to their families. 'Hokitika will be filled with miners wanting a good time. Not a safe place for women.'

'Don't worry about us,' Erenora assured him. 'Go to your loved ones.' As they separated, she made a vow to herself. From now on, she would not let her disguise slip again, the risk was too great. She *would* be Eruera.

The sisters turned south along the beach. How majestic the mountains were. They rose into the heavens like poutama, great staircases, foaming with snow.

Bowing before them, Meri raised her voice in karanga. 'E nga mounga tapu,' she called in the dawn light, 'oh, sacred mountains, we bring you greetings from your brother mounga, Taranaki.' In her usual simple, affecting manner she attempted to clear a safe passage for the three sisters.

Again, Erenora set the pace. Silently, Ripeka and Meri followed her. And it came to Erenora that she loved her sisters, and that she was the least among them. How would she be able to protect Ripeka, who was with child now, and Meri, who had a son waiting for her at Parihaka? She looked up at the towering mountains and the blue void beyond.

'If one of us is to die, let it be me,' she prayed.

2.

At this point, the question needs to be asked:

How many men from Taranaki were sent to the South Island?

Let me answer by dealing, first, with those men forcibly removed from Parihaka. Think of it: estimates of the permanent male population of Parihaka range between 600 and 800, but nobody knows for sure. Put that figure against the one for the numbers initially exiled to the South Island, over 420 Maori ploughmen in 1879 and a further 216 fencers in July 1880, and, well, you are already above the lower male number.

Then, however, you have to add the prisoners who *continued* to be exiled; some of those would have been supporters from Waikato and other tribes who were staying at Parihaka. Whichever way you cut it, Parihaka was sadly reduced. When you think of the implications for the future, the birth statistics must have taken a huge dip. How could the settlement survive?

Now, what of the other men who had begun to be sent to the South Island during Titokowaru's War ten years *before* the fall of Parihaka?

On this point, let me draw your attention to the excellent monograph by my friend Maarire Goodall. Speaking of Dunedin in particular, Goodall cites the case of 74 men from South Taranaki—supporters of Titokowaru—who arrived in Dunedin on the *Ran-*

gatira, along with 71 guards, on Saturday 6 November 1869:

> *A huge crowd thronged the wharf and lined the streets as the Maoris were taken to the prison, on its present site by the foot of Stuart Street. Some were fine, stalwart fellows, reporters noted; others, elderly and frail, able to walk only slowly. All were downcast. On reaching the gaol, they were given prison garb in exchange for their blankets and other clothes; and, the* Otago Daily Times *assured its readers, 'presented a much more comfortable appearance'. But within a few minutes of entering his cell, the first prisoner had died—Waiata, an elderly man serving a three-year term.*[18]

The prisoners were from Pakakohe, of Ngati Ruanui. Sometimes they were marshalled from Dunedin Gaol or from work at Andersons Bay—a mile or so away—at the inlet on the neck of the Otago Peninsula. Some reports state that they were held permanently in the caves at the end of Portsmouth Drive, but this is incorrect: it has been deduced that the three caves concerned were too small and probably used as offices or for storing equipment; a pole in one of the caves may have been used for chaining a prisoner for some infraction.

---

18 Maarire Goodall, 'Maori Prisoners in Our Midst', Witi Ihimaera (ed.), *Te Ao Marama Vol.2: Regaining Aotearoa—Maori Writers Speak Out*, Reed, 1993, p.41.

They worked with Pakeha convicts on constructing the causeway. Eighteen either pined away or succumbed to tubercular or bronchial ailments, before all who remained were formally released on 12 March 1872. In gratitude for the assistance of local Dunedin Maori, those who survived to return to the Taranaki changed their name to Ngati Otakou.

No women and children served with the Pakakohe prisoners.

It is likely that, despite the privations of their initial gaoling, two and possibly more of these Pakakohe men returned again as prisoners. This time, they came back as ploughmen of Parihaka. So, every gaol a Bastille? I know I'm being a Rottweiler; you can blame the mood I'm in.

How many Taranaki men kua ngaro ki Te Po? What *was* the number exiled to Te Wai Pounamu? Would a thousand be too high? And what about the number not sent to the South Island but gaoled in New Plymouth or other North Island prisons? The statistics are sketchy. We just don't *know.*

Perhaps some university historian, with a grant behind him or more funds than I can muster, might give some attention to these questions.

And now, treading the same Trail of Tears, came three Taranaki women.

3.

No wonder Whai was worried about Erenora and her sisters.

The road to Hokitika was crowded with young miners, riding horses or driving carts and raising dust as they raced into town. They threatened to run the women down in their haste, their thoughts on alcohol. Even on the outskirts of the town rowdy miners had already begun to celebrate, though not the birth of the Christ child; rather, they were intent on drinking themselves into a stupor.

'Hey, boy,' a voice shouted. 'Have you lost your senses? Get those women off the street immediately.' The voice belonged to the wispy-haired and nervous keeper of a dry goods store. 'The miners may be mothers' sons but come tonight they'll be an unruly mob.'

'Thank you for the warning, sir,' Erenora said.

Ripeka whispered to her, 'We'd better stock up while we can.'

'You'll be my last customers of the day,' the storekeeper said.

As he calculated the amount owing, Erenora asked, 'Perhaps you could recommend a safe route for us? We're seeking the gaol.'

'You'll be after Seaview Terrace on Misery Hill,' he answered, giving her a curious look. 'But I don't think they have any Maoris left inside.' He ushered

Erenora and her sisters out of the store, closed and padlocked the doors and then tested the windows again to make sure they were shut.

'Some of the prisoners may have been sent to another gaol in the South Island,' Ripeka told him. 'We'd like to know where.'

The store owner was on the point of venturing another possibility to Erenora but was warned by her look, *No, don't say it.*

'Well, good day to you then,' he said, 'and mark my words, boy, this isn't a good time for womenfolk to be about.'

'We followed the storekeeper's directions and were relieved to escape the township. The darkness was falling quickly and the wind was chill from the sea when we came upon the aptly named Misery Hill. The prison stood in a large clearing overlooking the ocean.

'Ripeka's early eagerness became filled with hesitation. "What if Paora doesn't forgive me?" she asked.

'As we approached the gaol, we saw a couple just in front of us. They were walking slowly, the old man supporting his wife, and as we drew abreast I lowered my voice and greeted them. "Good day to you," I said. They were a working-class couple, but wearing their best clothes. The old man was tall and barrel-chested; he looked as if could have been a prize fighter in his youth. "The same to you and your women," he answered, doffing his cap. His voice had an Irish lilt.

'"Oh, Seamus," the woman said. She had suddenly become affrighted by the prison: the entire circling wall, maybe 20 feet in height; the guard looking darkly down from the watch-platform, taking in our approach. Through the main entrance, I glimpsed an oblong-shaped building within. "Halt where you are," the guard ordered, his rifle at the ready. "The prison's closed to all visitors."

'"We were hoping to see our son," the old man said.

'"And I my husband," Ripeka added.

'"They're already locked in their cells," the guard answered. "You must come back in the morning when visitors are allowed to bring Christmas cheer to their imprisoned men."

'The elderly couple were disappointed, especially the woman, who dabbed at her eyes with a handkerchief. "We can wait one more day, dear," her husband comforted her. He introduced himself as Seamus Donovan, explaining he had come from Kumara with his wife to see their only son, Charlie, imprisoned for robbery and assault.

'"We met some of your Maori people," Mrs Donovan said, "when we came to see our Charlie, almost a year ago now. Charlie so admired them. He told us they were kept separate in a day room where they could be more easily supervised. They were always at their prayers and their hymns, always singing."

'Yes, I thought, *their voices would have called to God:*

'"Great Lord, you who flies on the wings of the wind, who unleashes the thunderbolt from the storming clouds, if it be thy will release us from those who keep us hostage! Return us, O Lord, to our iwi..."

'Mr Donovan enquired where we were staying for the night.

'"We've made no arrangements," I answered. To be frank, I hadn't given it a thought.

'"You'd best return to town with us, then," he said kindly. "The hotel Mrs Donovan and I are staying at has small but clean rooms and, who knows, there could be a vacancy. It might also be advisable, as far as the ladies are concerned, for you and me to combine forces. There's safety in numbers."

'I soon realised the wisdom of Mr Donovan's words. As we approached the main street of the town, I saw loud, drunken crowds moving through the pools of gas lighting from one hotel to the next.

'"I hope you're handy at fisticuffs," Mr Donovan said. "I will lead, the women will follow and you bring up the rear." I nodded but, even so, said to my sisters, "Keep your heads down and, Ripeka, hold tight to Meri and don't let her go." We began to shove through the groups of weaving miners. The commotion was extraordinary and the stench of vomit and sweat overpowering. I saw one young man open his buttons and piss where he was standing. Another staggered out of a hotel, downed his trousers and shat on the street.

'Meri raised her head. "No, Meri!" I cried. She had seen a young Maori woman, stupefied by liquor, being forced by her pimp to service men in an alley. "That could have been me," she whimpered.

'A voice rang out, "Hey, lads, more Maori whores!" Meri had been seen and young miners were soon lurching into my sisters. Mr Donovan and I began fighting for our women's lives. "Keep away," I shouted, punching right, left and centre. Mrs Donovan, Ripeka and Meri were also lashing out with their fingers and kicking with their feet. Mr Donovan was forging through the crowd, roaring, "Keep up, Mrs Donovan! Bring the ladies with you!" Together we gained the relative safety of the hotel. Did I say *relative?* The din inside was extraordinary and frightening. Already made almost insensible by liquor, some of the miners were taking any excuse to fight each other.

'And after all that, the hotelier told us there wasn't a room to be had. Mr Donovan said, "Look, boy, Mrs Donovan and I could share our room with you and your sisters. The price is already exorbitant and you'd be doing us a service by assisting to pay for it. Does that sound reasonable to you?"

'I nodded quickly, and we battled our way through the crowd and up the stairs. The Donovans' room was indeed small with a large bed that the women could share. There was no lock on the door. "Now you know why I suggested we combine forces," Mr Donovan said. Throughout the night, we kept guard shoulder to shoulder in the corridor, shoving away the drunks and louts who tried to get in. Sometimes I showed my knife as a threat. Both Mr Donovan and I were glad when, in the early morning, the hotel began to quieten down.

'I asked him about his son, Charlie. "We came all the way from County Cork," he said, "hoping to make a good future in Maoriland. We were gold mining but our claim was taken from us by a crooked land agent. When our darling boy went to get our papers back, his temper got the better of him and, well, one thing led to another, and he was charged with robbery and assault. Mrs Donovan and I know what it is to have your family gaoled wrongfully. She's taken Charlie's imprisonment very hard."'

4.

'The next morning, Christmas Day, we made a feast of our kai and the Donovans' food. On looking at the spread, Mr Donovan said, "To be sure, it is a banquet fit for royalty!"

'"Let's have a toast," Mrs Donovan said. She was becoming sentimental.

'Mr Donovan agreed, and measured out small nips from his flask of whiskey. "To family, friends and children," he said.

'We raised our glasses, and both Mrs Donovan and Meri burst into tears thinking of their sons.'

Around eight, the sisters returned with the Donovans to Hokitika Gaol. The morning was bright, the sky cleanly rinsed. A small number of other visitors, mostly women, were also on the road to Misery Hill. 'Merry Christmas to you,' they greeted each other. One wife had bravely brought her two children, who skipped along, eager to see their father.

The sisters may have been Maori and the other families the relatives of felons, but on that bright morning all celebrated their common humanity and fellowship. Erenora tried to put to rest her fears about what might lie ahead. Mr Donovan, however, was concerned about Ripeka's expectations. He whispered to Erenora, 'I do hope you have good news today.'

Shortly afterwards, they arrived at the prison. This was the moment all had been waiting for, but when the guard finally unlocked the gates, the sisters stepped back. And even though Ripeka's fingers dug into Erenora's arm, painfully so, and she said, 'I am dying of love to see my husband', she would not go through until all the other families were admitted.

'Come now,' Erenora said. She told the guard that she would like a word with the Hokitika gaoler.

'That's Mr O'Brien you'll be wanting,' he answered. As he took the sisters to the gaoler's office, Erenora saw her fellow visitors being reunited with their husbands. The children rushed to their father. Mrs Donovan clung to a fine-looking curly-headed boy.

'Mam! Oh, Mam!' he cried.

Mr O'Brien was in a relaxed mood, having eaten a good Christmas breakfast. He was not, thank goodness, as arrogant and abusive as the Mount Cook

222

superintendent. Instead, to Erenora's relief, he was a man who had dealt fairly with the Parihaka prisoners during their stay.

'They discharged themselves of their sentences to hard labour,' Mr O'Brien said, 'and they worked very hard indeed around Hokitika town.' He shook Erenora's hand with vigour and nodded to Ripeka and Meri. 'So you have come from Parihaka?' he asked. 'Is it true that Te Whiti had prophesied the prisoners here would be released when the moon turned red?' He chuckled, shaking his head with wry amazement. 'Came an eclipse of the moon and the next day, sure enough, I received the order that they were to be discharged! Did they arrive home safely?'

'Yes,' Erenora answered, 'but two men did not.'

'Two?' A shadow flickered over Mr O'Brien's face.

'Have you ever had a man here named Horitana?' Erenora asked, her heart beating fast.

'No, I would remember that name.' Erenora closed her eyes with relief.

'What about my husband?' Ripeka asked. 'His name was Paora. Perhaps he was transferred to another gaol?'

Mr O'Brien's eyes fell and he would not meet her gaze. 'That name,' he began, 'I do remember...'

5.

Truth to tell, Erenora had long had a premonition about Paora, but that did not make the news of his death any easier to bear. Immediately, Ripeka began to wail a tangi for him. 'Aue, aue te tane e, kua ngaro ki te Po.'

Mr and Mrs Donovan came to offer comfort. 'To come all this way, dear,' Mrs Donovan said to Ripeka, 'with so much hope in your heart...'

Mr Donovan took Erenora aside. 'Charlie told us that some of the Maoris died during the winter,' he said, 'I couldn't bear to tell you.'

'Could you tell me where my sister's husband is buried?' Erenora asked Mr O'Brien.

All the way to the cemetery, Ripeka couldn't stop crying. The sun was hot through the trees when the sisters entered the gateway looking for Paora's grave. They saw in the distance, slightly apart, the place where Mr O'Brien had told them Paora was resting.

Ripeka, filled with grief, stumbled forward, crying to Paora, 'Aue, husband, aue.' When she reached the mound of earth, she fell to the ground. 'You lie only six feet beneath me, and yet you are so far away.' Some kind soul had raised a white wooden cross. On it were inscribed the words:

PAORA, A DISCIPLE OF TE WHITI

Ripeka was in great distress, scraping some of the dirt into her hands and sprinkling it over her head. 'Te mamae ... aue te mamae...'

Meanwhile, what was Meri up to? She had wandered through the trees, picking small twigs of greenery. When she returned, she began to weave them into funeral chaplets. She placed one on

224

Ripeka's head, another on Erenora's and the third on her own.

'We will stay here for three days,' she said. 'And we will mourn Paora just as we would have done if he had died in Parihaka.'

Meri always surprised with her simplicity and sense of rightness.

And so began Erenora and her sisters' vigil at the graveyard.

Mr and Mrs Donovan came to say farewell before returning to Kumara. 'We'll bide a little time with you,' Mrs Donovan said, 'for surely the Irish and the Maoris are the same under the skin.'

After two hours, Mr Donovan coughed that it was time to go. 'You're a good lad, Eruera,' he said as he shook Erenora's hand. 'Look after your sisters.'

That evening the sisters wrapped themselves in shawls and slept in the cemetery. The sexton and gravedigger saw them the following morning, but did not disturb their grief. During that day, whenever people from Hokitika came to visit their own loved ones, they were greeted by Meri.

''aere mai e te manu'iri e!' she called. 'Come and mourn with us.'

Although the Pakeha were puzzled, not knowing Maori custom, they responded by bowing their heads and shaking hands. Some of the men, at the prodding of their womenfolk, left gold coins. 'After all, it is the Christmastide.'

The local vicar was soon told about the women and their guardian. He went to see Mr O'Brien. 'What shall I do?'

'I have already informed the mayor,' Mr O'Brien answered. 'Leave the boy and his sisters to their mourning. They will move on in due course.'

For the second night, the sisters slept in the cemetery, huddling for warmth in the blankets the vicar had brought them. But by the afternoon of the third day, Ripeka had not come to any peace with herself. She could not let Paora *go.*

'What are we to do?' Meri asked Erenora, concerned. 'We must go on to Christchurch. The miners are beginning to congregate for New Year. We should get out of Hokitika as soon as we can.'

Ripeka overheard her. 'Then leave me here,' she said to Erenora. Her grief had made her bitter. 'You never wanted me to come in the first place, sister, and I will be one less for you to worry about.'

'Ripeka, stop this,' Erenora said.

'And thank God that Paora is dead, Erenora, because this way he won't know the shame of my bearing a child of a rape ... I'm already soiled goods, aren't I.'

'No, Ripeka,' Erenora said.

Ripeka's hysteria continued to mount. 'Yes, go on without me. Isn't that what you've always wanted? Let me bear my devil's child where nobody can see it ... and, don't worry, I'll be able to look after myself ... there'll be other men who can have

226

me if they want to ... and when you get back to Parihaka tell them all that I died, Erenora, tell them that, like our ancestor, Poutini turned me into pounamu ... I don't care any more ... I don't care...'

Erenora slapped her, a stinging blow. 'But *we* care,' she yelled, shaking Ripeka. 'Meri and I are *not* going without you. Te mate ki te mate, te ora ki te ora, the dead to the dead, the living to the living. The time has come to carry on.'

With a cry, Ripeka collapsed into Meri's arms.

How long did it take before Ripeka relinquished Paora? It might have been an hour. Two hours. Finally, she saw a small breeze scattering fallen leaves like a benediction: *Go, wife.* She heaved a great sigh and, under the trees, with the sunlight slanting golden all around, she nodded.

Meri, trying to make her smile, began to tap her poi, persistent in the sunlight.

'Oh, you *two,*' Ripeka said to her sisters in exasperation.

CHAPTER NINETEEN

The Courage of Women

1.

Erenora and her sisters began the crossing of Ka Tiritiri o Te Moana, the Southern Alps.

Te ka'a o nga wa'ine, the courage of the women.

'It will be a tough walk,' Erenora said, 'and although it is summer, it will be makariri when we reach the top.' The flanks of the mountains looked daunting and precipitous.

The crossing followed an old pre-European trail once used by greenstone hunters moving from the West Coast to Canterbury. When Pakeha arrived, they expanded the trail to a bridle track. Then gold was discovered, and over 1,000 men, armed with picks and shovels, wrested the coach road from the mountains.

The sisters made good progress. Most of the horse-drawn traffic was coming from the Canterbury side. 'Hide!' Meri would yell whenever she heard the rumble of hooves and carts on the road. Having missed Christmas, the miners swept past whooping and hollering, wanting to be in Hokitika or Greymouth for New Year, but Meri wasn't taking any chances.

She also kept the sisters' spirits up. As they climbed the weaving, dizzying road she would exclaim,

'Oh, look! Titiro!' Everywhere the Christmas flower, the rata, was in bloom across the forest-covered hillsides. The mountain tops with their 'uka—or 'froth' as she called the snow—delighted her.

Came the first night, and the sisters huddled together to keep warm. Sharp stones from the track had lacerated Ripeka's shoes; her feet were bleeding.

'Here,' Erenora said, 'let me wash them.' She went down to the river rushing nearby and soaked her headscarf in the water. As she began to minister to her sister, Ripeka started to cry. 'I'm sorry, Erenora,' she wept. 'I didn't mean what I said about you at Hokitika.'

Erenora comforted her. 'I know you didn't. We are sisters.'

Their mood lightened, and they maintained good speed next day, with Erenora deciding the pace and her sisters following in her steps. Everywhere were deep gorges and spectacular rivers.

A few days later the sisters reached the summit of Arthur's Pass. 'Halfway there,' Erenora said as Ripeka and Meri did a little dance of joy.

'I knew it was right to karanga to the mountains,' Meri said. 'They are protecting us.'

They descended to the Bealey River, climbing again to Porters Pass. The only danger they faced was not of the human kind but from strong-beaked parrots which flew at them, crying, 'Keeaaa! Keeaaa!'

Then they reached Cass and, not long afterward, the Canterbury Plains, shrouded in mist, stretched before them.

2.

Wellington may have been Empire City, but to Erenora Christchurch, Otautahi, was like the city she had read about in John Bunyan's *Pilgrim's Progress.* After landing from immigrant ships into the chaos of a new land, the first citizens had set about building a place of splendid spires:

The City of the Plains.

'Maori were not as common in Te Wai Pounamu,' Erenora wrote. 'When Ripeka, Meri and I found our way to the dignified dark-grey cathedral, in its beautiful square, we were looked at curiously but not with overt animosity.

'We decided to go inside Te Hahi Nui to give thanks to God for keeping us safe. A choir was singing, such a heavenly sound. It was so good to be refreshed by hymn and prayer.

'As we departed I noticed a woman looking at us. Perhaps it was the feathers in Ripeka and Meri's hair that attracted her attention. She was on the point of approaching but was called aside by her companion.

'My sisters and I began to discuss our accommodation. "We can't afford to be wasteful," I said to them. "Let's camp on the outskirts of Christchurch." I wanted to save the money that we had for our return trip to Taranaki.

'"What if the police find us?" Meri asked nervously.

'"They won't," I answered. "Remember all those times when we were children, on the run from Warea, and made ourselves invisible in the bush?"

'"They might have dogs to sniff us out," Meri said. Hmm, I had never thought of that!

'We followed the glancing loops of the flax-bordered Avon out of the city; once upon a time, the area must have been a wonderful ma'inga kai. It wasn't long before we came to fine meadows, bright and open; a flock or two of sheep watched as we passed by. Following the glistening river took us to a potato field. The trill of the riroriro, the bird that signalled summer days, pursued us and, finally, we found a hollow that was warm and cosy for the night. We didn't think the farmer would mind sharing his potatoes with us so we dug up a few and roasted them on a fire, and then we bedded down, spending the night talking and laughing about our adventures. Sleep came easily and, the next morning, after a quick dip in the river to cleanse ourselves and revive our spirits, we returned to Cathedral Square.

'During the night, I had decided what I would do. "I want you both to remain in the square and wait for me," I said to Ripeka and Meri. "It's a lovely day and you can both rest in the sun."

'"Where are you going?" Meri asked, suddenly afraid.

'"To Addington Prison," I answered, "to find where the Parihaka men have been incarcerated. It will be quicker if I go alone."

'Alarmed, Meri looked at Ripeka. "What if something happens to us while you're gone?"

'*Typical,* I thought, *for my sisters to think of themselves. What about me!* I pointed crossly to the doors of the cathedral, "Run and seek sancluary inside."'

3.

Erenora was soon on the Lincoln Road to Addington, to the south-west of the city. She was in such a hurry, head down and intent on her destination, that she did not notice how quickly the environment around her had changed.

Suddenly, as she was crossing two iron tracks, there was a huge roaring sound and something monstrous, huge and belching smoke and embers, came out of a cloud to pounce on her. With a cry she flung herself to one side. And when the smoke dissipated, she took her bearings.

Where am I?

She was in a world such as she had never been before, a huge cacophonic railway junction of steaming, shunting trains and rolling stock. Of course she had seen illustrations of locomotives in books but nothing prepared her for the immensity of the engines, coaches and freight wagons. They were like her oxen, but they were also *not* like her beloved companions; they were malevolent, and they screamed so.

Except that in a brief lull, Erenora realised that they weren't screaming at all: the screams were coming from *her.* 'Mama, kei w'ea koe?' she whimpered. But her mother and father were gone, had been gone for many years now. *What did dead mean?*

'A moment ago I was in te Ao, the light,' she cried to herself, 'and now I am in te Po, the darkness.'

Yes, indeed, a few heartbeats before, Erenora had been in the presence of God; now she was in some phantasmagorical space at the edge of heaven, where bawling livestock, destined for slaughter yards, were being unloaded. From one of the trains came another kind of freight: prisoners under guard being delivered to the prison. And one of the guards had a whip...

Erenora put her hands to her throat. And then she saw the prison ahead and she had to stop and recover her breath—for it was designed in the same new Gothic style as Te Hahi Nui. But where one provided approbation and entry for those chosen by God, the other provided only moral disapproval and punishment for the fallen.

Disoriented and sobbing, Erenora stumbled across the maze of railway tracks and fell to the ground. Until that moment she had fortified herself with the unswerving belief that Horitana was alive and she would find him. After all, was he not one of the blessed? She remembered how, to Maori, even being put into the lock-up was regarded as a sentence of death.

'Oh Lord of Heaven,' Erenora prayed, 'have you deserted us?'

It had been a long time coming, this sudden collapse of her faith in God. All her life Erenora had been sustained by trust and courage. Now both deserted her. She couldn't move, and as her spirits descended even further, the question came to her:

'In this kingdom of the Pakeha, erected to the glory of God, where does the Maori belong?'

The question sank deep into her soul, and her thoughts became incoherent. What had the Confiscated Lands Inquiry said of the purpose for allocating reserve land to Maori:

To do justice to the Maori and continue English settlement of the country?

Erenora began to moan, swaying from side to side; she felt as though she were choking. All her life, she realised, ever since her mother Miriam had been cruelly ripped away from her, she had been fighting *for* her life. If confiscation continued, was that to be the future of the Maori, the iwi katoa of all Aotearoa? To be herded onto and live the rest of their lives in reserves ... or at the edges of the land, the fringes of the sea, the tops of mountains, offshore islands ... or to scrabble with others for scraps and pieces of unwanted broken biscuit, in the great cities of the Pakeha ... living at their outer limits where the Pakeha

234

always deposited his waste or the unwanted: the abattoirs, rubbish dumps, sanatoriums, cemeteries, orphanages, tips, brothels, asylums, gaols, poorhouses...

If Maori continued to fight against the Pakeha, would the price be deprivation of God's munificence and banishment, like felons, from his presence? Would Maori be erased all together?

And if this was the fate of Maori in God's kingdom on earth, would it be the same in God's kingdom in heaven?

The ground thundered around Erenora and she howled like a wounded animal, her hands over her ears and her eyes closed. That was when she heard Te Whiti's voice:

'Aue, Erenora, have you already forgotten that there will come a time when the days of our mourning will be ended? Our people also shall be all righteous ... we shall inherit the land forever ... A little one shall become a thousand and a small one a strong nation. Therefore, put aside your fears and rise up from the depths of your despair.'

From the death of her spirit came the birth of another.

'We are not forgotten by the great Ruler,' she said to herself.

Gathering her strength, she arose from the pit of her darkness. Her thoughts had betrayed only a momentary weakness. It would not happen again.

She looked around her. 'Make way,' she said. 'Let me through.'

4.

Erenora approached the portal of Addington Prison. She knocked three times at the doorway and a warder appeared on the other side. 'I would like to make enquiries about the Maori prisoners from Parihaka,' Erenora said in a firm masculine voice.

'The madmen?' the warder asked sharply. 'You can't expect any information without authorisation.'

How Erenora wished that Te Wheoro was with her. 'I have a letter of introduction,' she offered. She showed it to the warder. Yes, the government crest did the trick.

'Follow me,' said the warder, tight-lipped. He took her to an office and presented her to a prison official who appeared to be of higher standing. 'I am the registrar,' he began. 'You are from *Parry Hacka?*'

'Yes,' Erenora answered. 'I've come to ask about two men who may have been sentenced here along with the first batch of prisoners from New Plymouth Magistrate's Court on 26 July 1879.'

He looked her up and down. 'You are aware, are you not, that when the maniacs were brought here two years ago they were sentenced to hard labour? And then, for continuing disturbances, moved to Lyttelton Gaol?'

Erenora couldn't help herself; the offensive language was getting under her skin. 'I understand,' she said, raising her voice, 'the difficulties may have had more to do with overcrowding than with anything the men did to warrant further harsh punishment.'

The registrar gave her a sharp glance. 'You would do well to curb your tongue, young man,' he said. 'So you're aware that most were returned to the Taranaki? As for the rest...' He paused and with a grunt affirmed that he would answer her question. 'The madmen are all on Ripa Island.'

Erenora was astonished to receive any information. 'Ripa Island?' she pushed on. 'Where is that?'

'It was once a quarantine station in Lyttelton Harbour,' he said. 'Armed constabulary were assigned to guard the maniacs but more officers were added to cope with the ... increased ... numbers who subsequently came down from the Taranaki.'

'Were the prisoners Horitana and Riki among them?'

The registrar consulted his records, wetting his finger to turn the pages and trace down the list of names. Erenora wanted to jump across the counter, take the book from him and look for herself.

'The prisoner named Riki is still incarcerated on Ripa Island. As for any madman by the name of Horitana, I have no record of him.'

Erenora's heart flooded with both gladness and despair. 'Is there any hope of visiting the prisoner

Riki?' Apart from the joy that would give to Meri, Riki might know where Horitana was.

'No,' said the registrar. 'And that is all I will help you with.'

'I left Addington Prison, numb, and wandered aimlessly. I was happy for Meri, knowing that she would be overjoyed with the news that Riki was alive. At the same time, I was in shock and full of worry for Horitana. Where was he?

'Dazed, I sat by the side of the road, trying to decide what my sisters and I should do next. Obviously, there was no possibility of Meri seeing Riki and it would be best for us to return quickly to Parihaka before our money ran out. But what about my own quest for my husband?

'The sun was declining into afternoon when I made a decision. If Horitana wasn't in Christchurch the only other place where he could be was Dunedin. The time had come for me to continue on but, this time, alone. Therefore, on my way back to the city I made a detour to a shipping office. I thanked God that, with the addition of the coins from sympathetic settlers at Hokitika, there was just enough to purchase passage for Ripeka and Meri on a ship sailing from Christchurch to Wellington.

'I returned to Cathedral Square. Alarm filled me when I couldn't see my sisters. Where were they? I ran into the cathedral and, to my relief, saw them sitting in earnest discussion with a clergyman.

238

'"Oh, there you are, Erenora," Ripeka greeted me, as if I had just been for a walk in the park.'

The clergyman introduced himself.

'I'm Archdeacon George Cotterill,' he said. 'I'm a canon here, serving Bishop Harper, and I'm also diocesan secretary. One of our congregation, Mrs Platt, saw you all yesterday. She recognised from the feathers your sisters wear in their hair that you were from Parihaka. Knowing that I have a sympathetic interest in the Maori people of New Zealand and, in particular, the people of Taranaki, she advised me of your visit.' The archdeacon pumped Erenora's hand vigorously. 'The church is much alarmed at the way your men continue to be held without trial.'

'Thank you,' Erenora said. She didn't mean to sound ungrateful but she wanted to get Ripeka and Meri to one side so that she could tell them what she'd done. She hoped they would be obedient. But first she turned to Meri, 'Riki is alive and on Ripa Island.'

'Alive? And *here?*' Meri exclaimed as she burst into tears. 'Can I see him?'

Ripeka, although happy for her sister, couldn't hide a look of sadness. Why couldn't Paora also have lived...

'No,' Erenora answered. 'Absolutely not.'

Meri refused to take Erenora's word. 'You, of all people, you can make anything happen,' she said with determination. 'Don't say no to me.'

'Therefore,' Erenora continued, not heeding her, 'you and Ripeka are both returning to Wellington next week.' She gave them their tickets.

'I won't go,' Meri said. 'And only two tickets?'

'I plan to proceed alone to Dunedin,' Erenora answered.

'Oh, *I* see,' Ripeka said. 'When it suits you, you decide about me and Meri. Don't leave me in Hokitika but dump us both when we get to Christchurch.'

'You, Ripeka, are pregnant,' Erenora replied angrily, 'and you, Meri, should go back home and wait with your son for Riki's eventual return.'

But Meri was stubborn. 'I don't care if I have to wait for years. I'm staying until I see Riki.'

Although they were in the House of God, Erenora shook Meri hard. 'You and Ripeka are both holding me up and you *will* go back to Parihaka. Please be obedient, sister.'

In the silence that followed, Archdeacon Cotterill coughed. 'Actually, people in Christchurch do call the island Ripa but it's really Ripapa, and—' he paused '—there might be opportunity for Meri to visit before she and Ripeka return to Wellington.'

Erenora stared at him, her mouth open.

'Come back in two days,' he said. 'I'll see what I can do.'

5.

Two days? That would make it ... Sunday.

The sisters returned to their sleeping place in the potato field. Waiting for Sunday was agonising, but they filled in the time by taking walks together around Christchurch and its countryside. They talked about, oh, so many things: growing up as children together, helping to build Parihaka, getting married...

'We've never really had the time to korero, have we?' Erenora said, when one day Meri burst into tears.

'But we've always loved each other, eh,' Meri said, tapping her poi.

On Sunday, the sisters were up at dawn and, after morning prayers, struck their camp and made for Cathedral Square. Archdeacon Cotterill, waiting at the cathedral doors, looked very pleased with himself. 'I'm glad you're here early,' he said. 'Come along, we have a train to catch.'

A train? Very soon the sisters were being transported through Lyttelton Tunnel. As the train roared into the bowels of the earth, Meri clutched Erenora, afraid. 'Are we journeying to hell?' she asked.

On the other side of the darkness, however, was blessed sunlight. Lyttelton sprang brightly into view. The 'Liverpool of New Zealand' lay in a hollow surrounded by high hills. Ahead was the harbour.

'Here we are,' said the archdeacon. He hastened the sisters off the train and in the direction of

Gladstone Pier. Four large ships were being loaded with wheat for England, France and other parts of the world. And further along were the docks from which busy launches plied the harbour and the coast. Among the jostling boats a small vessel was waiting with a group of austere personages aboard and three women holding hymn books.

'We're joining the Lyttelton gaoler Mr Phillips, the chaplain Reverend Townsend, and members of the local Anglican congregation,' Archdeacon Cotterill explained. 'Reverend Townsend is my colleague and friend, and he's taking the service today on Ripapa Island.' He whispered conspiratorially, 'I obtained permission for you to come with us. He's relieved as his knowledge of the Maori language is limited.'

After hasty introductions, there was a lot of nodding of heads, and then the vessel cast off. Soon, it was making good way eastward across the harbour to Ripapa.

Archdeacon Cotterill engaged the three sisters in conversation. 'For many years,' he began, 'Kai Tahu used the island as a refuge whenever other tribes invaded Otautahi. The name Ripapa actually means "Mooring Rock", which is appropriate, don't you think?'

He was trying to keep the mood light, but Erenora could not help the retort that formed on her lips. 'If you're referring to its current use as a prison for Taranaki men, yes,' she said, 'but after

242

any invasion Kai Tahu could always return to their homes, whereas our men are not free to do that.'

Ripeka gave Erenora a warning glance. 'My brother does not want to sound ungrateful,' she told Archdeacon Cotterill.

The archdeacon accepted the comparison as a fair one and carried on in a conciliatory manner. 'Even for Pakeha, the island became a mooring place. About ten years ago, it was used for quarantining our new immigrants. We built a hospital and hostels for up to 300 people out there. But then the wars started in the North Island, and Parihaka prisoners were sent down here, so Ripapa went through a third incarnation—as an overflow prison for Lyttelton Gaol.'

'Over 150 to Christchurch in the one month of September 1880 alone,' Erenora reminded him sharply, 'including my sister Meri's husband, and many other men since then.'

At the reference to Riki, Meri gave a small sob.

Archdeacon Cotterill gave Erenora a sharp look. 'If your men are to be held anywhere,' he answered her, 'Ripapa is a better refuge than most.' He turned to comfort Meri. 'Do you know what the Pakeha immigrants called Ripapa?' he asked her. 'Humanity Island. Let us all hope that, as far as your husband is concerned, it has lived up to its name, eh?'

Suddenly, there was a scattering of sun-stars and against rising headlands Erenora saw Ripapa itself.

'We docked at the jetty to the island. Much to our surprise, another vessel arrived at the same time as us—and in it was a small group of Maori.

'"They're from Rapaki," Archdeacon Cotterill said. "Their hapu is Ngati Wheke."

'I walked across to them and we greeted each other. "We come to manaaki, to support, your people," their rangatira said.

'Together we walked to the gateway and into the prison yard where the service was to be held. The breeze was cool and invigorating and I could hear the prisoners singing in their cells:

'"O, Taranaki! Our w'enua, so lovely and lost! Hear our lamentation! Let the Lord inspire us all and give us the strength to shatter our vile chains! Let the wrath of the Lion of Judah cause our valour to awake, our courage to stir!"

'At the sound of the voices, Ripeka and Meri—especially Meri—started weeping. As for me, I could not help but wonder at the forbidding nature of the prison. The walls prevented any view from inside except through tiny slit windows. What was it like to be immured behind that stone? Our men were accustomed to the wide spaces of Taranaki, to forests and seas; here they could die of wondering whether that world was still there, and our sacred mounga holding up the sky.

'Then the men appeared, under guard, mustered to attend the church service. They were still singing and, as they passed by, Meri scanned their faces.

'"What joy to breathe freely in the open air!' they sang. 'Here in the sunlight is life!"

'And finally one of the prisoners looked Meri's way, saw her and gave a deep wounded cry. "It cannot be!"

'Although he was much changed, emaciated and stooped, Meri knew him immediately: her beloved Riki. Slowly, he stepped towards her. A guard went to stop him, but Archdeacon Cotterill intervened, whispering to Mr Phillips, who said, "Let them alone." In that precious space, Meri and Riki were able to embrace one another.

'"This must be a dream," Riki said. "Is it really you, Meri?"

'He turned to look at me and Ripeka. "And you, sisters-in-law, are here also?"

'I could not help but glance quickly at Archdeacon Cotterill and Mr Phillips to see whether or not they had overheard Riki's reference to me, but, no, we were sufficiently apart from them.

"You are in the light." Riki continued. "In prison, we are in darkness." Then his face blanched. "But why have you come?" He turned to Meri. "Has something happened to our son? You haven't come all this way to tell me—"

'"He's being well cared for," Meri reassured him, "but when Erenora left Parihaka to look for Horitana, neither Ripeka nor I could restrain ourselves from joining her. Even to spend just this moment with you has been worth our travails.

One day you'll be free and we shall all find peace."

'Riki began to moan with shame. He seized me and wept on my shoulder. "Aue," he began, "Horitana ... it may have been him who was on the same prison vessel that brought us all to Christchurch."

'"Then why isn't he here with you?" I asked, almost screaming with frustration.

'"Whoever the prisoner was, he was kept separately from us. Nor was he on deck when we were mustered and disembarked. But he sounded like Horitana when he cried out as we were leaving the ship, "Be of good heart, my fellow warriors", except that his voice was muffled, unearthly. We caught a final glimpse of the prisoner from far away—prodded by gaolers, stumbling along the dock."

'"Couldn't you tell if it was Horitana or not?" I asked.

'"No," Riki answered. "There was a blanket completely covering him and I thought ... he might be somebody else."

'"Who?" I asked, puzzled and confused.

'"There was a small coastal vessel waiting at the quay," Riki continued. "A stolid and sturdy man with a bald head was waiting. The gaolers gave the prisoner over to his care. I saw him sign some papers and shake the gaolers' hands. The prisoner was in great pain. It wasn't the chains that were so grievously afflicting him or the legirons he wore, but something else. I couldn't see what it was until he was being put onto the boat and the blanket fell away and..."

'"And?" I insisted.

'Riki paled. A shudder ran through him.

'"... it was te tangata mokomokai..."'

6.

Archdeacon Cotterill separated the sisters from Riki.

'We're here only by the good offices of Mr Phillips and Reverend Townsend ... you understand?'

'My sisters and I are most appreciative,' Erenora said, stepping away.

'Good,' the archdeacon answered, relieved. 'Let's proceed to the church service now.'

As the voices around her rose to praise God, Erenora prayed. 'Oh, Horitana, what has happened to you?' Her fists were clenched so hard, her fingers dug into her palms until they bled.

She seemed to hear his voice:

'Here in this void no living thing comes near. O, cruel ordeal! But God's will is just. I'll not complain; for He has decreed the measure of my suffering.'

After the church service, Archdeacon Cotterill approached the Lyttelton gaoler. Mr Phillips agreed that the three Taranaki visitors could exchange greetings with the other men. Erenora moved among them, offering words of courage and sympathy. 'Kia ka'a, kia manawanui,' she said to them.

And the men bore witness. 'The winters are bad, so cold, and of a kind we have never before experienced. Sometimes the only way to keep warm is to huddle together in our blankets. And can you see the walls around us? It was the same in Addington and Lyttelton too, where any infringement meant we were confined in incredibly small and cruel spaces where you couldn't see the outside world. Our cells had slop buckets but no running water. Our food was fit only for animals.'

Erenora shivered. 'You were never taken to work outside?' she asked. 'At Hokitika, the men at least worked in road gangs and had contact with the citizens of the town.'

'No,' the men answered. 'We were deprived of everything, even our own sense of respect. It was as if we'd been consigned to a pit, a hole in the ground—but at least on Ripapa, although no blade of grass grows, we're able to see the sky. Sometimes small birds fly through the barred windows. We feed them crumbs and, when the guards approach, we tell them, "Quick! Leave! Take messages to Taranaki that we survive." When you get back to Parihaka, give our wives the same messages that we give the birds, eh? That we do survive, Erenora, we *do*.'

Then it was time to leave Ripapa Island.

'Go home to Parihaka now, Meri,' Riki said as he clutched her. 'Await my return.' One last embrace, and Riki joined the prisoners as the guards took them back to their cells.

The sisters supported a sobbing Meri away from the prison. How good it was be outside. At the jetty, they said goodbye to the people of Ngati Wheke and then boarded the vessel taking them back to Lyttelton.

'Wait!' Meri cried.

From inside the walls came a low sighing, like a phantom moaning of the sea.

Meri's face was blinded by tears. 'They are men of Parihaka,' she said. 'They will never be lost to us.' She took out her poi, held them up to the sun and began to sing and dance:

'Takiri te raukura, 'aere koe i runga, 'uri 'aere ra i te motu e! Takiri te raukura, 'aere koe i runga, wai'o te ture kia rere i raro e! Let the raukura dance, go forth the raukura, fluttering above and arise upwards! Throughout the land let the raukura dance, fluttering above while the laws are fluttering down below! Let all know of your travails and be proud of you! Your mountain and your women salute you! If you must bow your head, let it be only to Taranaki!'

Then she collapsed, and Ripeka embraced her.

'When Kawa was born,' Meri sobbed, 'Riki was already in gaol in New Plymouth. My husband has never held his son in his arms.'

7.

On their return to Christchurch city, the sisters' hearts overflowed with gratitude for the kindness Archdeacon Cotterill had showed them.

He took Erenora aside. 'Young man, I've taken the liberty of purchasing you a railway ticket so that you can travel to Dunedin by train. No, don't thank me. As diocesan secretary there are some charitable opportunities I'm able to take advantage of and ... well ... this is one of them. You continue your journey. I'll see that your sisters are taken into church lodgings and I'll look after them until the time comes for them to leave. And regarding your men on Ripapa ... we know how harshly they're treated. Our church commission visits them regularly to ensure that the worst excesses of that treatment are minimised.'

After their evening meal, Ripeka looked at Meri and said, 'Well, before Erenora goes we had better shear our young *man* again, eh?'

Erenora's hair had grown to shoulder length. As they scissored and snipped, the sisters laughed and joked, but their hearts were breaking. When they had finished the job, however, e 'ika, they had done it with too much love. Erenora had to grab the shears and chop off two large hanks so as to look a bit more ugly and lopsided.

'There, that's better,' she said.

The next day Ripeka, Meri and Archdeacon Cotterill bade Erenora farewell at the railway station.

'Oh, do try to be brave,' Erenora said to her distraught sisters, 'and please don't cry so much.' But she wasn't feeling very brave herself and turned to the archdeacon, saying, 'You will look after them, won't you?'

Quickly she boarded the train, not wanting to look back. As the train left the station she kept thinking:

'If Ripeka and Meri can't even cut my hair properly, how are they going to get back to Parihaka by themselves?'

CHAPTER TWENTY

City of Celts

1.

Wellington, Christchurch and now Dunedin.

It was drizzling when Erenora reached the Octagon where the clock tower was striking the time for midday. The chimes were so loud and sonorous that Erenora had to put her hands to her ears. As she looked around she thought that no other city in New Zealand could be as wealthy or could compare with Dunedin's commercial and industrial mana, its power. Of all the three Pakeha cities in Aotearoa, Dunedin must surely be the greatest, the mightiest and the largest of them all.

There was a difference, though. The Pakeha who had built this city were distinctively Presbyterian Scots. They had created the Edinburgh of the South.

'Again, as a Maori, I was the object of curiosity,' Erenora wrote, 'but I noticed a strange difference. Perhaps it was because of their own difficult history with the English that the sober Scots citizens appeared to empathise with our own. The men in their suits tipped their hats to me and their women inclined their heads. They appeared to respect the Maori struggle for sovereignty and to acknowledge our mana.'

Erenora had sensed very quickly the empathy for Maori that came not only from the Scots but also others of Dunedin's liberal-minded citizens. In the case of the city's Maori leaders, Hori Kerei Taiaroa, the Maori parliamentary representative for the South Island, was exemplary in providing a lead for his Pakeha colleagues to follow. When, finally, the Taranaki prisoners' release was announced he actually travelled with them on the SS *Luna,* on 20 March 1872. The same spirited crowd that had welcomed them was there to give them a rousing send-off. His later speech attacking one of the West Coast Peace Preservation bills is a standout of the era. Among his Pakeha colleagues was Thomas Bracken, author of the words of New Zealand's national anthem and the originator, some believe, of the term 'God's Own Country'. The record shows that several other local MPs argued against the passage of those acts of legislation that gave the government the power to imprison Maori without trial.

'I was therefore grateful to discover this sympathy, and that it appeared to be shared by those whom I met on the street. One gentleman, in response to my request for directions to the Dunedin Gaol, shook my hand and told me he had been at Port Chalmers in 1879 when the first batch of prisoners had arrived from Wellington. "Judging from their powerful builds," he said, "it was clear that, if your warriors had wished, you could have easily defeated your foes." Another gentleman said, "I'm so glad that your people were treated separately. You're a nobler race than the murderers, robbers, conmen and shysters who are deservedly part of Her Majesty's population."

'And so I arrived at the imposing main entrance to the brick gaol on Stuart Street. A platform above and just outside the prison walls ran along three sides, and sentries were on patrol. My heart was thudding as a guard looked through the grating. I told him why I had come and he let me into a paved yard, scrupulously clean. Then another guard showed me to the warder's office. "If you wait here, the warder will attend to you."

'When the warder arrived, I told him why I'd come to Dunedin. He said, "Oh, but there are no longer any prisoners from Parihaka here."'

A huge wave of despondency engulfed Erenora. She could scarcely hear the warder's words. To have come so far...

'I like to think that your men were treated well by us,' he began. 'In Dunedin we regarded them as wards of the state and not as criminals, and, because of that, we practised open incarceration. They were employed on various public works outside the gaol, in particular the Dunedin Botanical Gardens. During the latter part of their sojourn with us, however, they worked further afield, around the harbour. On those occasions they were housed on a scow, the *Success,* which had originally been used for coastal trading. In the evenings, the local people said you could hear them singing their hymns.'

Erenora could not help but think of one of those hymns, one that perhaps had given the people courage and hope when they were building Parihaka:

'We trust in God's eternal aid! Upon the shores of Egypt He granted Moses life! He made the hundred men of Gideon invincible! If we trust in Him we will also be granted life and be made invincible, Glory to Him.'

Up to this time, Erenora had been buoyed by hope. Had she really come all this way for nothing? She tried to focus and, with a gesture of helplessness, interrupted the warder. 'Forgive me,' she said, 'but would you know if there was a prisoner by the name of Horitana among the men here? Was he returned to Taranaki?'

The warder looked puzzled. 'I knew all the men,' he said, 'and that name doesn't ring a bell at all.' He thought for a moment, then stood to consult a register. 'No, there was no Horitana sent here to Dunedin,' he confirmed. 'But...'

Erenora eyed him eagerly.

'... perhaps you should talk to...' The warder struggled with the pronunciation '... Te Whao? Although the other prisoners returned to Taranaki, he decided to remain in Dunedin among Otago Maori. He met a lovely Maori girl called Katarina. That might have been the reason why he didn't go back.'

Erenora's hopes rose. Te Whao had been one of the younger men chosen by Horitana to ride out of

Parihaka and plough the settlers' land. 'Do you know where I can find him?' she asked.

'Most certainly,' the warder smiled. 'At this time of day go to the bay where the *Success* is ... he's sure to be there. After the prisoners left, he became caretaker of the scow. He takes his job seriously. Take some tobacco with you—that will revive his memories.'

2.

'I hurried out of the city,' Erenora wrote. 'My entire search had now narrowed down to one man. Quickly I sought the place where the *Success* was anchored in a small bay. I made my way to the mooring and found a lone figure, like an eternal sentinel, huddling against the showery rain.

'I approached him slowly. "Tena koe, Te Whao." He was still young, but his eyes were old, as if his experiences had forever altered him.

'He looked at me strangely, not recognising me at first. I had to wait until he could see *through* my appearance. When he realised who I was, tears flooded into his eyes. "Erenora..." He hugged me tight but I was the one who held him up as he grieved for everything that had happened to us all.

'After a while I gave him the tobacco. He tamped some into his pipe, lit it ... and the memories came pouring out.

'"They used to give us tobacco all the time," he began, "the good citizens of Dunedin. When our

256

overseer called for a break and we downed our tools, they'd be waiting at the side of the road. While the overseer and guards turned a blind eye, the women would offer us soup and bread and some old Highland men sneaked us a dram or two of whisky. And, always, someone would offer tobacco."'

Let me explain the background to Te Whao's affecting narrative.

Although the very fact of imprisonment without trial and being forced to labour—slave labour—around Dunedin was harsh, one should remember that from the very moment the first Maori prisoners from Titokowaru's War arrived in Dunedin in 1869, they were treated with sympathy and honour. Among those who supported them were Pakeha like Isaac Newton Watt.

Watt's story is an interesting one. During the 1860s he had been a captain in the Taranaki Rifle Volunteers at the same time as Harry Atkinson, but whereas Atkinson became malevolently inclined towards Maori, Watt took the benevolent position. He married a Maori woman of the Waitara, Ani Raimahapa Paitahuna. They both left in the mid-1860s and migrated to the Bluff, as far away as Watt could get from the fighting. There, he took up a post as resident magistrate and, because he could speak Maori, he was put in charge of the Titokowaru prisoners.

Some nine or so years later, as Dunedin's resident magistrate, Watt did similar sympathetic service for the Parihaka ploughmen. When one named Watene died, it was owing to Watt's kind intercession that other Maori were allowed at the graveside to attend the service. Watt himself drove three of the prisoners, including the great chief Wiremu Kingi Moki Te Matakatea, from the prison in a hansom cab. Both Watt and Ani Raimahapa Paitahuna were buried in the same urupa as the Taranaki men who died in Dunedin.

Yet another official sympathetic to the Parihaka ploughmen was Adam Scott, the warder in Dunedin Gaol, perhaps the very one who had attended to Erenora's enquiry earlier that day.

The rain was falling, Te Whao making small holes in it with his words.

'We all suffered the bitter weather,' he continued, 'but our kindly treatment by the locals carried on and, well, I met my Katarina. And Mr Watt, Mr Scott and other officials, they ensured we had good meals. Not only that but they gave us pounamu to carve so that we would have something of value to take home with us.'

Erenora asked the question that had been lodged impatiently in her throat. 'Was Horitana ever in your midst?'

Te Whao took a long draw, then shook his head. 'We heard he was brought here from Christchurch by a small coastal vessel. It stopped long enough at Port Chalmers to take on provisions.'

'Where was he taken after that?' Oh, how Erenora's heart was beating!

'We think to an isolated island further south,' Te Whao answered. 'Rumour has it that there he's in the charge of a German overseer, kept in the hold of an old French explorer's ship that was wrecked on the island many years ago.'

Erenora tried not to show her pain, but Te Whao touched her hand with tenderness. 'That was long ago, Erenora—almost three years—and since then there has been no further word.' He looked into her eyes. 'You must face the fact ... with no news of him ... and the local people, my Katarina's people, they would have known ... he may be dead.'

Kua mate? Horitana dead? Erenora refused to consider it. *No.* Deep inside her, she knew he was alive. She could not give up on that. Never.

'You must come and stay with me and Katarina,' Te Whao insisted. 'Stay for as long as you want.'

For two weeks, Erenora grieved and wondered what to do. She oscillated between hope and depression.

'I won't give up,' she said to Te Whao one day while he was on duty. He was feeding a seagull, hoping to tame it. 'Even if Horitana is dead, well, don't our people say, "If you die a Maori the one great promise made to you is that your people will find you and bring you home?" Whether Horitana is alive or dead, I won't rest until I find him.'

With this resolve, Erenora remained in Dunedin. Sometimes she wandered about the city, searching through the great number of public houses for clues to Horitana's whereabouts. 'Have you ever heard of a German sailor?' she asked. 'Do you know an island where a French ship was wrecked?'

One day she made a special visit to Port Chalmers, where she asked directions to the cemetery. She found it as a storm burst overhead. Regardless of the sleet, she soon located the grave she was looking for. In this southern earth lay the Reverend Johann Friedrich Riemenschneider, born Bremen, Germany, August 1817, died Dunedin, New Zealand, August 1866. He had come from one side of the world to another and fashioned himself as much as possible into a faithful servant of God.

And only forty-nine when he died? Too young, too young!

Erenora sat down beside the grave and thought of her childhood in Warea. And then she patted the earth, 'Thank you.' All her life, Rimene's last words to her had been like a blessing, a feather cloak that he had cast across her shoulders. 'Leb wohl, mein Herz,' he had said. 'Go well, sweetheart.'

She made her way back to Dunedin and the *Success.* As soon as Te Whao saw her, he began to wave vigorously. 'Erenora! Erenora!'

She knew immediately that he had received news of Horitana. 'What is it? she asked. 'What *is* it?'

His eyes were shining. 'The German,' he began, 'the German, Erenora! One of Katarina's people saw him! He has arrived back in the port.'

3.

Erenora hastened to the waterfront and went from pub to pub asking about the German, without success. Perhaps he had already left or, maybe, Te Whao's informant had been incorrect. Had there ever been a German in the first place? Or had the whole story been a fanciful notion?

She was losing hope when, by chance, she saw a group of sailors clustered around the shipping office. Drawing nearer, she read the advertisement posted on the wall:

WANTED: PEKETUA ISLAND

A labourer is sought to assist the keeper in lighthouse duties on Peketua Island. No previous experience required. Suitable for a single man accustomed to his own company. Be warned: once the post is accepted there is no return to the mainland for a month. Apply at Imperial Hotel, Octagon. Rocco Sonnleithner

The name sprang out to her: Sonnleithner.

'Where the fuck's Peketua Island?' one sailor asked.

'The end of the bloody world,' another answered.

'I hear tell the German's a hard taskmaster,' said a third sailor. 'A big bugger like that, he'd whip you good if you slacked on the job.'

'But the money's good, mateys,' said the second sailor, 'and I hear that he has a beautiful daughter...'

Erenora's mind was in turmoil. What should she do? What if Rocco Sonnleithner wasn't the German rumoured to be Horitana's overseer? But what if he *was!*

The next morning, Erenora presented herself at the Imperial Hotel where she was shown to a large upstairs room. Fifteen other men, including the three sailors she'd heard talking the day before, were already seated. One aspect of the room struck her as being curious: all the curtains had been opened save one. The window it covered must have been ajar because every now and then the curtain shivered and billowed.

'Here comes the German,' one of the men whispered.

Erenora turned to look and, through the glass doors, saw a bald man of massive girth approaching along the hallway. As he opened the doors, the glass panels *flashed.* Next moment he strode past her in a cloud of body sweat. His clothes were ill-fitting, as if a tailor had thrown up his hands in despair but had tried to stitch together a suit that would cover that enormous bulk. He took one look at all the men including Erenora and spat out a curse, 'Ach herrje! What a useless-looking bunch.'

With a surly glance, he sat down on the other side of a desk. 'My name is Rocco Sonnleithner, but you can call me Rocco.' His voice was deep and thickly accented. 'You must all be rogues or vagabonds if you are so hard up that you want the job, eh? I will give a contract to the right man, a man who is willing to work hard, follow my orders, do shift work with me on the lighthouse six hours on, six hours off from dusk to dawn, and keep to his own company. You do your work and mind your own business and we will get along fine.'

Erenora's gaze was distracted by the curtain moving in and out.

'The days are your own,' Rocco continued, 'though there are some chores: firewood to be cut, repairs to equipment. Do not expect me to provide lively company. A boat comes every month to bring provisions. I will pay you two months in advance once we get to the island. Full payment for your stay will come to you after the third month. I will give preference to men who indicate they will stay longer than that. Is anybody willing to stay for six months?'

Several men swore at the terms, some kicking the chairs as they left. Four remained with Erenora—beggars couldn't be choosers. 'He's got us around his fuckin' little finger,' one of the men said.

'Any questions?' There were no questions. 'So, those of you who are left, you are willing to sign up for six months? If you're not, you should leave now as I am in no mood to entertain you.'

Nobody moved from their seats. 'Let me get the papers and, afterwards I will look at your details and make my decision on which of you gets the job.'

He got up and left the room.

Once Rocco had departed, the remaining men in the room began to smile and laugh among themselves. 'Bloody German, thinks he has one over me,' said one sailor, 'but I can take him on any time.'

Another, a tough-looking labourer, said, 'I hear he has his daughter locked up in his house but there's not a door that's been able to keep me out yet.'

A third man added, 'Perhaps she'll help to while away the days, eh, mateys?'

'What if she looks like the big fella?' asked the fourth.

'Who cares as long as she's a woman?' the first sailor laughed.

The labourer said, 'Sounds like an easy job to me—on an island where the police won't be able to find me and I can lie low and get paid for it.'

Erenora kept her own counsel.

Rocco returned, took his chair and smiled. Much to everyone's surprise, he addressed a question to the air. 'Meine Tochter, was sagst du dazu?'

Someone had been sitting behind the curtain all the time. A young girl's voice came back, clear, light, full of scorn. 'Vater, die Männer sind Bäsewichte, Dummkäpfe und verwegen! Willst du mein Urteil? Nimm den Jüngling. Take the young one.'

Rocco looked at Erenora. His expression was arrogant and his voice was tinged with a sneering tone. 'Der Jüngling ist ein Mai-or-ee.'

The young girl's voice came back quick as silver. 'Den, Vater. Den.'

Rocco weighed her words, which seemed to have hidden meaning. And Erenora, irritated by Rocco's ill-concealed contempt of her Maori identity, raised her voice in anger, though she took care to keep her tone low:

'Ein Maori, ja, I am a Maori, yes.' Desperately she flailed around for words. 'Es wäre jedoch ein arger Fehler Ihrerseits, wenn Sie mich deswegen geringachten, mein Herr. But it would be a bad mistake for you to discount me because of that.'

There was a small cry of delight from the young girl. Rocco was surprised at first, and his reply was tinged with mockery. 'Der Jüngling spricht wohl Deutsch?' He paused, taking Erenora in, and then he nodded. Moving quickly for a large man, he advanced on the four men in the room. 'Ach herrje,' he spat again, 'you are all worthless, stupid and presumptuous. Get out before I throw you out.' He turned to Erenora. 'You, boy, what is your name?'

'Eruera,' Erenora replied brusquely.

'You might not have as much muscle on you as the others,' Rocco continued, 'but you can speak a bit of German and that might make it easier for me when I give you orders. So ... I will give you the job and who knows? Perhaps, unlike the others I have employed before you, you will be intelligent enough to follow my instructions.' He grabbed Erenora by the neck and brought her face close to his, spitting as he spoke. 'If not, yours will be a miserable existence.'

'Take your hands off me,' Erenora snarled, shoving him forcefully from her. Caught off balance, he almost fell.

Surprised at the strength of her response, Rocco laughed. 'Perhaps I am wrong about your lack of muscle! Be at the docks first thing tomorrow morning and report to Captain Demmer, skipper of the *Anna Milder.* We set sail with the morning tide.'

Rocco showed Erenora to the door. Once it had closed behind her, she leant on it with relief. Then she began to shiver uncontrollably.

The end of the bloody world. What was it going to be like at te pito o te Ao?

Would Horitana be there?

ACT FOUR

Horitana

CHAPTER TWENTY-ONE

Horitana's Lament

1.

'Oh, valiant heart! Practise the art of forbearance!'

What, I hear you ask, of Horitana during all this time?

Imagine him cast into the deepest and darkest underground cavern, much deeper and darker than any cell in any castellated European fortress. Here, in a dungeon sculpted by nature, is a small stream, bubbling from some underground source. In the background are cold rocky slabs, seeping with moisture and covered in green moss. A flight of stone steps leads up from the cavern to a doorway. There's a large iron grille in the doorway; it is the only source of light from the outside world. But the sun's rays have not yet penetrated deeply enough, so Horitana stretches out his arms in entreaty:

'Aue, e Atua! O God! Kua ngaro a'au i te Po! How dark it is! Aue 'oki te pouri o tenei Ao! How terrible this silence!'

Pity him: he looks half-man, half-monster, the mokomokai appearing to be welded into his neck. Long strands of hair escape from the bottom of the mask like tendrils and it is not so silver now; the salty air has pitted and dulled its surface sheen. As for Horitana's body, although it is covered with a shredded blanket, you can tell that all the muscles have melted from it, leaving it skeleton thin; the skin is bleached, bleeding and ravaged with sores.

Although he is chained to a pole in the centre of the cave, Horitana is able to move to all its walls. His fingernails are long and curved, but some are broken. Over the years he has got to know well every nook and cranny, every crevice and protuberance. He has wrapped rags around his feet to stop them from being cut as he stumbles over the sharp gravelled floor; they are bruised and bloody where he has slipped and fallen. His toenails curl several inches long, and make it difficult for him to walk.

His sense of hearing is acute; so, too, his sense of smell. He knows that the cave is close to the sea. Even the mask can't obliterate the salt in the air that pricks his nostrils, or the booming of the ocean when there are storms. Indeed, Horitana's entombment in the sea cave is probably the reason why he has been able to survive. The foaming sea charges the air with oxygen; how gratefully he sucks the currents through the mokomokai's salt-encrusted silver lips.

On many occasions the ocean has thundered all the way into the cave, and Horitana has had to cling to the pole as the freezing water has risen. Sometimes the waves have reached right up to the mokomokai, and Horitana has often felt tempted to let the weight of it bear him under. Why should he still live when he already wears the face of a dead man?

Indeed, he tried to drown himself once. He sank beneath the water, screaming, 'Let me die!' but, choking and spluttering in unconscious reaction, he found the will to live.

The mokomokai is a terrible burden on his shoulders. To gain occasional respite he lies down. At other times he leans against a rocky outcrop and, right now, has found a ledge that can bear the corroded rim. Again he raises his arms to an unhearing God:

'Here in this void is my cruel ordeal! But Your will is just. E te Atua, 'omai koe to aro'a ki au. I'll not complain; for You have decreed the measure of my suffering.'

Horitana is not always alone. Seabirds have sometimes found their ways into the cave and, so also, the occasional barking seal. His most constant companions, however, are tuatara, the small scaly reptiles that move slowly around him. He killed one once, stuffing it through the mouth cavity of the mokomokai—and then he wailed for forgiveness from its brothers and sisters as they suddenly disappeared from the cavern.

'Come back!' he cried. 'Come back!' He realised they were the only living things that kept him company. After a while, they forgave him, skittering closer and closer.

He opens his manacled arms and sings to them:

'In the springtime of my life all my joy has vanished! Only truth and these chains are my reward. All my pains I gladly suffer; end my life in degradation; in my heart is this consolation—I have done my duty!'

A waiata addressed to tuatara? Truly this man, Horitana, is possessed of a rapture that borders on madness.

Suddenly the tuatara raise their necks, sniffing the air. They begin to cluster closer to Horitana, in the space where the sunlight will soon pour on him.

It is coming!

They start to clamber up the bony ladder of his breast, to the favoured place on his shoulders. They dig their claws into the parchment-thin skin, balancing one on top of another.

'Plenty of room, my little ones,' he chuckles.

And then ... the sun.

The daily warmth of the sun and the changing seasons, these are the markers by which Horitana measures his imprisonment.

There are also the moments when his gaoler arrives. Every week, Horitana waits for the sound of footfalls and the squeak of the opening door.

Listen: even now the gaoler approaches.

'Friend, kia ora,' Horitana calls.

His gaoler remains silent.

'Please talk to me?' Horitana pleads. 'All this time, and not one word do you give from one human being to another? Have mercy, korero mai, let me hear the sound of another human voice.'

There is only silence. Only blackness. And then comes the sound of the winch as Horitana's food is lowered down to him in a bucket. Sometimes there is also the swish of an extra blanket falling; the gaoler is not without kindness.

With a sigh, Horitana shares the food with the tuatara. Why do you think the colony has stayed with him? He is a generous master and lord of their domain.

'Te rangatira o nga tuatara a'au,' he sighs to himself. 'Behold, I am the king of the tuatara.'

The thought appeals to him and he begins to laugh and laugh, the sound echoing, chilling, finding no way out.

CHAPTER TWENTY-TWO

Marzelline

1.

'Just before dawn,' Erenora wrote, 'I made my way to the port. The *Anna Milder* was moored beneath a dockside crane. Captain Demmer was watching the stevedores at their work. They had already loaded most of the provisions on board, mainly sufficient fuel supplies to keep the lighthouse operational for three months and food provisions for the same period.

'I introduced myself to the captain. "I'd been told you were just a young 'un," he said. "Lad or no, you'd best supervise the loading quickly and don't take any nonsense from this lot."

'The stevedores had already loaded a pony trap and, as the sky turned turbulent red, I saw a frightened Shetland pony being hoisted on a winch from the crane. He was kicking and struggling in mid-air. I shouted to the men, "Wait." They were all standing on the dock but not one of them was on the *Anna Milder* to guide the poor creature down. I ran towards the deck and saw that there was a makeshift holding pen. I stood on the railings and motioned to the men to swing the pony out further, and then down—and he came to rest in the enclosure. Even when safely within, however, and despite the presence of bales of hay, the pony still bawled with fear. Quickly, I took off my neck scarf, tying it around his eyes as a blindfold. I was relieved that, after a short while, he calmed down.

'"You're the dark young bugger got the job with the German?" one of the stevedores asked. When I answered, "Yes", he thrust the bill of lading at me and said, "Be so good as to check that all provisions is aboard so me and the mateys can be off. The German's paying us little enough as it is, and fucked if we want to stay any longer than's required."

'I saw Captain Demmer looking at me, wondering how I would handle this. I knew he was doubtful of my abilities. "Don't let them pull the wool over your eyes, lad," he called.

'The stevedores thought I was ignorant, but they did not reckon with my mission education: six barrels of paraffin oil, some bales and sacks of food, equipment and three boxes marked "Miscellaneous" were not accounted for. "You thieving arseholes," I said, "I'll not have the master short-changed." I saw a lighter next to the *Anna Milder* and, despite the stevedores' cries of protest, stepped aboard and spied the missing items. "Put these back where they belong," I commanded, "or I'll have the wharfmaster onto you all. You'll get no pay until the job's completely and honestly done and, if it isn't, don't expect any other captain to employ you."

'I heard a chuckling sound. Unbeknownst to me or the stevedores, a carriage had arrived dockside.

In it was Rocco and, beside him, a very pale young girl all wrapped in furs against the cold. She was wearing a pretty hat and scarf, and her hands were in a warm muff.

'"Papa! Papa!" she said with delight, pointing at the *Anna Milder.* "Ist das mein Pony?" Her voice was light, lilting, and her words came out in a breathless rush. "Du hast es schließlich doch gekauft und den Wagen dazu. You bought him after all, and a cart too!"

'Rocco alighted from the carriage. Captain Demmer said to him with easy familiarity, "The lad is earning his keep, Herr Sonnleithner." Rocco appraised me critically, nodded and then turned on the stevedores. He spoke in rapid and guttural German, cursing them for being varlets, rogues and vagabonds, and they quailed before his wrath. "Eruera, confirm the inventory again," he said. "Are all provisions on board?" He noticed the boxes marked "Miscellaneous" and gave a *look* at the young girl in the carriage; she smiled. "Yes, the bill of lading is now complete, mein Herr," I answered. Rocco nodded, "Good. Tell these good for nothing oafs to be off and that their money is waiting at the hotel."

'Rocco turned his attention back to the girl. She had a trunk and hatbox which I brought aboard the *Anna Milder.* Then Rocco picked the girl up in his arms and carried her to where I was standing on the deck. "This is my daughter, Marzelline," he said. He lowered her down into my arms.

'His daughter? I could scarce credit it, so great was the difference. He was rough hewn but she was spun of fine silk.

'"Der Jüngling," she smiled. She was around sixteen, and her voice was lyrical and light. Her skin was pale, almost translucent, which is why her eyes by contrast seemed so clear and startlingly blue; I had never seen such a colour in all my life. Her face was framed by the pretty hat, so I couldn't see her hair but I imagined that it would be the same colour as her eyebrows, silver blonde and blending into her skin, making her look somewhat hairless.

'Flustered, I went to put Marzelline down on the deck. I was unprepared for her gasp of surprise and sharp instruction. "Nein, nein," she said. She clutched me, as if she would fall.

'I will never forget that moment as long as I live. Her long skirts ballooned as she slipped helplessly from my arms to the deck. Until that moment it had not dawned on me that she was crippled.'

2.

'You stupid boy,' Rocco snarled. He raised his hand and backhanded Erenora.

She fell to the deck but, hot-tempered, quickly got to her feet to defend herself against Rocco's second blow.

Marzelline put up a hand to stop the fight. 'It wasn't the boy's fault,' she said to Rocco. 'He wasn't to know about my legs—' she gave Erenora a smile

'—were you, Jüngling?' Then businesslike, she turned to Rocco. 'Now help me to the cabin. Don't you, the skipper and Eruera have more important matters to attend to?'

At her words, alarm spread over Rocco's face. 'Make haste, boy!' he ordered Erenora. 'Cast off the bowline!' The stevedores were jeering—'I hope you sink to the bottom of the sea, Rocco,'—but he ignored them. Once the vessel was free of the dock, he shouted to Captain Demmer to get under way. 'I'll not pay you more than contracted,' he said.

It all happened so quickly; the *Anna Milder* soon making midharbour.

'Why must we hurry?' Erenora asked the skipper.

'It's a long sail, lad, and we'll be battling the waves all the way,' he answered. 'We must get to Peketua by late afternoon otherwise it will be too dark and we'll have to stand off the island until morning—and that won't do Herr Sonnleithner's temper any good. Nor my pocket, if his threat holds to pay only for the transportation, and not for the time taken.'

'I was glad that we were leaving Dunedin behind. I had had enough of Pakeha cities and wanted only to be in the wilderness again. However, Rocco's temper still stung my cheeks and I knew that I needed to confront him as soon as possible; I ruminated on how I could ensure he never hit me again.

'For most of the journey, Captain Demmer sailed the *Anna Milder* close to the coastline, keeping it in sight and hugging it like a lover. Initially, I was forced to keep my wits about me because Rocco had me racing around the vessel checking that the ropes fastening the cargo were secure. Through a porthole I saw that Marzelline was having a grand time in her cabin, looking at herself in a mirror and modelling the lovely clothes she had bought in Dunedin. She had taken off her hat and her hair colour was indeed startling: a mass of silver-blonde curls like a doll's. You could tell from the way Rocco looked at her that he adored her. Every now and then I caught his glance too, and I knew he was watching me.

'I finally made my way to the Shetland pony's pen. The poor animal was looking very sorry for itself. I saw a brush and began to apply it with even strokes and talk to the pony. "Looks like you and I might have to be friends with each other, eh?" To be truthful I was feeling sorry for myself too.

'I don't know how long after it was that I saw Marzelline coming along the deck. Rocco was remonstrating with her, "Where are you going? To talk to the boy? Ach, he is nothing." Rocco wanted her to put on a hat to protect her skin but she shooed him away. She must have fitted herself with artificial limbs, which her long dress obscured; she was using crutches to balance herself. The deck was rolling and the wind was very blustery; I thought it would pick her up and she would be blown away like a delicate dandelion seedhead. I went towards her but she waved away my intentions to help.

'"We're both lucky, Eruera," she said conspiratorially as I arranged a couple of bales of hay for her to sit on. "The three boxes you saved have all of Papa's newly purchased books in them and three months' supply of his favourite cigars. And in one of the barrels those men would have stolen, Schnaps!" She grinned, licking the perspiration that beaded her upper lip. "Papa would have been insufferable without reading material and without his cigars and alcohol but, pooh!, he smokes in the cabin while he reads, and so drives me out."

'Marzelline had brought two apples. She gave one to the pony, which snuffled at the fruit and then gladly ate it. The other apple she polished and gave to me. "Here," she said. "I am so glad you are young. All of Papa's workmen have been so *old."* She made a face, crossed her eyes and made her tongue loll slack from her mouth.

'She made me laugh. At the same time, I felt a shiver of apprehension. I shouldn't get too close to Marzelline or allow her to get too close to me.'

Flights of birds, some high, some low, skimmed across the sky.

Under Captain Demmer's captainship, the *Anna Milder* forged on towards the south. The shoreline was spellbinding; truly Te Wai Pounamu was spectacular. Impenetrable forest and high ferns spread from the coastline upward to snow-covered mountain peaks.

Sometimes there were wondrous waterfalls, pouring down the ravines, as if the land was still rising from the sea.

And seaward, the vista was just as breathtaking. Schools of dolphins rose to pace the vessel and, every now and then, the surface would boil with shoals of fish. At one point, a huge pod of whales jostled the *Anna Milder,* finally speeding along an ancient migratory trail towards the Antarctic. Further out on the horizon, sailing in the same direction, were other ships, their canvas billowing as they made for Bluff.

Then the weather changed. Although the voyage had begun in sunlight, by early afternoon the sky had clouded over, the wind had turned cold and the sea was mounting. A storm was coming: the swell was extraordinary, lowering the vessel and lifting it as if the ocean was gasping for breath.

Captain Demmer ordered Erenora to do the rounds of the vessel and when she reported back he muttered, 'Good, she is nicely balanced as is and we can't afford to have any cargo shift on deck when we go through the reef.' He looked at the weather and gave Erenora a pitying glance. 'This storm is a harbinger of winter, lad,' he said. 'You're going to be living close with Herr Sonnleithner. Don't let him bully you.'

Suddenly the storm was upon them—violent winds and heavy rain. Erenora went to calm the pony and rig a shelter for him. Together they huddled beneath the canvas.

Then Erenora saw Captain Demmer waving to her. 'There's the reef and there's the island,' he yelled. 'Heaven help you, lad.'

Far away, looming high out of gathering gloom was a circle of light, like a full moon with an aureole around it. Below it was something dark and massive and, for a moment, Erenora could have been looking at a gigantic taniw'a, with a jagged backbone and tail threshing the sea.

'Yes,' Captain Demmer nodded, 'Peketua Island.'

3.

The waves were crashing against the ancient slab of the taniw'a's scaly grey breast. Silhouetted in the darkening sky, the body of the beast thrashed and curved around a small bay, the tail studded with dangerous rocks.

'Home,' Erenora heard a voice yell in her ear. It was Marzelline, standing beside her, utterly fearless. 'Isn't it wunderbar?' In preparation for landing she had changed into a seaman's hat and cape. She lifted her face to the stinging rain and gave a wild Walküre cry.

The taniw'a's eye transformed itself into the lighthouse's lantern. The powerful beam played across a sea broken by the exposed sharp points of the reef; waves were foaming around them. 'Don't worry, lad, there's a way through,' Captain Demmer said. 'What we have to worry about is on the other side of the rocks.'

Erenora saw what he meant. There was only a small gap in the taniw'a's tail. Beyond was a glimpse of a quay. 'You've got it easy,' Captain Demmer continued. 'You only have to brave the gap once.' The sea was smashing against the tail but storming through the small space. He lined the *Anna Milder* up with the gap and waited for the breast of a tide to take them through. 'As for me, I have to get in—and also get *out*.'

Captain Demmer never liked to wait. He felt the swell beneath the *Anna Milder,* went with the surge, 'It's now or never,' and grim faced, spun the wheel and steered the vessel straight for the gap.

A man appeared out of the driving storm from a makeshift shelter on the quay.

'Jack?' Rocco roared at him. 'Make the bowline secure, and now the stern. Danke.'

'Don't thank me,' Jack answered, 'the faster the vessel is unloaded the sooner I'll be able to get away from this fuckin' island.'

Rocco turned to Erenora. 'Carry your mistress off the boat,' he shouted. 'Take her to the shelter.' But Marzelline struggled in Erenora's arms. 'Nein,' she said impatiently when they reached the quay. 'Put me down. I will go the rest of the way to the shelter myself.'

Erenora lowered Marzelline onto the quay where she unstrapped her artificial legs; they would only slip in the rain. She pulled on heavy gloves and began to drag herself towards the shelter. When

Jack came to help her she said something that sounded strange to Erenora: 'No, Jack, it's over.' She saw that Erenora was eavesdropping and scolded Jack. 'Go and help Papa,' she said. As Jack shoved past Erenora he gave Marzelline a bitter glance.

'I can't keep the boat steady for too long,' Captain Demmer yelled.

Rocco appeared almost superhuman as he and Jack threw bales, boxes and sacks onto the quay. Erenora hauled them over to Marzelline to pack tightly into the shelter. By this time she was standing, having strapped on her legs again. 'Nur hurtig fort,' she reproved Erenora. 'Quicker! Quicker!'

Once that was done, the hard work of rolling the barrels of fuel up the gangplank began. A loud series of whinnies disturbed the work. 'What's that?' Jack asked. The pony had broken loose from his ropes and was up on his hind legs, trying to get out of the enclosure. 'Get the pony, Eruera,' Rocco yelled. 'Take him off before he jumps into the sea.'

The terrified creature baulked at the shifting boards beneath his hooves and Erenora had no other option except to ride him off the tossing boat. 'Don't do that,' Captain Demmer yelled, 'you'll only get killed.' But she leapt onto the pony's back and grasped his mane. Then, leaning down to unlatch the enclosure, she yelled into his ears, ''aere!'

With a cry of fear, the pony clattered up the ramp and onto the quay.

Erenora leapt down and slapped the pony on the rump, 'Good boy.' He ran along the quay and into the darkness. Erenora knew he would seek shelter somewhere; she would find him later.

'Now the pony trap,' Rocco instructed.

Through the icy pellets of rain and squalling wind, Erenora manhandled the trap up the ramp. 'I'll take it now,' Marzelline said, pulling it further into the shelter. Erenora joined Rocco and Jack in pushing the barrels of fuel onto the quay.

It seemed only a second before a warning cry came from Captain Demmer. 'The tide's turning,' he shouted. 'Get aboard, Jack!' The sea was rushing out, and the *Anna Milder* was beginning to strain on the ropes that tied her to the dock.

Rocco pushed the last barrel ashore and sat on it, panting.

'Where's my pay, you German bastard?' Jack yelled, aiming a fist at Rocco's face.

The big German fended off the blow and pushed him away. 'I'm a man of my word,' he said, handing over a wet purse. 'Every penny is there.'

Jack looked at Erenora before he boarded. 'All yours, mate, and you're welcome to it.' Then he called to Marzelline, 'I'd have stayed if you'd asked me.'

Rocco was laughing as he let go the lines. 'Goodbye, Jack,' he yelled.

The *Anna Milder* was scraping the bottom, but then a wave rushed in, buoyed her up and she managed to turn on the breast of the outgoing sea. 'Curse you, Rocco,' Jack said, 'you and your stinking island.'

From out of the darkness Erenora saw Captain Demmer waving. *Heaven help you, lad.* Then the vessel disappeared, sucked out from the shelter of the quay into the stormy dark.

Exhausted, Erenora crouched on the quay, but it wasn't over yet. Rocco spoke to his daughter. 'Are you all right?'

'Of course, Papa.' Shc was soaked through to the skin but seemed undaunted by the rain. Her fair curls were plastered to her forehead. She gathered her skirts together and, aided by her crutches, began to stump up the steps to open the stone cottage on the hillock behind the lighthouse.

Rocco took up a sack and indicated to Erenora that he should do the same.

'Follow your mistress,' he said.

CHAPTER TWENTY-THREE

History and Fiction

1.

From this point I have to confess something.

Throughout the first part of Erenora's narrative dealing with the history and events at Parihaka, I was able to keep fairly close to the way she told it in her manuscript. Again, when Erenora and her sisters left Parihaka I have kept for the most part to Erenora's record; my qualifications as a translator from Maori into English and an amateur historian were up to the task.

But I wasn't aware that Josie had been looking over my shoulder and, well, she's taken me to task. 'There's too much of yourself going into the kuia's story,' she said. 'Sometimes the way Erenora says things sounds more like you than her and, well, that goes for the story she's telling too. And some of the stuff about Piharo ... You make him sound like a really bad piece of work.'

My darling Josie always goes straight for the jugular.

Josie's observation has made me pause and think for a bit. I've come to realise that although I'm writing Erenora's history I'm doing so, unintentionally, in a fictional way. But just as I'm not a professional translator and historian, I'm also *not* a novelist. Why then, have I begun to treat history as an ouija board, putting my fingers on a glass and hoping that the spirit will lead the glass in the right direction?

Lying in bed with Josie last night, I was silent. But I felt I had to defend myself, so I waited for her to pay me some attention. 'All right,' she said crossly, putting aside the book she was reading, 'what are you brooding about now? Out with it!'

'Can I just treat Erenora,' I began, 'and her story as if she were some person walking through history—as if history was a *book?* No! History is a living landscape and Erenora really lived and breathed. She cried, she laughed, she experienced every human emotion. What other way is there to honour her in my version of her manuscript than, therefore, to also *imagine* how she really was emotionally?'

I pressed home my argument. 'Can I just treat Erenora factually? No! And Piharo, he was worse than I've written him! He was a sadist, but I didn't want to demonise him in the same way as Pakeha did Te Whiti and Tohu.'

Josie sighed, and I thought I had won, but when she picked up her book, I realised she was sticking to her guns. 'Your role should be as a recorder,' she said before she began reading again, 'not as a creator—or editor, for that matter.'

My darling is like this: stubborn, pedantic, won't let me hang one on her.

From this point onward, however, Josie will be happy—or happier.

Some years ago there was a development that lessened my need to involve myself so much in my ancestor's story. Remember that I told you our family's information about Erenora came from the unpublished manuscript in the St John's archives? Unfortunately, from the point where Erenora goes to Peketua Island, the manuscript was fragmented. We know that once upon a time she'd written an entire and full account—the binding proves it, with bits of the lost manuscript still attached—but, aue, most of the pages in the final quarter were missing.

Then came a new and surprising source of information that helped me to join the dots, as it were. This has lessened my propensity to imagine what happened and exacerbated my, well, penchant for creativity in fleshing out the characters involved.

Let me take a few moments to tell you about it.

2.

A few years ago I said to Josie, 'Why don't we go for a holiday to the South Island?'

Of course, she knew what I was up to: another of the research trips I'd been taking during my retirement to try to expand on my information about the Parihaka prisoners while they were in Te Wai Pounamu, and about the lives of Erenora and Horitana.

Josie has always encouraged my amateur sleuthing. For one thing, it means another holiday in the campervan we bought especially for the purpose; I hadn't realised that she felt so housebound when I was a teacher. For another, it provides her with the opportunity to bring along one of our ratbag mokopuna and show them the world, as well as to get them away from dope and gangs. This time we took along my son's no-hoper, Tamati, and Josie gave him the job of driving us to Dunedin. How we got there in one piece, I don't know. Josie should have known better than to offer the task to a boy racer.

Anyhow, my purpose in going to Dunedin was to follow up a lead on Rocco Sonnleithner. I discovered that there was a Donald Sonnleithner who lived in Maori Hill, a lovely established suburb overlooking the city. The surname was such an unusual one, I was sure there must be a connection. Rather than tell him I was coming—he might have said no—I decided to drop in on him. Maori do this all the time otherwise the person you're visiting might sneak out the back door while you're knocking at the front, thinking you've come to be paid back the money you lent him.

When we arrived in Dunedin, Josie immediately went to do some shopping for a nice warm coat, using the weather as an excuse. Tamati must have discovered some coven (or whatever) of boy racers, because he soon disappeared on me too. I decided that the walk would do me good so I made my way by foot to the address for Donald Sonnleithner listed in the telephone book. It was a good walk, almost an hour, and when I arrived I discovered a large two-storeyed

Victorian building of the kind Dunedin is well known for: you'd call it a handsome house, built for a highly respected merchant family. Solid brick, with a pitched tiled roof and diamond-paned windows, it was understated but with just enough quality to indicate that, actually, it was a cut above the rest.

Nothing venture, nothing win, I thought as I opened the gate, walked along a pathway between attractive gardens and rang the doorbell—it seemed to echo for ages, as if tolling back through time, but that's me again and my fanciful imagination.

Then, through the glass inset in the door I glimpsed the image of someone walking down the hall stairs ... and I stepped back, suddenly embarrassed that I had come without making an appointment. But it was too late: the door opened and a man stood before me, about my own age and height, sprightly with an enquiring air. 'Yes?' he asked.

As soon as I saw him, I knew he was Donald Sonnleithner and that I'd come to the right place. His eyes were so *blue.*

I must say I was so startled by those eyes—so clear, so bright, so deep—that I had to pause, searching for words. 'I'm sorry to call on you like this,' I began, 'but my name is...'

'I think I know who you are,' he said, raising his left hand to stop me, 'or, at least, where you've come from. Are you from the Taranaki?'

I nodded, puzzled. How could he guess that?

'I thought so,' and he smiled, though as Donald told me later, he also had to regain his composure. 'You must be a descendant of Eruera. Our great-grandmother, Marzelline, always said that one day someone from Eruera's tribe might pay us a call.' He opened the door wider. 'Do come in.'

Since that time, Donald and I have remained in contact and we have become good friends. One day, he sent me a copy of Marzelline's diary. Apparently, as for many young girls of her time, writing daily in it was a welcome pastime. It is from her strong, beautiful handwriting—in German, but Donald had translated it all into English for me—that I have been able to fill some of the gaps in Erenora's own shredded manuscript.

Some, but not all.

The narrative will be as historically seamless as my talent can make it, but be warned that my loyalty may still compel me to repair and gloss over any cracks.

Not only that; I love my ancestor.

CHAPTER TWENTY-FOUR

Island at the End of the World

1.

Throughout the storm, Rocco and Erenora transferred the stores from the quay to the cottage.

'Bring them through,' Marzelline urged Erenora. It didn't matter to the young girl that she was cold and wet, there was work to do.

Erenora barely had time to look at the interior as she ferried food—grain, molasses, lard, bacon, tea—from the quay to the pantry. Marzelline directed her where to put the other bales and boxes; Erenora marvelled at her energy and spirit as she methodically checked off the inventory.

'Now go back and get the rest,' Marzelline said, 'especially the sacks of flour and sugar before they get wet.'

Once the food had been safely stored, Rocco wanted to deal straight away with the barrels of fuel. 'I don't want any to be washed away by the sea,' he said.

'Can you manage, Jüngling?' Marzelline asked Erenora, her bright blue eyes shining with concern. She had finally taken time to remove her seaman's hat and cape and to wipe the rain from her face with a towel.

'Of course the boy can manage,' Rocco muttered. 'Come, Eruera.'

Lightning was crackling overhead as they braved the storm again. Erenora followed Rocco's lead, rolling the barrels along the quay and hauling them up a few stone steps to the lighthouse. Rocco opened the door to a wide circular floor. 'Stack the barrels around the walls,' he ordered. 'I am going aloft to check on the lantern.'

Erenora watched him ascend a circular staircase to the floor high above where the lighthouse's huge lamp was blazing over the sea. Then she went out to collect the remaining barrels. On every return she could hear Rocco stamping overhead and the occasional guttural swearword as he cursed Jack.

'Now go and find the pony,' Rocco said when he came down.

Shading her face against the rain, Erenora saw that the pony had found shelter beneath a large tree near the beach. 'There, there,' she consoled the shivering beast. She shepherded him to the small wooden barn close by the cottage. A milking cow was already in one stall; Erenora manoeuvred the pony into the second. Seven laying hens, guarded by a fierce rooster, clucked in the bales of hay.

The pony was wet, trembling with fear and cold, and Erenora was rubbing him down when Rocco entered. 'You sleep in the loft,' he said. 'It is comfortable and warm there and Jack will have left bedding for you. You take your meals in the cottage with me and my daughter. Tomorrow night you start your first shift as lighthouse keeper. Good evening.'

As Rocco brusquely took his leave, Erenora kicked him savagely in the back. The German turned to swing at her but discovered a butcher's knife at his neck. 'You've used physical force against me twice now, mein Herr,' Erenora said. She knew if she didn't take a stand against him now he would keep physically challenging her and, possibly, discover her secret. 'Don't do it again or I will stick you like a pig.'

Rocco looked at Erenora warily. 'The Jüngling fights back? So be it.'

They were interrupted by Marzelline; she had changed into dry clothing and pinned up her hair. She hesitated, knowing something had occurred between her father and Erenora—but Rocco made light of it.

He looked at her and smiled, good humoured. 'Eruera has just shown me he can look after himself.'

Marzelline nodded, 'I'm glad, Papa.' Balancing on her artificial legs and crutches, she had a pack slung across her shoulders. She put it down on a bale of hay, took out a large bowl and pitcher and began pouring steaming soup into the bowl. Then she took out two large pieces of bread from the pack.

'That soup is not for Eruera, is it?' Rocco objected.

Marzelline gave her father an impudent look. 'I bring replenishment for the pony, Papa!' she answered slyly. Her skin was shining, as if the storm had invigorated her. She whispered to Erenora, 'You have done better than any of the others already.' Then she turned to Rocco, 'Come, Papa, get out of those wet clothes before you catch a cold.'

Later that evening, staring out of the loft window, Erenora saw the storm was abating and the moon leaping high into a cloud-streaked sky. Had she made the right decision? What if the rumours that Horitana had been imprisoned on an island were wrong? If so, *she* would be the prisoner.

Glancing at the lighthouse, Erenora saw Rocco silhouetted on an exterior balcony below the lantern. She left the barn, ran swiftly through the rain to the lighthouse and made her first ascent of the lighthouse stairs.

'Show me what to do,' Erenora said to the startled Rocco, 'and then join your daughter for the night.'

'I worked my first shift that very evening,' Erenora wrote. 'I intuitively realised that if I didn't continue to take the upper hand, Rocco would ride me pitilessly morning and night. Better to get him to consider me, if not as an equal, at least not as an underling he could order around.

'The shift took me through to an hour after dawn when Rocco came to wind the lantern's operation down. You might have thought that he would be kindly disposed to me for having taken the initiative and worked on my first night on Peketua, but that was not in his nature. No, hard taskmaster that he was, he had me spending the day restacking the stores to his satisfaction. My only respite came when Marzelline took sympathy on me and brought me food again. "You must eat, Jüngling," she said, wagging a finger. "If you don't eat, how will you keep up with Papa?"

'"Don't call me Jüngling," I answered. "There are more than ten years between us." But Marzelline had already decided what and who I was, and she chose not to hear me.

'It was not until a week later that I was finally able to take stock of my surroundings—the island, the lighthouse, my new employer and his daughter, and my strange circumstances...'

2.

I was finally able to take stock of my surroundings.
Aue, describing Peketua Island is a true test, but from the fragments of Erenora's papers, and Marzelline's diary, we can surmise some details of Erenora's new world and build up a picture of it.

Of course the locational and topographical details of Peketua Island are well known. The name comes from the Maori god who was said to be the progenitor of all reptiles; he sculpted an egg out of clay and from it came the tuatara, Peketua's physical form. The island lies at coordinates 46° 47□S, 169° 10□E. Its area is 5.1 square miles, comprising a small plateau—the 'head' of Erenora's giant taniw'a—on which the lighthouse stood and a 'body' comprising a series of four hummocks each topped with a jagged pinnacle rising to the highest elevation of 240 feet.

Although small, the island's forested interior is difficult to access and, back then, it could not be traversed without difficulty. The quickest means of getting to the other side was in a small skiff with a much-patched but serviceable sail. Contrary winds made such a journey hazardous, however, and the best way was by foot, though walking was slow and meant having to negotiate jutting spurs and craggy cliffs.

As to the south-eastern side, where the lighthouse was, Erenora soon realised why its warning light was required. The outlying jagged rocks were scattered along the coast over a 5-mile stretch.

'It was Marzelline who was able to connect the myth of the island with reality. When I told her that the island was named after the god of reptiles she clapped her hands and answered, "Then the reefs are like scattered egg shells when the island was born and the foaming sea their discoloured albumen."

'I laughed at her cleverness. Yes indeed, in the agony of its birth throes Peketua Island had literally exploded out of its egg and sent thousands of broken shards across the sea. How ever had Captain Demmer navigated his way through the rocks?'

And then there was the lighthouse, Rocco and Marzelline's stone cottage—attractive in the daylight—and the small wooden barn close to it.

I don't want to provide a treatise on lighthouses, but some background might be in order, and I hope you'll indulge me as I've always been interested in these buildings. This fascination stemmed from the time when I was a young boy and my father, who liked comics, bought at the same second-hand store a small encyclopedia with highly coloured illustrations designed to enthral the young reader. Among the drawings were those of the Seven Ancient Wonders of the World. Can you name them? The Pyramid, the Sphinx, the Great Library at Alexandria, the Colossus of Rhodes, the Hanging Gardens of Babylon, pae kare, I can't remember the sixth one, but the seventh was my favourite: the Pharos of Alexandria, built in 247 BC and 460 feet tall, according to my encyclopedia. Not only could the light be seen 30 nautical miles away but—and this really appealed to my boyhood imagination—its huge lamp could act as a ray gun and burn any fleets attacking Alexandria.

You can see my point, can't you? From the very beginning of civilisation, lighthouses have been revered and regarded as important to humankind. They were *very* important to Pakeha when New Zealand was being discovered and colonised. Ships were the primary, and the fastest, means of trade, communication and immigration, but what a treacherous and hazardous coast. It's hard to credit, but over 1,000 ships were wrecked in the first fifty years of colonisation; that's, on average, twenty ships a year—imagine twenty planes crashing annually. No wonder that building lighthouses became a priority and that the first one was erected at the entrance to Wellington Harbour in 1848, only eight years after the signing of the Treaty of Waitangi. As for the lighthouse on Peketua Island, it was first lit nineteen years later, and its lantern was able to beam out to 20 nautical miles—not bad, eh. The lantern was fired an hour before dark and remained lit until an hour after dawn, but it also operated when mists or squalls affected visibility. To see a lighthouse, whether by night or day, was to know that a guardian was watching over your progress:

'I am here, pass by in safety.'

I like to imagine Erenora on duty at the lighthouse.

Snatching moments from her work, I picture her during the evenings going out onto the platform. She must have experienced some of her most sublime moments looking at that vast seascape, the stars above the ocean stretching into blackness. And during the days, peering through the telescope on the platform, she would have spied ships squeezing through the gap between sea and sky. They bucked through the waves, giving wide berth to the rocks and passed into the haze of the horizon.

Sometimes, when Rocco was not watching, she would swing the telescope landward.

If Horitana was here, where would he be imprisoned?

3.

'Rocco kept me so busy that I scarcely realised that three weeks had gone by. He was a tough taskmaster and he insisted on maintaining a daily routine.

'Most mornings, for instance, I was awakened by Marzelline's girlish laughter, "Papa, let me walk!" I watched from the window as, instead, Rocco carried his daughter down the steps from the cottage to the quay. He would seat Marzelline on the edge and, dressed in a voluminous bathing costume, he would leap into the freezing sea. Briskly he splashed around, blowing and puffing like a sea lion. Then he invited Marzelline to jump down into his arms. No matter what the weather, this was their regimen, their daily constitutional.

'There was a bell affixed to the doorway of the cottage and at 7.30 Marzelline would ring it for breakfast, "Eruera? Komm!" The kitchen was her domain and she cooked all the meals. She refused to let Rocco or me help her as she moved from kitchen range to dining table, ladling porridge or serving tea. Sometimes she was on crutches and other times she was in a wheelchair, always talking to herself. "Be careful now, Marzelline," she would mutter, "don't spill the milk! Oh, what a careless girl you are," she would cry, "you forgot to slice the bread!" I marvelled at her dexterity, though sometimes it failed her. Once I made the mistake of kneeling down to pick up a plate she had dropped. "No, Eruera," she pouted. "Your place, your job, is the lighthouse. My place, my job, is the kitchen."

'Following breakfast, Rocco spent most of his morning in the lighthouse. He liked to take the responsibility of maintaining the mechanism that rotated the lantern and refuelling the sixteen small paraffin oil lamps, each with its own lens, which turned inside. "If things go wrong while you are on duty," he said to me, "I have only myself to blame and I will not feel inclined to hit you—and invite you to hit me back." Rocco always had a list of other chores for me to do: keeping the interior of the lighthouse tidy, milking the cow, collecting and chopping firewood and fetching water from the well. The island was fortunate in having fresh water from an aquifer, an underground layer of water-bearing permeable rock.

'We were always busy in the mornings, even Marzelline, who had a little garden at the front of the cottage for flowers, and a vegetable garden and apple tree at the back. I liked watching her as she sat on a small cushion, pushing herself along the rows and weeding the potatoes, carrots and other vegetables. She was particularly proud of a windowbox where she carefully nurtured the aromatic herbs with which she seasoned our meals.

'Sometimes, rather than lay out lunch in the cottage, Marzelline would ask me to help her take a basket of food and drink to Rocco at the lighthouse.

"Papa? Papa!" she would call, until he appeared on the platform. "Is that my Rapunzel?" he would laugh, forgetting that I was there to eavesdrop on their intimacy. "I let down my hair!" He had constructed a pulley system from the platform with a chair on which Marzelline could sit and be raised to the top.

'Over lunch of cheese, sausage, bread and drink, Marzelline and her father would chatter away and often they played board games or read. Once lunch was finished, Rocco would rest: sleeping or reading or relaxing with one of his cigars. As for me, I took up fishing from the skiff that was moored at the quay. "Look, Papa! Eruera caught another fish!" Marzelline would exclaim when I arrived at the house with my catch. I think Rocco was jealous that I was such a good fisherman but, to be truthful, the island's waters were so plentiful that anybody with a hook and line could catch something.

'Sundays were special days. After lunch Rocco dressed in black coat and white shirt, and Marzelline joined him in the sitting room where they read to each other from the Bible. Come the evening, we would have dinner early in the cottage and, an hour before dark, Rocco lit the lantern and stayed on duty until midnight.

'Then he would come and wake me. "Eruera! Boy! Do not let the lantern go out or it will be the worse for you."'

Although the pony had been broken in—Marzelline christened him Napoleon—one of Erenora's first duties was to make him amenable to the harness and trap. He was not a large animal, but Rocco appeared to have an antipathy to horses. 'You do it,' he said to Erenora.

There was a long sandy beach on the other side of the quay. On the first day of training, Erenora introduced Napoleon to the harness while Rocco and Marzelline watched from the hillside. When Erenora placed the harness on the pony's back he recoiled; pulled across the sand, Erenora hung onto the reins for dear life.

Over the next few days, Erenora tried the harness on Napoleon again and again without success. 'What if the pony won't submit?' Marzelline asked her father.

Rocco gave Erenora a strong glance. 'Eruera will do it,' he told her.

It was only a matter of time, especially when Erenora had a brainwave. She took Napoleon into the surf and hitched the trap to him there. The water level was up to the axles and, this time, the pony couldn't bolt. He gave Erenora a withering, defeated look: *unfair.*

'Can I drive him now?' Marzelline asked. 'Can I, Papa?'

Rocco lifted her into the seat. When he and Eruera went to walk beside the trap she set her chin with determination. 'Nein. I go by myself,' she muttered, as much to herself as to them. With that, she sent the pony trotting down the beach.

Watching her, Rocco looked at Erenora and spoke gruffly, 'If ever my daughter wanted to go further than the cottage I always had to carry her,' he said. 'Now she can ride to the end of the world.' It was the closest to a thank you that Rocco had come.

The next Sunday, Erenora pressed home her advantage. After lunch, Rocco and Marzelline settled down to reading their Bible to each other. 'May I join you, mein Herr?' Erenora asked.

'I thought you Maoris were heathens,' Rocco answered, astonished.

'I was brought up by Lutherans like you,' Erenora said.

Rocco paused, thinking.

'Oh please, Papa,' Marzelline teased him. 'I get so tired of your droning voice!'

Rocco tried to look disapproving but, eventually, he frowned and nodded his head. 'But I am master,' he said to Marzelline, wagging a finger, 'you are mistress—and Eruera is our servant.'

'Not in the eyes of God,' Marzelline said.

And that was that.

4.

'And so,' Erenora wrote, ' my relationship with Rocco settled into a better pattern of acceptance.

'He even trusted me enough to pull one of his teeth. I had to use two sets of forceps and he battled me all the way and, at the end, he lifted his fist! And he also began to trust his daughter to me on occasional afternoons. Sometimes when he was resting, I prepared Napoleon so that Marzelline could drive the trap along the beach. "Is that all right, mein Herr?" I would ask. And Marzelline would confront him, "It had better be!" She soon became more adventurous, forcing the pony up the sand dunes into rock caves. One day I forgot she was crippled and chastised her, "You try to walk before you can run." We both laughed at my innocent remark.

'Soon afterwards, the ease into which Marzelline and I had grown was illustrated when she asked, "Eruera, would you help me from the trap? I think I will go for a swim." The day was dull and the breakers were surly, but Marzelline wasn't deterred. To speak plainly, I suspect she desired physical contact: she had an affectionate heart and loved to have me swing her down onto the sand—"You're so strong, Jüngling!" On that occasion, Marzelline was wearing her artificial legs but, as she undressed to her underclothing, she nonchalantly took them off in front of me; they were kept on by a tight girdle around her thighs. She unwrapped the bandages from the stumps and, looking at me, said, "You can touch them if you like."

'I did not take up Marzelline's offer. I felt a slight sense of unease. We belonged to different worlds and this offer of intimacy was dangerous.

'She began to prattle on. "You know, people feel sorry for me but I'm not sorry for myself. After all, I don't know what it's like to have legs, this is all I've ever known. I only wish..." she bit her lip and her eyes welled with tears "... that I wasn't such a burden to Papa."

'"A burden?" I asked, astonished. Anybody could see that her father worshipped her. His eyes were always upon her, watching her every movement with undisguised wonder.

'With a cry of self-pity Marzelline propelled herself savagely through the surf. She went so far out into the waves, as if she wanted to drown herself, that I leapt in after her.

'"Oh, Eruera," she sobbed as I carried her out of the water, "don't you understand? Papa gives up his own life for me! Everything, for me! He buries himself away from the world just for me!"

'She held onto me so tight, and there was such strength in her arms, as if she never wanted to let me go.'

'Perhaps it was Marzelline's self-pity that propelled her questing spirit. Wilfully, she wanted to prove to her father that he did not always have to look after her.

'There was a path from the cottage along a steep cliff-face. One day while we were out on the cart, despite my entreaties she forced Napoleon to mount the path. When we got to the top, the view was breathtaking. But Rocco had witnessed the ascent, and a light began to flash from the cottage: *Return immediately*.

'When I delivered Marzelline to the house, he was furious. "Didn't you see how dangerous the path was, you stupid boy?" he shouted. "And you, daughter, you went too far. You could have been killed."

'Marzelline stood her ground. "Papa, you must let me grow up," she said with determination. "You can't always tell me what to do and where to go."

'That started a fierce argument, the patriarch trying to impose his will on his daughter and Marzelline rebelling against him. I couldn't follow all their rapid German but at the climax of their altercation Marzelline screamed at him, "And what happens when you die, Papa? How will I manage to survive if you don't allow me to find my own independence?"

'The thought shocked Rocco so much that he paled. In vain entreaty, he put his arms out to her.

'"No, Papa," she said. "*No!*" and she pushed him away.'

CHAPTER TWENTY-FIVE

A Walk to the Other Side of the Island

1.

The first month drew to an end, with winter closing in. Erenora had kept close watch on Rocco, waiting for him to disclose another role, as gaoler on Peketua Island. While out with Marzelline, she had also made quick searches along the immediate beach to see if there were any secret places a prisoner might be kept. But Rocco's anger when Marzelline had taken the cliff path with Napoleon had put paid to any wider search.

If Horitana was here, where was he?

Finally, with great daring, she decided to raise the subject at supper.

Rocco mocked her. 'Me, a gaoler for some secret prisoner?'

Erenora almost believed him.

'Then one day,' Erenora wrote, ' Marzelline drove Napoleon at a fast canter along the beach to the very end.

'Although there was a spur that blocked any further advancement, there was also a short tunnel to the other side. Most times the sea was too high to allow you to go through it but, on this particular day, it was a very low tide—down to only a couple of inches of water.

'Marzelline was feeling impatient that day. She was looking particularly pretty and tossed her curls, saying, "Ach, Eruera, don't you think that sometimes our world is too small?" She was still chafing at the limits her father placed on her independence, and I was cross with her that we had gone so far. "I'm late for my shift," I said. Pouting, Marzelline turned the trap homeward.

'We were making our way back to the cottage when, in the distance, there was a *flash* from the clifftop. Marzelline took out her mirror and replied. "It's only Papa," she said. "He hasn't waited for you. He's started his long nature walk. He must trust you, Eruera."

'I was instantly alert. "Where does he go?"

'"Once a week he walks to a special place on the other side of the island to watch the seabirds. He likes to look at the birds, the penguins, seals and sea lions—they're all of intense interest to him." Then she pursed her lips and watched until Rocco had disappeared. "Good," she said, "the mice can play!" She looked back at the hole—it was still fairly close—and I could see her scheming. "Let's go back." She shook Napoleon's reins, turned him around and uttered her wild warrior cry.

'"No!" I shouted. What if we were trapped by the incoming tide? Or if the cart hit a submerged rock and threw Marzelline into the waves? "Don't go any further," I called, but Marzelline took no notice. The water sprayed around Napoleon's hooves and the wheels of the cart, and then, through the hole Marzelline drove the cart. Quickly I splashed after her.

'"What took you so long?" she laughed when I joined her. "Isn't it beautiful on this side?"

'"You could have been killed," I answered angrily.

'"Poor Eruera, I scared you." Taking no further notice of me, she urged Napoleon out of the shallows onto the sand.

'Ahead was a brackish lagoon separated from the sea by snags and ridged sandbars. It was the kind of place where the detritus of the ocean was brought by swirling currents. Trapped in a bowl made by sheer cliffs leaning against the sky, the currents had no option but to drop their rubbish: piles of drift-wood, mainly, and the bones of a giant whale.

'Marzelline drove Napoleon along the rim of the bowl until we came to a fall of rocks, caused by the eroding sea. "We'd better turn back," I said to her. "The tide is coming in fast."

'She nodded, "Ja, mir ist sowieso langweilig. I'm bored anyway. Nur totes Zeug hier. There are only dead things here." Then something caught her attention. She shaded her eyes and pointed at it. "What's that?"

'I was looking at her and I swear that the first time I saw the remains of the old wreck was when they appeared in her clear blue eyes. I followed the direction of her gaze.

'The hulk must have been there for many years. It looked as if, once upon a time, it had had three masts. Driven by countless storms, it had been pushed against the cliffs and come to rest in the sheltered hook of the lagoon. Only the stern and part of the upper deck and upper gun deck were exposed; most of the wreck was skeletal or buried in water and sand. On the stern was some faded lettering:

VICOMTE DE BRAGELONNE

'"Oh," Marzelline said, "it must have been a French ship."

'*Vicomte de Bragelonne.* I remembered the rumour about Horitana being held in the hulk of such a ship. Could he have been kept in the stern? I left Marzelline in the cart, then splashed swiftly through the shallow water to the hulk and clambered in.

'"Eruera?" Marzelline called. She sounded petulant, as if cross that she couldn't accompany me. I heard her encourage Napoleon to catch up.

'First I searched the upper deck and gun deck, but it was silted up and awash with water. I then turned to investigate the great cabin at the stern. The floor had collapsed long ago and one side was completely exposed to the elements. Nobody could possibly have been imprisoned there.

'Then I thought of Rocco—*nature walking, once a week a long walk to the other side of the island while I am on duty*— and my heart quickened.

Perhaps Horitana had been moved.

2.

'I took Marzelline back to the cottage.

'"Won't you stay and keep me company while Papa is away?" she asked.

'"No," I answered. "I had best be about my other chores."

'She pouted a little but her moods were always mercurial. "Never mind," she said brightly, "I'll make you a lovely pudding for supper." I left her humming in the kitchen and, with relief, set off at a run along the cliff path. The lighthouse would just have to look after itself.

'The sky was pearly, washed with pink and purple. When I reached the top of the cliff I thought I'd lost Rocco: after all, he had quite a lead. Then, far off, I saw a faint *flash* of sun reflecting off the spyglass and realised that good fortune favoured me. I ran, moving fast to make up the time between Rocco and me. About twenty minutes later, perspiring heavily, I reached the spot where I'd last seen him and then, ten minutes later, I was just in time to see him strike purposefully north-west across the island. He must have been this way many times before: the grass was flattened, and he had chipped away scrub and branches to give him easier passage.

'The physical characteristics of the other side of the island came as a revelation to me. There was a view over the stormy 7-mile passage that separated Peketua Island from the South Island. Oddly enough, the currents must have been as rough there as they were on the seaward side of Peketua. Their eroding force had created a coastline that had collapsed into a series of offshore pinnacles and sea stacks. Thousands of seabirds, obviously nesting there, wheeled above them.

'Rocco came to a vent going down through a major fracture in the cliff; I presumed it had been created by some age-old volcanic activity. He sat there for a while, then began to look through his spyglass. I was disappointed: so he had come only to do some nature watching after all. But no, all of a sudden he began to carefully climb down a natural staircase in the cliffs. Then he disappeared.

'I made my way after him to the rocky steps. I was tempted to follow him—but what if I met him on the way back? I decided I had to bide my time and come back another day.

'But I knew, with certainty, that this *was* the island.'

CHAPTER TWENTY-SIX

Rocco and Marzelline

1.

Do you want to see a photograph of Rocco and Marzelline?

It was given to me by Donald, and must have been taken about five years after the events I'm telling you about, when Rocco left the island and began an export business in Dunedin.

The photograph was taken for the *Otago Daily Times.* It shows Rocco as a successful merchant shaking the hand of the mayor and surrounded by employees of Sonnleithner Agricultural Supplies. He is a tall, solid man, with a very serious expression, and he has what was once called a mutton-chop beard—it covers most of his lower face. What is telling, I think, is the way the other men in the picture are standing: like the mayor, they're not looking at the photographer but, rather, at Rocco. Certainly there's a softness in his eyes, but he must have been a man whose authority was respected and admired. Judging from some of his public pronouncements that I've read, pompous though they are, he had made himself into a man of influence.

Marzelline is standing in front with her father. Her back is straight, and you can just see the walking stick on which she's supporting herself. She looks as if she has taken a quick deep breath and instructed the photographer, 'Take the photograph now, sir, in case I lose my balance!' Despite the strain of maintaining the pose, Marzelline manages to look surprisingly composed, and both the camera and the man behind it are in love with her. They've organised a penumbra around her, bathing her in light. She is already other-worldly to look at, but the halo highlights her pale skin and the startling silver-blonde hair. Although the photograph is not in colour, you can tell that her eyes must indeed have been striking. And while all the men are looking at Rocco, his gaze is directed at her.

Marzelline is wearing the latest fashion, a beautiful floor-length light-coloured Victorian gown with a beaded bodice and sleeves; around her neck is a locket, tied high on her neck by a velvet ribbon. There are signs that in maturity she will incline to plumpness but at this moment she's revealed as having an unusual and singular beauty. There's something else too: a huge reservoir of strength.

Such a girl would indeed have the Walküre's cry within her.

2.

How had Rocco and Marzelline come to be in New Zealand?

To tell this story, for which Donald supplied the background, I have to remind you that the dynamic imperialism which marked the New Zealand Company's colonising zeal was not only attractive to pioneers of English, Scots and Irish extraction. By virtue of the company's efforts in Germany, two parties of German migrants were attracted to settle at its second town in Nelson.

Most of the Germans in the first party originated from the Rhenish provinces and were led by entrepreneur John Nicholas Beit, with whom they sailed from Germany in 1842 on the *St Pauli.* Beit had purchased land at Moutere for the purposes of wine production. Unfortunately, their arrival in June the following year coincided with the so-called Wairau Massacre in which, for a long time afterwards, the Ngati Toa chief Te Rauparaha was blamed for murdering a number of prominent townsmen. The incident must have caused the German settlers great anxiety: they had been motivated by economic opportunity and deep idealism—among their number were four Lutheran missionaries of the North German Missionary Society: J.H. Trost, J.W.C. Heine, J.F.C. Wohlers and J.C. Riemenschneider. Of them all, the Reverend Wohlers became the best known, labouring among Maori in the south. The last-named was, of course, the same man who later left Nelson and became Rimene of Warea.

By the way, the second German party disembarked a year later, in September 1844. They were led by Count Graf Kuno zu Ranzau and, unfortunately, *their* arrival, too, coincided with disaster: the collapse of the New Zealand Company's operations in New Zealand. Undeterred, and with better capital behind them, the immigrants established a small settlement named Ranzau and added their industry to the making of New Zealand.

Rocco Sonnleithner came to New Zealand on the *St Pauli* with his family; he was five when they landed. When his parents moved to Ranzau he went to the Lutheran school at nearby Sarau. His love of reading developed there but he was not a good student and drifted into engineering; he worked on bridge construction in the district.

A few years later Rocco met his wife, Lotte, and they married at St Paul's Church in 1866. He could hardly credit his good fortune: although she was almost ten years older, a schoolteacher in her mid-thirties, she was regarded as a classic beauty. 'What do you see in me?' he asked her. She replied, 'A good man, hard-working, who will make a good father.' The truth was that Lotte had had many suitors but none had been considered suitable by her repressive, cultured and sophisticated parents. Rocco was her last chance.

Because Lotte had married against her parents' wishes, there was a falling out. 'You will either accept my husband,' Lotte told them, 'or that will be the end between us.' Not even her pregnancy appeared to change her mother and father's view of the marriage, so Rocco decided to leave Ranzau and seek his fortune on the goldfields of Central Otago. He tried to convince Lotte to stay with her parents in Ranzau, but she had had enough. 'They have already turned their backs on us,' she said.

Marzelline was born while her parents were panning for gold. From the moment Lotte and Rocco saw their daughter, they were struck by love for her. Lotte had the child she had always craved. As for Rocco, he never ceased to wonder that such a daughter could be the product of loins as rude and ugly as his.

3.

Let me go back to Erenora now.

'As it happened,' she wrote, 'my intention to explore the place where Rocco had disappeared was both thwarted and, ironically, propelled by the arrival of the *Anna Milder* on its monthly visit. I was pleased to see Captain Demmer but I felt some frustration that time would be taken up with unloading the provisions that had come with him.

'"How is Herr Sonnleithner treating you, lad?" Captain Demmer asked. I told him, "We've reached an accommodation with each other." Even so, the captain made an offer, "If you want to come back with me, step aboard now."

'I shook my head. How could I do that? I was so near to discovering whether Horitana was here. Then Captain Demmer put a hand in his breast pocket and brought out an envelope. "I have a letter for you," he said to Rocco. At the sight of its seal, Rocco's face drained of colour.'

After the *Anna Milder* had been unloaded and made her way from Peketua Island, Erenora took a rest in the barn. When she looked into a mirror she saw that her hair was getting long and decided to cut it before dinner.

'I was at this task when Marzelline found me. "Would you let me do it?" she asked, her eyes shining. "I trim Papa's beard and what remains of the hair on his head. Please, Eruera, please!" She was so insistent that I said yes.

'At the end of the haircut Marzelline gathered the tresses in her palms and brought them to her lips. "Mmmmn, your hair smells beautiful," she said. Then, just before she left, she asked me a very strange question. "Eruera, do you think I am pretty?" In her voice was all the yearning for affirmation felt by a young girl who does not know that she is, yes, lovely. I wanted to say, "Yes, you're pretty, Marzelline, and some day some fortunate young man will come along and take you away with him." But before I could do that she gave a gasp of horror as if she had un-masked something about herself she had not intend-ed—or was frightened that I might say something she did not want to hear. "No, Jüngling, don't tell me!"

'She opened the door and stumbled back to the cottage.'

That evening, at dinner, it seemed that everyone was agitated for one reason or another. Among the provisions landed was a very fine bottle of brandy. Despite Marzelline's remonstrations—'Papa, wait until after dinner,'—Rocco started drinking immediately after the *Anna Milder* left the quay.

By the time the meal had been served, he was already stupefied with liquor. He began to sing a drunken ditty.

> *Hat man nicht auch Gold beineben, kann man nicht ganz glücklich sein—*

Rocco was also smoking a cigar, waving it around in the air and sprinkling ash all over the food. In a temper, Marzelline pulled the cigar from his mouth and threw it out the window.

'Du kannst gehen,' she told him. 'Geh! You can go, now, and smoke your stinking cigars in your lighthouse.' She turned on Erenora, her temper overflowing with some imagined slight. 'And you too, Jüngling, geh doch! I wish I'd never met you.'

The atmosphere was so strained that escaping it was a relief. Erenora went to the barn where, for want of something to do, she began to groom Napoleon. Afterwards, she climbed to the loft. From her window she could see the light in Marzelline's bedroom and, on the lighthouse's platform was Rocco, singing his drunken heart out.

> *Traurig schleppt sich fort das Leben, Mancher Kummer stellt sich ein—*

Suddenly Rocco gave a yelp; the sound of a crash followed. Rushing outside, Erenora saw that Rocco had tripped and fallen on the platform.

Marzelline opened her window. 'I don't care if Papa is hurt. He can stay in the lighthouse for all I care.' Slam.

Erenora sped to the lighthouse, climbed to the third storey and saw, with relief, that Rocco was okay. He had managed to sit up and when Erenora tried to persuade him to go inside, pushed her away. By now he was maudlin. 'I don't want you. I want my Liebling ... meinen Liebling...' He looked at Erenora and pulled her close. 'My Liebling ... such a beautiful baby...' His breath was reeking with alcohol. 'What happened to her was all my fault...'

Then Rocco told Erenora how Marzelline came to be crippled.

4.

Rocco was on top of the world.

He had been panning the Shotover River for a year, drawn to his particular claim by the story of two Maori who had found gold nearby. One was a renowned swimmer who dived in to rescue his dog on the opposite bank. Where the dog was, the Maori also found gold, and he took 300 ounces in one afternoon. The location was forever after known as Maori Point.

Rocco's own pannings were not as substantial but they were sufficient enough for him to take a trip, every now and then, to Charlestown at nearby Skippers Canyon. There, the gold was weighed at the assayer's office and a note issued for him to deposit in the bank. He wasn't like other men, greedy for wealth; very soon he planned to sell the claim to someone else and take Lotte back to Ranzau. 'Perhaps your parents will welcome us back, now that I am a man of means,' he told her.

'No, Rocco,' she answered, 'the fault was never yours. It was mine for choosing to leave them.'

Nevertheless, Rocco was determined to try for reconciliation with Lotte's parents. After all, they had a granddaughter now.

> *Doch wenn's in den Taschen fein klinget und rollt, Da hält man das Schicksal gefangen—*

Whenever Rocco went into town, Lotte always accompanied him. It was the middle of autumn, and Charlestown was loud and busy. Rocco was delighted at the price he was offered for his gold dust. He set about replenishing his supplies and joined a few other miners who were drinking at one of the pubs. When he rejoined Lotte, he was filled with love at her own delight: at the local dry goods store she had found some pretty fabric to make into a skirt for herself and a matching one for Marzelline. 'And I found these for you, Rocco,' she told him as she showed him two cigars.

Rocco saw that the sky was changing colour, blanched, as if it was about to faint. He had left their departure a little late. 'We had better head home,' he said. Marzelline was sleeping, so Lotte placed her in blankets on the buckboard and stepped up on the cart beside Rocco.

As they drove out of town, Lotte told Rocco, 'I have a good husband and a lovely child. No woman could want more in her life.' She threaded an arm in his.

Macht und Liebe verschafft dir das gold,
Und stillet das kuhnste Verlangen—

It was a blessed afternoon and the trees were ablaze with red and golden leaves. Rocco, however, was somewhat disconcerted by the weather. The air had dried out, as if sucked of moisture, and the sky had now turned a virulent white. There was a lot of static in the atmosphere and even the two horses were becoming skittish.

It all happened so quickly. One of the wheels dropped off the cart; it tipped, dragging the rear axle, and Lotte almost tumbled out. She gave a little squeal and then a laugh, 'What's happening?' She heard Marzelline crying. 'Have you had a fright, Liebling?' she smiled. While Rocco brought the horses to a halt, she climbed carefully over the seat to comfort her daughter.

The cart had come to rest on a bluff overlooking the river. The road wound around the cliff and, in the distance, Rocco could see his claim. Humming, he stepped down, preparing to prop up the axle and repair the wheel.

The lightning came from nowhere. The air crackled and danced all around the cart, sparking along the iron frame, traces and even the hooves of the horses. The animals took fright and bolted. 'Nein,' Rocco screamed, 'Nein.' He began to pursue the runaway cart, glimpsing Lotte's frightened face as she held Marzelline in her arms. 'Rocco? Rocco!'

There was a corner ahead. The horses, blinded by the lightning, went straight over the edge of the cliff, dragging the cart with them.

For a moment there was silence. The sun came out, flooding the landscape with golden light. A bird even began to sing. And then, faintly, Rocco heard Lotte calling, far away, and he stumbled to the cliff and looked down. The cart had come to rest at the edge of the river. One of the horses had broken its neck in the fall. The other was still in the traces, kicking and trying to get up.

'Oh, Lotte,' Rocco whimpered. He clambered and fell down the incline. The cart was lying on top of her and Marzelline. Where he got the strength from he didn't know but as he pulled the cart off his beloved wife she gave a gasp and blood poured from her mouth. She coughed, labouring to breathe, and words struggled up from her throat, 'Is Marzelline all right?'

The little girl was unconscious, but breathing—and her legs were crushed.

Tears shone in Lotte's eyes. 'I thought I would be here to look after you both always,' she wept.

Every word was accompanied by a small gout of blood. 'I thought I...' She was desperate to say more, but the blood was in the way. Rocco was looking into her eyes when she sighed, and then she was gone.

Rocco unhitched the remaining horse, wrapped Marzelline in her blanket and rode as fast as he could back to Skippers. The doctor took one look at her legs and said, 'I will have to take them off at the knees.'

The next day, Rocco buried Lotte in the cemetery in the town. There weren't many mourners: the doctor and his wife, a scattering of townspeople who came out of respect. The afternoon after the service, he signed over his claim to a neighbouring miner. 'I don't want money for it,' he told him. When Marzelline recovered from her operation, he purchased a buggy and took her away with him.

So Rocco's wanderings began. He decided not to return to Ranzau but instead set out for Dunedin. It was difficult for a man with a small child to find a job that suited—he wouldn't let anybody mind her. Eventually, he found the position of lighthouse keeper. This gave him the isolation he craved for himself and his daughter.

Marzelline didn't speak until she was six. When she did her first words were clear and concise. 'Wirst du mir vergeben, Papa? Will you forgive me?'

5.

Rocco's mood changed from maudlin to morose. He began to sing more wildly, the words spat out with bitterness and loathing.

> *Das Glück dient wie ein Knecht für Sold, Es ist ein schünes Ding das Gold—*

Having heard Rocco's story, Erenora was reminded of her own mother, Miriam, deprived, like Lotte Sonnleithner, of the chance to watch her daughter grow into womanhood.

Exhaustion made Rocco turn from his singing and the memories and look at Erenora. 'I am not a good man, Eruera. Because of me, my own wife died. I crippled my daughter and now ... now I am to be made complicit in something just as terrible.'

'Yes?' Erenora answered, holding her breath.

'The rumour is true,' he said. 'I am not only a lighthouse keeper, Eruera. I am also a gaoler.' He was almost asleep on his feet, groaning from drunkenness.

Erenora stifled a cry, then fiercely she began to shake him. 'You have a prisoner here?'

Rocco stirred, and shook his head to revive himself. 'I have never liked the job,' he slurred, 'but I am well paid. The man was a political agitator, one of your own kind, so that was my reason for agreeing to keep him under my care. He was shipped to the island in great secrecy. His place of incarceration is a cave by the sea, at the bottom of a cliff on the other side of Peketua. I visit him once a week to take food to him. But not for much longer.'

'What does he look like?' It was lucky that Rocco was so inebriated. One glance at Erenora, and her love and concern for Horitana would have been revealed.

'I have never seen his face,' Rocco answered, belching. 'He is padlocked into a silver *thing.* His suffering has often moved me but, after all, he must have done something really serious to merit such punishment. I am strictly forbidden to speak to him or help him. Even so, I have had some moments of weakness for the poor fellow—and I have gladly given him food and drink. It will soon be all over with him. Er sterb' in seinen Ketten. He will die in his chains.'

With a drunken gesture, Rocco gave Erenora the letter that Captain Demmer had handed to him:

I am sending a man on a chartered vessel who will take care of your prisoner. You are to give him up to my man's care. It is time for him to be added to my collection. In preparation, dig a grave for him.

The signature made Erenora gasp. *Piharo!* So he was behind Horitana's punishment.

'What is the deed the writer speaks of?' she asked Rocco.

'Although he has paid me well to guard the prisoner,' Rocco began, 'I draw the line at murder.'

'Murder?' The word froze Erenora's blood.

'For the past year he has been sweetening my position by offering me an extra purse if I kill the prisoner. In letter after letter he has ordered me to take on the job of executioner. He has fulminated against me, accusing me of lacking courage. I have refused to comply. Now he sends a cut-throat to do his purpose.'

Erenora watched Rocco as he subsided into his self-pity.

'Whatever happens will happen,' he groaned, 'and who knows when this man will come? Tomorrow or the day after? Meantime, I had better attend to the lantern.'

'No, mein Herr,' Erenora answered. 'I will take over looking after the lighthouse for the night. You go to bed.'

'Where?' Rocco asked. 'Marzelline is certain to have locked me out. By the way, she knows nothing of this. Eruera, I warn you, do not tell her. I would not want her to think less of me. I am her father, not a killer.'

'I will take you to the barn now,' Erenora nodded. 'Can you stand up?' She put her shoulders under his arms to help him. The changed position made Rocco vomit. 'Ach, I am sorry, Eruera.' But after that he was better able to stagger with her through the trapdoors and down the stairs. 'You are a good boy,' he said. 'No wonder my daughter is fond of you.'

Together, under the moonlight, they wove their way towards the barn. They paused at an outside pump where Rocco washed his face and mouth, trying to recover.

'I am sorry, Eruera,' he said.

Panting, Erenora helped him to the barn, pushed him up to the loft and put him to bed. She hoped he would soon fall asleep. She needed time to think, to come up with a plan. But in his drunken stupor, Rocco looked at her, dazed and puzzled. 'Eruera...' Before Erenora could stop him, Rocco kissed her. It was not a kiss of friendship and nor was it pleasant, tasting acrid and bitter. Propelled by some need for expiation, it was deep and long.

And moaning with sexual need and desire, Rocco began to pull Erenora down into his powerful arms.

'Nein,' she said. Her voice was sharp, like a rifle shot.

Rocco looked at her, horrified, and then fell back, dead drunk.

CHAPTER TWENTY-SEVEN

Marzelline's Diary

1.

You can understand Rocco's dilemma, can't you, eh. He had sensed Erenora's innate femininity.

As for Marzelline, was it any wonder that she had fallen in love with Eruera? She was an impressionable young girl alone on an island where the only other men had been her father and the labourers he employed to help him; none of them had been a Jüngling.

In Marzelline's diary there's an entry that shows her feelings for Eruera.

'Mir ist so wunderbar, es engt das Herz mir ein. I feel so strange, my heart is gripped. I am in love! He is the Jüngling who came to help Papa in his lighthouse duties. His name is Eruera, and he is a Maori. I wish I could draw his portrait: he is slim and has wide shoulders tapering to a small waist. He is taller than me but not as tall as Papa.

'Despite his dark colouring, Eruera is most handsome to me. He has glowing eyes and full lips and his hair is the shiniest I have ever seen on a man. O namenlose Pein! How I wish he would look kindly on me, not as a friend or as his employer's daughter but as a sweetheart.

'Does he have such thoughts for me? I must admit that there are times when he is holding me in his arms and looking into my eyes that I see ... tenderness. Die Hoffnung schon erfüllt die Brust. Hope already fills my breast with inexpressible delight! How wonderful to imagine how we could be if we were ... dare I say it ... man and wife? In the peace of quiet domesticity we would wake in each other's arms. Each day would be filled with joy and love. And the nights ... I tremble to think of the delights we would find in each other! Ja, ja, er liebt mich, es ist klar, ich werde glücklich sein.'

As for Erenora, her mind was in turmoil. In particular, she was seized with rage against Piharo.

'Monster! How my blood boils at your cruel revenge! Did not the call of pity or the voice of humanity ever touch your vicious mind?'

She began to sob, but then regained her composure. What was the use of spending precious time railing against Piharo? Gathering her strength, she drew courage from what she knew she had to do: rescue Horitana from the assassin and get him away before the chartered vessel arrived. If possible she would do it in the morning. She looked at the turbulent sea, and the dark furious night.

'Yet, though hatred and anger storm through your soul like relentless ocean waves, Piharo, in me a rainbow arches over the dark sky.'

She saw a star burst in the darkness. And now, look! It was creating a pathway through the dark.

'Come, Hope,' Erenora prayed. 'Do not forsake me. Oh, star, brighten my goal. Let me not falter. Strengthen me in my resolve, Amine.'

2.

Erenora did not know that the government had decreed the release of Te Whiti and Tohu and, therefore, of all other Parihaka prisoners. Piharo must have feared that questions would be asked about Horitana's whereabouts. It would be only a matter of time before the authorities traced him to Peketua Island.

This was why Piharo decided to send an assassin.

The next morning everyone was subdued. Rocco was groaning with a terrible headache. He heard Marzelline calling for him, 'Papa? Where are you?'

She was on her crutches and, when she saw him walking unsteadily from the barn she gave a cry of distress. 'Oh, Papa, are you all right?'

At breakfast, Marzelline was also apologetic to Erenora. 'Sometimes I can be a bad girl,' she said. When Erenora rewarded her with a smile of forgiveness Marzelline's mood immediately lightened.

Rocco was still feeling under the weather and staggered away to retch his guts out. When he returned he said, 'Eruera! What did I do last night?' He appeared to have no recollection of taking her in a passionate embrace, but he did recall showing Erenora the letter and taking her into his confidence. While Marzelline was busy in the kitchen he whispered, 'I must go to the cave this morning,' he said, 'to prepare the prisoner's grave. I am not feeling very well. Ach! It has to be done.'

'Perhaps I can help you,' Erenora suggested. 'Would that make it easier for you?' Had all her attempts at creating trust between them paid off?

Rocco hesitated for a moment, then nodded. 'Bring two shovels and a lamp.'

Erenora could hardly believe the turn of events, or conceal her impatience. Once breakfast was over, she ran to the barn to collect the grave-digging implements. Rocco was waiting for her at the door of the cottage.

Just before they left, Marzelline gave a huge cry and flung her arms around Erenora. Her eyes, so blue with the sea and sky, brimmed with tears. 'Eruera! Eruera!'

Erenora looked at her, uncomprehending, but held her tight and stroked her long, silky hair.

'I have a feeling I will never see you again,' Marzelline said plaintively. As Rocco and Erenora left, she waved from the doorway, waving, waving until they could no longer see her.

'The day turned wet and merciless. All the way across the island, the weather was stormy. Ka patupatu taku manawa, my heart was pounding with fear, joy and trepidation. I could not believe that very soon my quest for Horitana would be over. What would I do if it wasn't him? It had to be him!

'I was carrying the two shovels and Rocco the lantern. As we leaned into the driving wind, Rocco shouted instructions. "The prisoner is chained but his hearing is acute. Do not step too close to him, and on no account are you to utter a word to him. When I tell you to dig, do so."

'We came to the top of the cliff. From there I could see the wild ocean roaring through the passage. Seabirds were riding on the stormy winds above, crying across the clouded vault of the sky. Rocco motioned me towards the cliff where I saw the steep set of steps. Oh, wilful Fate! If I had been behind him, I could have pushed him and he would have pitched headlong in a long helpless fall to the sea far below. But the opportunity was lost ... and I would have to bide my time.

'Halfway down the steps I saw the entrance to a shaft. A sense of dread overcame me when I saw the door, which had a grille in it. As Rocco opened it my heart heaved with anticipation and fear. I swayed, almost fainting.

'"Come inside," Rocco said.

'For a moment I was overcome by a gust of foetid wind that came up from the cave. I went through and, on the other side, rested against the wall of the shaft, waiting for my vision to adjust to the gloom. I saw that Rocco had cut a staircase to enable our safe descent. "How cold it feels," I shivered. Rocco, oblivious, had descended.

'Taking a deep breath, I followed him. The steps were dangerous and wet. Moss lined the sides all the way down. With shock I had a hideous realisation: I had come to dig the grave of my husband. If I did not succeed in rescuing him, it would indeed become the place where he would be laid in the earth.

'"Stop," Rocco ordered. We had reached the bottom of the staircase where there was complete blackness. The unbearable stench of animal urine, excreta and putrefaction almost suffocated me. Every now and then came the low boom and hiss of the sea and the crunch of pebbles shifting in the eddying currents, but no amount of sluicing by the sea would ever cleanse the underground latrine. Then Rocco lit the wick in the lantern. It flared in the dark...

'And I saw the prisoner.'

3.

Erenora stifled a cry. The rumour was true:
Te tangata mokomokai.

He was chained to a post in the middle of the cave. Was he man or beast? His head looked like some corroded *thing* and he was cloaked with...

Erenora gave an involuntary gasp as the cloak *moved.* She saw then the tuatara that clothed the prisoner's body, holding on with their claws, their bellies pulsating against his skin. As soon as they saw the light of the lantern, they began to slip away from him until the floor of the cave was *seething* with more than a hundred tuatara, like a grey, writhing carpet piled at the prisoner's feet.

'Vielleicht ist er tot?' Rocco muttered. 'Perhaps he is dead already?' He lit a firebrand on the wall to give further light in the darkness. He bade Erenora follow him across the floor of the cave.

Their footsteps were loud on the gravel. The tuatara slid away from the sound.

'Was this the moment that I should kill Rocco?' Erenora wrote. 'I raised my shovel to strike him down but...'

The prisoner spoke in the darkness. His voice was muffled. Erenora could not recognise it.

Who has arrived to visit me?' He sniffed the air. 'Ah, it is my old friend, my gaoler. But surely you come out of time?'

Erenora's heart filled with aro'a. She could not resist giving a small cry and, immediately, Horitana was alert, straining at his chains. 'Who is that? Gaoler, who have you brought with you? Why won't you speak to me?'

Rocco motioned to Erenora to back away beyond the reach of Horitana's chains. He kicked at the floor of the cave until he found a spot where the gravel appeared soft. 'Eruera, dig,' he ordered.

At the sound of the shovel, Horitana rushed toward Erenora. His chains prevented him from coming further and he gave a cry of pain. 'Who are you? Speak to me, please, let me hear the sound of a human voice. Take pity. Speak. Korero mai.'

Erenora went to respond but Rocco put a hand over her mouth. 'No. Keep digging.'

And Horitana exhaled a deep sigh. 'At long last, death? I thank you, gaoler. But am I not to have a final meal before you kill me? No?'

The tuatara were circling back to him. 'It sounds as though I will be leaving you all soon,' he said to them. 'Who will look after you when I am gone?' He called to Rocco, 'Hey, gaoler, I will save you all your labour. After you kill me, leave my body to be feasted on by my friends.'

Suddenly, Rocco gave a cry. 'O, armer Mann.' He threw his shovel to one side.

'I had been wondering how I could overpower Rocco,' Erenora wrote, 'when I saw him turning away, his back to me. This was it.'

With a hoarse, guttural moan, Erenora raised her shovel. Screaming for release, she brought it down on Rocco's head.

He collapsed, stunned. 'Eruera, have you gone mad?'

'There was blood on his head and shoulders and arms,' Erenora wrote. 'I was screaming and screaming, and the prisoner in his mokomokai was wailing and the tuatara were slithering all over the cave, climbing the rocky walls, trying to get away. But then—'

Erenora began to sob. She put her shovel down.

'I can't do it,' she said to Rocco. 'I can't stop a murder by committing a murder.'

She thought of her mother, Miriam, killed so long ago in Warea. *Mama, kei w'ea koe?*

She looked at Rocco, tears streaming down her eyes. 'And I can't make an orphan of a young girl who lost her mother, by killing her father.'

She knelt on the ground. 'Mein Herr,' she wept, 'I place my life and the life of my husband in your hands.'

4.

Rocco gave a cry. 'I knew it,' he said. 'I knew the emotions I had for you were those of a man for a woman. What is your name?'

'It is Erenora.'

Rocco gave a gasp. 'And the prisoner ... you say he is your husband?'

Erenora nodded her head hopelessly. 'I have been looking for him for a long time. Even just to spend some last moments with him, to touch his face, to caress his skin, to hold him, has made my search for him worthwhile.'

Oh, even wounded Rocco could have overpowered Erenora easily enough. He could have bound her so that when the assassin arrived he would have two victims, not one, to dispose of. But Rocco had already come to his own decision:

'*O, armer Mann,*' he had said when he threw down his shovel. 'Oh, you poor man.'

'I don't know how long I lay weeping.

'Rocco had become silent but the prisoner was agitated. "Taku 'oa wa'ine? My wife? Is she here like an angel to escort me to heaven?"

'Then Rocco spoke to me. His voice was hoarse but the accustomed gruffness had gone. "Welch unerhörter Mut, Erenora," he said with wonder, "what unheard of courage." His voice softened further, as if peace was coming to his soul; all this time he had been greatly troubled by his conscience about the prisoner and now he was being delivered from it. "I cannot believe that a woman as you," he continued, "would go to such lengths to save a criminal with blood on his hands. In my heart of hearts I have suspected this accusation wasn't true. And now, Erenora, you are willing to sacrifice yourself and him to me and place yourselves at my mercy? That only confirms your and the prisoner's goodness."

'He helped me up and smiled gently. "Your husband has suffered long enough. Perhaps he will forgive me for my role as his gaoler. Here is the key."

'All I could do was sob as Rocco put the key into my hands. And then I tried to put the key into the padlock of the mokomokai. Aue, after all these years the padlock had rusted. With a cry of frustration I

338

pushed Horitana against the rocks and, taking up my shovel again, struck the padlock.'

The sound boomed and echoed around the cave, but the deed was done. The tuatara disappeared into the gloom.

'No, wait,' Horitana said.

Erenora looked at the man in the mask. He was panting, holding tightly to the pole, whimpering.

'I have lived so long in the mokomokai,' he said. 'It has been like an old friend. Let me say goodbye to it.' He began to caress it with tenderness, and then he gave a sigh of acceptance.

'And now, you who have come to release me of it, lift it off my shoulders.'

Erenora put her fingers under the rim.

'I took off the mokomokai.'

And Horitana gave a huge, painful sob.

At the final moment when the prisoner's face was revealed, Erenora became afraid. Again the same doubt: What if it wasn't Horitana?

His face was entirely covered by a thick beard and his hair was long, lank. The skin beneath was pale, scabrous and scaly. He would not look up. He buried his face in his hands.

'Horitana?'

At the sound of Erenora's voice, the prisoner pushed the hair out of his eyes. He gave a cry as the light from the grille of the doorway beat down upon his face and he reeled away from her. 'Is it really you, Erenora, here? Oh Lord of Heaven, why do you punish me so?' He was shielding his eyes.

Erenora took a few steps after him but he pushed her away. 'You're not dreaming. I am here.'

He cried out again, 'Erenora?' and he looked at his hands. 'You, the first person I have touched in three years ... and I push you away?' He collapsed onto the floor.

All Erenora could think of was that he could not recognise her. 'My hair will grow again,' she said.

Then she realised that Horitana was blind.

Did that matter? Horitana and Erenora embraced each other tenderly. In that second touch of skin on skin, Horitana knew it truly was her.

'We have met again in darkness,' he said as he pulled her forehead close to his. 'The first time was when we were together in the darkest pit at Warea. The second came when you rescued me from the dead in the trenches, and now you descend into the darkness to me again. You, my courageous wife.'

Erenora pressed her nose against his and, oh, it was as if all the years melted away. Her heart, how it fluttered, ka patupatu tana manawa.

'I am sorry it has taken me so long to find you,' she answered, brushing away their tears. ''oki mai taua ki te Ao marama. Let us return now to the world of light.'

With Rocco's help, Erenora guided Horitana from the cave where he had lived for so long. But at the threshold, the opening to the outer world, he backed away, crying, 'The *sun...*' Erenora ripped off her sleeves and bandaged Horitana's head.

Only then did they leave the darkness.

Just in time. On the horizon was a ship.

As fast as he could, his head aching, Rocco hastened them down to a cove. 'Wait here,' he said. 'Hide and, later, I will bring the skiff.'

'How will you explain to the executioner?' Erenora was panicking. 'When you take him to the empty cave he will know Horitana has escaped, and will come looking for him.'

'I will tell him that Horitana overpowered me today but I was able to fend him off ... and a wave, rushing into the cave, swept him away,' Rocco answered.

'He will want to see the body.' Erenora could not quite believe that they would get away with it.

'That will not be possible,' Rocco said. 'The currents ... there's a storm coming too ... the tide will have taken him miles away by now.'

'But he will find the mokomokai in the cave,' Erenora answered, 'and realise that your story wasn't true.'

'You must go back and get it,' Rocco said firmly. 'There is time.'

With a sigh Erenora made herself believe Rocco's story. 'But what about Marzelline?' she continued. 'When I don't return with you...'

'I will not destroy her girlish dreams,' Rocco answered. 'I will tell her there was an accident when you and I were returning from the cliffs. I tripped and would have fallen over. You reached out your hand, saved me, but at the expense of your own life. You pitched headlong onto the rocks below. Nobody would have survived the fall.' He was in a hurry now. 'Geh, Eruera, leb wohl,' he said. 'Goodbye.'

Erenora took a deep breath: yes, it could work.

She gave Rocco a grateful look, and then spoke again. 'Mein Herr, you must take your daughter back into the world.'

Rocco's eyes widened and he shook his head. 'Nein! Nein! She would know only heartache. Would a man ever look her way? Knowing that she is a cripple? No. I do not want Marzelline to experience the world's cruelty.'

'You are wrong. ' Erenora took his hands in hers. 'You must take the chance. Your daughter is stronger than you think. Give her the opportunity to *live.*'

And Rocco finally admitted the truth about his fears.

'What if I lose her ... as I did her mother?'

CHAPTER TWENTY-EIGHT

A World Saturated in the Divine

1.

Well, time to tie up the loose ends, eh?

While Erenora was away from Parihaka, William Hiroki—the Maori who had killed a surveyor named McLean and sought protection from Te Whiti—was hanged. His trial had begun on 3 May 1882, and he was found guilty of murder and sentenced to death at 8 a.m. on 8 June 1882.

Te Whiti and Tohu were shipped from Wellington to Addington Gaol in Christchurch, arriving there on the government steamer *Hinemoa* on 27 April 1882. Regarded as prisoners at large, they were shown the Canterbury Museum and the Kaiapoi Woollen Mills, the Christchurch Railway Workshops and the telephone exchange. When asked what he thought of these wonders, Te Whiti answered that he thought the Pakeha had some useful technology but so did the Maori.

The prophet leaders were moved throughout the South Island to Timaru, Dunedin, Invercargill, Bluff, Queenstown and Oamaru. Wherever he went Te Whiti was called 'The Lion of Parihaka' and attracted a large following; some he regarded as nga tangata tutua, ill-mannered. No matter the hospitality, Te Whiti always asked why he had not yet had a trial.

The visit to Dunedin is of special interest. Escorted by their gaoler, John Ward, the two prophets stayed at the Universal Hotel. While there the two prophets were guests at the Kai Tahu meeting house—Te Wai Pounamu—at what was known as Otakou Kaik (a Pakeha contraction of the Maori word Kaika), a couple of miles past Port Chalmers. The house was associated with the well-known local Ellison family, who had so kindly assisted the first prisoners from South Taranaki nine years earlier. Their journey to the Kaik was to visit their kinsman and relative, Raniera Erihana—Dan Ellison—whose wife, Nani Weller, was from Kai Tahu.

Te Whiti and Tohu ended their travels around the South Island at Nelson, where they were placed under house arrest for eight months. In October 1882, a comet illuminated the sky each evening. I wonder what interpretation Te Whiti made of the comet's appearance, he whose name meant 'The Shining Path of the Comet'? The thought haunts me: I can imagine him staring up at that apparition, his face impassive as he watches the comet opening all heaven's gates, listening to the music of the universe and seeking divination.

Then, in 1883, Te Whiti and Tohu were told that the government was burying the past and letting them go back to Parihaka as free men. Te Whiti was not persuaded. 'If the grasshoppers find good new grass, they will come,' he said. 'Nothing will prevent them.'

On 9 March the prophets saw their beloved Taranaki Mountain from the deck of a government steamer. The dawn came up and, behold, the mounga began to *shine* with the promise of a new day. Although they were home, however, the government extended the legislation to restrain them for another year; if they kicked up any fuss they could be arrested again.

Their return signalled the further release of hundreds of the Parihaka ploughmen, fencers and farmers still in South Island gaols. Gradually those who had been freed began to arrive back at the kainga. A poi song was composed to honour Te Whiti:

'Tangi a taku i'u e w'akamaru ana ko au pea e ... My sorrow is ended now that I may stand with you, the bargeboard of our house Miti Mai Te Arero ... Here the white feather is in its place—'

Harry Atkinson was still around to harass them. He was back as premier for three further terms before finally being ousted in 1891 by John Ballance and the Liberals, the first organised political party in New Zealand.

2.

From the time Erenora had begun her quest, it had taken her two years to find Horitana. They returned to Taranaki at the beginning of 1884. I wish that her unpublished manuscript was intact because it would have given us clues as to her remarkable journey bringing Horitana home. All I have are local South Island Maori sightings and stories that tell of a young Maori—some say a young man, others a woman—leading a blind man northward from Peketua Island to Dunedin and Christchurch and thence, with the aid of Archdeacon Cotterill, by ship to the North Island.

I can imagine them both, approaching Parihaka, and the tataraki'i, sensing their arrival, beginning to open their shimmering wings, whirring in the dazzling sunlight, whirr, whirr, *whirr.*

Erenora was overjoyed to see Ripeka and Meri. Ripeka was the mother of a son she was passing off to everyone as Paora's; Meri and Riki's son, Kawa, was now a boisterous little boy who loved to watch his mother swinging her poi.

'You got back safely,' Erenora exclaimed. 'Ever since we parted, I've been so worried about you both. If anything had happened to you, I...'

The two sisters looked at each other. 'She never thinks we can do anything without her,' Ripeka sighed. 'She forgets we are women of Parihaka.'

Although they made light of their odyssey, let me tell you that Ripeka, Meri and Erenora were not the only Parihaka women who made remarkable journeys to the South Island looking for their men.

Some, dangerously, set out alone and never returned. Happily, Horitana gradually regained sufficient sight to be independent, although he could never go out into the strong light for too long. There were many hot sunny Taranaki days when he preferred to stay inside in the cool, quiet and dark. He bore, for the rest of his life, the scars on his shoulders where the mask had rested. The experience of having spent so long in the damp cave never left him; no matter how valiant his heart, its rhythm was forever weakened, and he was plagued with breathing problems and rheumatism. And sometimes he would murmur softly in his sleep, in a loving way, and stroke the air delicately with his fingers. Erenora was puzzled until he explained:

'It is just my little tuatara family. They come to me in my dreams and like to nestle against my skin.'

3.

One day Erenora saw Piharo. Although Horitana's sentence was no longer in force, Piharo still had power and might continue his vendetta against him. She had also heard that Piharo had a reward posted for any Maori to advise him of her own return.

After brooding for a week, Erenora realised that the time had come to pay Piharo a visit. She risked discovery by riding through the twilight, hoping she would not be seen, and making a reconnaissance of the substantial house that he had built: stone and brick, paved with Italian tiles and filled with chandeliers and other sumptuous objets d'art. Even the garden had been finished, with a maze and fountain in the middle of it, appearing as if it had always been there.

The purpose of her visit? In her heart of hearts she would have dearly liked to meet him, persuade him to let bygones be bygones and to cease his vendetta, but she knew he would never do that. In her darkest despair, she thought of killing him, stealing into his bedroom while he slept, but that would lead to a hunt for the murderer—and, anyway, she couldn't take another person's life, even Piharo's. Such an act would have undone everything that Te Whiti stood for, all the suffering his followers had gone through in the name of peaceful protest.

She therefore decided on teaching Piharo a lesson of such power that it might dissuade him from visiting any further vengeance upon herself and Horitana. But how could she gain entry during the day when his farm manager, labourers and servants surrounded him? Even during the evenings there was always candlelight in his bedroom. Did Piharo never sleep?

Erenora could wait no longer. During a bitter cold night filled with a blizzard off the sea, she rode to Piharo's house again. Shouldering the knapsack she had brought with her, she moved swiftly through a grove of trees at the back of the building. Branches were being flung into the air and the darkness was filled with calling moreporks. The storm made it easier for her to enter unheard through the rear terrace windows. Once inside she made her way up the staircase and stepped into Piharo's bedroom. It was ablaze with flickering candles, so many of them. How could Piharo sleep with so much light? And yet he did, his eyes shut tight.

He had been reading an elegant volume of poetry. He looked so harmless, his chest rising and falling, yet this man was filled with malevolence.

Erenora gently prised the book from his grasp and went to work.

Piharo tossed and turned in his sleep. He dreamt that spiders were crawling over him and woke up to find that he was already restrained by Erenora's ropes.

'I hear you've been trying to find me,' Erenora said. 'I decided to save you the trouble by coming myself.'

Piharo tried to shout for help but it was too late; Erenora placed a kerchief around his mouth and tied it tight. 'I don't plan to kill you,' she said. 'After all, if I did that I wouldn't join Horitana in heaven when we die.'

Erenora moved around the room, cupping the flames of the candles and blowing sharply on them. As each one was snuffed out, Piharo began to moan. The smoke from the candles drifted in the air. She left two alight so that she could see what she was doing—and opened the knapsack. In it was something heavy and monstrous.

'In Maoridom,' she said, 'we always say that you must be careful of any evil you do lest it be returned unto you.'

Piharo's eyes spilled with tears of terror when he saw the silver mokomokai he himself had designed. His heart began to race and, by the time Erenora lifted his head from the pillow to padlock the mokomokai to him he was in a catatonic state. Even so, he formulated in his head three words:

'No, please don't...'

Erenora blew out the first remaining candle. She was not to know that Piharo had a particular affliction, claustrophobia, nor that he was afraid of the dark. Then she blew out the second flame.

'... not eternal darkness...'

He was dead when his servant found him the next morning.

4.

Erenora and Horitana helped Te Whiti and Tohu to repair the village that John Bryce had desecrated. They were happy and God smiled on them: they had four children.

My w'akapapa goes back to the second boy, Whatarangi.

In 1886, Te Whiti began a new ploughing campaign; he had already resumed the 18th of the month meetings. Despite his limited sight, Horitana led the ploughmen as he had done in earlier days. Te Whiti was gaoled, along with Titokowaru. Oh, this is another story that would make you weep: for instance, during the imprisonment, Hikurangi, Te Whiti's wife died and he was not allowed to return for her tangi'anga.

Following the imprisonment, Te Whiti and Tohu, with the help of a man named Charlie Waitara, using Maori money, added gas lighting to Parihaka, many fine European-style buildings, a water supply and a metalled road. Dan Ellison continued his visits from the South Island and also subsidised the rehabilitation of the kainga from his own pocket.

One of the great glories of Parihaka became its fine orchestral marching band, playing triumphant fifes, trumpets and drums at tribal gatherings.

On 18 June 1888, the great militarist Titokowaru died. Even so he prophesied, 'I shall not die, I shall not die. When death itself is dead, I shall be alive.'

Incredibly it was not until 12 July 1898 that the last of the Parihaka prisoners returned home to the kainga, bringing to a close nineteen years of imprisonment of Parihaka men, some of whom had been only boys when they were exiled.

Meanwhile, all John Bryce's kereru were coming home to roost. In 1886, he took the historian G.W. Rusden, whose work has been quoted in Erenora's story, all the way to the High Court of Justice in London in one of the most famous libel cases in New Zealand. Specifically, Bryce contested the report in Rusden's three-volume history of what had happened in 1868, during Titokowaru's War, when the Kai-Iwi Yeomanry Cavalry unit attacked Hauhau warriors. Rusden had included women and children in the incident; Bryce denied direct involvement.

Bryce may have won the case but for the rest of his life he fought a rearguard action on his crumbling reputation. In 1903, possibly still seeking approval from New Zealanders, he wrote, 'With the feet of 20th century tourists on the very summit of the mountain, we may well hope that the occult and malign spirits will now retire into a necromantic night and trouble the sunshine no more.'

He still hadn't got it.

EPILOGUE

Always the Mountain

CHAPTER TWENTY-NINE

The Radiance of Feathers

1.

Glory to God in the highest, and on earth peace, good will toward men.

And to women, too. There's not much more to tell you.

Tohu Kaakahi died on 4 February 1907. Mourners tell of the coming of a cloud in the shape of a waka, with a solitary paddler, which, when it arrived above the marae, stayed for the entire tangi'anga.

Te Whiti died nine months later, on 18 November. How significant that his death came a few hours after the special Sabbath he had instituted some forty years before. Mourners both Maori and Pakeha travelled to Parihaka to pay tribute to him as he lay within a radiant penumbra of white albatross feathers. Taare Waitara, who delivered the eulogy, said:

'Let this be clearly understood by all Maoris, Pakehas and all other nations. The white feather is a sign that all nations of the world will be one, black, red and all others who are called human beings. This feather will be the sign of unity, prosperity, peace and goodwill.'

So far in this story I have resisted drawing the parallel between Te Whiti and the great Indian statesman, Mahatma Gandhi, whose methods of passive resistance gained acclaim some years later. Gandhi knew of the Parihaka story through Irish leaders who had visited New Zealand raising money and support for the Irish Home Rule movement; he came into contact with them when he was on a visit to London.

With pride, I make the connection now.

A few years later, Erenora's adoptive mother, Huhana, died at Warea.

The one compensation for that sadness was that on their way back from the tangi Erenora saw five of the bullocks which the constabulary had earlier herded away from Parihaka before Erenora had shot their companions; they were being taken to the knacker's yard. Of course they were very old now, but they knew her still. Erenora paid top money to save them.

After all, they had been her beloved companions.

Loving till the last, Huhana had left Erenora her little patch of land with a small w'are on it, a cow bail, hens and a vegetable garden. It was the place where Erenora had been born and grew up and, although she and Horitana were sad to leave Parihaka, they decided to take the children there. One bright

354

day they set off, herding the bullocks before them. They remained there until the end of their lives.

It belongs to me and Josie now. Every summer we like to close our bungalow in New Plymouth and spend time on that ancestral land with all its memories. We'll never sell it.

Never.

In 1913 John Bryce died, and then the Great War began in the Northern Hemisphere and, well, that took the attention of New Zealand away from domestic matters.

As for Parihaka, Te Whiti had prophesied that it would progress through three stages before the arrival of Aranga, the day of resurrection and harvest. He added, 'Those who are bent by the wind shall rise again when the wind softens.'

I like to think that Aranga, the day of resurrection and harvest, has arrived.

Indeed, Horitana himself took on this symbolism to explain to Erenora how he had managed to survive his terrible ordeal of the mokomokai and imprisonment. 'I always lived in hope,' he said, 'and when I was brought before the court that was my day of betrayal. The placing of the mokomokai over my face, on that day I died. Then you came and resurrected me. The rest of our lives will be our harvest.'

As for our mountain, the New Zealand Geographic Board decreed in the 1980s that it could be called either Egmont or Taranaki. I'm happy to say that both Pakeha and Maori prefer to call the mounga Taranaki rather than using the name of a man who never visited New Zealand.

Doesn't Taranaki look beautiful in the twilight? Look at how it is *shining!* And below it is Parihaka, triumphant, clustered around the three main houses of Toroanui, Te Paepae o te Raukura and Te Niho o Te Ati Awa.

Stand on, oh great houses, stand always, stand forever.

The mountain has seen it all. People around here always say that if you want to know what happened, ask the mountain.

2.

But ... you should always leave the best for the last, eh?

A few months ago I paid a visit to Donald Sonnleithner. Josie and I went down to Dunedin with three busloads of descendants of the eighteen prisoners from South Taranaki who had died there. It was local historian Denis Harold who had some years earlier discovered the men's burial places and, ever since then, there have been visits to the graves to remind the men that they are not forgotten—nor their connections with Pakakohe and Patea. One of those visits included Bill Dacker and writer Jacquie Sturm—one of the prisoners had been an ancestor of hers—and Janet Frame was with her.

Anyway, on the recent visit—Sir Paul Reeves was with us—we unveiled a memorial and, afterwards, I gave Donald a call to invite myself over for a glass of wine from his fine cellar. He had a lovely warm fire going in the living room and, very soon, between sips of wine, he began to tell me what happened to Rocco and Marzelline following Erenora's escape with Horitana from Peketua Island.

I say 'escape' but, of course, Marzelline didn't know this. She thought that Eruera had died on the island and, in her diary, she simply writes:

'Der Jüngling ist tot.'

You can imagine how difficult it was, therefore, to hear Donald on that wintry evening, telling me of Marzelline's grief when Rocco told her Eruera had drowned.

'She insisted on searching the coast,' he said.

I nodded, thinking that when Marzelline didn't find his body, she surely must have uttered her Walküre cry. If ever she had found Eruera I'm sure she would have taken him proudly to Valhalla.

'Eventually,' Donald continued, 'Rocco took Marzelline away from the island and brought her to Dunedin. Here, he began a company importing agricultural machinery to New Zealand. As you can see from the house'—Donald waved his hand to take in its understated grandeur—'he became very successful. As for Great-grandmother, after all she was sixteen and she began to heal. I don't think she ever forgot Eruera but life has a habit of moving you along, doesn't it? Very soon she became immersed in Dunedin society and, when she was nineteen, she caught the eye of, and eventually married, a gentleman from Somerset called Quentin Fellowes. The marriage was, from all accounts, a happy one and from them both branched our family like a lovely spreading tree. Great-grandmother took over the importing business when Great-great grandfather took ill, and he lived with her and Quentin, delighting in his grandchildren, until the end of his life. The oldest male child of every generation has taken his surname, Sonnleithner.'

That evening, Donald and I talked further about Rocco and Marzelline. Donald regaled me with stories of his great-grandmother's beauty, charm, wit and huge business acumen. However, he had always sensed that there was more to the story of Marzelline and Eruera than was contained in her diary.

Yes, he had been patient. But this time, he *pushed* me.

'There's always been something that has puzzled me,' he began.

He got up from his chair, stoked the fire and then went to his bureau. Picking up Marzelline's diary, and nudging his reading spectacles onto the bridge of his nose, he thumbed through the pages.

'It's a diary entry from 1914, in which Marzelline mentions how, with two of their children, she and Quentin were on a motoring holiday through the North Island. They were in the Taranaki and, there, they had an interesting meeting by the side of the road...'

He began to read from the diary.

3.

Im Frühling, komm! Frühling streu ins Land deine Blüthen aus ... O springtime, come! Strew your blossoms over the land...

'It was a day in spring,' Marzelline wrote. 'How beautiful that part of the country looked! It took my breath away, with Mount Egmont cleaving the blue sky apart and the blossoms drifting across the plains.

'We were driving to New Plymouth and had just passed a small Maori farm. A man was in the field behind a plough being pulled by two bullocks. Following him was a woman whom I presumed to be his wife, bending and planting seeds in the furrows.

'Ach! Something happened to the car because, all of a sudden there was a *bang* and it stopped dead in its tracks. Of course Quentin, who was never any good at mechanical matters, tried to fix it. I had to tell him, "Be off with you and find a mechanic!" He took my remonstrations in good humour and was fast down the road. Meanwhile, I had a good novel to read and the children began to play in a nearby paddock.

'All of a sudden I saw the Maori couple coming along the road. The man must have been in his late sixties, his wife was a little younger. "Tena korua," I greeted them.

'The woman said, "Your husband called by to ask if we could look after you and your children while he was away. Well, we were just about finished the ploughing anyway and so..."

'She had a pitcher of water and she offered some to me. "Thank you," I said.

'Her smile was graceful and she hadn't really seen my face. But when I lifted the pitcher to drink, she gasped and spilled the water. She looked at me as if she were seeing a ghost. "Your eyes! They were always so blue!" I was puzzled and concerned, but she quickly covered her agitation. "It's nothing," she said.

'She gave the pitcher to her husband. "Take some water to the tamariki," she said. He nodded and went into the paddock where the children were playing. "Are you children thirsty? This is good wai, comes straight off the mountain!" He had brought a spinning top with him and he put it on the ground and showed them how to make it spin by using a whip made of flax. His wife and I stood watching him. "Your husband is so patient," I told her. She put an arm around my waist in a gesture of friendliness.

'Very soon, I saw Quentin coming back along the road in a cart with a young mechanic. Thanks goodness he hadn't had to go too far—and that nothing major had happened to the car. In those days, automobiles were rare in country areas, but at least the mechanic knew what he was doing. After a bit of tinkering, he asked Quentin to get into the driver's seat while he cranked the car. What a relief! The engine burst into life.

'"Children, quickly!" I called. They came running from the paddock. Over the loud din of the engine, Quentin tried to give the old Maori couple some money but they wouldn't hear of it. We thanked them, though. The woman reminded me of somebody. Just as we were leaving, she smiled and cried over the engine noise, "Hasn't it been lovely to spend a moment together in the sun?" Then she reached for my hand and clung to it. "Are you happy?" she asked. I was startled. "Yes, of course I am." Then she asked, "Is your father still alive?" I wondered how the kuia had known Papa. "Yes," I answered. "He was a good man," she said.

'Afterwards I wondered about her remark. More intriguing was when she cupped my face in her hands and traced my chin.

'"How pleased I am that you have found a good husband," she said. Then she kissed me lightly on the cheek.

'"Leb wohl, mein Herz. Go well, sweetheart."'

Donald put the diary down.

'You know...' he began, 'that diary entry has always puzzled the family. The Maori woman seemed to be acquainted with the lives of Marzelline and Rocco. How?'

He was looking at me, but I shrugged my shoulders and kept my silence.

Then Donald told me that at Marzelline's death a locket containing dark hair was buried with her. 'We've always believed it belonged to the Maori boy that Great-grandmother met while she was on Peketua Island with her father,' Donald said carefully.

All along I'd told Donald that I was a descendant not of Eruera but of a person whom he took to be a separate identity, Erenora. How could I tell him that Eruera hadn't been the person Marzelline thought he was? That he hadn't died?

Should I tell Donald the truth? Or should I maintain the fiction? Such a moral dilemma! Even though I was only an amateur historian, did I not owe it to history to tell the truth?

I realised that Rocco himself offered an answer. He had obviously not told his impressionable young daughter that the boy had been, in fact, a woman. Perhaps Rocco had loved Erenora also. If it was good enough for Rocco to keep the secret out of love for his daughter, I would too. And Erenora, as well, *she* had chosen not to disclose the truth when she met Marzelline on that spring day in 1914 and, as you know, I love my ancestor.

Wasn't that what history was, after all? A matter of perspective, determined by whoever told it? Even if it wasn't, surely it was better for me to leave Donald's family with the story of a Maori boy who was Marzelline's first love and, from the sound of it, had held her heart always?

Wasn't it their history, not mine?

'Well?' Donald asked. 'So who was the woman Great-grandmother Marzelline met that day?'

The coals crackled in the grate. The flames flickered and then settled into a warm glow as I told Donald the truth.

AUTHER'S NOTE

I have always loved political opera, in particular Ludwig van Beethoven's *Fidelio.* Indeed, inspired by *Fidelio,* in 1993 I wrote an opera libretto, *Erenora,* recasting Beethoven's heroine as a Maori woman.

Sixteen years later, in 2009, I began a collection of novellas called *Purity of Ice.* Realising that an opera production of *Erenora* in New Zealand was unlikely to happen, I decided to turn it into one of the novellas but giving the original libretto a preceding context: the extraordinary events of Parihaka and the exile of the prisoners of Parihaka to the South Island.

Sometimes, however, things don't turn out the way you intend them to. The novella kept on growing as I continued my exploration of the intertextual techniques, multiple narratives and perspectives that I had begun to develop in *The Trowenna Sea* (2009). In this case, I was particularly fascinated about the possibilities of further acknowledging the boundaries between fiction, history and biography by making visible historical and biographical material and using footnotes. And, of course, there were the intersections with *Fidelio* to consider.

The novella was still growing when my good friend, agent and mentor, Ray Richards, to whom this book is dedicated, finally suggested that I extract *Erenora* from the completed collection and publish it as a separate book. It became *The Parihaka Woman.*

ACKNOWLEDGEMENTS

Although *The Parihaka Woman* is, above all else, a work of imagination, I have attempted to maintain it within an accurate historical context.

For tribal aspects and oral narrative, I am particularly grateful to Ruakere Hond (Taranaki, Ngati Ruanui me Te Ati Awa) and my friend Miriama Evans (Ngati Mutunga) who advised on the Parihaka and mana wahine aspects. Aroaro Tamati (Taranaki, Ngati Ruanui and Te Ati Awa) also read the manuscript. The main texts consulted, as far as Taranaki and Parihaka are concerned, were G.W. Rusden's three-volume *History of New Zealand,* (mainly Volume 3), Chapman & Hall, 1883; and James Cowan, *The New Zealand Wars: A History of the Maori Campaigns and the Pioneering Period,* two volumes (mainly Volume 2), Government Printer, 1922–23. Now out of print, these texts were consulted at Wellington Central Library.

Other texts consulted from my own personal library for more specific detail were Dick Scott, *Ask That Mountain,* Heinemann/Southern Cross, 1975; James Belich, *Paradise Reforged: A History of the New Zealanders from the 1880s to the Year 2000,* Penguin, 2001; Hazel Riseborough, *Days of Darkness: Taranaki 1874–1884,* Penguin, 2002; Danny Keenan, *Wars Without End,* Penguin, 2009; Rachel Buchanan, *The Parihaka Album: Lest We Forget,* Huia, 2009; Kelvin Day (ed.), *Contested Ground: Te Whenua i Tohea—The Taranaki Wars 1860–1881,* Huia, 2010; Michael King,

The Penguin History of New Zealand, Penguin, 2003; Jane Reeves' essay, 'Exiled for a Cause: Maori Prisoners in Dunedin' in Michael Reilly and Jane Thomson (eds), *When the Waves Rolled In Upon Us: Essays in Nineteenth-Century Maori History* by History Honours Students University of Otago 1973–93, University of Otago Press in association with History Department, University of Otago, 1999; and Bernard Gadd's essay, 'The Teachings of Te Whiti O Rongomai, 1831 1907', in the *Journal of the Polynesian Society,* Volume 75, No.4, 1966.

Hazel Riseborough's text requires special mention. I agree completely with her approach, as articulated on p.9, that 'Archival material is a totally inadequate source from which to draw a "Maori" perspective of the Parihaka years ... What he [Te Whiti] is purported to have said, and more importantly to have meant, has come to us almost exclusively through European reporters dependent on European interpreters of varying ability and persuasion.' In her book Ms Riseborough practises what she preaches by showing admirable discipline and restraint in *not* offering too many instances of what Te Whiti said. When one couples this with the moving and generous offerings by Te Miringa Hohaia of waiata surrounding Te Whiti and Tohu, you realise how refined and layered Maori language is.

I also consulted some internet sites on Taranaki and on Te Whiti, Tohu Kaakahi and other real figures, notably the online *Dictionary of New Zealand Biogra-*

phy on teara.govt.nz and the Ministry for Culture and Heritage's NZHistory.net.nz. I apologise in advance for any omissions in acknowledging sources.

The story of Parihaka is never-ending. I look forward to the day when a son or daughter of the kainga writes with the resources available from their elders.

All errors of fact or interpretation are my own.

Special mention must be made of Te Miringa Hoha-ia, Gregory O'Brien and Lara Strongman (eds), *Pariha-ka: The Art of Passive Resistance,* City Gallery Wellington, Victoria University Press for Parihaka Trustees, 2001 (especially the essay by Hazel Riseborough). This publication, which was the joint winner in the history section of the 2001 Montana New Zealand Book Awards, accompanied the exhibition of the same name at the City Gallery, Wellington. Held between 26 August 2000 and 22 January 2001, the exhibition was the most significant event in recent years in terms of bringing the story of Parihaka before the public gaze.

The exhibition later travelled to other galleries, including the Dunedin Public Art Gallery, from 26 November 2002 to 10 February 2003, where a new component, *Te Iwi Herehere, Nga Mau Herehere Torangapu,* was added. Put together by Bill Dacker, *Te Iwi Herehere* conveyed the story of the Maori political prisoners from Taranaki in Otago 1869–1982. It was supported by the Dunedin Public Art Gallery and the Otago Settlers Museum and remains the most complete statement to date about the Otago prisoners.

Adam Gifford knocked on my door and supplied me with information on the Parihaka prisoners in Dunedin; Dick and Sue Scott read the manuscript and gave me their aroha; Bill Dacker, author of *Te Mamae me te Aroha: The Pain and the Love,* (1975) a history of Kai Tahu whanui of Otago, 1844–1994, took valuable time to generously assist with information that he could well have withheld for his own research and publications. Karin Meissenberg and Cath Koa checked the German reo to ensure that it conformed to the South German dialect of the period.

Grateful thanks to the University of Auckland for superlative support, and to Harriet Allan and her staff at Random House New Zealand. Harriet suggested that Anna Rogers edit the book and it has benefited from her painstaking editorial analysis.

I also record my gratitude for the funding support of the New Zealand Arts Foundation, 2009, Creative New Zealand Te Waka Toi, 2010 and the Premio Ostana (Italy), 2010.

Finally, I must acknowledge Te Haa o Ruhia and Turitumanareti, the dream swimmer. I thought you had left me forever, but you are beside me still.

CHAPTER NOTES

Prologue: Taranaki

CHAPTER 1: ALWAYS THE MOUNTAIN

The derivation of 'Taranaki': in Maori 'tara' means mountain peak and 'naki' is thought to come from 'ngaki' meaning 'shining'. See 'New Zealand Volcanoes', on the GNS science website,www.gns.cri.nz, accessed 19 December 2009.

Erenora is the Maori transliteration of Leonore, which is the German variant of the French Eleanor, meaning 'shining light'. Leonore is the heroine of Beethoven's only opera, *Fidelio* (Op.52), 1805–06.

The Last Samurai, Warner Brothers, 2003, was co-produced by and starred Tom Cruise and was directed by Edward Zwick. This epic film was set in the samurai culture of nineteenth-century Japan. Irony: how come the story was not set among Taranaki Maori of nineteenth-century Aotearoa? Where is Kimble Bent when you need him?

The Wiremu Kingi Te Rangitake quote, 'I have no desire for evil...' comes from G.W. Rusden, *History of New Zealand,* Chapman & Hall, 1883, Vol.1, p.631. The incident of the women facing off the surveyors was published in the *Southern Cross* and is also cited in Rusden, Vol.1, p.631.

For further reading on J.F. Riemenschneider see W. Greenwood, *Riemenschneider of Warea,* A.H. &

A.W. Reed, 1957, and T.A. Pybus, *Maori and Mission-ary: Early Christian Missions in the South Island of New Zealand,* Reed, 1954.

Act One: Daughter of Parihaka

CHAPTER 2: FLUX OF WAR

The Great Maori Land March of 1975 was led by Dame Whina Cooper (1895–1994) from Te Hapua to Wellington. The marchers arrived at Parliament on 13 October where a petition signed by 60,000 people was presented to Prime Minister Bill Rowling. The march was a defining moment in Maori history, marking a new era of Maori land rights protests, and political, economic, social and cultural activism.

Horitana is the Maori transliteration of the name Florestan, who is the hero in Beethoven's opera *Fidelio.* The Maori name should really be Horetana but I decided to be kind to readers by opting for Horitana, a name easier to look at and pronounce.

CHAPTER 3: TE MATAURANGA A TE PAKEHA

The incident of the rapa is cited by W.H. Skinner, *Pioneer Medical Men of Taranaki,1834–1880,* New Plymouth, 1933, p.94.

The description of Te Karopotinga o Taranaki is drawn from various sources, including G.W. Rusden, other texts listed and internet sources.

CHAPTER 4: OH, CLOUDS UNFOLD

The quote from the *Nelson Examiner* is cited by Dick Scott in A *sk That Mountain,* Heinemann/Southern Cross, 1975/p.23.

The physical description and biographical information about Te Whiti o Rongomai in this chapter and throughout *The Parihaka Woman,* and the physical description of Parihaka, have been primarily sourced from oral information supplied by Ruakere Hond but also from G.W. Rusden and other texts listed and internet sources.

For a more comprehensive account of Titokowaru, no more fascinating account exists than James Belich's *I Shall Not Die: Titokowaru's War, 1868–1869,* Bridget Williams Books, 1989.

The description of General Gustavus von Tempsky is based on internet sources.

CHAPTER 5: PARIHAKA

The political and social contexts for this chapter have been primarily sourced from Ruakere Hond and G.W. Rusden but also Dick Scott, Hazel Riseborough's *Days of Darkness: Taranaki 1874–1884,* Penguin, 2002, and others mentioned.

Dick Scott expanded his 1954 *Parihaka Story* into *Ask That Mountain,* published in 1975. There are also some radio items on Parihaka in New Zealand broadcasting archives, two of special interest by Haare Williams and Selwyn Murupaenga. I must not forget, either, Harry Dansey's play, *Te Raukura: The Feathers of the Albatross,* a few years later in 1974, the first published play by a Maori.

Regarding the term 'demilitarised Maori zone', Rachel Buchanan alternatively offers the wording, 'right in the middle of the confiscated zone', in her *Parihaka Album: Lest We Forget,* Huia, 2009, p.39. Take your pick.

'The ark by which' is cited in Dick Scott, *Ask That Mountain,* pp.105–06. 'What matters to us': J. Caselberg (ed.), *Maori Is My Name: Historical Maori Writings in Translation,* Dunedin, 1975, p.136, is cited in Rachel Buchanan, *The Parihaka Album,* p.26. Both utterances were made on 1 November 1881 before the invasion of Parihaka. By the way, when you are researching you come across such good old friends, now gone. It was John Caselberg who took me over to Otakou Kaik when I was Burns Fellow at the University of Otago in the 1970s.

See Te Papa-Tai Awatea/Knowledge Net for biographical information on Alfred and Walter Burton and their photo graphy firm; the photograph which the anonymous narrator describes is based on 'A Parihaka scene in the eighties', Alexander Turnbull Library, reproduced in Dick Scott, *Ask That Mountain,* p.39.

'Softly you awoke my heart' and 'And I, dearest wife': the exchanges between Erenora and Horitana are modelled after the aria, 'Mon coeur s'ouvre a ta voix', Camille Saint-Saëns, *Samson et Dalila,* libretto by Ferdinand Lemaire, 1877, Act 2, Scene 3.

CHAPTER 6: A PROPHET'S TEACHINGS

Tohu Kaakahi's haka is cited in Dick Scott, *Ask That Mountain,* p.37. Maori and English from Whatarau Ariki Wharehoka, to whom Scott dedicated his book.

'The twelve tribes of Israel' comes from the *New Zealand Herald,* 21 June 1881 and is cited in Bernard Gadd, 'The Teachings of Te Whiti O Rongomai, 1831–1907'.

'I do not care' is cited in Dick Scott, *Ask That Mountain,* p.79.

CHAPTER 7: WHAT WAS WRONG WITH A MAORI REPUBLIC?

The 1881 census statistics come from the *Auckland Star,* Issue 4109, 22 June 1881, p.3; also 'Vital Statistics for May', *Evening Post,* Vol. XXI, Issue 146, 24 June 1881, p.2.

'The land is mine...' is taken from G.W. Rusden, *History of New Zealand,* Vol.3, p.261.

One surveyor reported to the West Coast Commission Report in 1880: 'The natives came to remove my camp, and I was very much pleased with their quiet behaviour, the utmost good humour prevailing on both sides', cited in G.W. Rusden, *History of New Zealand,* Vol.3, p.260.

'Ich hab auf Gott' is from Beethoven's *Fidelio,* Act 1 trio.

Act Two: Village of God

CHAPTER 8: DO YOU KEN, JOHN BRYCE?

The description of John Bryce uses G.W. Rusden, Dick Scott and other texts listed.

For an interesting government perspective on Hiroki, see R.R Parris, Land Purchase Commissioner's supplementary report to the Under-Secretary, Native Affairs, *Appendices to the Journal of the House of Representatives,* G.I.1882, New Plymouth, 23 May 1882.

Although Erenora explains that the name Piharo is derived from the Maori word 'piharongo' (a very hard black stone used for making implements—H.W. Williams, *A Dictionary of the Maori Language,* 1957) the name is also used to maintain the parallel with Beethoven's *Fidelio.* Piharo is the Maori transliteration for Pizarro, the governor of the Spanish state prison in which Beethoven sets his opera.

Piharo's motto, 'Fais ce que voudrais', also happens to be the motto of The Hell-Fire Club: Marjie Bloy, 'The Hell Fire Club,' www.victorianweb.org. Bloy gives the motto as 'Fay ce que voudres'.

CHAPTER 9: THE YEAR OF THE PLOUGH

The main source for the historical context remains G.W. Rusden, but other important informants in constructing the context for the fiction were Ruakere Hond, Miriama Evans, Bill Dacker, Dick Scott and Hazel Riseborough.

'I want you to gather the men' is after Dick Scott, *Ask That Mountain,* p.55.

'I Te Raa o Maehe' is cited in a number of references. The full waiata is printed in Miringa Hohaia, 'Ngaa Puutaketanga Koorero Moo Parihaka', in Te Miringa Hohaia, Gregory O'Brien and Lara Strongman (eds), *Parihaka: The Art of Passive Resistance,* City Gallery Wellington, Victoria University Press, Parihaka Pa Trustees, 2001, p.48. Hohaia's use of double vowels has been retained. In his note to the song, Hohaia wrote: 'This song ... was composed by Tonga Awhikau, a returned ploughman who died in 1957 aged 104. He is remembered for leading the land struggle in the 20th century. People flocked to hear his oratorical skills and to see this charismatic tamaiti rangatira noo Taranaki (child leader of Taranaki).'

Te Miringa Hohaia was involved in Taranaki land claims all his life. He was director of Taranaki's Parihaka Peace Festival when he died on 7 August 2010. Tariana Turia, Maori Party co-leader and local

MP said, 'This is a terrible loss for the people of Taranaki and the nation.'

This would be a good time to also mention Auntie Marj, a great kuia of Parihaka, who died during the writing of *The Parihaka Woman.* Beautiful and proud, we will always remember you, kui.

'He hoped, if war did come' is cited in Dick Scott, *Ask That Mountain,* p.56.

The 'death blow' comes from Rusden, Vol.3, footnotes, p.319 and p.324. The Taranaki desire to strike a death blow to the Maori race was widely proposed. Rusden references Arthur Atkinson, a large Taranaki landowner, as proposing 'Extermination'.

'Gather up the earth' comes from the Reverend T.G. Hammond's unpublished typescript, 'Maori Legends and History, Te Whiti and Parihaka, The Passing of Tohu', Alexander Turnbull Library; cited in Dick Scott, *Ask That Mountain,* pp.55 and 56 (footnotes).

'My weapon was the plough' is cited in Hazel Riseborough, 'Te Pahuatanga O Parihaka', Hohaia, O'Brien and Strongman (eds), *Parihaka,* p.28. The ploughman who said these words was anonymous.

'If any man molests me' and 'Go, put your hands to the plough' are cited in G.W. Rusden, *History of New Zealand,* Vol.3, p.272.

CHAPTER 10: TE PAREMATA O TE PAKEHA

Bill Dacker provided valuable oral insights into the Maori parliamentarians in the years surrounding Parihaka.

'... indispensable for the peace' and the Stewart denunciation are cited in G.W. Rusden, *History of New Zealand,* Vol.3, p.279.

CHAPTER 11: SAGA OF THE FENCES

The political and social contexts for this chapter have been primarily sourced from G.W. Rusden but also Dick Scott, Hazel Riseborough and others mentioned.

'... every gaol a Bastille' is after Dick Scott, *Ask That Mountain,* p.81. 'My heart is glad' is from the same source, p.89.

'Though the lions rage' is from the *Wanganui Chronicle,* 3 November 1881, cited in G.W. Rusden, *History of New Zealand,* Vol.3, p.412.

CHAPTER 12: 5 NOVEMBER 1881, TE RA O TE PAHUA

The dramatic historical sequence of the invasion of Parihaka has been told most graphically by G.W. Rusden. Subsequent tellings by Dick Scott, Hazel Riseborough, Ruakere Hond and others listed have also been used as a context for Erenora's own version.

'The man that is come to kill' is cited in G.W. Rusden, *History of New Zealand,* Vol.3, p.398. 'If any man thinks' is cited in Dick Scott, *Ask That Mountain,* p.107.

'Takiri te raukura', transcribed and translated by Ngati Mutunga in 'Historical Account' in the Deed of Settlement, 31 July 2005, pp.49–50, is cited in Rachel Buchanan, *The Parihaka Album,* pp.25–6.

Details of constabulary and settler camps are taken from Hazel Riseborough, 'A New Kind of Resistance', in Kelvin Day (ed.), *Contested Ground: Te Whenua i Tohea—The Taranaki Wars 1860–1881,* Huia, 2010, p.248.

'Be of good heart and patient', 'Be not sad' and 'Why are you grieved?' (this last by an anonymous woman) are cited in G.W. Rusden, *History of New Zealand,* Vol.3, p.417.

CHAPTER 13: THE SACKING OF PARIHAKA

The account of looting the Parihaka houses comes from Colonel W.B. Messenger of the Armed Constabulary, as recorded by James Cowan in *The New Zealand Wars,* Vol.2, Government Printer, 1922–23, p.506.

The details of the forcible removals of 'strangers' are summarised from Dick Scott, *Ask That Mountain,* pp.126–30. The destroying of the wairua incident is cited in Hazel Riseborough, *Days of Darkness,* p.170.

'Prey to kites and crows' is after G.W. Rusden, *History of New Zealand,* Vol.3, p.324. Don't you just love that poetic phrase?

CHAPTER 14: A WIFE'S DECISION

'I am indeed of stout heart' is a line from 'Takiri te Raukura', cited in Rachel Buchanan, *The Pariha-ka Album,* p.91.

Act Three: Three Sisters

CHAPTER 15: THE MURU OF PARIHAKA

The Waitangi Tribunal Report, 1996, was the first historical investigation into confiscations from the 1860s to the present. The Taranaki claims were heard in twelve sittings, involving thirty-three research reports from Maori and Pakeha experts such as Hazel Riseborough, a stalwart in telling the story of Taranaki. By using the word 'holocaust' in its report, the tribunal, as Rachel Buchanan writes, inflamed New Zealanders.

'Ko tama wahine' is cited in Dick Scott, *Ask That Mountain,* footnote, p.181. Miriama Evans similarly offered advice on mana wahine of Taranaki.

CHAPTER 16: THE QUEST BEGINS

Historical and geographical information in this and subsequent chapters has mainly been sourced from Maurice (Moss) Shadbolt, text, and Brian Brake, photography, *Reader's Digest Guide to New Zealand,* Reader's Digest, 1988. This book, which provides comprehensive historical notes and concise details on main cities, towns and important landmarks in New Zealand, as well as stunning photography, kept me on track in endeavouring to imagine Erenora's, Ripeka's and Meri's odyssey to Wellington and thence to the South Island. Like John Caselberg (see notes to Chapter Five), both Moss and Brian were close friends of mine, now gone. Moss was outraged at what had happened at Parihaka; I like to think he was looking over my shoulder as I wrote

The Parihaka Woman.

'Soon arrived at Ohawe' is cited in Shadbolt and Brake, *Guide to New Zealand,* p.138.

On Mete Kingi see Steven Oliver, 'Te Rangi Paetahi, Mete Kingi—Biography', *Dictionary of New Zealand Biography,* Te Ara—The Encyclopaedia of New Zealand, updated 1 September 2010. Oliver says, 'In general, Mete Kingi was in favour of the sale of land, so long as enough was retained to provide for Maori welfare.'

'The Pakeha is burning the bush' is from Malcolm McKinnon, 'Manawatu and Horowhenua Region—Rapid Change, 1870–1880 and 1880–1910', *Te Ara—the Encyclopedia of New Zealand,* 22 December 2009.

For further reading on the Kapiti Coast see Wattie Carkeek, *The Kapiti Coast,* Reed, 1968, and Olive Baldwin, *Celebration History of the Kapiti Coast,* Kapiti Borough Council, 1988.

CHAPTER 17: EMPIRE CITY

This chapter was originally titled Va Pensiero after the Chorus of the Hebrew Slaves sung in Giuseppe Verdi's opera, *Nabucco,* libretto by Temistocle Solera, 1842. The intention here, as with the interpolation of the aria from *Samson et Dalila,* is to maintain the subtextual connection of Maori as the children of Israel suffering the oppression of the Pakeha (Egyptians) with the Old Testament parallels, in this case, of the Israelites under oppression by, respectively, the Philistines and Babylonians. Incidentally, when I was a young boy growing up in Waituhi in the 1950s, one of the earliest tunes I ever heard was 'Va pensiero', played as a waltz by an orchestral trio with one of our old koroua, Snapper, on the accordion; people danced with great dignity. As an adult, when I heard the chorus again, this time sung on record, I was puzzled: how come an Italian chorus was singing my koroua Snapper's tune?

Source reading for Wellington included David Hamer and Roberta Nicholls (eds), *The Making of*

Wellington,1888–1914,   Victoria University Press, 1990.

On Te Wheoro I consulted Walter Hugh Ross, 'Te Wheoro Te Morehu Maipapa, Wiremu' from *An Encyclopaedia of New Zealand,* edited by A.H. McLintock, originally published 1966, *Te Ara—the Encyclopedia of New Zealand,* updated 23 April 2009.

The sources for information on Mount Cook Prison included James Mackay to the Hon the Native Minister, 'Maori Prisoners at Mount Cook Prison', *Appendices to the Journals of the House of Representatives,* 1879; and Helen McCracken, 'National Art Galley and Dominion Museum (Former)', New Zealand Historic Places Trust/Pouhere Taonga, 10 September 2008.

'Fly, our thoughts' is after 'Va pensiero', Chorus of Hebrew Slaves, Guiseppe Verdi, *Nabucco,* Part 3, Scene 2.

CHAPTER 18: EVER, EVER SOUTHWARD

Grateful thanks to Bill Dacker for assistance and information in creating the context for the story of the Parihaka prisoners exiled to the South Island. For further information see Maarire Goodall, 'From Prisoners in Our Midst', Witi Ihimaera (ed.), *Te Ao Marama Vol.2: Regaining Aotearoa—Maori Writers Speak Out,* Reed, Auckland, 1993. Like John Caselberg, Maurice Shadbolt and Brian Brake, Maarire Goodall is another of the friends and colleagues who once inhabited an earlier life, and I pay tribute to him.

Sources for the 'roistering township' of Hokitika included Philip Ross May, *Hokitika: Goldfields Capital,* published for the Hokitika Centennial Committee by Pegasus Press, 1964. The description of Hokitika Gaol comes from Colin P. Townsend, *Misery Hill: Seaview Terrace, Hokitika, 1866–1909: The Home of the Dead, the Mad and the Bad,* Leon G. Morel, 1998. I located Mr B.L. O'Brien as the Hokitika gaoler via a long search through http://paperspast.natlib.govt.nz.

'Great Lord, you who flies' is from Verdi's *Nabucco,* Part 1.

Chapter 19: The Courage of Women

The main descriptions of Arthur's Pass are drawn from Shadbolt and Brake, *Reader's Digest Guide to New Zealand,* pp.268–70 and Wikipedia, 'Highway 73'. Descriptions of Christchurch are based on James Cowan, *The City of Christchurch,* New Zealand City Series, Whitcombe & Tombs Ltd, 1939.

The section involving Erenora's emotional breakdown in Addington is taken from Howard McNaughton's superb essay, 'Re-inscribing the urban abject: Ngai Tahu and the Gothic Revival', *New Zealand Geographer* 65, 2009, pp.48–58. Some of the themes and wording in *The Parihaka Woman* take their inspiration from McNaughton's work.

After a frustrating hunt for a book titled *Addington Prison* (all I had to go on was that it was softback,

119 pages), in the end the detail for the gaol in the 1880s was obtained from a number of small references such as Mike Crean, 'Addington Jail's Strange History', *The Press,* 5 August 2002, Howard McNaughton's essay (see above) and other general references on Christchurch itself.

Te Whiti's encouragement, 'Aue, Erenora', comes from one of the passages of the Bible, Isaiah 60. The passage provided the words for a Parihaka poi chant.

Archdeacon Canon George Cotterill, the Reverend John Townsend and Samuel Charles Phillips were all real people. Their roles in Christchurch and Lyttelton were deduced from investigation on http://paperspa st.natlib.govt.nz. It took quite a while.

For information on Lyttelton Harbour, Lyttelton Gaol and Ripapa Island I read John Johnson, *The Story of Lyttelton,* Lyttelton Borough Council, 1952; W.H. Scotter, *A History of Port Lyttelton,* Lyttelton Harbour Board, Christchurch, 1968; David Gee, *The Devil's Own Brigade: A History of the Lyttelton Gaol, 1860–1920,* Millwood Press, 1975; 'Ripapa—an ideal pa site', www.doc.govt.nz, accessed 14 October 2010. Prisoner conditions also extrapolated from descriptions in Dick Scott, *Ask That Mountain,* p.84, citing a *Press* report and, pp.85-86, a *New Zealand Times* report.

'Oh, Taranaki!' and 'Oh, what joy' are after 'Va pensiero', Verdi, *Nabucco,* Part 3, Scene 2.

'Here in this void' is after 'Gott! Welch Dunkel hier!' from Beethoven's *Fidelio,* Act 2, Scene 1.

For 'Takiri te raukura' see the notes to Chapter Seven. The final lines are interpolated as Meri's. I felt that at an emotional moment of farewell like this, she would want to utter something powerful.

CHAPTER 20: CITY OF CELTS

Grateful thanks again to Bill Dacker who, via email correspondence, provided me with many details for this chapter and ensured its accuracy. For information on Dunedin, David Stewart and Robin Bromby's *Dunedin, Historic City of the South,* Southern Press, c.1974 was the main source, but other texts also assisted in assembling the setting.

L.C. Tonkin's *Dunedin Gaol in the 1870s: some notorious inmates,* L.C. Tonkin, c.1980, reprints a series of articles published in the *Otago Guardian,* 1873, possibly written by W.J. Perrier or J.J. Utting.

'The rain was falling, Te Whao making small holes in it with his words': this is an allusion not a quote, to a line in Hone Tuwhare's famous poem, 'Rain', from *Come Rain Hail,* University of Otago, 1970; Hone lived in Dunedin for some years. While I'm at it, I could mention another allusion to this same poem at 'Embers from the beach fire burnt tiny holes in the dark' Chapter Seventeen. Other allusions exist throughout the novel, e.g. to William Blake's *And did those feet in ancient time,* 1804, (best known as the anthem *Jerusalem,* composed by Sir Hubert Parry in 1916), and so on.

'We trust in God's eternal aid' is after Verdi's *Nabucco,* Part 1.

The material on Isaac Newton Watt builds on an email exchange with Bill Dacker and that on Adam Scott is from Stuart C. Scott, *The Travesty of Waitangi—Towards Anarchy,* Campbell Press, 1995, p.117. The author, Adam Scott's grandson, writes, 'The Scott family was in no doubt but that the attitude of their father to his Maori charges was entirely benevolent, as was that of the Dunedin community as a whole.'

D. Harold, *Maori Prisoners of War in Dunedin 1869–1872: Deaths and Burials and Survivors,* Hexagon, 2000, provides further information on the earlier Taranaki prisoners. See also Edward Ellison, 'The Northern Cemetery', Southern Heritage Trust, Historic Event, Parihaka, 2003.

Rocco is the name of Florestan's Kerkermeister, or gaoler, in Beethoven's *Fidelio;* he has the same function in *The Parihaka Woman.* I have given him a surname, Sonnleithner, after Joseph von Sonnleithner, who wrote the opera's German libretto. The original French libretto, which had been used for two previous versions of the story, Pierre Gaveaux's *Leonore, ou L'amour conjugal* (1798) and Ferdinando Paer's better-known *Leonore* (1804), was written by Jean-Nicolas Bouilly.

Act Four: Horitana

CHAPTER 21: HORITANA'S LAMENT

This is the *Fidelio* act. In Beethoven's opera, set in late eighteenth-century Spain, the heroine Leonore has been searching for her husband, Florestan, whom she knows is imprisoned somewhere for his political activities. Thinking that she has found him in a fortress near Seville, she takes on the guise of a young man and obtains employment as a prison guard. Her sole objective is to rescue him. Although I did, indeed, set the libretto of Erenora in a prison, for the purposes of *The Parihaka Woman* I placed the action on Peketua Island.

'Aue, e Atua', 'Here in this void', and 'In the springtime of my life' are from Florestan's aria, 'Gott! Welch Dunkel hier!', from Beethoven's *Fidelio,* Act 2, Scene 1.

CHAPTER 22: MARZELLINE

The *Anna Milder* is named after the 19-year-old soprano who sang the role of Leonore at the premiere of Beethoven's *Fidelio,* on 20 November 1805. Captain Demmer is named after Friedrich Christian Demmer, who sang Florestan in the premiere.

Marzelline's entry into *The Parihaka Woman* completes the parallel with the main cast of Beethoven's *Fidelio:* Leonore, Florestan, Pizarro, Rocco and now Marzelline, Rocco's daughter, 'seine Tochter'.

Walküre is the German for Valkyrie, the mythological warrior women who choose proud warriors, slain in battle, and take them to the hall of death.

Jack is named for Jaquino, listed as doorkeeper in Beethoven's cast of *Fidelio.*

CHAPTER 23: HISTORY AND FICTION

Donald Sonnleithner is based on a dear friend and librarian whom I met during my time as Burns Fellow at the University of Otago in 1975.

CHAPTER 24: ISLAND AT THE END OF THE WORLD

The topography of the island is modelled after descriptions of the various outlying islands as detailed in 'Offshore Islands and Conservation: New Zealand's Subantarctic islands', www.doc.govt.nz and other sources.

For the Pharos of Alexandria see Michael Lahanas, *The Pharos of Alexandria, the first Lighthouse of the World,* Hellenica, 2010, especially for its imaginative illustrations. Also useful is Jimmy Dunn, *Pharos Lighthouse of Alexandria,* Tour Egypt, 2010.

The Peketua lighthouse is modelled on the Dog Island and Centre Island lighthouses, built in 1865 and 1877 respectively to mark the dangerous water in Foveaux Strait between the South Island and Stewart Island. Maritime New Zealand is the source for descriptions of the lighthouse and its operation in such articles as 'Lighthouses of New Zealand and History of Lighthouses in New Zealand', maritimenz .govt.nz. I could not have imagined what life might have been like for Rocco, Marzelline and Erenora on a lighthouse island had it not been for Helen Beagle-hole's superb *Lighting the Coast: A History of New Zealand's Coastal Lighthouse Systems,* Canterbury University Press, 2006.

CHAPTER 25: A WALK TO THE OTHER SIDE OF THE ISLAND

Le Vicomte de Bragelonne is the title of the trilogy by Alexandre Dumas, père. The third novel is *L'Homme au Masque de Fer.*

CHAPTER 26: ROCCO AND MARZELLINE

The New Zealand-German back-story for Rocco and Marzelline comes from research I conducted while writing my previous novel, *The Trowenna Sea* (2009). It is a fascinating story, worthy of a novel of its own. For further information, see Joy Stephens, 'German Settlement in Nelson', the prow.org.nz and 'The Settlement of Nelson & German Immigration to Nelson', ancestry.com.

Rocco's wife is named after Lotte Lehmann, a famous mid-twentieth-century interpreter of the role of Leonore in Beethoven's *Fidelio.*

'Hat man nicht', 'Traurig schleppt', 'Doch hn's in', 'Macht und liebe' and 'Das Glück dient wiäre strophes from Rocco's 'Gold Song', in Act 1 of /e-lio.

CHAPTER 27: MARZELLINE'S DIAℕ

With the words 'Mir ist so wunderbar' Marzelliȵ launches the quartet in Act 1 of Beethoven's Fideli. 'O namenlose pein!' are the words of Leonore in thä quartet.

'Die Hoffnung schon' is from Marzelline's first act aria in Beethoven's Fidelio and 'er liebt mich' are her words in the Act 1 quartet.

'Monster! How my blood boils' and 'Yet though like ocean breakers' are after Leonore's great Act 1 recitative, 'Abscheulicher! Wo eilst du hin', from Fidelio. 'Komm, Hoffnung', 'Come, Hope', is the aria that follows.

Rocco's words, 'Vielleicht ist er tot?', are from Act 2, Scene 1 of Fidelio and 'O armer Mann' is after 'den armer Mann' in the same scene. 'Welch unerhörter Mut' are Pizzaro's words in the quartet, Act 2, Scene 2.

'Geh, Eruera, leb wohl': this constant refrain in Erenora's life, 'Live well', is used again here to give radiance to the end of the chapter, which is constructed like a long, shining aria.

CHAPTER 28: A WORLD SATURATED IN THE DIVINE

The details of Te Whiti and Tohu in the South Island come from John P. Ward's *Wanderings with the Maori Prophets, Te Whiti & Tohu (with illustrations of each chief): being reminiscences of a twelve months' companionship with them, from their arrival in Christchurch in April 1882, until their return to Parihaka in March 1883,* Bond, Finney, 1883. Ward was appointed interpreter to Te Whiti and Tohu from their arrival in Christchurch in 1882 until their return to Parihaka in March 1883.

For the Otakou Kaik, known by Maori simply as the Kaik, see W.A. Taylor, *Lore and History of the South Island Maori,* Bascands, 1952.

'If the grasshoppers' comes from p.133 of Ward's *Wanderings with the Maori Prophets.*

The extract from the famous double poi, attributed to Te Whetu and as given by the Reverend Paahi Moke and first published in Dick Scott's *The Parihaka Story,* 1954, is cited in Dick Scott's *Ask That Mountain,* 1975, p.146.

For the Parihaka aftermath G.W. Rusden and Dick Scott are the main sources of the summary.

'I shall not die' is cited by James Belich in 'Titokowaru, Riwha—Biography, Dictionary of New Zealand Biography'— *Te Ara Encyclopaedia of New Zealand,* updated 1 September 2010.

The return of the last Parihaka prisoner is cited in many texts, including 'Parihaka: History of Parihaka', parihaka.com.

'Bryce the Bravo', *The Tribune,* 1890, cited in Dick Scott, *Ask That Mountain,* 1975, p.160. Bryce's 'With the feet of 20th-century tourists' was published in *The Press,* 27 March 1903 and is cited in Dick Scott, *Ask That Mountain,* 1975, p.6.

Epilogue: Always the Mountain

CHAPTER 29: THE RADIANCEOF FEATHERS

Opening quote from the King James Bible, Luke 2:14.

Information on the passing of Te Whiti and Tohu is from Dick Scott, *Ask That Mountain,* 1975, p.192-95; and 'Let this be clearly understood', Taare Waitara's eulogy, is cited on p.195.

'Those who are bent by the wind'—Tariana Turia, co-leader of the Maori Party, quoted this saying of Te Whiti's on 18 November 2003, on the occasion of the second reading of the Ngati Tama Claims Settlement Bill.

'Im Frühling, komm!' is from Dimitri's aria in Act 1, Scene 4 of Franz Lehar's *Tatjana.*

'Leb wohl, mein Herz', for the final time in *The Parihaka Woman,* 'Go well, sweetheart': a mihi aroha to all those descendants of Parihaka.

Na reira, apiti 'ono tatai 'ono, te 'unga mate o te wa, 'aere, 'aere, 'aere. Apiti 'ono tatai 'ono te 'unga ora, katoa, tena koutou, tena koutou, tena tatou katoa.

Books For ALL Kinds of Readers

At ReadHowYouWant we understand that one size does not fit all types of readers. Our innovative, patent pending technology allows us to design new formats to make reading easier and more enjoyable for you. This helps improve your speed of reading and your comprehension. Our EasyRead printed books have been optimized to improve word recognition, ease eye tracking by adjusting word and line spacing as well as minimizing hyphenation. Our EasyRead SuperLarge editions have been developed to make reading easier and more accessible for vision-impaired readers. We offer Braille and DAISY formats of our books and all popular E-Book formats.

We are continually introducing new formats based upon research and reader preferences. Visit our web-site to see all of our formats and learn how you can Personalize our books for yourself or as gifts. Sign up to Become A (RHYW) Registered Reader.

www.readhowyouwant.com

Made in the USA
Middletown, DE
11 December 2021

55140927R00225